T0287742

THE RADICAL NOVEL RECONSIDERED

A series of paperback reissues of mid-twentieth-century
U.S. left-wing fiction, with new biographical and critical
introductions by contemporary scholars.

SERIES EDITOR

Alan Wald, University of Michigan

LAMPS AT HIGH NOON

LAMPS AT HIGH NOON

Jack S. Balch

Introduction by Michael Szalay

University of Illinois Press

Urbana and Chicago

Frontispiece: Photo courtesy of Michael Balch.
Introduction © 2000 by the Board of Trustees of
the University of Illinois

Library of Congress Cataloging-in-Publication Data
Balch, Jack S., 1909–1980.
Lamps at high noon / Jack S. Balch ;
introduction by Michael Szalay.
p. cm. — (The radical novel reconsidered)
Includes bibliographical references and index.
ISBN 0-252-06939-0 (pbk. : alk. paper)
1. Federal Writers' Project—Fiction.
2. Strikes and lockouts—Fiction.
3. Art and state—Fiction.
4. Authorship—Fiction.
I. Title. II. Series.
PS3503.A5514L36   2000
813'.52—dc21   00-033795

P 5 4 3 2 1

FOR MRS. GEST

CONTENTS

INTRODUCTION

Michael Szalay

In the summer of 1935, President Franklin Roosevelt created the Federal Arts Projects as a subsidiary of the Works Progress Administration. This country's first and to this date most comprehensive national arts program, the Arts Projects were comprised of the Federal Theater Project, the Federal Art Project, the Federal Music Project, and the Federal Writers' Project. On September 12, the projects received their final executive approval and began dispensing work-relief to the tens of thousands who would eventually find employment on them. Roughly one year later, on October 27, 1936, a handful of writers employed in the St. Louis office of the Missouri Writers' Project—Jack Balch among them—took to the picket line. Balch's *Lamps at High Noon* (1941) is the only novel we have about this strike; indeed, it is the only novel to treat comprehensively *any* aspect of the Federal Writers' Project. But more than this, Balch's novel, an early and unique document in this century's "culture wars," is without peer in its critical engagement of the economic constraints and political exigencies that have vexed debates over the federal funding of art since the New Deal.

The issues involved in the strike—treated below—were at once humdrum and fantastical: recriminations over pilfered hotel receipts and reports of political assassinations swirled about as Balch and some dozen of his colleagues picketed the projects. Reporting on these events in *New Masses* on November 17, 1936, fellow striker

Jack Conroy framed the work stoppage in terms that resonate with recent controversies over the National Endowment for the Arts. To Conroy, the strikers had been unfairly censored in their efforts to compile the Missouri state guide, part of the American Guide series that was the principal product of the Writers' Project. Working for the state, Conroy insisted, should not have required conforming to its political sensibilities. He asks, "Does the administration, through the Federal Writers' Projects, intend to stimulate and foster writers, or is its purpose to stifle and emasculate them, close their mouths, keep them in intellectual bondage and submission twenty-four hours a day? Those of us who went at the job of writing the American Guide with the determination to make it a full-bodied, rich, and recognizable picture of life in the United States—the land, its people, their customs, their folk-lore—would like to know."[1]

This question might well have been asked by Charlie Gest, the wide-eyed and well-intentioned protagonist of *Lamps at High Noon* who confronts firsthand the project's sometimes underhanded efforts to monitor the political views of its writers. Modeled on Balch, Gest is assistant director of the Writers' Project in Monroe (a fictionalized version of St. Louis) and watches helplessly as his boss denies employment to leftist "troublemakers." But while an undeniable concern in *Lamps at High Noon,* this kind of discrimination is itself only a symptom of a deeper problem. The project workers are censored at all because, far more ominously, their project is not public in any clear sense; Balch's workers find it next to impossible to determine where the government that employs them ends and where a more powerful world of special interests begins. Balch's strikers fault national project director Jonas Colon (based on actual project head Henry Alsberg) for failing to protect the autonomy of the project from the corrosive influence of back-room boss Joe Tremaine (based on Thomas Pendergast). Dubbed by one historian "the most powerful person in the history of the state," during the twenties and thirties Pendergast ran the Missouri Democratic Party as well as numerous state businesses and corporations.[2] Like Pendergast, Tremaine is involved with virtually all political and economic activity in Missouri, and the project is no exception. Colon thus appears as a Tremaine stooge, unwilling to confront a political machine that had recently thrown its considerable weight behind President Roosevelt in the 1936 presidential elections. Tremaine is particularly hard to fight because he works within the established channels of government. Unchecked by the regulatory mechanisms of the New Deal, Tremaine consolidates his stranglehold on Missouri while working on behalf of Washington. This was the case with Thomas Pendergast as well, who dispensed federal largesse as if it were his own. Pendergast's Ready-Mixed Concrete Company—like Tremaine's—supplied virtually all of the concrete for Missouri's WPA building projects. Because of corporate tie-ins like these, he was able to dictate much of the hiring and firing that took place on the project. In fact, Pendergast personally appointed the head of the Missouri Writers' Project, Geraldine Parker, who ran project manuscripts by him for his approval before sending them on to Washington. To take but one example, all mention of silicosis poisoning from state mines was deleted from the final copy of the state guidebook as a result of Parker's deference to Pendergast.

Tremaine's political appointees are largely unsympathetic to the authors' project they run and barely conceal their glee as it collapses of its own weight. "Now you take when we put dough into a road project," one such official tells the striking WPA writers. "We put down a road—let's say we spend a hun'er' thousan' on it. When it's down, it's *down.* You can *feel* it. You can *ride* over it. It's there. The public knows what the money has gone for—" (383). There is little sympathy for the writers' strike, the official maintains, because the public is justifiably more comfortable spending government money on roads than on the arts. He asks the strikers, "What've *you* fellas got to show when you're through?" (384). Nothing that warrants the expenditure of public money, reasons the "middle-aged wheelhorse" (382). "Look at it thisa way," he expounds. "I go to a tailor. See? I tell him I want a suit of clothes. See? I tell him what kind of clothes I want, and I tell him what kind of style and cut. It's up to him to make me the kind of suit that I want. If I don't like the suit that he makes me, I don't have to buy it. And I can get me another tailor" (384). One of the strikers replies that the authors' project should be thought of as something like a national museum. "There's a man named Rockings who maintains a private art gallery down at the State Capitol," he begins. "It's considered one of the finest of its kind in the country, and a quarter gets you in. Okay. You know yourself that not all the paintings in that gallery have been found acceptable by everybody. And yet, the *gallery itself*—" (384). Before the project worker can finish, the official interrupts with a knowing wink: "Between you and me—pardon me, ladies—I wouldn't hang them things in my bathroom" (385). Even these sentiments were scripted by Pendergast, who only reluctantly allowed Parker to include mention in the Missouri guidebook of native son Thomas Hart Benton, the painter whose works were collected in the actual museum to which Balch alludes. The political boss was reportedly furious with the painter because his recent work, especially *A Social History of the State of Missouri,* had criticized his machine's role in the state.[3] "I wouldn't hang him on my shithouse wall," Pendergast told Parker. "How about writing about our wonderful roads instead?"[4]

The public record since the New Deal is littered with such high-minded aesthetic appraisals, offered by those who would mete out standards for what kind of art the government should and should not support. A Pendergast protégé since the mid-thirties, when the political boss pushed through his bid to become Missouri's senator, President Harry Truman volunteered in 1947, "I am of the opinion that so-called modern art is merely the vaporings of half-baked lazy people."[5] This same year, a Republican representative from Michigan, George Dondero, defended Benton-style realism from the ascendant forces of abstract expressionism. Even as the CIA paraded the work of ex-WPA artists like Jackson Pollock across Europe as exemplars of cutting-edge democratic culture, and even as hordes of Americans avidly consumed Pollock's forms, Dondero burst forth that such "Communist art, aided and abetted by misguided Americans, is stabbing our glorious American art in the back with murderous intent."[6] Aesthetic canons may have changed since the cold war, but the overall tenor of the conservative hostility to funding the arts certainly has not. In 1989, Republican senator Jesse Helms held forth that "the avant-garde in the art world mock art that is beautiful and uplifting—even as they extol so-called art that is shocking and depraved." Offering an erudite proof of this dictum, Helms decreed of Andres Serrano, the NEA-funded creator of the controversial "Piss-Christ": "he is not an artist, he is a jerk."[7]

Whether the defensive reflex of a reactionary cultural sensibility or emblematic of more popular American taste, such off-the-cuff dismissals are easily laughed off. But *Lamps at High Noon* refuses to offer a self-satisfied account of either the Writers' Project or its legacy. Instead, Balch's even-handed novel, often full of self-doubt and recrimination, helps show why the federal funding of art has proven a trigger-point issue in American cultural politics. Awash in the kinds of bureaucratic inefficiency we have come to expect from popular representations of government agencies, Balch's author's project is also hamstrung by the priggish aesthetic predilections and incipient nativism of a middle-brow booboisie. But as much as Balch's *Lamps at High Noon* seems to catalogue the forces that militate against a national arts policy, it is still more deeply concerned with the left and its relation to the New Deal. Amazed by the often seamless rapprochement between Washington and Tremaine, Gest is absorbed by the difficulty of effecting a similar relationship between the state and the left. What kinds of sacrifices are made, the young administrator asks, and what benefits are received, when the left turns from uncompromising revolutionary politics and enters the administrative corridors of "big government"?

* * *

While Balch's experiences on the Missouri Writers' Project exposed him to the compromise and red tape of government service, his experiences earlier in life left him no less expert in the often bloody requirements of actual revolution. In fact, the relatively modest scale of events in *Lamps at High Noon* does not begin to do justice to the strikingly varied and often danger-filled life of its author. Jack Balch was born Yaakov Balokofsky in London on April 9, 1909. According to Jack's son Michael, in 1917 Jack's father, Shmuel—one of seven Jewish Russian brothers, all of them tailors— joined the "Jabotinsky Brigade" of the British Army, the 38th Battalion of the Royal Fusiliers, housed within the City of London Regiment. Conceived by Ze'ev Jabotinsky, one-time Russian Marxist and eventual founder of the Zionist Haganah, this all-Jewish volunteer unit was organized to assist in the British Army's liberation of Palestine from the Ottoman Empire. After the British succeeded in securing what would become Israel, the unit disbanded amidst recriminations that the British were not prepared to follow through on their commitment, formalized in the Balfour Declaration of 1917, to an independent Jewish state. While many in the 38th left the British Army and returned to London, some were redeployed, like Jack's father, who was sent with the British Expeditionary Forces to the port of Archangel in 1917. Soon thereafter, Jack and his mother—fleeing London amidst Zeppelin bombardments—shipped to Archangel to join Balch's father. Michael Balch reports that after being stopped on the North Sea and held at gunpoint on the deck of a German submarine, mother and son arrived in Russia—only to find the Soviet Revolution in full swing. The Expeditionary Forces had by this time left Archangel in disarray and relocated to the Black Sea port of Odessa. After more than a year of precarious travel across war-torn Russia, Jack and his mother finally caught up to Jack's father. Young Balch would then serve as something of a mascot for the British Navy in Odessa. Showing sailors the town, translating for them based on the Russian he had picked up on his trek across the Ukraine, the child was unofficially adopted by the crew of the HMS *Pegasus*.

Only ten at the time, Balch would later consider his experiences in Odessa some of the most formative of his life. His firsthand ex-

posure to senseless atrocities in Odessa would lead to the deep impatience with self-interest and petty factionalism so evident in *Lamps
at High Noon.* Recalling his political education in what had once
been the "Paris of the Ukraine," Balch writes:

> What the political people said by way of explanation and nec-
> essary conclusions to be drawn I could only guess at the time.
> We saw this: That the Ukrainian Nationalists killed Jews; that
> the Germans, who used to kill both Nationalists and Jews, had
> got so accustomed to being killed themselves that they'd quit
> killing others and were thankful for small favors granted them
> by way of food and shelter; that the Bolsheviks killed officers,
> speculators, and foreign interventionists; that the Whites
> killed Bolsheviks and workers; that the French, British, Greek
> and other Western Armies killed anybody who moved against
> them after they'd moved in; that dribbles of Chinese and
> Mongolian mercenaries, who'd come a long way to look out
> for their employers' interests and for personal loot, killed any-
> thing, whether it moved or not; and that private citizens, sin-
> gly or in bands ranging up to 10,000 arranged themselves in
> doorways, cellars, and rooftops every time the city began to
> change hands, to kill the people moving out and to strip them,
> their wagons and horses or whatever could be moved.[8]

Balch would never shake this experience, which colors even the office
politics of *Lamps at High Noon.* Gest is more than aware that the
bureaucratic abuses perpetrated by the leadership of the local WPA
simply do not offer the kind of moral clarity surrounding events
elsewhere in the world. But as rife as they are with the pathos of
senseless bloodshed, Balch's recollections of Odessa do strike a chord
with the internecine maneuverings of *Lamps at High Noon.* Describing the novel's "bizarre and discordant amalgam of humanity and
politics," the dust jacket of the Modern Age release reported, "There
is a brilliant quixotic scapegrace, a famous novelist, a prominent
socialite, a paretic, a lovelorn psychopath, a labor spy, an ex-banker—these and more, all under the buffoonish Director, Mr. Hohaley of the Old South, a sycophant appointed by the local political
machine." Fred T. Marsh struck a similar note when he described

Balch's novel in the *New York Times Review of Books* as "An improvisation of considerable virtuosity, often entertaining but frequently offending, a medley of stunt passages, occasional scherzos of imagination, bits of mad waggery, stretches of crudeness and thunders on the left, echoes of everything from everywhere, witty and tender, blatant and brash by turns, [but] at the same time not without serious intention."[9] Undeniably informed by a radical, socialist sensibility, *Lamps at High Noon* is also part absurdist theater, which is no doubt why it was reviewed as graciously and as frequently as it was in the liberal press. *Lamps at High Noon* is not a call to revolutionary action. Like his experience in war-torn Odessa, Balch's fictional medley is awash in self-interest to the point that its politics, completely and utterly local, verge on irredeemable chaos.

Odessa was not the only locale to offer the young Balch visions of political dissolution and its attendant barbarities. Finally reunited in Odessa in 1918, the Balch family journeyed to Constantinople, where they might well have witnessed the death throes of the Ottoman Empire. When the Balchs arrived, the city was being torn apart in a feeding frenzy of western colonialism. In 1915, the French, British, and Russians had divided up the city on paper even as the Ottomans remained in place. For the next five years, Greek, French, British, and Russian forces vied with the nationalist armies of Mustafa Kemal, who slowly but surely consolidated his hold on what would become Turkey the year the Balch family departed for the United States. After more than three years of wandering dispossessed across two continents, the Balchs booked passage to New York, arriving on Ellis Island in 1920.

Balch gave up his swashbuckling lifestyle only gradually. A successful amateur boxer and a regional wrestling champion (he wrestled for money at county fairs), he joined the merchant marine in his teens and voyaged extensively around Europe, Asia, and South America. After his return to the United States, Balch worked as a gravedigger, a printer, a carpenter, and a shipping clerk. Inspired by his wanderings, the twenty-two-year-old Balch published *Cas-*

tle of Words and Other Poems (1931), a collection of sonnets and rhymed lyrics. Eager musings on innocence, love, and absent objects of desire, the preponderance of poems in the volume are romantic in tenor. The volume begins with a "Prelude," whose first stanza opens:

> Weary are the feet that falter
> Through the caverns of the night.
> Seeking entrance to your alter [*sic*]
> Goddess! beautiful and white!
> Weary are the feet that falter!

As the volume progresses, the poems become darker and more concerned with revolutionary politics. "Revolutionist's Mother," which recalls Balch's experiences in Odessa, offers one example:

> "Christ is dead and we are risen,
> Muzhik, worker, from our prison,"
> Sing the soldiers as they go.
> "Kill the Czar for fertilizer,
> You will never make him wiser,
> Sweep him under with a hoe,
> From the bones potatoes grow."

"Revolutionist's Mother" is the only poem in the volume explicitly concerned with the left. But the penultimate work in the volume, the resigned and foreboding "Impressions," offers a prolegomenon for the more political writing to come. "Impressions" is a study in myopia and factionalism; the poem analogizes the lover's body to the political body, in effect staging a breakdown of the starstruck voice that characterizes so much of the volume:

> Cities are muscles on the torso of the world.
> Little red-man-corpuscles push them up,
> Little white-man-corpuscles push them down.
> There are no corners to cities; they spiral and leap, flame
>   and flare.
> Out of cities come strange music:
> Music of god-builders, god-breakers, music of sensitive
>   dreamers.

> All of the music is beautiful, all of the music is love
> music.
> But men love different music.

Embraced in such different form by so many, "love music" begins itself to seem a site of contest between red and white (political) cells.

As the thirties drew on, Balch became more and more absorbed by radical politics. Three years after publishing *Castle of Words,* he joined the St. Louis Union of Writers and Artists and began attending meetings of the local John Reed Club, where he met Jack Conroy, Orrick Johns, Joe Jones, and Wallie Wharton. Balch would become particularly close with Conroy, whom he helped to organize and then edit *Anvil.*[10] Balch would remain an editor of *Anvil* until it was absorbed by *Partisan Review,* contributing during this time to both magazines as well as to *New Masses.* In attendance at the First American Writers Congress, held in May of 1935, the iconoclastic Balch spoke out against hampering proletarian short fiction with canned "red-flag" endings.[11] By now, he loved music very different from the kind found in *Castle of Words.* Where that volume is lyrical, romantic, and nostalgic, Balch's writing throughout the thirties is gritty and sometimes unpolished, given to dialect and unmediated working-class points of view. On the strength of this writing, and at the young age of twenty-six, he was appointed assistant director of the Missouri Writer's Project in 1935, soon after which he became involved in the strike that is the subject of *Lamps at High Noon.* In 1937, Balch's short story "Beedlebugs" was collected in *American Stuff,* an anthology of work from those employed on the WPA Writers' project.

After leaving the WPA in 1940, Balch worked as a reporter for the *St. Louis Star Times* until 1944, at which time he became a drama critic for the *St. Louis Post-Dispatch.* While in St. Louis, Balch became close friends with Tennessee Williams (he would later pen a biography of the playwright) and began writing and directing plays of his own. In 1948 Balch moved to New York, where he continued to produce his work off-Broadway. His experience with theater soon led him into television, a medium in which he blossomed. Balch worked as a television director throughout the fifties, directing award-winning shows for ABC, NBC, and WPIX. During this time he continued to write his own plays, many of which he produced for a new generation of TV programming geared to nationally broadcast one-hour and half-hour plays, such as "Studio One," "Kraft Theater," and "Matinee Four-Star Playhouse." One of these plays, "Elijah and the Long Knives," was produced by ABC and awarded "Best Television Play of Any Network" during the 1954–55 season; it was reprinted in numerous anthologies, including the *Hastings House Anthology of Best Scripts of the Year.* In 1959 Balch became editor of *The Theatre,* a monthly review of drama, comedy, and music eventually driven under by *Theatre Arts,* a journal for which he then served as drama editor. Late in life, the multifaceted Balch would change media yet once more. By the time of his death on August 15, 1980, he was an accomplished painter, having shown in galleries in New York, Los Angeles, and Israel.

* * *

Balch realized early in his literary career that writers on the left were passing up an opportunity to engage what were then entirely new forms of American government, those later associated with the welfare state. In his short story "Take a Number, Take a Seat," published in the *Partisan Review* in 1935, an aspiring writer is treated like chattel as he waits to meet with a relief worker dispensing coupons for the local food market. Despite his anger, the character finds himself musing, "what great story-stuff this is." Even as he fumes at the agency's indifference, he thinks to himself that "the trouble with Farrell's shortstories [*sic*], those I've read, that is, there ain't none of his lumpens ever come in contact with social service, Conroy has nothing to say about this either." "Gloating . . . in the name of this field's virginity and the worth of all this to me in the realm of stories yet to be written," the young writer finds the hook that will sell his stories.[12]

Balch was certainly correct that the left tended at times to give the New Deal less than serious attention. Jack Conroy parodied Balch's story with "Pay a Nickel, Take a Seat." Here, Balch's "social service" turns up as a public restroom. Indignant at finding all of the stall doors locked, Conroy's character lets fly with a tirade in defense of Communism.[13] Literary editor of the *New Republic* and one-time fellow traveler Malcolm Cowley helps explain why New Deal relief agencies might have seemed so trivial to Conroy: "We were, at the time, so dismayed by the jackbooted march of the fascists in Europe that, once more, we paid less than the proper attention to events in Washington."[14] "For most Americans," remembers Robert Warshow, the atmosphere of the thirties "was expressed most clearly in the personality of President Roosevelt and the social-intellectual-political climate of the New Deal. For the intellectual, however, the Communist movement was the fact of central importance; the New Deal remained an external phenomenon, part of that 'larger' world of American public life from which he had long separated himself—he might 'support' the New Deal (as later on, perhaps, he 'supported' the war), but he never identified himself with it. One way or another, he did identify himself with the Communist movement."[15]

At the close of the thirties, even after eight years of Roosevelt, few writers on the left had taken up the New Deal in explicit fashion. John Dos Passos would soon begin his New Deal trilogy, but the author had by this point long since repudiated the left. In Caroline Slade's *The Triumph of Willie Pond* (1940), the ailing Willie Pond digs ditches for the WPA as his family, monitored at every turn by intrusive welfare agencies, bemoans the indignity of working for the government. Alexander Williams's potboiler mystery *Murder on the WPA* (1937) takes place on the Federal Writers' Project but is devoid of serious political content (its burlesqued fascists notwithstanding). Norman Macleod's *You Get What You Ask For* (1939) fictionalizes the author's experiences on the Writers' Project, but the novel is more concerned with representing the alcoholism of its protagonist than his experiences with either the left or the WPA. Better-known radical novels would treat these topics, but only in a passing manner. Richard Wright was a member of both the Communist Party and the Illinois and the New York Writers' Projects, and touched on the relation between the left and New Deal "social services" in *Native Son* (1940), where Bigger Thomas is courted by Party activists while on relief assignment at the Daltons'. Also a veteran of the Communist Party and the Writers' Project, Meridel Le Sueur had by the end of the thirties begun serializing *The Girl,* whose heroine delivers her child at the doorstep of a New Deal social agency from which she has just escaped. But these exceptions aside, the New Deal offered largely uncharted terrain for the radical novelist at the close of the decade. *Lamps at High Noon* is thus almost alone in situating a late-thirties interest in Communism within the context of governmental politics and policies; Balch's is one of the few radical novels of the thirties or forties to examine in any depth the sometimes compatible, often conflicting spheres marked out by the ideology of the left and the more prosaic world of civic and municipal New Deal politics.

The Federal Writers' Project was the preeminent meeting ground between the New Deal and the left during the Depression. Though New Deal officials vociferously denied that project workers let political affiliations color their work, few bothered to deny that many of the thousands receiving a government check on the project were actively involved on the left.[16] Communist influence on the project did become a heated topic in 1938, when Congressman Martin Dies (D-Texas) began to investigate the issue with the House Committee on Un-American Activities.[17] But there was a surprising amount of political tolerance on the project during its early years. Even Henry Alsberg—who received his official appointment as national director of the Federal Writers' Project on July 25, 1935—had an unambiguously radical background. A self-proclaimed philosophical anarchist, the young Alsberg wrote glowingly about the Russian Revolution. Though he later disowned the Bolshevik cause,

Alsberg remained largely if limply sympathetic to the left while running the projects.

Alsberg was able to accommodate so many of the left in part because—unlike the Theater and Arts Projects—the Writers' Project did not allow its writers to produce original material. While the WPA was overseeing the construction of countless roads—so impressive to Balch's fictional city official—the Writers' Project was putting together a public monument whose content carefully skirted divisive political issues. This was the American Guide series, a compilation of every state's history, folklore, and cultural and natural resources. "The plan," project director Jonas Colon explains,

> was this: to produce The Story of America. Not just the history, not merely the politics, the economics, the village folklore, the literature, but the whole thing. Think of it, to tell the story of AMERICA! What a huge job this was!
> To the end that the plan might succeed, the creative forces of the nation were being mustered. (35)

To Gest, this endeavor is every bit as necessary as other public works: he reasons that as a result of WPA efforts "America will have, for always, things now that it never could afford: Hospitals, schools, roads, books, theater, most of all, a research, a consciousness and a possession of culture." "In the midst of a depression," he concludes, "we are allowed to hand ourselves riches we could never *afford*" (229). Gripped with enthusiasm, Gest sees the Guide series as the quintessential modern epic: "Homer, in ages past, laid down the Odyssey of Ulysses like a carpet over the fields of Greece and the people came out of their warm caves in the city and wept at its dark strange beauty. Mr. Roosevelt, we who were about to die, salute you. Lo and behold, the story of our people. And what's more, in goddam fine prose too" (104–5).

Numbered among those who actually did produce this fine prose were some of the country's most accomplished and most promising writers: Conrad Aiken, Nelson Algren, Saul Bellow, Maxwell Bodenheim, Arna Bontemps, John Cheever, Jack Conroy, Edward

Dahlberg, Floyd Dell, Ralph Ellison, Kenneth Fearing, Zora Neale Hurston, Claude McKay, Tillie Olsen, Kenneth Rexroth, Philip Rhav, Meridel Le Sueur, Margaret Walker, Richard Wright, Frank Yerby, and Anzia Yezierska. Charlie Gest is not himself a particularly distinguished writer when he is asked by Washington to become the assistant director of his state project. Rather, he figures among the thousands of workmanlike talents for whom the project offered a chance to break into what had become a cutthroat profession. By 1933, the combined revenue of American publishers had dropped by more than 50 percent since 1929. Whereas 214 million new books were sold in 1929, only 111 million were sold four years later.[18] In fact, there were only fifteen authors in the United States in 1934 who sold more than fifty thousand copies of their books. Royalties of well-established writers, whose books customarily sold over ten thousand copies, had by 1935 dropped 50 percent below their 1929 levels.[19] The *Partisan Review*'s 1939 survey of the decade's most prominent writers was conducted with just this problem in mind. James Agee, Wallace Stevens, William Carlos Williams, John Dos Passos, Gertrude Stein, Henry Miller, Lionel Trilling, Robert Penn Warren, and R. P. Blackmur were among "the representative list of American writers" who were asked, in addition to other questions, "Have you found it possible to make a living by writing the sort of thing you want to, and without the aid of such crutches as teaching and editorial work? Do you think there is any place in our present economic system for literature as a profession?" The vast majority (thirteen of fifteen) said that they had never been able to make their living exclusively by writing, and that laissez-faire literary patronage was not then—and never had been—able to support literature as a profession.[20]

Given these conditions it is hard to overestimate the impact the Federal Writers' Project had on Depression-era writing. "More than any other literary form in the thirties," declared Alfred Kazin in 1942, "the WPA writers' project, by illustrating how much so many collective skills could do to uncover the collective history of the

country, set the tone of the period."[21] But the profound influence
Kazin rightly notices had as much to do with the steady salary paid
writers as the project's bureaucratic orchestration of "collective
skills." Earning somewhere between $20 and $25 for working
roughly twenty hours a week, writers were given the opportunity
to produce their own material even as they earned what by Depression standards was a comfortable income. The modern writer would
thus become what Malcolm Cowley in 1954 called "the salaried
writer . . . a new figure in American society."[22] Government officials waxed eloquent praising this new form of employment. Art
critic and adviser to the projects Forbes Watson confessed, "It may
sound dull and bourgeois to remove the artist from the high plane
of romantic finances, which never freed him from worry or kept his
feet on solid ground, down to the lower work-a-day plane." All the
same, he reasoned, a salary "freed [the artist's] imagination from the
irritating interruptions certain to enter into the working life of a
man who does not know how he is going to pay rent, his bills for
materials, and the grocer."[23] "Nothing like it, to my knowledge,
has ever been in history," declared Edward Bruce, painter and another adviser to the projects. "The very method of payment is democratic. The artist is paid the highest craftsman's wage allowed under
existing conditions and the product of his work becomes the property of government."[24]

When Gest first hears that he has been hired as the assistant director of the newly formed state "Authors' Project," the sheer novelty of the enterprise makes it difficult to explain matters to his
family. Asked what kind of job he has just been offered, he is "perplexed with how to explain, 'it's—it's for the Government, you
might say.'" "A detec-uhtif!" his sisters blurt out, "A G-man!"
Charlie continues, "it's like in France—or Russia, where the Governments are interested in art academies." He goes on, "The Government is going to pay writers to write. It's a new policy, under
Roosevelt. . . . All over the world educated people have been laughing at America." Charlie's always colorful mother cannot help laugh-

ing herself. Shaking her head, she asks, "The Government will pay you money to write—a story?" Charlie responds by asking his mother and sisters if they have ever heard of Shakespeare, Maxim Gorki, Sholem Aleichem, or Spinoza. "They were young men once," he declares. "They had mothers. Sometimes they were hard up. It was different in those days, though. They didn't have the hard times we have now. Even so, there are a lot of Gorkis we never heard anything about" (15–16).

As so often turns out to be the case in *Lamps at High Noon,* Gest's idealism is off the mark. The Authors' Project—like the Writers' Project—remains an enterprise in unemployment relief more than a full-blown effort to support the arts. Gest "wanted to think of the Project as a writers' job and himself a writer and the others writers. Fellow-craftsmen. And words and thoughts developing between them slowly and with care, and with dignity, as those things should. That's the way it was in his father's shop. All craftsmen, workers, and proud of it too." Instead, "it was a shock to him to think how much *charity* went into this job" (79). Gest soon discovers that the projects are not concerned with nurturing the next generation's Maxim Gorkis. Nor were the Writers' Projects themselves: in the words of George Biddle—a friend of Roosevelt's who helped conceive of the idea for the Arts Projects—the government did not intend in its programs "to discover Michaelangelos, but to put needy artists intelligently to work."[25] As Archibald MacLeish would later put it, Roosevelt did not expect "the projects to produce paintings or plays or books or records of the first importance. Certainly it was with no such purpose in mind that the projects were established."[26]

It became clear at the very start of the project that work on the guide books would have to accommodate a wide range of talent and training. In September of 1935, Alsberg wrote that those eligible for the program included not only "writers and research people but librarians, architects, reporters, lawyers, and others whose classification indicates education that would make them useful to us."[27] Two years later, Alsberg further suggested that even the writers and researchers themselves need not be especially gifted to be useful, announcing at the Second American Writers' Congress that "we must get over the idea that every writer must be an artist of the first class, and that the artist of the second or third class has no function."[28] But the problem as Gest eventually sees it in *Lamps at High Noon* is that there are deplorably few artists of any rank on the project. Gest confesses to Jonas Colon that, out of the hundreds working at his office, only about six writers would end up actually writing the state guide. This exclusive concentration of talent would not be such a problem for the young administrator were it not for the fact that his office was turning away numerous qualified black writers. Gest muses that the project is "built on sand. For while two-thirds of the Project workers were either illiterate or totally incompetent for the work to be done, there were now—just one instance, he thought gloomily—exactly eighty applications in the files from Negroes and not one of them would be used, he was sure. Forty of these Negroes were college graduates; twelve of them were Ph.D.'s" (211). Anticipating pressure from the Washington office to employ black writers, project-head Hohaley—the effete southern gentleman for whom James Branch Cabell represents the pinnacle of literary achievement—puts his maid on the payroll. Hohaley tells her to go in every two weeks to collect her check, but otherwise, to continue her labors at his home.

That Hohaley is a buffoon should not suggest that his cavalier racism is in some sense idiosyncratic. The New Deal had an often embarrassing record with black Americans. Black Americans turned to the Democratic Party in record numbers during the New Deal, and as Lizabeth Cohen observes in her history of the New Deal in Chicago, the WPA was "one of the New Deal programs most responsible for orienting blacks toward the federal government."[29] But while the Roosevelt administration eagerly embraced the black vote, its programs often offered little to this constituency. The Social Security Administration did almost nothing to help the black community, which was crippled by an unemployment rate between

40 and 50 percent. Helping only those who were already steadily employed, the administration offered limited assistance at best to those who were out of work or to nontraditional laborers: out of the 5.5 million blacks working in 1935, roughly 2 million were in agriculture and another 1.5 were in domestic service; neither group was eligible for benefits.[30] The National Recovery Act, to take another example, was derisively referred to as the Negro Removal Act, and the WPA persistently doled out undesirable jobs to its black workers, when these workers were employed at all. To be sure, not all the WPA state projects were equally racist. A small but important group of black writers (Arna Bontemps, Ralph Ellison, Chester Himes, Zora Neale Hurston, Claude McKay, Margaret Walker, and Frank Yerby, for example) would credit the Writers' Project with having provided them an invaluable and uniquely formative experience. Richard Wright therefore introduced Henry Alsberg at the Second American Writers' Congress as being responsible for one of "the most interesting experiments in the history of America."[31] Writing in *Opportunity* in 1935, the black critic Robert Weaver expressed similar if less enthusiastic support for the New Deal. Blacks turned out in such large numbers for the New Deal, he explained, because even the uneven succor offered by its programs was better than the cold comfort of laissez-faire. "It is impossible," he reasons, "to discuss intelligently the New Deal and the Negro without considering the status of the Negro prior to the advent of the recovery program. The present economic position of the colored citizen was not created by the recent legislation alone." Pointing out the persistent discrimination on agricultural and housing projects, Weaver nonetheless concludes, "given the economic situation of 1932, the New Deal has been more helpful than harmful to Negroes. We had unemployment in 1932. Jobs were being lost by Negroes and they were in need. Many would have starved had there been no Federal relief program."[32]

Charlie Gest would find little solace in these words, though he docs do his best to hire black Americans on the project. Given to self-doubt, Gest questions his commitment all the same. "If blood could be shed in Spain, and for no reasons other than men's blindness, greed, and cruelty, then why not understand that ink could be spilled wastefully here? And men deprived of the right to work, i.e., *rights?* Negroes, for instance, are not allowed to eat in restaurants with white men in this town. But since when have I quit eating in restaurants? Where do you make a beginning?" (213). As it was, Balch was conscious of treating "the problems of the project and the idea of the project in the first place . . . with sympathy, to say the least."³³ But somewhere over the course of Gest's agonized mental meanderings—from Spain, to black workers' rights, to segregated seating in restaurants, and then to his own decidedly liberal guilt concerning where he eats his own meals—the project strike emerges as a displacement of more pressing political concerns. Hence Gest's palpable unease: he cannot outpace the nagging suspicion that the issues at stake in the work stoppage are not the ones that most need addressing. Hence one take on the novel's title: like a lamp that burns bright at high noon, the strike is misplaced if not altogether irrelevant, not unlike the "gesture" or "jest" buried in Charlie's patronymic.

The strike is by no means capricious or unimportant; Gest and his compatriots are unequivocal in their belief that labor has the right to strike. Tremaine only helps consolidate this commitment; he is as unalloyed an example of American despotism as workers on the American left were likely to find. Visiting Tremaine's stronghold in Johnsburg (Kansas City), Gest is brought to a sky-scraper window by an ally of Tremaine's. "Look," the wealthy banker points out, "There lies a great city below you. Three hundred and fifty thousand souls. Each year for twenty-six years one man has organized it, made it possible for it to continue living with justice and bread for all. Given it its laws" (134). You can embrace the organization, he makes plain, or be plowed under. Cast in this light, Tremaine is an example of the kind of American fascist who so preoccupied the popular imagination in the late 1930s, from Shagpoke

Whipple in Nathanael West's *A Cool Million* (1931) and Berzelius Windrip in Sinclair Lewis's *It Can't Happen Here* (1935) to D. B. Norton in Frank Capra's *Meet John Doe* (1941). Faced with such a figure, Jonas Colon's sympathetic assistant turns to the darkening political atmosphere in Europe and compares the strikers' efforts to those of the Loyalists in Spain.

But this analogy—which works by comparing Washington's employment policies to Madrid's brutal repressions—seems only to leave the strikers on still more dubious footing. In point of fact, their city "is not Spain," writes the national headquarters of the Writers' Union—which decides not to back the strike—"nor is the Authors' Project the same as the Chevrolet factory" (380). Gest is himself paralyzed with doubt concerning the strike, and not simply because he is unsure how to picket successfully a federal relief agency that cannot be threatened with the prospect of lost profits. Moreover, the details surrounding the strike are anything but unequivocal. A flamboyant loose cannon who spearheads the strike and steals documents from Thorton Hohaley's desk that suggest he has been pilfering from the project, Lloyd Matson admits to having become a Communist simply because he saw it as the best way to rankle his boss. "Each of us has a *true* reason for joining [the Party]," expounds Matson, "regardless of what *sounds* good" (250). When Tremaine has Matson fired for his actions (or, more accurately, when Matson is fired for a reason invented to distract attention from Hohaley's petty thievery), the strikers are placed in an uncomfortable position. They know Matson to be a shady and self-aggrandizing character and suspect that he deserves to be fired; at the same time, they fear a dangerous precedent is set when the Tremaine machine terminates his employment with the spurious accusation that he sold pornographic photographs to co-workers.

The incidents surrounding the real-life dismissal of Wayne Barker, the WPA worker on whom Matson is based, were still more fantastic. According to Conroy's *New Masses* article, Barker was actually fired because he had used Henry Alsberg's name to obtain information for a *New Masses* article of his own, published on August 25, 1936. The article, written under the pseudonym Michael Hale and titled "Fifteen Leading Jews Marked for Death," was an exposé of one James True, a "key man in the dissemination of anti-Semitic literature" and "the pet Jew-baiter of Republican super-patrioteer groups." According to Barker's article, True was planning to assassinate fifteen leading Jewish American figures at the heart of what he called "the Jew Deal," among them Supreme Court justices Louis Brandeis and Benjamin Cardozo, Harvard law professor Felix Frankfurter, Secretary of the Treasury Henry Morgenthau Jr., and the ambassador to France, Jesse Isidor Strauss. Barker reports True as saying, "There are about fifteen of them who run things here and are part of an international alliance who plan to wreck Christianity and the world. Now the thing to do would be to get them out of the way. If these big Jews were bumped off, then we wouldn't have any trouble. They ought to be put in their graves."[34] Neither Alsberg nor Parker ever made official mention of Barker's article, which does not show up even tangentially in *Lamps at High Noon*. At the same time, the novel does find Gest repeatedly denying that he is Jewish. At the start of the novel Gest is coming home from a drinking spree when he is stopped by a local policeman. The situation feels implicitly menacing; even the approach of the officer is "very frightening" (21). When Gest is abruptly asked, "Jew?" it seems only natural that he should reply, "Oh, no, sir. French. Part French. Part Swedish" (22). Monroe may not have been Spain, but Balch makes clear how imminent an American Third Reich sometimes seemed to those who were Jewish in the thirties.

Despite all of this, Gest refuses Matson's cynicism. Most of all, he remains committed to the idea that with the appropriate coaxing the New Deal might implement many of the left's social programs. The failure to produce such a rapprochement between left and center, Balch further suggests, stems from a lack of vision in both camps. Blacklisted for fighting Tremaine's machine on behalf of labor, Clyde Harkins thus blames Tremaine's power not on a craven New Deal but on the tendency of radical activists to miss the forest through the trees. He lashes out at the naive Charlie Gest:

> Communists! Don't tell me about your Communists! I know all about your Communists. What were they talking about when Tremaine was swinging the State Legislature like it was his kiddy-car? They were talking about the coolies in China. When the big fight came up in '33 (I bet you don't even remember it) over the stuff Tremaine was pouring into the state highways, giving us the biggest automobile fatality list of any state in the Union, what were the Communists talking about? History will hold Goering responsible for the Reichstag fire, they were shouting. Who gave a damn about coolies and the Reichstag? Who even knows where China is? (139)

Needless to say, Harkins once gave a damn, but he remains bitterly impatient with the left's approach to people like Tremaine. "I am not a Red," the disillusioned radical concludes. "I'll tell you what I really am. Are you ready for a big surprise? Hold your breath now. I'm just a plain middle-class liberal small businessman kind of a Democrat who believes in the Constitution and the Bill of Rights. Yes, can you feature that? Just a plain Democrat" (142).

Harkins's words wear well today, when the academic left seems relatively uninterested in the beleaguered welfare state, the rapidly dissolving legacy of the New Deal. Eager only to theorize "capital," many on today's left seem equally uninterested in taking up the corporations that replaced the modern-era political machines. As cultural critics we know that "late capitalism" has a "logic," but we know relatively little about how it is organized on the ground; consequently, even as recent criticism has turned en masse to the products of the contemporary culture industry, one is hard-pressed to find work on the multinational media monopolies that produce such ostensibly popular artifacts. If the contemporary left is able to afford this kind of apathy, Harkins's vitriol helps explain why the old left could not. Though it is not a direct allegory of the Hitler-Stalin Pact, *Lamps at High Noon* speaks to the notorious détente between Germany and the Soviet Union far more coherently than it does to the Spanish Civil War. Published a full five years after the strike, and two years after the pact would so disillusion its author, Balch's novel is a case study in the price paid by the left for involvement with an unambiguously capitalist state. If writers are going to work for the state, Harkins therefore suggests, they should know how it works and who runs it—they should learn to negotiate its Byzantine corridors with the same fervor they bring to intellectual debate.

Charlie Gest's feelings toward the Writers' Project move from uncritical exuberance to hardened skepticism as he learns to do just this. Gest wants desperately to believe in the New Deal; he has the ecumenical passion that he calls "the desire for faith" (80). Only reluctantly does he confess to himself that its programs are as potentially dangerous as they are salutary, that its good intentions do not always overshadow the abuses it tolerates on the way to realizing those intentions. Only slowly does he come to see Roosevelt as what a wizened neighborhood philosopher calls "the Pharaoh-Moses." The old man maintains that "Roosevelt, above all Presidents since Lincoln," possesses a kind of schizophrenia bound to "drive mad the greatest." He explains, "The role of Pharaoh is to rule: to sit like Jehovah's bad conscience on the place of power; that of Moses—for Jehovah can be good too, although very seldom—is to smite at him who rules: to rebel, to give blows back" (170). *Lamps at High Noon* is filled with similarly torn and ambivalent representations of the New Deal. Departing for his visit with Clyde Harkins, Gest is asked to describe his employer by a local civil servant:

> "We're beginning to get a lot of government men nowadays. How was Washington, when you left it?"
> "Painted white, like a hospital."
> "Sick house. Eh, sir?"
> "Depends on the view. House of mercy. Either way." (116)

Unaware that Harkins has been blacklisted, Gest is at this point still sanguine about the New Deal. But white blood-corpuscles, he would soon discover, had won the day over red; the result was hardly "the music of sensitive dreamers" referred to in Balch's "Impressions." *Lamps at High Noon* starts with the festive jubilance of a local Recovery Parade, replete with dances, bands, and the mayor proclaiming "how Roosevelt has brought recovery" (13). It ends in failure and disappointment; though he is hired back as a regular worker after the strike, Charlie's mother dies in a "sick house" of her own at the close of the novel. Helpless and trapped, waiting to die in terror, she seems to embody the fate of those who would look beyond the family for relief.

The Federal Writers' Project would carry on until 1943, when it was dissolved into the War Services Subdivision of the WPA. By then, all of the volumes of the American Guide series had been published. Missouri had successfully produced its own state guidebook two years earlier; *Missouri, a Guide to the "Show Me" State* was published the same year as *Lamps at High Noon.* The guidebook was something less than a monument to Kazin's "collective skill": whereas Gest confesses to Jonah Colon that it would take only six writers to compose the guide, it ended up taking even fewer for the actual guide. The Missouri guide was written almost entirely by Harold Rosenberg of the national office, in part because the strike had left material from the Missouri office in disarray.[35] The guide does not itself make mention of the strike. It does, on the other hand, offer something of a political obituary for Thomas Pendergast, whose fortunes began to wane shortly after the conclusion of the writers' strike, when he came under extensive investigation by the FBI. The guide reports, "In 1938, more than 100 members of the Pendergast political machine of Kansas City were indicted for vote frauds in the city elections and for income tax evasion." The matter is concluded abruptly, in what has to stand as one of the guide's less compelling gestures to the ineluctable progress of democratic, liberal government: "Once given an opportunity, Kansas City repudiated the machine government."[36]

Notes

I would like to thank Alan Wald, Douglas Wixson, and Michael Balch for their help researching this piece.

1. Jack Conroy, "Writers Disturbing the Peace," *New Masses* 21 (Nov. 17, 1936): 13.

2. Richard Kirkendall, *A History of Missouri,* vol. 5, Missouri Sesquicentennial Series, ed. William Parrish (Columbia: University of Missouri Press, 1986), 5:4.

3. Ibid., 5:200.

4. Monty Noam Penkower, *The Federal Writers' Project: A Study in Government Patronage of the Arts* (Urbana: University of Illinois Press, 1977), 164.

5. Gary O. Larson, *The Reluctant Patron: The United States Government and the Arts, 1943–1965* (Philadelphia: University of Pennsylvania Press, 1983), 60.

6. Ibid., 34.

7. Jesse Helms quoted in *The Culture Wars,* ed. Richard Bolton (New York: New Press, 1992), 78, 30.

8. Jack Balch, *St. Louis Post-Dispatch,* Apr. 11, 1944, 1.

9. Fred T. March, "First Novel by a St. Louisan," *New York Times Book Review,* June 1, 1941, 7.

10. For an account of Balch's relationship with Conroy and the St. Louis John Reed Club, see Douglas Wixson, *Worker-Writer in America: Jack Conroy and the Tradition of Midwestern Literary Radicalism, 1898–1990* (Urbana: University of Illinois Press, 1994), 259, 295, 306, 351, 359, 371, 383, 384–85, 395.

11. See *The American Writers' Congress,* ed. Henry Hart (New York: International, 1935), 178.

12. Jack Balch, "Take a Number, Take a Seat," *Partisan Review* 2 (Apr.–May 1935): 66, 67.

13. Reported in Wixson, *Worker-Writer in America,* 432. (Wixson incorrectly states that Balch's short story appears in *New Masses.*)

14. Malcolm Cowley, *The Dream of the Golden Mountains: Remembering the 1930s* (New York: Penguin, 1964, 1980), 283.

15. Robert Warshow, "The Legacy of the 30's," *Commentary,* Dec. 1947, reprinted in *The Immediate Experience: Movies, Comics, Theater and Other Aspects of Popular Culture* (New York: Doubleday, 1962), 35.

16. The four sections of the Federal Arts Projects received just over $27 million out of the almost $5 billion allotted for the WPA in its first year. The initial six-month budget of the Writers' Project came in at just under $6,288,000 for an estimated sixty-five hundred writers; during the course of its eight-year existence, an average of forty-five hundred to fifty-two hundred people were at work for the FWP, as compared with the 2,060,000 workers who drew salaries each month from the WPA in general.

17. Critical opinion varies considerably over the extent to which writers affiliated with the Communist Party and other politically radical organizations embraced New Deal ideology while working on the Writers' Project. Michael Denning notes the large numbers of radical writers employed by the WPA only to confirm the right-wing assumption that these figures "infiltrated" the government and other such organs of the cultural apparatus (*The Cultural Front* [New York: Verso, 1996]). Douglas Wixson suggests just the opposite, namely that "the United States government filled a vacuum created when the left largely abandoned its sponsorship of worker-writing" (*Worker-Writer in America,* 421). Helen Harrison contends that "In the early 1930s, a significant number of American artists who were aligned, either practically or theoretically, with the Communist Party became supporters of the New Deal. Artist members of the John Reed Club, a party directed cultural organization, were enjoined to develop 'revolutionary art' as a vehicle for the type of social change that had transformed tsarist Russia into the Soviet Union. Yet many of them found Roosevelt's 'peaceful revolution' worthy of the highest accolade they could bestow on a subject: its inclusion as an affirmative theme in their work" ("The John Reed Club Artists and the New Deal: Radical Responses to Roosevelt's 'Peaceful Revolution,'" *Prospectus* 5 [1980]: 241). Robert McElvaine concurs when he notes that "leftist intellectuals were basically in tune with the values of the public aspirations of the New Deal. Franklin Roosevelt often employed the same class-oriented rhetoric and symbols that the leftists used. The leftists were calling for a liberal socialism, while FDR was offering a social liberalism" (*The Great Depression, America, 1929–1941* [New York: Times Books, 1984], 206). As Paula Rabinowitz reports, David Lawrence blames the Writers' Project in particular for diluting the

radicalism of the literary left of the period: "Lawrence answered his own query, 'Who Slew Proletcult?' by blaming the appointment of writers sympathetic to the CPUSA to positions of power in the Federal Writers' Project of the Works Progress Administration (WPA), an action that tempered their radicalism" (Rabinowitz, *Labor and Desire: Women's Revolutionary Fiction in Depression America* [Chapel Hill: University of North Carolina Press, 1990], 30).

18. Alan Filreis, "Stevens, 'J. Ronald Latimer,' and the Alcestis Press," *Wallace Stevens Journal* 17 (Fall 1993): 181.

19. Penkower, *Federal Writers' Project,* 5.

20. *Partisan Review* 6 (Summer 1939): 26.

21. Alfred Kazin, *On Native Grounds* (New York: Reynal and Hitchcock, 1942), 501.

22. Malcolm Cowley, *The Literary Situation* (New York: Viking Press, 1954), 176.

23. Forbes Watson, "A Steady Job," *American Magazine of Art,* Apr. 1934, 168.

24. Edward Bruce, "Implications of the Public Works of Art Project," *American Magazine of Art,* Mar. 1934, 114.

25. George Biddle, "Art under Five Years of Federal Patronage, *American Scholar* 9 (July 1940): 333.

26. Archibald MacLeish in *New Republic,* Apr. 15, 1946, quoted in Jerre Mangione, *The Dream and the Deal: The Federal Writers' Project, 1935–1943* (New York: Little Brown, 1972), 349.

27. William F. McDonald, *Federal Relief Administration and the Arts* (Columbus: Ohio State University Press, 1969), 681.

28. Cited in *The Writer in a Changing World: The Proceedings of the Second American Writers' Congress,* ed. Henry Hart (New York: Equinox, 1937), 245.

29. Lizabeth Cohen, *Making a New Deal: Industrial Workers in Chicago, 1919–1939* (Cambridge: Cambridge University Press, 1990), 268.

30. Gwendolyn Mink, *The Wages of Motherhood: Inequality in the Welfare State, 1917–1942* (Ithaca: Cornell University Press, 1995), 137.

31. Cited in *Writer in a Changing World,* 241.

32. *A Documentary History of the Negro People in the United States, from the New Deal to the End of World War II,* ed. Herbert Aptheker, 4 vols. (New York: Citadel Press, 1992, 1974), 4:174, 179.

33. Unpublished and uncollected letter from Jack Balch to Jack Con-roy, Mar. 21, 1941.

34. Michael Hale, "Fifteen Leading Jews Marked for Death!" *New Masses* 20 (Aug. 25, 1936): 8, 9.

35. Penkower, *Federal Writers' Project,* 164.

36. Workers of the Writers' Program of the WPA in the State of Missouri, *Missouri, a Guide to the "Show Me" State* (New York: Duell, Sloan and Pearce, 1941), 58.

Bibliography

Selected Works by Jack Balch

"Beedlebugs." In Federal Writers' Project, *American Stuff: An Anthology of Prose and Verse by Members of the Federal Writers' Project with Sixteen Prints by the Federal Arts Project,* 180–85. New York: Viking, 1937.

Castle of Words and Other Poems. St. Louis: Bromberg, 1931.

Lamps at High Noon: A Novel. New York: Modern Age, 1941.

"Looking for Elmer." *New Masses* 17 (Oct. 22, 1935).

"Odessa: Tough and Beautiful City Possessed, for a While, by Many." *St. Louis Post-Dispatch,* Apr. 11, 1944, 1.

"A Profile of Tennessee Williams." *Theatre* 4 (Apr. 1959).

"St. Louis Idyll." *Partisan Review* 1, no. 4 (1934): 43–47.

"Singer of the Gumbo." Review of *Road to Utterly,* by H. H. Lewis. *New Masses* 16 (July 9, 1935): 24–25.

"Take a Number, Take a Seat." *Partisan Review* 2, no. 7 (1935): 59–69.

"Telephone Call." *Anvil,* Jan.–Feb. 1934. Reprinted in *Writers in Revolt: The Anvil Anthology,* edited by Jack Conroy and Curt Johnson, 16–18. New York: Lawrence Hall, 1973.

Reviews of *Lamps at High Noon*

Anonymous. *New Republic* 104 (June 30, 1941): 898.

Anonymous. *New Yorker* 17 (May 31, 1941): 70.

Anonymous. *St. Louis Star Times,* Dec. 18, 1941.

Bauer, Robert. *Accent* 2 (Autumn 1941): 62.

Feld, Rose. *Books,* May 25, 1941, 8.

Marsh, F. T. *New York Times Book Review,* June 1, 1941, 7.

Rankin, R. B. *Library Journal* 66 (May 15, 1941): 463.

Smyth, Frances. *Saturday Review of Literature* 24 (June 14, 1941): 10.

Other Sources

Conroy, Jack. "Writers Disturbing the Peace." *New Masses* 21 (Nov. 17, 1936): 13.

Hale, Michael. "Fifteen Leading Jews Marked for Death!" *New Masses* 20 (Aug. 25, 1936): 8, 9.

Mangione, Jerre. *The Dream and the Deal: The Federal Writers' Project, 1935–1943.* New York: Little Brown, 1972.

Penkower, Monty Noam. *The Federal Writers' Project: A Study of Government Patronage of the Arts.* Urbana: University of Illinois Press, 1977.

Sporn, Paul. *Against Itself: The Federal Theater and Writers' Project in the Midwest.* Detroit: Wayne State University Press, 1995.

Wixson, Douglas. "Jack Conroy and the East St. Louis Toughs." *New Letters* 57 (Summer 1991): 29–57.

——— "'Very Penniless If Fairly Philosophical Victim': The Jean Winkler Correspondence about Jack Conroy and the Ill-Fated Missouri Writers' Project." *New Letters* 57 (Summer 1991): 61–87.

——— *Worker-Writer in America: Jack Conroy and the Tradition of Midwestern Literary Radicalism, 1898–1990.* Urbana: University of Illinois Press, 1994.

BOOK ONE

PART ONE

"Where are you going?"

Mrs. Gest looked up suspiciously from the potatoes she was peeling. Her eyes were contemptuous, black, ready to anger.

"It's two o'clock," Charlie answered as sullenly. "Maybe the mailman's been here."

Always wanting to know where he was going!

He ran down the stairs. Her voice followed him down: "A *bundle* of letters." The words in Yiddish carried an indescribable irony.

Halfway down, he made out three white objects. He ran faster. One of them turned out to be the gas and electric bill for Mrs. Cohen who shared the apartment with them; another turned out to be their own gas and electric bill. He cursed. He was always expecting a letter—from where he didn't know. But at the sight of the third his heart stood still, then began to race like mad. It was a long white official-looking envelope.

"Anything for us?" his mother called.

She too was always expecting something.

"The gas and electric bill."

He lit a cigarette, took a long puff. No hurry, no hurry . . . all the time in the world! He slit the corner of the envelope by sticking a key into it and jerking.

3

"Dear Mr. Gest," he read, "Your name has been suggested in connection with a branch of the National Authors' Project we are about to start in your state. Although details of supervision and personnel have not been settled as yet and, indeed, the project has not altogether been decided on as yet, we may be in a position to offer you a place as a supervisor in your city at the probable salary of fifteen hundred dollars a year. Should you be interested in this type of work, kindly write giving full particulars."

He stared at the signature. "Jonas B. Colon, Director."

"What are you doing there?" his mother's voice came.

His answer came automatic.

"I'm taking a shave," he answered rudely.

Fifteen hundred a year. Holy Jesus! Twelve into fifteen goes one, carry three, twelve into thirty goes two, carry six—one twenty-five a month! Over twenty-five a week! Five dollars a day!

He walked slowly back up the stairs. Take your time!

"How much is the gas and electric?"

He looked at his mother sitting at the table with the paring-knife in her fat hand. "Fat like a hog," she was fond of saying, "but ask the doctor—I aint healthy." His eyes took in the dark rings cutting into her fat cheekbones like gouging fingers, the pile of dirty dishes waiting in the sink to be washed, the line of socks and underwear hanging on the "summer" porch. "It's for two months," he said steadily, "three dollars and sixteen cents."

She cursed. "A fire on them! Every month we got less to cook, and every month it's higher."

He walked steadily to his desk and slipped a clean sheet into the typewriter.

"Dear Mr. Colon: In answer to your letter of November the twenty-seventh—"

"We suffer from the want of bread," said his mother, staring with hatred at her ancient enemy, the desk, "we suffer till the soul goes out of us—and he *writes!*"

—"may I say with all the emphasis possible that I certainly do

4

need"—he thought a moment, crossed out the *do need*—"am interested—"

"It makes a difference to him, does it, that a penny comes to us like a hot coal in the belly! That the poor old man holds on to his tortured job by a soaped straw; that I don't know how we'll get coal this winter!"

"For God's sake," he roared, "let me alone!"

"Swearing comes to the shameless barefoot who lies on his father's old bones. Let me alone, he tells me. Die, he says!"

"—in your proposition."

Next paragraph.

"Enclosed, should you be interested in my work, are two short stories published in the last three years. The one called "Her Lips, Her Hands" was given a star for distinguished rating in Mr. O'Brien's yearly anthology of *Best American Short Stories*. The other, I understand, was to have been included in another anthology, but was forced out because of some other material."

He paused to think, in despair at his language, which seemed inept and cold, and started a new paragraph: "I left highschool in my third year because of family economic conditions—"

Oh, Christ! What rot!

He yanked the sheet out of the typewriter, crumpled it into the wastebasket.

"Got a nickel, Ma?"

Her voice was as harsh as his own.

"Work, you'll have a nickel."

He went to the purse.

"I took a nickel."

She continued to peel potatoes, her mouth, as she bent over the pan, compressed, the somber lines cutting into the fat flesh. He watched her for a moment, fighting an insanely ecstatic desire of a sudden to stay her busy fingers and scream out the news.

Steady, boy, steady. All the time in the world!

"I'll be back in a minute," he whispered.

5

All the way down the stairs and into the street his pace was even. Then he began to run. Faster! Faster! Three little boys playing cops and robbers in the sun stopped to stare and whistle. Tony the barbecue man yelled "Eh, where you go?" but got no answer. One of the Blond Wop's girls prepared to tap at the window, but he passed too quickly. He ran into the drugstore. "Calley 061 . . ." His hands trembled dialing the telephone; he strangled a mad impulse to shout . . . "Elizabeth? Listen, Elizabeth!" He got hold of himself. "What're you doing tonight, my pet?"

He made his voice masterful, calm, still with a quiet joy in it. "You seem to be in a good mood," she said.

As usual, she seemed glad to hear from him. At the same time, there was that impatience with him too. He knew just what would impress her.

"I just sold a story to *Saturday Evening Post*," he said recklessly. "Of course," he said, "there's some changes they want made, so they're holding up the check until then. Meanwhile—"

"Meanwhile?" She laughed.

"Listen," he said. He lowered his voice, whispered: "I'm a bad man. I dream of you, my crunchy slut, particularly as night falls. That's why I sleep all day."

"So?"

"Well?" he said. "Huh?"

"All right," she said. "Tonight at ten. Pick me up at the church. You know where it is."

"Okay," he said. "At the church. At ten. You'll know me by the Bible in my hands."

He put the receiver back on the hook. For a moment he frowned at an invisible reflection of himself in the depths of the booth. *Saturday Evening Post!* He shouldn't have said that. Well, he had. And he was to meet Elizabeth tonight! He hadn't expected that at all. He was lucky if he got to see her once in two weeks. Lizzie. The job. Thinking of Lizzie and her golden brown

6

length, the lithe walk on her and the cool solid breasts, the job became more real. He laughed aloud. He pulled the letter out of his pocket, read it right there in the booth.

"By God!" he said. "Well, by God!"

HE WALKED STEADILY DOWN THE STREET BACK TO THE HOUSE, restraining a mad impulse to shout, to run, as the full import of the communication came slowly and then with a rush to him. His pulses beat as he thought of what could be done with a steady job and steady dough coming in. First thing, that was one thing sure, his mother was going to the hospital for two weeks for a rest. Second, his dad would quit his job and by God! there'd be one hell of a sweet long rest for him before anybody'd even begin to hear of his getting another job again. Thirdly, Elizabeth and he—

O Elizabeth!

In spite of himself his steps quickened as, in an uncontrollable bolt of fancy, he visualized and endured his mother's objections to his plans for their welfare.

"Goddamit," he heard himself thunder, "don't you realize we can afford this splendor now?"

He appealed to his dad and kid sisters, standing around with shining eyes full of adoration.

"Did you ever see such an idiot as this fool who gave me birth? It's like casting pearls before swine! Twenty-five bucks a week, I'm telling you! Yeah, rolling in like a march of the drunken sailors!" He got mad as he contemplated her stubbornness. "Careful, hell," he growled at her imagined admonitions. "Please try to understand that YOU DON'T HAVE TO SCRUB ANY MORE!"

Afraid to look into those shining eyes too long, he jumped from one reform to another. Items of diet for his mother in line with the doctor's hitherto impossible instructions. And what unheard of items he could think of! New dresses and shoes for the

7

kids and movies twice a week, an extra blanket for little Janice these winter nights, an unabridged dictionary for himself as a start . . .

And if only the job kept up, then, then—

Oh, there was no end to possibilities, no end, no end! And he looked about him with generosity and warmth for the whole neighborhood. These cobblestones, these bits of grass growing so strangely between the pavement bricks and around the fire hydrants, what love of them did not fill his heart at this moment! What ugliness, what misery and twisted growth did he not sweep away in an instant!

An old, well-nigh forgotten, dream of his highschool days came back to haunt him with its first loveliness and pity. In this dream, he saw the twilight of humanity, when the whole world had grown old. There they sat, his father, his mother, his childhood friends and playmates, and all were gray and finished now. And beside each grieving figure was the boy or girl he had been. These children still played and sang their songs, but the elders who were the children asked themselves where their lives had gone. Then the child who was himself took him by the hand and began to lead him. Instantly, the other children had their elders by the hand, and all were moving, traveling, running down the gray slopes. The further they moved, the faster they ran. Soon each pair began to merge, was one.

There were no fathers, no children, none hurt or to be hurt, none groaning, none lame, but a host of eternally youthful, eternally strong young men!

Tears came to his eyes! Such crazy extravagant thoughts! And from where? The merest lead for a job, not even a job as yet, and to be aroused so easily! And in superstitious fear, he tried to hold down his soaring hopes, tried too to keep from looking at these rows of box-like houses with his understanding, as on places haunted by the curse of the dreams that died in them. . . .

IN THIS MOOD, DEEPLY MOVED, ALTERNATELY EXCITED AND depressed, he came back to the house and was amazed to see that the landlord's car was standing at the curb. What the hell is this —the first of the month? His face freezing into a sullen guarded mask, he went up the stairs. The kitchen door was open and—a sound to start snowballs growing in his stomach—he heard his mother crying.

"What's the matter?" he demanded, coming into the room.

"He asks what's the matter, the philosopher!" his mother answered.

The landlord leaned across the table. He spread one withered hand on it in a gesture of firmness and condolence. Eighty-nine years old, he was a great favorite among the poor Russian-Jewish women who rented from him. They loved to hear him tell how he had refused to sanction his sons' wives' schemes to retire him from the active management of his buildings. They loved to hear him tell how he had come across the ocean sixty-five years before without a penny to his name, with nothing but an ambition to work, to make good, to succeed. They loved to hear this particularly when their husbands and sons were in the room to hear.

They were awed to know that he came from Switzerland, and could not speak a word of Yiddish.

"God love me! Where is Switzerland?" they would ask each other.

Charlie, like the rest of the men, who felt they knew what was what, hated him and considered him a trouble-maker. "Stingy son of a bitch," they would say of him. "Eighty-nine years old, may he spit gold! And still making money."

They all knew the story of the landlord's "man," Poor Bill, the carpenter who had lost his memory. Poor Bill slept in the basement with the rats, had appeared one day from nowhere, not knowing who he was, and had been sleeping there ever since. He cleaned ash-pits for people, did odd-jobs to keep alive. One day the boss gave him the job of fixing the Gests' roof so it wouldn't

9

leak when it rained. This was during the summer. When it was finished, Poor Bill had come for his pay.

"You'll have to wait for the rainy season so's I can see whether you did the roof a good job," the landlord, it was known, had said.

The incident lent itself well to dramatization.

"*Nu, nu,*" one would say, presenting Poor Bill's side of the argument, "suppose, may the hour never be, the job is found out not to be a good one?"

"In that case, may the hour never be, as you say, you can tear the work off again."

"And it can rain in good, like before."

The landlord's name was Kleinschmidtt, with two *t*'s. The money didn't mean anything to him any more, he had told Poor Bill; with him it was the business principle involved. His greatest ambition was to live to be one hundred years old. The women looked at his full white head of hair and rosy cheeks and confided to each other: "May such things be said of *my* sons!" And although *his* mother had now been buried for more than half a century, their eyes still clouded fondly as they thought of a mother's feelings as she gazed on such as he.

The men all lived for the day he would fall down a ladder and break a leg.

He leaned forward now and spoke in his careful, faintly German-like accents: "Don't worry, Mrs. Gest. Do I look like I will throw you out tomorrow? The money is good, I know it."

"My Charlie wants to know what's the matter here," Mrs. Gest said bitterly. "God wanted to bless me—he sent me a Charlie for a son!"

"It aint good for you," said Mr. Kleinschmidtt; "look at me. You should *never* worry."

"Lives in the house. Eats. Sleeps. Does he care what goes on?"

"Don't worry. Don't worry. Am I putting you out on the street?"

"From the cradle to the grave we slave. Why do we do this foolish thing?"

Confused and undecided, trying to come to a decision from which he shrank, Charlie went into the bedroom and began to rummage in the closet. Should he tell her, or should he not? But suppose there was no job, after all? Come to think of it, why should there be? Had anything real ever existed for him, outside of his warped imagination? Kleinschmidtt! He shook his head, a deep slow anger stirring in him. . . .

Anger is my only son

he improvised:

Anger is my only son
And I love my son
But it's not too late
For birth control

he laughed. Pretty lousy. Still, it was a good thought. *Anger is my only son.* Poor bastard, behold your father! Well, it was worth saving, some day he'd do something with it. . . .

Dear dear Mother.

He pulled a shirt off its hook. Then he got a pair of pants and went into the toilet. He put them on. In a minute, he came out, got the coat to match the pants, and put that on. He stood in front of the mirror and looked at himself. Drawing his eyes away from the broad dark face that persisted in staring back at him, he looked up and down his body and concluded that, under the artificial lights of the streets at night, Elizabeth would not know that the coat was cleaner than the pants. On his way back to the kitchen, he looked surreptitiously at the clock.

The landlord, meanwhile, was about to make one of his famous points and had grown into the merriest of humors.

"Your husband makes how much, twenty? Twenty-five dollars a week?"

"Fifteen—if he works a whole week."

"All right. Fifteen. That's even better. He's making fifteen today and yesterday he made twenty. So you think that you have lost a lot of money. Well, let me tell you. I got a friend, used to be worth four hundred thousand dollars. FOUR HUNDRED THOUSAND DOLLARS. A lot of money, yes? All right. Well, the crash came in 1929—I bet you have already forgot about that crash— and he lost two hundred and fifty thousand dollars. TWO HUNDRED AND FIFTY THOUSAND DOLLARS. *That's* money. And you're worrying!"

He turned humorously to Charlie.

"It is the same here. *I* got to wait for my money, and *she's* worrying."

Charlie's "son" leaped like a stab of indigestion.

"You got a hell of a lot to worry about, haven't you?"

The old man flared. "You just bet I have, young man." He smiled again at Mrs. Gest, although a trifle forcedly, and concluded: "Take the advice of an old man. Let those who *have* money worry about money."

JANICE AND CLARA, SUFFERING FROM NOTHING AS YET BUT overflowing spirits, rushed into the house.

"Teacher says that it's everybody's duty to go to the Recovery Parade next Thursday, and it'll be a lot of fun."

"How can it be a lot of fun if it's gonna be a duty?"

"It aint the same thing, Stink-face! It aint like you have to wash your face behind the ears."

Ordinarily, Mrs. Gest, a true mother, entered into their activities with an enthusiasm to match their own; these included every detail of their school lives, the reading and minute discussions of all the murder and passion crimes in the newspapers and the latest gossip from Hollywood. The Recovery Parade, that lovely and tinsel make-believe in the wicked city that the newspapers and the radio were playing up, concerned her too—but today, sick and harassed more than usual, their words cut like knives aimed at her body.

"Mad ones!" she shrieked. "You are Jewish children! And it bothers you what the *Goyim* do, have fun, duty—may they be a sacrifice for you!"

In this state, the children knew better than to cross her openly. One might as well cross the moon or the sun, or a bad grade in school—not that they had thought of it in just those ways. "She's crabby," they thought, dismissing the matter from their minds, with the reservation, "All right for her; wait till she asks us to read the paper to her," and went into the "middle" room, whence presently their whisperings, effervescent, arose again, flowering soon into shouts.

"Just like in the Mardi Gras in New Orleans when they got floats and flowers and everything, they're gonna have it here. And they're gonna have a big dance in the streets and there's gonna be bands and then afterwards they're gonna have folk dances and a performance by the ballet dancers and the Mayor's gonna speak and tell how President Roosevelt has brought recovery—"

Clara had been waiting with her mouth pursed. Now, as Janice paused for breath, she said scornfully, "How can they have flowers in winter?"

"Oh, my head!' Mrs. Gest suddenly moaned.

Her face, as she bent over the steaming peas and carrots of the supper soup, suddenly seemed to Charlie, in spite of the fatness of her cheeks, more haggard and worn than he had ever seen it, and a wave of such tenderness and pity for her came over him that his heart seemed to close like a fist, and, more than anything else, he wanted to say the words that would bring her comfort.

It was no use, he decided, he had better tell her.

"Listen, Ma. I—I didn't mean to tell you this until I was sure, b-but, listen, I—I think I've got a job."

She looked at him with hard wet mistrustful eyes from which he found himself flinching.

"A job!"

"No kidding, Ma, I'm pretty sure—"

"Like you always get a job!"

"This time it's different, Ma. I—I got a sure tip. I—I didn't want to tell you until I m-made sure."

Now that he'd told her, he wished he hadn't. Suppose something went wrong? Suppose they decided not to have a project after all—what, for that matter, was a project? What kind of work would they want him to do? And how did he know he could do it?

"I didn't mean to tell you," he muttered resentfully, "but you're always worrying so much about everything. How do you think I feel when I see you going around here with a face like a funeral!"

Against her will she was impressed. "Tell me, Charlie, I'm your mother. What kind of a job is it?"

Her words irritated him.

"What's your being my mother got to do with it?" he shouted. "Why do you make everything sound so goddam personal? So mystical. It's a job, that's all. The way you act, you make it sound as though I'm getting married. Or running from the police."

"God forbid!' she exclaimed. Irrelevantly, she smiled. "What big words you use. Like elephants. Who understands them? I bet you anything you like you don't understand them yourself."

"All right," he said, trying to keep from smiling himself, "I don't understand them."

They looked at each other shyly, as though about to romp together. Mrs. Gest's eyes began to grow red.

"You were always a good boy, Charlie. Everything I give him," she said, to the wall, as though it were a third person, "he eats. Not a complaint. He leaves my plates clean like they was scrubbed."

The girls had drawn closer, wooed by the strangeness of the conversation.

"Charlie," wheedled Mrs. Gest, catching him by the sleeve and trying to caress his head, "tell me, give me pleasure! What kind of a job is it?"

"Well," he hesitated, flattered by the attention and perplexed with how to explain, "it's—it's for the Government, you might say."

"For the Government!"

"A detec-uhtif!" Janice screamed.

"A G-man," burst from Clara.

"You see," he said, ignoring them, "it's like in France—or Russia, where the Governments are interested in art academies. In France, if a writer—"

"Writer?" said Mrs. Gest.

"Well, what's wrong with that? The Government is going to pay writers to write. It's a new policy, under Roosevelt. . . . All over the world, educated people have been laughing at America."

"France. Russia. Roosevelt." Mrs. Gest shook her head. "The Government will pay you money to write—a story?"

It certainly sounded preposterous, as he knew. Why did he sound so insincere, even to himself?

"Look, Ma," he said angrily. "Did you ever hear about Shakespeare?"

"Yes, I heard about him."

"We heard about him too," Janice and Clara shouted.

"All right. Did you ever hear about"—he searched for a name that she might recognize—"Maxim Gorki? Sholem Aleichem? Spinoza?"

"*Nu?*"

"Well," he stuttered, "they were young men once. They had mothers. Sometimes they were hard up. It was different in those days, though. They didn't have the hard times we have now.

15

Even so, there are a lot of Gorkis we never heard anything about. . . ."

He began to talk fast against the look of suspicion beginning to appear on her face.

"Who cared anything if a man starved—"

"One thing," said Mrs. Gest. "On my life—I should die if it isn't true—you aint fooling me about the job?"

He hated this oath, a favorite of hers. She asked a man to "swear" as though, if he did, then she knew things to be all right. Logic meant nothing; arguments were like guns, to get you out of tight places.

"For Christ's sake," he shouted, "why the hell should I fool you? What the hell do you think I'm getting out of this?"

"On my life?—swear!"

"Aw, for Christ's sake!"

Furious with himself, not looking at her, he flung himself into the next room, picked up a book he had swiped from the library that day. It was *Swann's Way,* by Marcel Proust. He was reading it to study Proust's style. But he could not concentrate on it, get past one page, and he put it down, going to his desk:

"Dear Mr. Colon: This is to say that I have received your kind letter of the—

"Dear Mr. Kleinschmidtt: Now is the time for all good men to come to the aid of the party now is the time for all good—"

How the devil did he ever expect to be a writer when he couldn't even write a letter? Irrelevantly, he thought, How the hell can anyone do anything in this crazy house! He was conscious of the kids' chattering, back to the damned and double-damned Mardi Gras and the Recovery Dance, his mother's silent scrutiny of his back. He added the sheet to the other spoiled ones, and got up.

"Aint you gonna stop for supper?"

"I aint hungry."

"As long as I cook for you!"

"I told you I aint hungry."

"Put on your coat. It's cold outside."

"Hell, don't I know it's cold outside?"

Now that he had told her the news, he had but one wish—to get out of the house. He had done his best. She could make what she liked of what he had told her.

"When did you hear of this job, this prosperity?" his mother asked.

He did not answer.

"Didn't you maybe get a letter that Clara could read to me?"

"I didn't get a letter."

"Will you take us to the Parade next Thursday?" Janice said. "Will you?"

"Next Thursday is a long way off," he said. "Maybe next Thursday I got to see a fellow."

Mrs. Gest couldn't see why he shouldn't swear if he was telling the truth. "Some fellow he's got to see," she sped him maliciously, "a fellow who lifts his skirts."

On the landing, he paused and thought a minute. No dough. He went across the street to Tony's barbecue place. The place, as usual, was crowded with Negroes who came, not for barbecue, but for the ten-cents-a-half-pint whisky Tony served in the back room.

"Hello, Curly," a black girl said, leaning back slovenly on a chair and carelessly gapping her legs at him. Couples danced on the floor, pressing hard against each other and standing in one place. He stared at the black girl's thighs and gasped as he thought of Elizabeth. Pressing through the hot throng, he made his way to where Tony declaimed to his sycophants.

Tony waved his hand. "Be witchyou in fi' minutes, Charlie," he said, and immediately came over. " 'Ow you? 'Ow you mother and family?"

"All right. Say, Tony, can I ask you a favor?"

"What you want, Charlie?"

"I—I'm going to work for a newspaper next month. C-can you loan me—a buck?"

"Sure. Here, Charlie."

"I won't be able to pay you till I get paid, you know. Maybe not till next month."

"That's all right, Charlie, my friend."

As he went out the front door, past the black girl, he heard Tony's shrill harsh voice: "You see that fella? That's one-uh fine Jew-boy! Smart. He will amount-uh something."

"GOING TO THE PARADE THURSDAY?" MRS. COHEN ASKED AT the corner.

A buck. Man, it aint chicken! Ha, ha.

"What parade?" he said.

As usual, the Blond Wop's girls started tapping. The way they sat behind their curtains, they could never see who was coming until he was almost past. The only thing they could tell was whether it was a man coming, by the sound of the steps. But mixed crowds sometimes fooled them.

"Why the hell aint you making plans to go to the parade?" Charlie shouted. "I'm going. The Mayor's going."

"Go to hell, screwy!" the girl answered.

He stopped in at the Greek's. The Greek's was a place that had one fine thing about it. Come in six years running. Then stay away six months. Then come back. Nobody would ask you where you'd been. Nobody would give a damn. Be saying hello to a fellow for six years. Disappear. Come back in six years. Hello, he'd say.

Early as it was, a bunch of the fellows were standing around the nickel machine.

"Gimme a shot," he said, in the joint's tough manner.

The Greek poured it out. Charlie laid a dime on the counter. The slug threw a good hot streak down his throat.

"Another one, Charlie?"

18

"Go ahead. I'm in the bucks."

The second shot followed the first. Charlie put another dime beside the first.

"Fill 'er up again?"

"No, two's enough. I'm saving my money for the parade. Got my eye on the dance with all the dolls on it."

"What dance is that?" somebody asked.

"Aint you heard?" the Greek said. "The *dime*-a-dance!"

A couple of the guys drifted up to listen. They were anonymous dark fellows, could have been Greek. Italian. Jewish. Might even have been Armenian. Not a one of them had a last name.

"This is the *Recovery* Dance," Charlie bantered back. "You pay for the dance, but you keep the doll."

That was the way to tell them.

"Don't let your mama find you at Blondie's," the Greek came back.

"Eh, buy me a drink," Tommy Put-Put said.

"Give this man a drink," Charlie said. "The drink will be on me." He put still a third dime down and sauntered off with an air.

It was early yet. Half an hour at least before he could even think of going out to meet Elizabeth. He took a look at the game on the machine. Nothing doing there. Too early for the bigshots with the two bits jackpot habit. Nothing here but the jitney boys and the matchstick fiends.

He looked at the matchstick game for a minute. He deliberately kept from thinking of the Project. He wanted it to soak in first.

The way you played the matchstick game was like this. You put a bunch of matchsticks or toothpicks down on the table, any number. Then you started the game by picking up some of them, no more than three. Then the fellow or fellows you were playing with picked up some. The idea was to make the guy who was to be the loser pick up the last match. Like drawing the short straw. You could play ten games of this a minute. After you'd played a number of games, somebody would start getting nuts before he could quit the game and he'd start a fight.

He hung around until the first fight was about to start.

"All right, Dago," somebody suddenly shouted.

"Your ass," said the dago.

"*Your* ass."

The Greek came over.

"What's the matter, boys?"

"He's trying to give me the silver-lined douche-bag."

"Gentlemen, I got to go," Charlie said.

Nobody paid any attention to him.

He exited, whistling. . . .

"Shine, mister? One nickel, one beer, one smile from yoh best gal!"

The colored boy sat like a king on his wooden stand.

"Shine 'er up?"

He climbed up on the box. The colored boy kneeled at his feet.

"How's business?"

He felt full of curiosity.

"Gittin' mighty cold. People don't like to shine they shoes when they gotta sit in the cold."

The muscles on his shoulders, as he worked, rippled like snakes. His hands tightened like locks around the silken cloth.

"Ever do any fighting?"

"Fight women."

"Boy, you got arms like Dempsey."

"Yas, suh! One nickel, one beer, everybody happy like winning jockey!"

"Wouldn't you rather be fighting than sit here in the cold?"

"Me?" the laughter was derisive. "Hell, I was bohn to sit in the cold."

When Charlie looked back at the corner, the shoe-shine boy was stamping his feet and flinging his arms about him.

20

The drinks had gone to his head. He jingled the coins remaining in his pockets and felt himself lord of the universe. The crowds were catsup to his nostrils. He walked down the crowded street, taking in the high-yellows and the newspaper vendors with impartiality, and sang a song he had heard in a saloon once. The noise he made was just one of the many noises of the street, but he thought of it as the key to the whole.

> Oh, my name is Samuel Hall, Samuel Hall,
> Oh, my name is Samuel Hall, Samuel Hall,
> Oh, my name is Samuel Hall,
> And I hates yuh, one and all,
> Damn your eyes!

A car pulled up behind him with a jerk. He jumped, expecting the police. It was a man and his girl in a thirty-five Ford. Regular symphony hounds. They got out, the girl standing poised in a fur coat and a kerchief tied around her head while the man locked the door.

> Oh, the sheriff he did come, he did come,
> Oh, the sheriff he did come, he did come,
> Oh, the sheriff he did come,
> But he looked so goddam glum,
> Damn his eyes!

This time it was the police. Their habit was to cruise about very slowly up and down the streets, very slowly, very deliberately, watching everything. Cars attempting to pass them would honk their horns impatiently, then, suddenly realizing it was the police, would jam on the brakes, following humbly. Before a long slow line of cars could gather, though, a careless hand would move out from the driver's open window and a round sweep would say, in effect, Pass. At other times, you would be in a grocery store or the drugstore and suddenly, from behind the partition in the back, would stroll an officer. Very frightening. Or you would find them in saloons or the backs of the movie houses of the neighborhood, leaning on their big arms, but never too busy to look at you. Just let them get you for something. . . .

"C'mere, you!"

They had singled him out from the throng. Him they had chosen.

"Wotcha name?"

"Charlie Gest, sir."

"Jew?"

"Oh, no, sir. French. Part French. Part Swedish."

"Whenja git out?"

"Get out of where?"

"You know where—*stir?*"

"If you mean prison, the penitentiary, officer, I've never been there."

"Where yuh goin'?"

"I'm off to visit a young woman whose hand I shall ask in marriage."

"Listen, punk, you gittin' smart wit' me?"

"Oh, no, officer."

"You aint goin' to no nigger gash-house?"

"Uh, uh."

"Well, wotcha do fuhr living?"

"Me? I'm a writer." May as well be modest. "I write books about nature. The last book I wrote, it was in three volumes. A trilogy."

"Books, huh?" the detective's voice was incredulous, but friendlier. "That's a pretty swell racket, huh? Make lots of money?"

"Well, it depends on the popular taste at the time. Some of my books don't sell as well as others, but then—it's all in a lifetime."

"Wotcha say yuh name was?"

"Gest. But I don't write under that name. Proust. That's the name I write under. Marcel Proust. All my books are in the library."

"You got a regular publisher for them books? Like Macfadden like in *True Detective Stories?*"

"Oh, yes. This is a Government house. The National Authors' Project of Washington, D.C."

The cops told him to be good, and left. The crowd which had gathered dispersed, disappointed.

> I saw Mamie in the crowd, in the crowd,
> I saw Mamie in the crowd, in the crowd,
> I saw Mamie in the crowd,
> And I hollered right out loud,
> "Hey, Mamie, aincha proud?"
> Damn her eyes!

CHARLIE HAD HARDLY BEEN GONE TEN MINUTES WHEN THERE came a knock at the door, and without further ado, in walked Harry Goselkin. The sisters looked at each other with a grin. Mrs. Gest was glad too to see those haggard cheeks and the high curved bald forehead that bulged out from the head like a mountain. He looked like a genius, but a bigger fool never breathed. But just now he was most welcome, not only because he was the man Mrs. Gest "planned" for the next-door widow, Mrs. Cohen, but because his arrival was opportune to drive away the sparkle of hope that Charlie's news had kindled, and that she could hardly trust herself to believe in.

"Look who's here!" she ejaculated gladly. "Harry, what brings you here?"

She gave her face a quick rub, hoping to erase the tears that had been dribbling down it, but he noticed nothing. His eyes, which seemed to hold infinite depths of slyness and of wisdom, revealed nothing, really, but a great greediness.

He jerked an explanatory shoulder in the direction of the corridor.

"Where is my fortune?" he smirked, in a whisper because of the thin walls. "Is she at home?"

"Foolish man! Where else?"

Janice and Clara, studying their expressions in the mirror in the bedroom, crept closer. They were at an age when all experiences were occasions for awe and entertainment. They wore the same big eyes and interested expressions for all occasions, whether it was for the doctors who came to examine their mother's groanings, for the mother-cat in the attic upstairs waiting for her litter to be born, or for the lady from the relief come to ask questions.

They listened to everything with avidity.

"Your fortune!" they heard their mother whisper. "Foolish man to hesitate! The money waits to be spent. She sits there like a blind dog with her bone."

"If it's so good," said Harry, with a shrewd look, "it will wait."

The whispering made everything real mysterious.

The children felt just as they did at a movie. The face of their mother, leaning forward excitedly and whispering, while her hands wove nervously in her lap with a deeper excitement; the complacency with which Harry was now removing his coat, walking on tiptoe to hang it carefully in the closet before moving up to the mirror to regard his vain countenance; the knowledge of the shrew who even now sat on the other side of the door, pathetic in her desire to catch the least word of the conspirators; the certainty with which they both knew she was listening—all these factors gave the girls the same feeling as when the teacher was telling them some story that was real spooky, or when, in the movies, the good woman, the "girl," is standing with her back to the wall in an old castle, and on the dark wall behind her a hand starts moving toward her throat. . . .

Janice whispered into Clara's ear: "Do you think he'll marry her?"

"Ssh!" Janice hissed back.

"Sit, be easy," they heard Harry's gloating counsel. "If you

24

have a cup of coffee, pour a cup. She has waited so long, the dried onion, let her wait some more."

. . . They sat and drank coffee.

"Do you think, no fooling, that this once-upon-a-time beauty really has two hundred dollars?"

"Do I think—? With my own eyes I have seen it, I should have it in the bank!"

"Aw!" said Clara.

"Ssh!" hissed Janice. She explained fiercely to her sister. "She's making it up, dummy. Don't you see, she's got to pretend that the widda's got two hundred dollars."

"If she's got the money," Harry was saying, "why should she work for someone else—a woman her age! Tell me that, not that I call you a liar, that hour should not be! Why doesn't she open herself a little business?"

The children's minds worked busily with their mother's.

"Why should she work? . . . Why *shouldn't* she work? Should she take a chance on losing every penny, her a greener? Or should she sit in the house and wait for you to give her ideas what to do with herself maybe?"

Harry brought up another objection. "I don't know. Two hundred dollars. What is that? Can one buy a store for two hundred dollars?"

Mrs. Gest now spoke with genuine enthusiasm. "One works," she said vigorously. "One pushes himself up. You need to go to a show?" (The children's eyes blazed scorn with hers at those who needed to go to shows.) "Don't go to a show. Stay home. Sleep on the table. Try, try—there is nothing a man cannot do, if he only tries!"

Her voice, unknown to herself, had risen until it could be heard plain and loud. The children heard a faint scratching sound from the other side of the wall, and gripped each other's arms. In their imagination they could see the widow rising from her knees. They could see her going creakily to the mirror . . .

25

powdering her nose . . . dabbing her hair . . . turning her head from side to side in an anxious effort to ascertain the faithfulness of the dye . . . pulling her rag of a dress into shape . . . taking a last excited look at herself . . . turning, with a properly innocent smile, to the door. They shuddered deliciously. ". . . Here she comes," they said inside themselves.

There came a knock.

"Come in!" called Mrs. Gest. She bustled for another cup, the lines of recent misery completely gone from her transformed face, her eyes dancing with girlish glee.

Harry lifted his eyes haughtily to the ceiling.

"Am I maybe in the way?" said the widow, framed in the doorway.

BY THE TIME CHARLIE GOT TO THE CHURCH WHERE ELIZABETH managed the church activities of a group of rich children and taught them the story of Jesus Christ and the example of His life, the drinks he had taken had begun to wear off, and the letdown—because he had not eaten before leaving the house—was making him hungry.

He was still too early. For the tenth time, he took the letter from his pocket to read the amazing words.

Come, now, could it be possible, then, that his "chance" had come?

". . . The project has not altogether been decided on as yet . . ." He kept returning to this phrase.

The trouble is, he thought soberly, I've been out in the cold too long to believe in heat any more. Is that a fire down there? Is that what they say? I will get excited about it, but still I will not truly believe that it is a fire. I will keep circling it, though, just outside the light.

There are millions like me, he thought. We live pressed next to each other like sardines in a box. There are private and invisible hills running through the center of the city. Desert areas

26

spread through the downtown sections and the skyscrapers are ghosts. Each man howls on a short-circuit and the shock returns into himself.

I shouldn't have told Ma, he thought. I shouldn't have said a word. When the fox scents food, he doesn't run yelping over the neighborhood, telling of the vague rumor. He crouches low to the ground, sticks out his nose and follows the trail. If nothing's at the end of it, only he's hungry.

But the weather, which was turning colder by the minute, was real enough. Cold weather meant that it would be too cold to go to the park tonight. It was to the park, of course, that he'd hoped to lure Elizabeth.

God's free boudoir where, as a boy, he had often come with other boys to spy on the couples on Murdock Lane.

> Our Father, which Art
> By all accounts
> In the dollar sign,
> Give me this day the big chance
> To pay my own way,
> So that I may not feel dirtier
> Than the next fellow!

Listening to the rising wind, he thought it best to turn up his coat-collar. Meanwhile, he waited—as he always seemed to be waiting—for the hour to strike. His thoughts were a queerly assorted mixture, a sort of swing orchestra, wherein a high quavering note fought tooth and nail for supremacy with the low wah-wah keys, the melody being tossed from the brass—his mother—to the saxophones—Elizabeth, perhaps—while the strings, not taking sides, but whanging away for all comers, were first the project and a glittering hope, then himself asking Elizabeth to come to the park and lie with me and be my love, himself walking down the street looking at the comfortable closed-in houses, himself, the project, Elizabeth, snapshots too with no

27

rhyme or reason out of his childhood. . . . Presently, from the immense doors, swung open as though to expel hundreds of gingham-gowned and frock-coated celebrants, Elizabeth come.

Watching her tall slim figure approaching, he straightened up, and his heart beat faster. She was what he was waiting for. Come closer, blue-green eyes! Sway to me, through me, marble-ass!

"Well, Mr. G.," she said gaily, waving as she caught sight of him, "you finally made it. Congratulations."

"Huh?" he said.

He had almost forgotten what she referred to.

"And *The Saturday Evening Post* at that," she laughed. "My, my, what must you think of the capitalistic system now, my bucko!"

He put one arm around her waist as they walked and let it slip to her hip.

"Your voice is like your breasts," he said. "Full, rich, wonderful, with absolutely no meaning in it at all. That's the only reason I let you talk."

"My," she said, "how you turn a compliment."

"Yep," he said, "down at Police Headquarters, they have me labeled Alias Lord Chesterfield."

"Seriously, though, I'm very much pleased with the sale of the story. I'm taking you to see Professor Blakey. He wants to feed us tea and purr over you."

"I can't show him the size of the check," Charlie said. "Will he require an apology for that?"

"We'll be there in another minute or two," she replied sweetly, "and in the meantime, if you can disengage yourself from certain portions of my anatomy that I am too much of a lady to specify by name, I wish you'd clean up your suspicious little proletarian mind and put a smile on your face."

"When I first started writing," Charlie said, sticking his hands in his pockets, "it was as though my whole life had suddenly become clear. The things I couldn't have . . . I was sixteen at the time and had just returned from the coast from running away from home to discover that my Pa'd been out of work and they'd had to sell Janice's crib. . . . The things that I wondered about by myself. . . . I saw that if I wrote about them— and then, the things I'd always wanted to say to my folks, do for them. . . . If I wrote about things, held a mirror up to the stinking mess . . . and I thought people would be glad—what the hell, here's the truth, they'd say, the man's a writer, and that's no apple butter! The first story I published, I took it around to all my friends—but all they asked was How much did you get for it—and my mother was pleased at first. 'My God,' she said, 'we'll be rich.' But after a while—"

"The thing I like about you," Elizabeth said, "is your really beautiful irrelevance. Now what on earth has all this got to do with a visit to the eminent Professor Blakey to receive congratulations on your crashing the holy citadels?"

"Well," he said, "you're not bad at compliments yourself. The thing that's got me worried is, first, I can't show the little bastard a check and, secondly, if for some reason the *Post* decides not to use the story after all, I don't know how to undo this forthcoming visit, which he will then undoubtedly rue as a waste of his time."

She stopped.

"Wait a minute," she said slowly. "You *have* sold a story, haven't you?"

"Sure I have," he said, "and when I make my first hundred thousand, I will buy you a bag of peanuts and put your name in electric lights on Broadway."

"Ah," she said, "there's my pretty boy! There's my little genius."

OUTSIDE THE GEST "RESIDENCE," AT ABOUT THE TIME THAT Charlie, his congratulations received and all opinions delivered, was saying good-by to Elizabeth at her door but had already taken hours doing it, everything was shadows, not a living dog, to use a common phrase, was on the street. The stores, the saloons, the gambling house—everything was closed, all people seemed asleep. No light even in Tony's place. It was a dark world, a fearful life, in truth, this poverty-stricken street twice as desolate as any wickedness needed. By day, at least, one could talk to someone; but at night, with not a policeman about, and with the winter coming on, men's hearts turned against one another. . . .

Long after her husband had told her the news from his shop and gone to bed, Mrs. Gest was still awake. The evening that had begun in such merriment and joyousness when he had come home to be told that Harry Goselkin had, at last, consented to take Mrs. Cohen to the show if she paid the admission and that —guess what, you'll never guess—Charlie was about to get a job had ended in this:

"The boss took me off five dollars and said he was lucky he could still hold the store open, the way the customers pay him!"

Had anybody ever had such misfortunes to contend with? It seemed that no sooner had you survived long enough to hear some good news, than bad news came along. Charlie's job! Even if it came, what would she do till then?

Tomorrow she had to make her weekly visit to the clinic. No wonder she hated them. Doctor Marvin—that famous specialist of everything but how to make enough to live on—would ask her had she been worrying, had she been eating herring again, was she sending out her washing instead of doing it herself, did she understand that her life was a flickering candle that she must guard against all suddenly opened doors and drafts? . . .

She thought of the long ride out to the hospital on the street-car, the transferring, the fifty cents you had to pay admission, then the long wait till the doctor could see you. And for what? So he should stick his needles into you that made you want to vomit, and the children should shout at her not to eat herring?

She blundered back and forth, back and forth through the rooms, feeling a heavy growth in her as of tears. One time she fixed the blanket over the children's forms, wriggling even in sleep; another time she put a couple of pieces of coal into the stove, placing the precious fragments with care. A visit to the kitchen confirmed the already certain fact that the faucet was still leaking, and she fixed a dry rag to catch the sound.

It was at times such as this, in the long midnight hours when all others were asleep and only she waked, that the waters of her life parted and she saw the rock bottom on which she walked.

A screech to freeze the soul as a taxi full of wild boys careened around the corner drove her to the window again to see that the white old man was still lying in the gutter. First the street had been totally empty, nothing on its accursed black length but the whine of the wind, scratching like a cat. That, and the occasional rumble, awaking wild hopes that it was Charlie returning, of streetcars running east or west two blocks over on Hudson Avenue. Then there had been this old man!

If it wasn't an old man lying in the gutter, it was always a black man beating his woman or a policeman beating a black man!

At first, she had thought the old man must be dead. He lay so peacefully, only a dead man could lie so. But there had been something too grotesque in his position, half in the road, half on the pavement, for him to be dead, and the arm flung over his eyes seemed too protectively arranged for one who might have no further need of fear.

A full second had passed as his open mouth had stared back at her, and, oh, those moments before she had seen that it wasn't Charlie, come to a bad end! Oh, her mother's heart that everything could stab until she had realized that it was another drunkard, such as the street threw up every night as a sewer throws up bad smells!

As she recalled this agony, the agonies of other nights when she had waited up for Charlie came back to her, and soon, soon, if only the flesh endured, the girls would grow up and then, misery! For them too she would be waiting up. At the thought, she had to look at the time. Two o'clock. How could the soul stand such heaped misery! Was not the soul flesh, like blood? He had lied to her, Charlie had! He had no job, he had said he had a job only to stay out late again! She knew it, she knew it!

"Come to bed," her husband said, waking momentarily.

"Go!"

She shuddered at the thought of the horrible treachery of her children. What would happen to them when she was not here any longer to stay awake and pray for them and keep them from harm?

"What are you waddling around like a duck for? In the house are no worms. Come to bed!"

"Cold-blooded one! Do you care what happens to the house? Your son—dragging his frozen bottom from one saloon to another—does he care? You'll both live to be a hundred!"

"Tomorrow you'll be gasping like a fish! Come to bed!"

At this, she felt the heaviness climbing to her throat. Only God was her friend, God—and tears. But bitterness, too, rose in her; bitterness as she thought of the girl she had been, the sweet strong girlhood with laughter on its lips, a girlhood that had been sucked up and eaten, as the maggot eats the apple, by a man who was not a man but a fool, and by children for whom she had borne untold sufferings, but who had turned out to be, not children, but stones—vipers she had nourished with her heart's blood. . . .

"You come from work," she shouted, as the clock ticked, tic-toc, each stroke echoing a blow in her temples, "you see nothing. As long as there is that to stuff your snout with, and a paper to read. It bothers you that my head bursts, and I don't know which way to turn first? It worries you that we got debts, and I don't know from which one to hide my shame?"

32

She stared at the shadows through the window, at the moon peering in like an evil eye over the roof-tops, the same moon that bathed the beds of the rich and her mother's grave—

"I don't know where to give myself an advice," she babbled, "so lone in the world. . . . Like grass. Like a stone. And nobody has pity. . . . Nobody. . . ."

At the sound of footsteps far up the street, she threw the window wide open. She waited. The footsteps drew nearer, each step ringing clear on the cobbled street. Then the walker lifted a thin quavering voice like an unhappy dog's:

> Peanuts—
> Who wantsa buy mah nuts . . . ?

She fell back, trembling.

"Momma, my dearest," she moaned in the Yiddish tongue, the language of lamentations, "didn't you know the truth! . . . On bended knees you begged me—Where are you going, foolish one? you said. . . . What far fortune will you find? . . . When shall my eyes behold you again, my daughter?—You should see me now, Momma. . . . You should only see what a finish is coming to me. . . ."

Her voice grew quiet, almost confidential.

"What then?" she assured the Unseen Listener. "Is He an unjust God? A"—she groped for words—"a—a God who doesn't know what He is doing? . . . Rest easy, Momma. He knows. He forgets nothing. . . . For every one of your dear tears He will pay me. . . . For every tear. . . ."

GOD—THERE CAN BE NO DOUBT OF IT—WOULD "PAY" HER, as Mrs. Gest expected, but, having all her lifetime in which to work, He may not have been in a hurry to mint His coins all at once, for, if He may be assumed in His traditional style, He was at this moment looking over the shoulder of Jonas B. Colon as that worthy sat in his office in Washington, D.C., working far into the morning and, not only just looking, but prodding him on, supplying him from His infinite reservoirs with the energy to carry on until his secretaries and subordinates should arrive with morning coffee and cognac and take over.

The building in which Colon sat had been the play-house once of an American President who loved good times, willing women and men about him who were fat and of a co-operative disposition. Nothing remained now of that time but the winding stairways, that persisted in charm and an atmosphere of intrigue although they had been scrubbed clean with disinfectant and the paintings removed from the walls. The rooms—halls, really—were covered with heavy mahogany desks, swivel chairs, steel filing cases and cabinets, typewriters, draftsmen's tables, maps and all the other paraphernalia of a gigantic and up-to-date office. The building also housed half a dozen other agencies of the Government's program. It was within ten minutes' ride by taxicab of all the monuments in the district, the White House, or the Post Office.

Colon, a tall slight man in his middle forties, was a famous foreign correspondent who had just returned from Europe to take over the post. There was so much to be done, but those who had sent for him felt that he was the man to do it, and they may well have been right. Insatiably he tore at the stacks of letters, communications, and telegrams before him, marking this with a scrawled JBC, that with an X, the other with a REF. Before him, on the wall, was a huge map of the United States, with redheaded pins stuck through the maps of one-third of the states, green pins through the others. Two hundred men and women had been and were being put on the Authors' Project in New York, a skeleton force of supervisors and secretaries was winging its way to California, with stops and arrangements to make en route in New Mexico, Texas, and Arizona; Iowa, Illinois, and the great wheatladen states of the Northwest were being covered; even the remote reaches of Alaska and the Indian depths of the Florida swamps had not been forgotten.

The plan, essentially, was this: to produce The Story of America. Not just the history, not merely the politics, the economics, the village folklore, the literature, but the whole thing. Think of it, to tell the story of AMERICA! What a huge job this was!

To the end that the plan might succeed, the creative forces of the nation were being mustered. The various authors' organizations had been approached, their lists ransacked. Before Colon lay a mass of telegrams and letters. One from a world-famous novelist in the Far West said simply, "Splendid. I accept." An editorial writer on a New York metropolitan newspaper wrote asking for full particulars for a Sunday column to be entitled, "Americans to Know Themselves." Chambers of Commerce had responded, pledging the use of their facilities. Libraries. The Historical Societies of various states. The universities.

Much had been done. Much remained to be done. Colon, working like mad, was not even quite sure just what had to be done. He was the executive, the man who stood at the main switch, ready to flood the land with light. Beneath him, tier below tier in an ever-widening arc until the whole resembled some imagined pyramid of effort and desire, were executives on executives, secretaries on secretaries; beneath these the agencies of relief, of expenditure, the forces of the elected Government who'd hired him and his staff; below them the masses, hungry for employment, culture, self-knowledge, who'd put his employers into office, hiring the hirers; under all these the land, the wide wonderful land, with the illimitable continent-wide farms on it, the cities, the big cities and the little cities, the cities with the Dutch names, the English names, the Indian names and the French, the factories, the mills, the adobe huts of the craftsmen, the fishing villas on bamboo legs of the creoles, the skyscrapers that looked at each other across the telegraph wires between New York and Chicago, San Francisco and St. Louis; and under all these, under the earth, the dead, the fragrant dead of the Americans of all races, intangibly rising through the wheat-roots and the unmined coal, the uncollected songs, the mystic and the mighty traditions. . . .

Yes, the mystic and the mighty traditions. That was it. Southern style golden fried chicken, for instance. Was there not something profoundly American in that? Colon was, among other things, an accomplished gourmet of European foods. He had eaten in the famous dining rooms and equally famous off-street dens in a dozen capitals. The grimy chips-and-fish of London, the delectable octopus and old wines of Naples, the shashlik of the Caucasus and the sticky sweets and bitter coffee of Pera, native as the flash of sun on the domes of the mosques. A monograph of his in an esoteric Parisian monthly of a decade before was famous in certain quarters for his dissertation on food. A tone poem of the rhapsodies of the belly, one critic had called it. A vindication of European culture by knife and fork and under the chef's hat, another had said.

The famous Colon smiled wryly, thinking of this European culture. Verlaine. Léon Blum. The Passion Play at Oberammergau. Walks by the civilized lake in Switzerland under the ice-white mountains and talks with Einstein. Dim but returning memory of an exclusive from Mussolini for the American Babbitt-press on that gentleman's renunciation of the Socialist Party. Long heated talks and exciting ideas in the cafés of Geneva after the sessions of the League of Nations. Russian girls of the old nobility in Constantinople, who thanked you for entertaining them some nights away from the English sailors on shore leave. Wilsonian idealism, in whose accents responsible statesmen had whispered in his ears the material for those witty, allusive articles of his. . . .

Rotten. Rotten.

With all the beauty and the erudition, what had happened in Europe? How was it that he'd suspected nothing, known nothing,

36

trusted until the very end? Where were all the wise men, why were the shrugs and the subtle triple implications of no avail when the storm burst? From where the age-old cry "Jew! Jew!" in pleasant Vienna as a mob pursued an old man and tore his beard? In what inferno was brewed the castor oil vats of Italy? And Hitler—where was Beethoven's spirit that day? The gentle German folk?

Almost wistfully, he lifted his eyes to the great pin-pricked map of America.

What is the capital of California?

I don't remember, if I ever knew.

What is the population of Albany, New York?

I don't know.

Is it possible to tell a Negro of Mississippi by his speech from a Negro of Alabama?

Search me.

What are the chief products of St. Louis, Missouri?

One really can't let it go at Lindbergh and beer.

Who, besides Al Capone and Samuel Insull, lives in Chicago? Carl Sandburg?

Well, who else?

I never knew.

Name three American rivers besides the Mississippi and the Ohio.

I don't remember.

We were the generation that thought America was dull and all alike, no difference between the places and the people, and went to Europe, wooing the Venus de Medici and compliment- ing the dark thoughts of assassins and the bouncing of brains on dadaist platforms because they were exciting. . . .

He caressed the telephone by his side.

I could call Seattle, Portland, and their voices would fly the Rockies, clear as birds.

It was exactly four o'clock.

37

He dialed Information in the building. The night watchman answered.

"Has Mr. Colon come in yet?"

The watchman's voice was full of outrage.

"I'm verra sorry, Sor, but I can't be giving you information."

Mr. Colon leaned back in his chair.

"Of course not," he murmured to himself.

BUT GOD, IF WE MAY ASSUME HIM A LITTLE FURTHER, WAS NOT yet through for the night. How did He know that Charlie, dismissed at last by Elizabeth, would go straight home? True it was that Charlie had no money, but there were ways of getting around this fact, and it costs nothing to walk aimlessly through the streets, a pursuit in which Charlie excelled, or to step into the Greek's place to swell the admiring gallery that every night whiled away the idle hours watching the jackpots of their financial betters at the five-balls-for-a-nickel machine. Perhaps He did know that Charlie would go straight home, but wanted to make sure. That He could take a certain pleasure in setting the stage is shown in an episode from His younger days when, for the furtherance of His purposes, He appeared before a forebear of Charlie's, Moses, in a burning bush. . . . At any rate, as Charlie—who still believed in a certain amount of free will—stood on the corner waiting for a streetcar and thinking it was up to himself to decide whether or no he wanted to ride home in style or to spend his remaining dime for a package of cigarettes and take a chance on bumming a ride home on one of the cattle trucks that, at about this time, rolled by en route to the West Side stockyards, God decided the issue by making him aware that his head contained lice.

To Charlie this phenomenon bore no aspect of the miraculous. Feeling an itching in his scalp, he attributed it immediately to his sisters, who had often come home from school with hair lice, contracted from a towel communally used. He scratched, as a matter of course. He probed with his fingernails. And sure enough, he found one. Standing under the light, he looked at it. Huge and black, it wriggled with hundreds of legs. He rolled it gently between his fingers so as not to crush it, feeling its silky texture, barely fuzzy, while his mind stepped aside and invited his nausea to come forward. Then he flung it from him in an excess of disgust. Not seeing where it fell, he stood in the wind sweeping his clothes with his handkerchief. Then he threw away his handkerchief. But the die was cast for God's purpose.

He wanted nothing now but to get home and soak his head in boiling hot water. And so he waited impatiently for the streetcar that would speed him, among other things, to his mother's relief.

"Goddam. Oh, goddam!" he said, not knowing, of course, what he said.

The car took him down to Grant Street without a stop, as though understanding that he must get home right away. All that time, he scratched. He was the only passenger, and so he could scratch. He scratched, and watched the motorman's neck, which was red and fat. Then, at Grant, a drunk got on, and tried to talk the motorman into letting him stay on without paying. First he wheedled, then he demanded, then he said if the conductor would give him his name he'd send him the ten cents in the morning. He said he knew the conductor was an Irishman like himself, and that the Irish had to stick together. Just to show he was an Irishman himself, he said he'd give him his name. This, it turned out, was Pat Malone. Finally, when even this was of no avail, he began to curse:

"Why, yuh Jew shon uh vuh bitch, I godda haffa mind ta slap da holy living soup outa yuh fat ass!"

The conductor didn't say a word. Just kept on looking where he was driving and stopping at each corner for the bum to get out. Then, just when Charlie was getting pretty impatient with the car's progress, it stopped, as though finally, at Monroe. There were two cops standing on the corner.

The conductor pointed. "See them?" He spoke without the slightest trace of malice. "You gettin' off, Lousy?"

Lousy knew his right name, even if Charlie almost jumped. "Don't go gittin' hard onna old guy, Mishta," he said. "How yuh know I aint yuhr old man?"

"I'm waitin'," the conductor said frigidly.

"I'm goin'," Lousy said. "Don't go gittin' hard now."

"Step lively!"

He waited courteously till the drunk was safely off, then started up the car with a jerk. Charlie watched the drunk weaving in the roadway, and heard the loud voice of one of the cops telling him to C'mere!

"Lousy bastard," the conductor said calmly. "I toss 'em out every night. Aint a night aint one of 'em don't get tossed offa this wagon. That scrawny motherlover's been on here third time this week."

How could the conductor know that his action and words were the instruments of Providence perhaps; was he not behaving—by his own statement—as he had behaved at least three times this week? How could he know that the matter would work to strengthen a perversity in Charlie, thus assuring that even now in this hour, while he sped to Mrs. Gest's rescue, he should store up more fuel for the burning up of his mother, who "owed" a debt to God? For Charlie reverted now to thoughts that often haunted his actions—that, as a poet has said, "A man's a man for a' that," a view which bound him to the underdog, when he should have been preparing mentally to travel with another kind of a dog.

"What's the difference if they ride?" he asked coldly.

The conductor laughed at such naïveté. "What's the difference! How do I know he aint a fink the company sent to put in a report on me?"

"A fink?"

"Sure—a fink. That's what they call the lousy bastards."

40

"They wouldn't be sending them out like that, would they—getting them drunk and dirtied up on purpose?"

The conductor shrugged his shoulders. "I give up tryin' to figure out finks a long time ago. Aint no use figurin' nuttin'. Best thing is, to play safe. Then nobody's got nuttin' on yuh."

Charlie, in this statement, thought he saw the height of the unreasonable. "Suppose a guy really needed a ride?" he asked. "Suppose he really needed it, I mean. Left his wallet home, say—or didn't have one, and it was a cold night?"

"Aint no skin offa my tail," said the conductor, supremely convinced of this by life. "Jesus Christ Himself—how would I know He wasn't a fink?"

At which the perversity began to work:

"How do you know *I* aint one?"

The conductor looked at him—a long sidewise look.

"You aint got nuttin' on me if you was the chief of the finks."

Charlie got up to go, touched the bell for Wharton Street. The car began to slow down. "I got this on you—" he said with relish, "what you said about finks. If I was a fink, I wouldn't want to be called that. And I don't think the company would like it." He watched the skin growing pale on the conductor's fat face. "The fact is," he added with deliberateness, "the company wouldn't like it at all."

The conductor's face had the expression of the damned.

"Listen," he quavered, "I got a wife and four kids, and I can't afford to be tossed offa the job. I—"

Charlie afforded himself the emotional luxury of getting off the car as slowly as possible.

"As a matter of fact," he said regretfully, "I'm not a fink at all. But I can tell you this, that so long's there are men like you, the books don't mean a damn thing."

Immediately, he regretted having told the conductor that he was no fink. Hell, he should have let him keep on thinking that his Doom had come. He visualized the conductor, his car put

41

away, wending his weary way home, the bitter thoughts beating at his hitherto impregnable brain. Fifteen years' service—no, make it twenty!—and now disgrace. His wife. His children; all of them crying, of course, with that fidelity to actuality that made such fiction seem so unreal to most editors, as though life is a formula worked out by esthetes. And why not write it, come to think of it! For fifteen years Jonathan Thimblewit had served his masters faithfully, and now, as his hand unerringly guided the car, of which he was chief engineer and custodian, to the termination of its final run, his honest features twisted in a smirk of pleasure as he visualized the pension that then would be his for the rest of his life. . . .

The story would be the story of a man who had a job and one who had no job, and how each turned lousy in his fashion.

At the corner of Demeter, thoroughly absorbed in the technical problem of the plot, he lit a final cigarette, gave his head a vigorous scratch and, a minute later, threw the cigarette away. By now his footsteps would be within his mother's hearing, and he tried to walk softly. When he saw his mother's face at the window, he abandoned this pretense. He put on a puzzled smile.

"Why aint you asleep, Ma?" he asked, his words sounding false even to himself.

"May your children suffer like you make me suffer, that's all I wish you!" she screamed back, in this wise passing on to him a curse that would not become fully effective—as she realized— until he should have taken her place in the ranks of the world's incurables. Her voice, which had cooed to him in his cradle, was hoarse, wild; her eyes, as she glared down at him, full of torture and hate.

He threw a quick glance at an old man lying in the gutter, fumbled for the latch, closed the door behind him, and fastened the rope before passing through the yard. He climbed the stairs with sinking heart, seeing how dark the neighbors' houses were and trying to guess vainly at the time. The front door was already open, and as he came in and closed it, he heard his father speak up.

"Sarah"—how tired his voice seemed—"it must be almost morning. I beg of you, let there be sleep."

"A job he was going to get! A job—in gambling houses and among the red lights, may he be cursed with the curse he will bring home one day! A job—you'll yet see what kind of a job he will give this dark house! All kinds of diseases and lice! And the police will yet bring us news of this fine fellow. . . ."

All her fears were pouring out of her, like the blood out of the wounds of a dying man. Without a word he handed the letter from Mr. Colon to his father and said, "Read it to her!" Then Elizabeth and the drunk, the motorman and the lice, the whole evening forgotten, he crept silently to his bed. The last thing he heard as he fell asleep was his father getting up to sit on the edge of the bed and fumble for a match and his mother's voice describing the gambling dens in which she imagined he spent his time. How good it was to lie between the cool sheets, to close your eyes and let the cool sleep come!

He dreamed first that he floated face down on a smooth illimitable gray sea merging smoothly with a gray slightly sloping land that stretched back to illimitable horizons that moved, with no change, into gray dead skies.

Down the slopes came a tall gaunt woman with sightless staring eyes. She stood on the sea's edge, waiting a sign from him, but he could not speak and she could not see. He floated before her, some intangible current carrying him, his arms and legs rigid, knowing he must surely perish if she did not see him. This moment stood suspended for a long time. Then she turned and began to glide back into the distances from which she came, and, some rite fulfilled, he slowly began to sink. Then he was seeing her flickering form through veils of unrippled water. Then she was gone, and the waters closed over his head.

Next he dreamed that he had awakened and was lying on his

43

back in bed. He opened his eyes. A woman with blazing red eyes stood directly above him. The blazing red eyes were the first thing he saw. Then he saw that she had a dagger in her hand poised to plunge into his heart. As long as he kept his eyes open—this was the rite of the dream—so long was he safe. But as he recognized her, a wave of horror passed through his body. It was his mother. The dream, which he had had before, ended with recognition.

He awoke. He heard his mother groaning, mumbling in her tortured sleep. Was this a dream too? If he pinched himself, would he wake? No, this was the truth! The stove crackled out its little song; the furniture, ugly flowers of the fire's little glow, thrust out its bulk from the shadows; his father snored. Hearing a voice in the emptiness outside the window, he got up to look.

The white old man he had noticed that evening on coming home still lay on his back, but a slim, broadshouldered form kneeled over him. Broadshoulders' voice floated in softly on the running wind.

"Roll over now, Fat," he was whispering. "Git ovah on yoh side now!"

His hands gently urged, and Fat, sound asleep or dead drunk, rolled over heavily at the suggestion. Broadshoulders' hands went deftly into his right-hand trousers pocket.

"Easy now, fat old man!"

His fingers moved with the delicacy of a dream. "Come again, Fat. Roll over!" Fat groaned, tried to sit up, but Broadshoulders' fingers were at his chest, softly insistent, and in a moment he fell back. "Roll over!"

The old man rolled.

"Damn!"

Broadshoulders stood up and the dream ended. He began to kick and stomp. He kicked the old man swiftly and savagely in the side, then he lifted his heel and brought it straight and

44

repeatedly down on his face. The old man's face fell away and black running lumps broke out on his dangling features. Broad-shoulders kicked and stomped expertly for ten or fifteen seconds, then, as rapidly, he turned and walked away. At the corner, looking neither to right nor to left, he disappeared. Then, as Charlie still watched, his mother let out a sharp cry in her sleep, as though of warning, and he blundered back to bed.

He dreamed that he lay in bed trying to get to sleep, but could not. What the hell's the matter here? he asked himself in his sleep. There was something surely under the sheets. He put his hand down with the palm flat and began to sweep, searching. Loaves of bread in the bed? It didn't make sense. Ma, he was about to call out, complaining, what the hell am I doing with loaves of bread in the bed? But suddenly they began to move. They moved, and they began to crawl up on his body! Good God! They were beginning to sprout legs under his touch, they were growing longer and thinner. With a yell, he realized what they were—lice! And he woke up, his body bathed in cold sweat.

As he sat on the edge of the bed, wangling a cigarette from a depleted pack in his pants pocket, the events of the preceding twenty hours flooded back into his mind. He sat staring around at the objects in the icy rooms; then, the cigarette lit and drawing, went to the window. The lifted shade revealed a cold sun rising on a wet washed-looking world. The fat old man had vanished, a battered hat sole evidence that he had ever been. Across the street a shade now lifted, revealing a woman in a chemise over which was thrown a man's coat. Up Demeter Street, hurrying toward the streetcars, came a throng of men and women, each hurrying separately, with drawn faces and shoulders bent to fight the morning cold. It was a strange sight, and he stood at the window watching a morning earlier than he had seen in many months. Back of him, the alarm clock suddenly rang, and his father stirred. . . .

45

PART TWO

It was a week later, Thursday, the day of the Recovery Parade. The city was hung about with flags and pennants for the occasion. The downtown stores were boarded up with stout smooth planks against the gay and somewhat rough hundreds of thousands of celebrators expected to view and join in the proceedings. Schools were hotbeds of insurrection all that day and every policeman on the force was shining his badge and shoes.

It was a great day all right, but in the home of the Gests it was The Day of Days.

Charlie had received an answer to his letter to Colon.

REPORT TO MR THORNTON C HOHALEY NEWLY APPOINTED LOCAL DIRECTOR, the telegram had read, 600 JUSTICE BUILDING DECISION IN HIS HANDS HE MUST APPROVE YOU

"Try, try," Mrs. Gest sped him. "Fall on your knees," she urged. Her blood remembering ancestral tribes prostrate in their deserts, their hands knocking on the stones before an implacable but Hebraic Jehovah, "beg him," she implored, "be not stiff-necked. Tell him our woes, consult with him—"

Charlie laughed shortly, straightened his tie, pocketed the half dollar she pressed into his hands.

"Yes, Ma, I will try. On my knees I'll consult him. With my pants rolled up."

HE STOOD BEFORE THE JUSTICE BUILDING AND LOOKED UP AT the huge pile, on the sixth floor of which, room 600, his fortunes lay. So this was it, huh? No Columbus, peering quizzically and with anxiety through his telescope at the misting pencil line of the horizon, the dagger-point of mutiny held at his back by his followers and dependents, by the planks under his feet and

46

the weather, could have wondered more than he. No Balboa, silent on a peak in Darien.

He hated the place, he wished he did not have to go into it.

It is difficult, perhaps impossible, for those who are themselves employed to understand completely this complicated feel ing that ravages the breasts of the jobless as they stand at last on the threshold of the life that exists about them everywhere and every day and yet is always for others, never for them.

The unemployed meet with each other on the streets. About them swirl the men with suitcases, briefcases, portfolios; the men in overalls; men who have to do with the buildings going up, coming down, the real estate transactions, the gains, the losses, the robbing, the cheating, the editing of newspapers, the greasing of cars, the skilled operation of restaurants and picture shows. . . .

"How you doin'?"

"Aw, fine!"

They both laugh raucously.

Don't crap me, brother.

"My wife was just talking about you folks yesterday."

"That's funny. We was just talking about you."

They observe the girls, the wind smacking at their breasts and thighs, on their way to or from offices, off to lunch, to bed, to the latest matinees.

"Boy, that's all right."

"Not bad," they say.

"I could do me with a piece of *that.*"

"Who couldn't?"

Who *you* crapping?

"Well, drop over to the house some time."

"Soon's I get the chance."

That's right. When you aint *busy.*

"Well, see you in church."

"Yeah. That's right. *Church.*"

47

They go their ways, bearing themselves broadly in a narrowing space. They look in the windows of jewelry stores. It's another crowd that's doing the marrying now. Occasionally, they take in a show, trying to remember themselves in the fantasies before them. Let Ford or Chevrolet come out with a new model, they fly into inexplicable rages in saloons over the differences. They lust for suicide over the Want Ads and plot vaguely whom to take with them.

MY NAME IS CHARLES GEST, HE SAID INSIDE HIMSELF. I AM twenty-four years old. I am a writer. I am full of crap. I would like to be out in a boat with Joan Blondell. Keats is my favorite poet. I am nothing, I have done nothing; if I walked into a river, the doctors would hold her pulse and my mother would grieve. I knew a fellow once who had a strange ambition. He was a hardware merchant. A puny generous fellow who was afraid of hoodlums and would pay your way to shows to have company. He had had gonorrhea four times. If it were not for his older brother, he used to say, he would have failed in business long ago. His ambition, he told me, was to walk into a poolroom on Hudson Avenue full of guys playing pool, with his hat-brim turned down and his overcoat collar turned up, a cigarette dangling from the corner of his mouth and behind him a sergeant of police and a squad of cops. He would walk through the place, the cops remaining respectful and silent at the door, and the guys would be frozen where they stood. One with the billiard cue halfway to the ball. Another with his mouth open and his eyes lifting. A third with a coke in his hand. He would walk from one to the other, looking them long and cool in the face. Then, cool and hard, sort of casual, you know, nary a change in expression, he'd say, "This aint him, Sarge." He would pause, look around him, flip the smoke in a wide arc, turn then, the cops parting silently to make an aisle for him.

At the door, he'd turn, looking back, sweeping the place slowly with this stare, then, out he'd go. . . .

He seemed suspended forever in a one moment of always.

"Sixth floor," he said aloud to the elevator girl.

She turned and looked at him. He pushed back to the rear of the car, pulled hard on his cigarette. She was a Negro, one of the light-skinned and lithe kind who are so frequently to be found in the more genteel white buildings. He knew that she could see he was not a judge, nor a lawyer. She had fine breasts, the hard scornful eyes of the belonger. He tried to look like a witness, an important harassed witness.

"This elevator don't go but to the fourth floor," she said, a trace of contempt in her voice.

He walked up the two remaining flights, walking slowly to give himself time to think and also in order not to become hot and sweaty; for the rules of this game he was playing were that you must look your best, and you mustn't stutter or be caught with your pants down, and the flights were long.

Five more minutes, he thought, and I'll know. . . . Five more minutes, and he propelled himself forward. He felt himself on an operating table, and the question was, would he make it? If only he knew what the man upstairs looked like, what he was. But that man was not and could not be a person, could not be a mind speaking English words with whom you could talk. He was an abstraction, a myth about to become flesh, and on this abstraction depended so much. Suppose the director didn't like him, for instance. . . . *Director!* The very word! . . . Suppose he knew that you were supposed to be a radical of sorts. Oh, if only Colon had written more, given him time, prepared him. He needed time. He closed his eyes and stopped on the stairs a moment.

"I'm insane," he said aloud. "What's the point of all this, why not go in? You fool, you've got it, YOU'VE GOT A JOB!"

The door said SIX, and he opened its mahogany magnificence

49

and stepped out of the marble corridor into—a huge and empty floor, unfinished, resembling a barracks room. 600! The whole floor was a room. At the far, far end, beneath the one window thrown open, he saw two figures—a man and a woman. They sat at a desk behind an improvised wooden railing. The air about them was a frieze of cigarette smoke.

He walked toward them, aware that he had the whole floor to cross and that they had stopped whatever they'd been doing and were watching him. As he got close, he couldn't help it, he broke out into smiles.

"How do you do?" he said.

He was actually inaudible.

"Mister Gest, I b'lieve," the man said.

Hohaley—it must of course be he—got up as Charlie came to the partition and put out a hand for him to shake. *His hand was put out first,* Charlie noted. He saw a large pair of extraordinarily lucid but very cold black eyes, and felt a fat but vigorous hand shake his. Then, as he took the seat to which Mr. Hohaley waved him, he began to see the rest of the man. Mr. Hohaley was of medium height, between thirty-five and forty, tending to fat and to large pores and evidently very vain, for the large pores— after shaving—had been smoothed with somewhat too much powder. The powder had begun to streak a bit, giving the face a peculiarly dirty-looking appearance, which was even underlined by the brilliance of the eyes. Charlie looked again at the man's eyes and remembered the fatness of the hand-shake, and it suddenly came to him that Hohaley looked more like a woman than a man. The hint of femininity was furthered by the way Hohaley held his cigarette. The director's right arm rested on the broad arm of the chair, the other, pinching rather than holding the cigarette, waved to and fro through the air with coquettish rather than emphatic gestures.

Charlie examined him with extreme caution.

"So you are Mister Gest," he cried now. "Well, I declare, Sir, I never would've b'*lieved* it. My, how *young* you are."

Charlie, hearing these lilting rhythms with wonderment, got ready for Mr. Hohaley to pause and ask him how old he was then. He wet his lips, ready to make himself say "Twenty-four" and say it clearly, but the director had not paused and he held himself tense, listening to him rush on.

"I have had the pleasure of knowing a great many writers, but very few of them have been old men. It seems as though times have changed. In the days when America was young, why it took a man until when he was maybe a granddaddy before he had become an author who was accepted as such, whereas now, with America growing middle-aged and more settled than it once was, the men of letters are getting much younger."

Mr. Hohaley began to laugh. He threw his head back, showing rows of even teeth, nicotine-coated. His neck was creamy-white (why do I notice the bastard's *neck,* Charlie wondered), unlike his face, which grew red as he laughed; but it was just as fat. He noted with terror that the eyes remained just as cold as before—as though they sat by themselves and had nothing to do but watch.

"I will never forget one occasion, however, when I had the pleasure of meeting the youngest writer of them all, even younger than you seem to be, Mister Gest. Can you imagine who that was?"

Charlie cudgeled his brain, feeling that somehow it was enormously important that he know. But Mr. Hohaley told him, to his great relief, before he could think of a single name—one that would need to be, he was certain, famous.

"It was a man named James Branch Cabell. Oh, yes," he said, laughing at Charlie's incredulous expression, "I know full well that, in point of years, Mister Cabell is reckoned among the Deans of our literchure (It's a *Southern* accent, Charlie suddenly shouted inside himself!), but," a tap here at the forehead, "I am referring to his *mental* age. . . . What do you think of Mister Cabell's writings, Mister Gest?" he suddenly asked.

The question put Charlie in a sweat. He felt a slow trickle of anger in his veins. How was he to know whether the remarks on Cabell's age were meant to be complimentary or otherwise? He decided to play safe.

"Well," he said, "of course, Mr. Cabell's has not remained the last word in our fiction, but he has written some very fine stuff. His *Jurgen,* for instance, has—"

"Just as I was saying to the gentlemen," Mr. Hohaley broke in. " 'Of course,' I said, 'Mister Cabell has written some of the best American fiction of the time, and to give one illustration, there is his *Jurgen,* which I have treasured and kept by me always,' but that does not give him the right to be a boor (he pronounced it bu-w-uh), or to go off the deep end, does it now?"

This statement sounded as though it might be a question, and Charlie did not dare not answer. Could there possibly be a double meaning in all this? Could it be that, in some way, *he,* not Cabell, was the real subject of this conversation? "Of course not," he stammered, adding, as Mr. Hohaley beamed on him and seemed to wait for more, "My God!"

"I can see that you are a gentleman," Mr. Hohaley said softly. He felt the director's eyes opening wide on him and he thought— the thought came to him not in a picture, but in words—"I am being invited to enter into them: they are saying Come on in, deep, *deep";* and, as tactics, he knew that he should be doing just so, but he could not. He did not dare, so apparently cold and watchful did the eyes remain. Nor did he want to. He dropped his own eyes on the pretext of looking for a cigarette in his pockets, but felt that the director must see how the evasion had been made, and thought himself flushing.

"Well, sir," the other resumed smoothly, and exploding in

laughter, "there we were, all of us, some twenty gentlemen of M'ssippi and Mister James Branch Cabell, whom I had invited as I thought he would add to the gathering and—oh, I *beg* your pardon—"

Charlie stiffened in alarm.

"—I had forgotten. You must forgive me, Sir. I was referring to my country home in M'ssippi. This was when Mrs. Hohaley was still alive (*Mrs.* Hohaley, Charlie thought, astonished instinctively that such a person had existed). Can you forgive me for not having mentioned the unfortunate circumstances that the house is no longer in my possession and that I cannot invite you therefore to drop in should you ever find yourself in its vicinity?"

"I would have liked to accept the invitation," Charlie muttered.

"You, too, Miss O'Hara, please accept my apologies and my regrets," he said.

Charlie turned and for the first time looked at the woman. Miss O'Hara turned out to be very young and quite pretty. Twenty perhaps. Strawberry Irish. With a lingering gaze of her own.

"Again I beg your pardon, Sir. Mister Gest, this is my sec'tary, lovely Helen O'Hara." He dwelt on the syllables. "Miss O'Hara, this is Mister Gest. You had better take a good look at him, Miss O'Hara. From now on, he's in the picture."

In the picture!

"How do you do?" Charlie said foolishly.

"Isn't he wonderful?" Miss O'Hara said. "Don't you love working for Mr. Hohaley? He just hired *me* today."

"Come in, Sir," Mr. Hohaley suddenly boomed, "come in, come in. Pull up a chair."

Charlie looked up to see a strange figure advancing from the door, something all arms, legs, and jaw. As the figure drew closer, he saw that it was a young man, younger even than himself, tall, some six feet, blond, with a hawk-like incredibly eager face. His walk was a sort of a shamble, with which he made great progress. Also, it was quite silent, although the legs and arms seemed to proceed independent of each other and the head jerked from side to side in a manner of greeting.

"You, I presume, are Mister Lloyd Matson?"

Matson screwed up his lean face into a thousand wrinkles and gave Charlie a prodigious wink with the side of his face away from Mr. Hohaley.

How did he dare! And hadn't the director seen this gesture? Perhaps he had. You couldn't tell from his face.

"Yessir," Matson said meekly. "Bob Gans of the *Star-Globe* called you about me."

Mr. Hohaley frowned. "I was aware of that, Sir."

Matson groaned, shook himself like a dog, and winked at Charlie again. "Gosh," he said, "I sure am sorry, sir."

"Bob is an old friend of mine and recommended you very highly," Mr. Hohaley said severely.

"That's what Bob said, sir," Matson said, grinning deferentially.

"Yes," Mr. Hohaley said. He pointedly dismissed the subject. "I was telling these folks about a party we gave—when Mrs. Hohaley was alive—at which I had the pleasure of James Branch Cabell as a guest. Won't you feel more comfortable sitting down, Sir?"

Matson sat down.

"Well, Sir," Mr. Hohaley said, after a pause, and addressing himself mainly to Charlie, "there we were, as fine a lot of gentlemen as ever were seen in M'ssippi. There was Jed Harness, whose grandfather was the commanding officer at Hellasburg in the Civil War; there was Murt Calloway, whose boast it is that he has built all the roads in the state that are worth traveling over; there were bankers, contractors, at least one lawyer whose

54

opinions a Supreme Court Justice once stopped over at Horse's Hollow to hear. . . ."

Matson leaned forward in his chair, put his elbows on the tops of his knees, thrust his head forward, and stared upward intently at Mr. Hohaley, paying him a kind of homage. Charlie noticed that if Mr. Hohaley's eyes were cold, Matson's were clever.

"In short, everybody of consequence. There they sat, and ate of the food my good wife had provided, and enjoyed our wines." He looked at Charlie and smiled. "And presently the table was cleared away, and they brought out their cigars and over the black coffee there was the finest, most interesting talk you ever could hope to hear. Everybody joined in it, giving of their valuable opinions, gained in years of LIVING—all, that is, but Mister James Branch Cabell. He sat at the end of the table, the one man I had thought would contribute most to the conversation, and said nothing. So finally, when there was a lull in the talk, a lull during which everybody began looking over in Mister Cabell's direction, and fidgeting, wondering why he was so unwontedly silent, I stepped in and said, 'And, Mister Cabell, what does one of our foremost novelists and men of letters have to say to us?' To which Mister Cabell then looked about him and deliberately said, 'In the presence of this brilliant company, Mister Hohaley, I have nothing to say.' "

At this point, a knock was heard at the door. Because the room was so large, the knock sounded large and hollow and reverberated like thunder. There was a silence. Everybody looked at the door. Then a scratching was heard. Somebody was trying to get in.

"Mister Matson, Sir," said the director, "would you be so kind . . . ?"

"Sure thing," Matson said.

He rose and sprinted at the door like an athlete. He hurled himself on the handle, yanked it open. In stepped a tall woman, a stick-like figure. Matson caught her by the arm and hurried her forward.

"Oh, I'm so sorry," the new arrival said. "I—I couldn't get the door opened."

"That door is heavy," Matson announced, as though justifying her.

Charlie looked away, afraid he would wink again.

"Thank you for your kindness, Sir," Mr. Hohaley said to Matson. "And what can I do for you?" he asked.

"My name is L-Lucille Turnbull," the tall woman said.

She was about thirty-five years old, although, because of the perfect symmetry of her face, it was hard to be certain of this. Her figure was angular, seeming to stick straight up and down inside her thin shabby coat—a shabbiness emphasized by the hairy fur piece around the neck. Her voice was quiet and she held her hands loosely clasped together in front of her. A long faint scar showed whiter than her skin on the right side of her face. Only her eyes were eloquent. They were green, slightly prominent and somewhat wet—the eyes of one who might have been standing in the cold a long time. "I'm from the Library Society. I—I have been making myself useful as a sort of Social Relations to Miss Englewood. I sort of see people for her, and . . ." Her voice trailed off.

"Oh, yes," the director said heartily, "yes. I see. I see. We were just discussing literchure. Won't you join us?"

Matson leaped to his feet. "Have a seat," he offered.

"Thank you," Miss Turnbull said, not taking her eyes off the brilliant-eyed fat man. "I'd rather stand. . . . I thought—that is . . ."

Again her voice trailed off. She stood there looking at Mr. Hohaley, her eyes shining.

"Twelve o'clock," Miss O'Hara suddenly announced.

"Well, folks," Mr. Hohaley said, standing up, bringing them all to their feet, "I don't know when I have enjoyed myself more

56

than today or when I have met a more intelligent group of people. We will certainly have to resume this conversation later in the day when, I trust, you will allow yourselves to be my guests for supper and, may I say, somewhat of a celebration of the launching of our great enterprise. No place like over the cocktails to get business done. And now I must rush."

"I sometimes write something for the *Republican Ladies' Bulletin*," Miss Turnbull said. "Social news. You know—"

"Splendid," Mr. Hohaley said. "I suggest you do something on the Project for it. I'm sure you will be most valuable."

"I could go and tell a lot of people about it this afternoon," Miss Turnbull suggested.

"Very well. That will be fine," Mr. Hohaley said.

Miss O'Hara was thumbing through a notebook. "You're due at the Mayor's office in fifteen minutes," she said.

Mr. Hohaley laughed. "Yes. And in half an hour I must see the Adjuster. We must get desks, typewriters, files, people from the relief rolls. . . . And then, remind me, Miss O'Hara, I must call the Gov'ner long-distance. Then I b'lieve I have an appointment at my tailor's. After which, gen'lemen"—he turned to Charlie and Matson—"I believe that we have an engagement to celebrate this happy occasion. Naturally, you will all be my guests."

"I'd love to go to the Parade," Miss O'Hara begged.

"We will decide in due time," Mr. Hohaley said, smiling.

"And don't forget," Matson said, screwing up his eyes and gleefully rubbing his hands together, "we want to hear the rest of the story about James Branch Cabell."

He laughed. "I hope, gen'lemen," he said, "that you will not find my narrative powers too dull." He frowned, and looked about him. "Remember one thing . . ." he said deliberately. Everybody immediately looked very serious and sober, completely attentive. "Our work is not for now. It is for all time, for fifty years from now. Fifty years from now there will be no

57

Communist Party, no Socialist, no Democratic or Ree-publican, but there will always be this state. By the same token, governments in Washington will come and go, but here in this state is where we continue to live. And it is this state, and *us,* that we are here for, to put it down in words."

This was the first definite thing he had said pertaining to the work for which after all Charlie had been hired, but it was awfully general. Is there something I'm missing here, Charlie wondered? He tried to add up the director's cool *sexy* yet lustless eyes, his ambiguous but somehow meaningful monologue on Cabell and the twenty "gentlemen" of Mississippi and his warm invitation to them to be his guests at a "celebration" with the fact that he'd asked no questions of him, or of anybody, and indeed did not seem to want any information—but it made no sense. And what about the "apology" for not being able to invite him to be his guest at his old home in Mississippi? Was the man a fool? No, Charlie could not believe that. Or maybe *he* was the fool. He was conscious again suddenly, as he had often been in the past, of an essential ignorance on his part—no, not necessarily an ignorance, but an *innocence,* of life. I go my restricted way, he thought, knowing nothing of how it is with the rest of the world, building up my little fictions which, when I feel sufficiently energetic, I write up into little short stories which the editors, naturally, promptly reject.

The director certainly meant something by that last speech though; he was sure of it. People do not speak for absolutely no reason. Nor do they seem to be what they are for purposes other than their own. And if the director did mean something and the words could be taken at their face value, then he did not agree with them. No Communist Party in fifty years? No Socialist? Democratic? Maybe not, but there would be parties. The fat old man lying in the gutter, and Broadshoulders, "rolling" him—they would have parties, and on opposite sides. He and Kleinschmidtt—they would never see eye to eye with each other, he was sure of that too. And between the streetcar conductor and Jesus Christ would always stand the figure of a Fink. . . .

As to the director, there was the personal disturbing question. The question was rhetorical, not intended to make sense.

They all walked down the stairs together and got into the elevator. To add to Charlie's bewilderment, an old whiteheaded man leaning on a cane, who turned out to be a judge and to know Mr. Hohaley, greeted him, lending him greater reality than Charlie's thoughts.

"Why, *Billy,*" the Judge said, the coquettish little name falling strangely on Charlie's ears, "why Billy-boy, of all people!"

"Judge Williams," Mr. Hohaley exclaimed, drawling the title.

"I heard you gave up the house," the Judge said.

"Yes, yes. Yes," the director drawled, "I did that."

So there had been a house.

"Too bad," the Judge said.

"Yes, wasn't it."

Charlie could hear no sorrow in the voice of either. Their speech was as stylized as a sonnet or a five-course ham dinner. The director had exhibited more sorrow at not finding it possible to invite Charlie. . . .

Yet their manner managed to be dramatic in the extreme.

"So good to see you again," they were saying almost at the same time. "*Marvelous,* Judge. . . . *Wonderful,* Billy-boy!"

They held hands for a moment, and Charlie, fascinated, would not have been surprised if they had kissed. In fact, he was surprised when they did not. And yet, he was not altogether surprised. Hohaley impressed him as being not so much sexy as sexless. Yet he was feminine. Could a man be womanish without being womanly? The soul of a woman in the body of a man, but a man's body which is—disinterested? Yet there had been a Mrs. Hohaley!

He had no time for further reflection. As they all got out of the elevator, Mr. Hohaley turned the Judge by the arm and

59

made him look at the at least partly self-conscious little cluster.

"Judge," he said, "I want to introduce you to some of the most brilliant young people of our day. They are writers, members of my administrative staff."

He called them off by name, informally, turning, as he did, to regard each with those amazingly lucid and watchful eyes.

"How do you do?" Charlie said, when it came his turn. He put his hand in the Judge's soft white one and shook it for a moment, feeling a vague but deep sort of shame at the manner of the introduction. "Most brilliant young people of our day!" Was this really true? Could these words be considered the deepest sort of kindness and encouragement, non-critical, to say the most; or were they not, rather, the most refined sort of cruelty? On the whole a pretty cheap form of fun at the expense of people who were poor and, but half an hour ago, jobless.

The others, however, did not seem to think them so, and again he felt that he had to suspend judgment. In a peculiar sort of way, quite new to him, he found that he was enjoying this experience. He had never had anything quite like this happen to him.

"Dee-lighted," the Judge said in answer to each name. "Dee-lighted." Everybody beamed, and Matson, whom Charlie watched closely for a reaction, ventured the breezy statement that, now that they were all in the same building, the Judge must come up to inspect the project some time; perhaps, as he, Matson, was among other things a publicist, the Judge would consent to pose with Mr. Hohaley for a picture which then could be released to the press for the kind of publicity that would do the best good?

"I'll be glad to," said the Judge.

"Wonderful," said Mr. Hohaley, with great gusto.

He waved his hand gaily, taking hold of the Judge's with the other. "See youall at three," he said. A large, fantastic creature, he moved majestically away under the brim of an enormous fedora, surely the only one of its kind in the city. On either side, scattering like carrier pigeons to left and to right before they'd reached the corner, moved the Misses O'Hara and Turnbull. Not until they had all disappeared into the crowds beginning to gather and clog the streets for the Parade did Charlie turn his eyes to Matson and draw his breath.

"LET'S GO," SAID MATSON, AT ONCE.

Charlie felt himself to be ready for anything. Without a word, he allowed himself to be seized and hurried, he knew not whither.

They plunged into Kenzie Street, where Matson made an abrupt turn and they went east. Matson, nearly a head taller than Charlie, took long loping steps that carried him as though on roller skates, and Charlie found himself almost running to keep up. Looking sideways, he found his companion's face convulsed with what appeared to be glee. He kept screwing up his eyes and every now and then let out a sort of howl or neigh of delight.

From the business section, with its careful and select restaurants, its business fronts, expensive parked cars and general air of well-being, the two now entered a poorer section, the transient quarter. Signs announced that two eggs, bacon, coffee and doughnuts were served here for fifteen cents, there that clean beds, STAG, might be had for twenty cents on up. Cheap mixed hotels with black barkers outside who tried to pull you in with "you can't miss what we got to offer you" were uniform at fifty-yard intervals, and labor employment agencies dotted the area. Sad-eyed Mexicans in sombreros and bleached overalls sat on the sidewalks waiting for something to show up. The smell of drunkards' vomit rose from the pavements underfoot.

"How'd *you* get on?" Matson suddenly asked, still chuckling.

"They wrote me from Washington," Charlie said, expecting now to hear something.

"They did?" Why was Matson so amazed? "Say, who's your pull?"

"I don't know about pull. I'm a writer. This is a writers' project, isn't it?" he asked sharply. "If anybody spoke up for me, I don't know him. Besides, he spoke up for me for the proper reason."

Matson chuckled. "The three biggest words in the English language are *if, pull,* and *in.* I don't know where your pull comes from, although it must be pretty big if it's from Washington. If you don't want to tell me, that's all right. There's enough for everybody, as the man said to the mob who came to help him rape his wife." In flight he looked sideways at Charlie, resembling what the latter imagined a faun must look like—a faun mixed with satyr. "You know where *my* pull comes from?"

"Sure. From Bob Gans."

"Right. And you know where Old Man Hohaley's pull comes from?"

Charlie was curious. All the same, he answered, "He's probably an administrative type. Seems to be ("among *other* things," he almost added). Probably from that. Might even be a very good administrator. What's wrong in assuming that the 'pull' comes from that?"

Matson tore a cigarette out of its pack and thrust it into Charlie's mouth. "Here," he roared, swooping and with one movement lighting a match on the pavement before him, hopping to avoid falling over his own feet, and thrusting it under Charlie's nose. "Let me give you a blaze! . . . He likes you, my friend. His eyes are watering for those curly black locks and those brave brown eyes of yours. You're a writer, eh? Do you know poetry? Well, so do I. 'His eyes hath thee in thrall,' " he misquoted, "that's what. Did you see *his* eyes, boy? That's where *his* pull comes from."

Charlie began to laugh and improvised:

Eyes may kiss
And eyes may woo,
But eyes alone
Will never do.

"Exactly."

"You're nuts," Charlie said. "Aren't you?"

"Each to his own pull," Matson roared, "live and let live. So long as there's plenty, plenty for all." He pulled at Charlie's sleeve. "Aley oop! In here."

He turned in at a hotel that said MEN ONLY in front and flew up the stairs. Charlie went after him, stumbling at first on the ragged carpet. He got to the top in time to see Matson going into a room to the left and followed him in. Matson pulled a shade, drawn to protect the linoleum on the floor from the sun. An un-made bed, a cockroachy-looking washstand, a marble-topped low chest of drawers, a HOME, SWEET HOME sign on the wall, and a newspaper-covered table gave themselves stolidly to his gaze.

"Watch the birdie," Matson shouted. He drew a suitcase out of the closet and began piling stuff into it pell-mell from the chest of drawers and clothes hangers on the wall.

A chalky-faced woman appeared in the doorway.

"You leaving?" she asked bleakly.

"His name is Horatio Alger," Charlie said gravely. "He's on his way UP."

The woman gave him a look. "Yeah. And you're the Prince of Wales. . . . You owe me for four days," she said to Matson.

Matson pulled a crumpled dollar-bill out of his pocket and gave it to her.

"You got twenty cents change coming," she said. "I would like it if you draw the shade when you get ready to leave."

"Ready now," Matson shouted. He fastened the clasp on his suitcase and rushed from the room. "Keep the change," he yelled. "Send my mail to the Martin with it."

63

At the bottom of the stairs, he searched his pockets. "I got two-bits. How much dough you got?"

Charlie went into his pockets. "Fifty cents."

"Hand it over."

Charlie handed it over.

"Taxi!"

The cabbie jammed on his brakes and the car came to a screaming halt. A Mexican, slumbering on the sidewalk, jerked convulsively at the sound and leaped to his feet, screaming *"Eh, hombre! hombre!"* at the top of his voice. Believing a riot, a holdup, or perhaps an ambulance call to be in progress, Mexicans, drunks, and ragged little boys began converging on the spot as fast as they could from all directions. Heads appeared at upstairs windows and neighborly cries and curses flew from mouth to mouth. "What's up! What's up!"

"Pile in," Matson ordered. "Martin Hotel. . . ." As the taxi drew off, he leaned out of the window and began waving his hand to everybody. "Good-by," he shouted. "Good-by, Brother. Take care of Sister."

The taxi went three blocks, made a sharp left turn and drew up in front of the swanky Martin Hotel. The cabbie leaped out of his seat, ran around the back, and opened the door with a smart flourish. The two young men stepped out of the car and Matson pressed Charlie's half-dollar into the cabbie's hand. A bellboy rushed forward, the cabbie handed Matson's suitcase to him, and the procession entered the lobby. "Look distinguished," Matson growled and made for the desk, where he immediately signed the register.

"I want a room with a bath," he demanded, "and I want it on the outside, because I'm used to the New York streetcars." The desk-clerk nodded complete understanding. "Do you have a good bar and restaurant here? Don't crap me now, my friend. I'm here to set up a Project employing hundreds of people and I expect to have to do a great deal of official entertaining. Also, do you

64

have a thirty-minute cleaning service here in connection with the hotel?"

"I'm sure you'll find everything satisfactory here, Mr. Matson," the clerk said.

"Fine. That's how I'll want it. Gest, have the boy take up my bag."

"Take up his bag," Charlie said.

"I expect to be here pretty permanently," Matson said. He made as though to reach at his hip pocket. "You want me to plunk something down now?"

"That will not be necessary, sir."

Matson, frowning absorbedly and stalking with the importance of a financier of the first water, entered the elevator. After him came Charlie. After him came the bellboy. The lift shot up and a moment later the door opened, and the procession moved with a dignified beat through subdued corridors softly drowned in deep rugs and colors unobtrusive as rich relatives. From over the opened transom of a near-by room came the tinkle of glasses and the rich crescendo of sated feminine laughter. The air of the place breathed luxury, sensuous promise, and comfort. The bellboy deposited a key slickly in a keyhole, smiling like a magician, and threw open the door with a flourish. He preceded them into the room, threw open the windows and patted the welcoming committee of towels on the rack, numerous and large enough to greet all comers.

"Will that be all, sir?" said the boy.

Matson threw him the two-bits. "That will be all," he said.

The bellboy closed the door after him and Matson immediately went into the next phase of his transformation. Dashing into the bathroom, he turned on the hot and cold faucets in the bath. Emerging, he shed himself rapidly of his clothes, letting them drop around him as he got them off. In a minute, a creature of skin and bone, he stepped to the telephone. "Room service," he barked. "Presto!" he said to Charlie. . . . "Room service? Send

65

a boy up at once for a suit of clothes, a shirt, and a tie to be pressed, cleaned, and returned to me in half an hour. Also, let's have a bottle of Scotch. Any good Scotch will do. Send up some white soda and some ice. Thank you." He returned to his clothes, wrapped his underwear, which was filthy, in a newspaper, and flung the package into the wastebasket. The suit he placed on a chair next to the door. To this he added a shirt and a tie from the suitcase. "For the bellboy," he said, and dived for the bathroom. Instantly Charlie heard a splash, and by that he knew that Matson had arrived.

He walked over to the bed. It was a broad double job, mute and appealing as a woman in the grass. He jabbed it with a finger. A tiny squeak, muffled, as though it had a cushion stuffed in its throat, arose, and the bed gave. He put his hand down, palm spread, and pressed. The bed sank. He removed his hand. The bed came back. He sat down and bounced. The bed rode like a clipper.

A knock.

"Come in," Charlie said.

It was the bellboy bearing the Scotch, soda, ice, and glasses on a tray. Respectfully, he deposited the whole on a side-tray near the bed. Charlie indicated the pile of clothes on the chair. "The master," he pronounced, "would like to have these back just as soon as possible." The bellboy's eyebrows went up a bit at the "master," and he started to give Charlie what has been known for centuries and in all lands as the "eye." "Drink hale, drink hearty," roared Matson at this moment, arising from his bath. The bell-boy, reassured, gathered the clothes and departed.

Charlie poured himself a tall tumbler, neat as a maiden with her skin pulled tight about her.

"Ah-h," he breathed.

He poured another.

"Obviously," he said then, speaking as attorney for the bellboy and the worldly order of things he represented, "the gentlemen

66

were already drunk when they arrived. . . . Asked by reporters who met them at the docks what they thought of the Statue of Liberty," he continued aloud, "they said they were sure she was a good girl and did she have a girl friend."

"Now," said Matson, dashing into the room and unwinding a wet trail of narrow aristocratic-looking hoof-prints as he came, "the next step is to get dressed. And then"—he pounced on the bottle and tilted it to his mouth—"a visit to Clemm's is indicated. . . . No, you don't," he shouted as Charlie again reached for the bottle, "I have need of you in the next half-hour and total spiffli-cation before then, therefore, is *verboten*."

He caught sight of himself in the mirror. "Nice mirror," he said.

After this, he put one hand before him, one hand behind, in a dancer's pose. Holding his toes straight before him and advancing by a series of stiff formal movements of the knees and calves, he celebrated himself and in the manner of Bing Crosby sang a hoarse impromptu which he called "Clothes Make the Man."

A few minutes later his clothes were brought back. As he dressed, he gave Charlie his instructions.

"I will appreciate it," he said, "if, on leaving the hotel, you immediately return to the Project and there wait for a telephone call from the Credit Department at Clemm's. This call will come in about half an hour from the time you get there, if you don't loiter on the way. They will ask you to vouch for me and I shall expect you to do the same."

Presto! A few minutes later saw the two young men entering the lobby from the elevator. In spite of Matson's admonitions, Charlie, giving himself the character of a man who could drink indefinitely and still remain erect, had had two more drinks and the raw hot stuff on an empty stomach was now having its effect. Not precisely drunk, nor yet sober, he was in that delicious state which, normally, is maintained only by geniuses, certain young women with great capacities for love, children on picnics, and

67

beggars who have, after long and hazardous apprenticeships, at last grown old in their profession and shed all early dross. In other words, he had attained that precarious balance between the absolute and the relative wherein good and evil kiss and make up, and men acknowledge no yesterdays and no tomorrows, spending each moment for what it is worth and, in turn, accepting impressions and experience without stint or fear. Gazing boldly and with confidence to left and to right, Charlie, on Matson's heels, marched to the street, exchanging secret glances with every woman under sixty who passed. There he linked arms with his companion. And so, a twin picture of happiness and well-being, they kept together until they had arrived at a point approximately halfway between headquarters of the Project and that headquarters of the local well-dressed man, Clemm's. Surveying each other then with jubilant eyes, they clasped hands long.

"And here we part," said Matson, beaming tigerishly. "I to Clemm's, you to your post."

"I can't quite believe it," Charlie exclaimed. "Tell me, Matson, are you real? I mean *really* real? Or aren't you real at all? Just a newsreel maybe. . . . Or perhaps just reeling?" He giggled. "Were you actually born? Do you have forefathers? Or are you merely a cross between the creations of a number of playful spirits?"

Matson, highly, nay, tremendously pleased with such a rewarding audience, affected a deep frown. "It is plain to see that you've led a starved life, if the small transactions of the past few minutes can fill you with such exaggeration."

"No," Charlie said. "I mean it. Really. Ha, ha, *really* again. I'm like the guy in the poem. I walk like a lion, but I'm as timid as any maid—"

"Who ever heard of a timid maid?" Matson exclaimed. He whistled at a pair of fat ankles that passed. From above the ankles came a scandalized voice:

"Watch who you whistlin' at, hoosier!"

68

"See?" Matson said. *"Timid maidens!"*

Charlie leaned on him in helpless laughter.

"There are so many questions I want to ask," he said, trying to show the seriousness of this desire while the mirthful tears ran down his cheeks. ". . . I feel the need of being so careful. On the one hand, you know . . . and then, on the other hand . . . and then again, people don't just open a door and say 'Come in, your pay will be one fifty a month' and 'As for me, I'm off on vacation, so don't stop me to ask what you're supposed to do to *earn* your money.' But *you*—"

"There, there," said Matson, "is that what's frettin' us? Do we really have QUESTIONS? And want ANSWERS? All in good time, then. Matson will explain the facts of life to you when he gets back. Matson will—"

Charlie stood and shook with laughter.

"Ha, ha, ha, ha."

Matson joined in.

"Ho, ho, ho, ho."

And so they parted. . . .

Back at the Project again, Charlie walked back and forth between the window and Mr. Hohaley's desk and waited for the telephone to ring. Of its eventual ringing, he had no doubt. Meanwhile, to amuse himself and also, perhaps, in his search for information, he opened the drawers in the desk and looked at some of the letters therein. Applications. To Mrs. Roosevelt. To Mr. Colon. To Mr. Harry Hopkins. Tales of distress. Tales of woe. All in carbon copy and relayed per this secretary and that until finally they had reached Mr. Hohaley. "Dear Sir: This is to apprise you—" Yes, he thought happily, talking with tenderness to the tubercular man with five children, the middle-aged spinster whose company had folded and didn't know what to do, help is on the way. Help is coming. Idiotically, he found himself chuckling as his thoughts flew back to Matson. The astonishing great callow youth, with his winks and his Aladdin transformations (first he is a ragamuffin, next he might be—who knows!—a Beau Brummel, a dandy, a fop in knee pants and a beard), had vastly taken his fancy. . . . One, two, three, he counted, when I get to seventeen the phone will surely ring. He let ten minutes go by. . . . Sixteen, seventeen, eighteen—the phone rang.

For good luck, he let it ring again.

"Hello-o-o," he said, speaking in a soft, soothing tone.

The voice of a diplomat, self-assured yet ingratiating, came over the phone. "Lemme talk to Mr. Gest, if he is in."

"Whom shall I say is calling?" he whined.

"Mr. Abrams, Credit Department, Clemm's Stores!"

No less, the voice implied.

"Just one moment, please."

He lit a cigarette. "Yes," he said abruptly. He bit the word off crisp, like the important opening note in a musical arrangement. "Gest is speaking."

"Mr. Gest?"

"Mm-hmm."

"Mr. Gest, I am sorry to trouble you, sir, but we have a Mr. Matson here in the office who wants credit for thirty days and claims that he is an employee of your organization—"

"Quite right. Mr. Matson is almost more than an employee. He is one of our best men. Assistant State Supervisor. Working out of Washington. He—"

"That's all we wanted to know, thank you very much, Mr. Gest. Sorry again to have troubled you. We have to check through when—"

"Not at all. Know just how it is. Used to be in the business myself. In Philadelphia. Incidentally, about young Matson. I'll tell you a little secret about him. He's really incognito. Incog-nito. . . . Yes. Father's one of the biggest men in the country. Dollar-a-year man variety. Matson's really just down here for the experience."

70

"Thanks for the tip, Mr. Gest. Young Matson won't be disappointed in us. Thanks again. If ever we can be of similar service to yourself . . ."

After hanging up, Charlie waited a moment. Then he called up the store where his father worked. The boss's ill-natured voice:

"What do you want?"

"May I speak to Nussim?"

"Just a minute."

Nussim came to the phone.

"Hello?"

The sober little voice of a workingman, a non-reductible voice, one of the loudest therefore in the world.

"Hello, Pa. This is Charlie. Can you hear me?"

"Yes."

"Everything's all right, Pa. I'm on."

"I hear you, Charlie."

The wonderful confident words. "Tell Ma when you get home."

"All right."

That was that. He could imagine the reception of the news at home. His thoughts returned to Matson, as to the lesser but more bearable glory. It gave him real pleasure to think that Matson, in all likelihood, would walk out with the store. It pleased him to think that the next time he beheld his new-found friend, that worthy might be wearing a tuxedo, with a gardenia in his lapel and a wreath about his head. In fact, he was hoping that it might be so. Such an attire, he was sure, would be the final touch to top off the miracle of his transformation and make it flesh.

FROM FAR BELOW, TINY AS THE SOUND OF COCKROACHES RUNning across kitchen floors, came the sound of police whistles. He went to the window. The sun, balanced like some trained impossible seal on the edge of the facing-west skyscrapers, shot light into his eyes. Automobile horns, like frogs native to the urban jungle and to no other place, were beginning to honk, taking up the sound from each other. In the east, from the armory on Brenton, a cannon, silent except on the Fourth of July, went mad with joy, seemingly at its resurrection, and began pounding rhythmically at thirty-second intervals. Cars going west in five lines jammed the broad highway. South- and north-bound traffic, stuck fronts to sterns like so many coupling worms, kept doggedly inching forward. . . .

There was a scratching at the door back of him.

"Coming," he said. For no particular reason, he laughed out loud. Yes, there was a reason why he laughed. How very odd to be opening the door from the *in*side! Dreams had been more real.

Sure enough, the scratcher turned out to be Lucille Turnbull.

"Hello," she said, looking at him with those eyes wet with perpetual and fixed adoration.

He bowed low. "Come in, fellow-worker, come in." Grinning: "You and I, Miss Turnbull, let us go to the window. Below, the populace gathers, a good omen, as though to do us honor. Perchance we shall behold Matson, floating on his new camel's-hair coat among the clouds."

He walked by her side, square beside her towering frail figure. Obediently she trotted to the window. There she stood, unseeing.

"I don't know what Mr. Hohaley will think of me," she said miserably. "I didn't speak to anybody about the Project."

This omission, he saw, must be treated as though it were the height of the dreadful. As he replied, he suddenly thought of Matson. Had he appeared to Matson as Miss Turnbull appeared to him? He was in a mood for irony. But how dreadful *that* was to think about! Then could Matson have been as anxious as he? And whom did Matson have to question anxiously?

Is it to laugh? Is it to weep? Languorous, in this lull between

72

battles past and yet to come, he chose laughter. He would prefer to laugh. Yes, that he would.

He restrained himself.

"You *didn't?*" he asked curiously. "Not to one living soul?"

Shure and its mud ye have in your brain, me bhy, for it would hardly be a *dead* soul she had not told.

"I wouldn't take this omission to heart," he said hastily, his mouth twitching. "After all, this is the first day. There must be granted a period of preparation. If necessary, I will intervene with Mr. Hohaley. . . . Girding of the loins, you know. Very necessary."

It seemed that she had not heard him.

"I'm so unhappy," she said. "Mrs. Arnold wasn't home. Mrs. Van Der Gilt wasn't home. Her maid told me that she had gone out of town for the week. And naturally I couldn't tell the maid about the Project. She wouldn't have been interested."

"How do you know she wouldn't have been interested? I knew a maid once who was interested in Einstein. I lost her because she said I couldn't understand what she was talking about."

Under his banter, he was beginning to wince. The old nervous jitters of the unemployed rushed forward to seize on him, boon companions of a lifetime of malice and insult, perjury and injury. They had needles ready to puncture the balloons he had borrowed from Matson to ride on. Would nothing hold her off, this ill-bred bitch?

He had a picture in his mind of Lucille going about trying to tell Mrs. Arnold about the Project. Mrs. Van Der Gilt. The picture was gruesome. For Christ's sake, what would she have told them? What could she have told them? And what did they have to do with it?

Lucille going from door to door on Millionaires' Row (naturally, somehow, the Millionaires'), ringing bells, waiting patiently for the maids to appear. "Uh, hello, my name is Miss Lucille Turnbull. The Library Society —uh, excuse me, no—the Authors'

Project sent me." I'm to tell Mrs. Mush all about it. I'm to fall on my knees. Help, help. Mr. Hohaley has given me permission to do this. He heard this, my humble suggestion, and said it would be all right, go ahead, Lucille. . . . And the mistress never home. The mistress out playing golf. The mistress in bed with her sons' young college friends, all of them. The mistress is too too busy in the parlor, she is pressing her platinum tresses. Old Lucille with the sniffles, beginning to weep. "Move on, Miss," says the policeman, "you can't weep here, you know."

He hoped that he was imagining things. With all the venom at his command, he felt that he hated the snifflers, the weepers. He was feeling pretty cocky and he wanted to keep feeling that way. Hell, he thought, I could have pleased the old lady ten years ago by opening a grocery store and living the life of a solid citizen. With what, he did not ask himself. In hell, he reflected, there is torture and gloom but also dignity. Without dignity, there was only hell.

Matson had endeared himself because he seemed to have pride, a certain flair. The *gesture* is not to be despised. It is the camouflage of a proud heart.

"Are you sure that that was the reason you lost her?"

"Lost who?"

He was lost in abstractions.

"The maid. . . . Maybe you had wronged her, and that's why you lost her. You just don't know what women have to go through. All you men are alike." Torrentially, she burst into tears. She really seemed to be suffering, and he began to feel ashamed of himself. "Oh, what a life I've led," she finished irrelevantly, "what a life! What a life!"

She *has* been wronged, he thought. A trite word, but suffering is real. "Do you want to tell me, Miss Turnbull? Would it help?"

It would indeed. He had an uncanny feeling that she had no other story to tell.

74

"Do you know Jim Hudson, down at State Hall? . . . I thought maybe you would, from his pictures in the papers. He's a big politician now, but in those days he was just a clerk, a *young* clerk, just out of law school, on his way up, and, oh—what is your name again?—Gest? Oh-h, Mr. Gest, he loved me so much. You wouldn't think it to look at me now, would you, me so plain and all; if it wasn't for Mr. Hohaley, he is *so* wonderful. . . . In those days Jim was tall and very handsome, he hadn't put on any weight as yet. . . . He wanted to marry me."

The words came out with a rush and her eyes wove bright garlands and sad posies about the scenes she described.

"But you know how it is with a young girl—a young girl in those days (Oh, those days, she wept, those days, those days!). I wanted a career. Yes, Mr. Gest, I wanted to be a writer. Are you a writer, Mr. Gest? You are? What do you write, may I see something you have written some day? Can I have an autographed copy of your first book? I am also a writer. I even wrote a poem this morning, to Mr. Hohaley. I was too flustered to show it to him. . . . Oh, no, not me, I am not a writer, I never was a writer, oh, I don't know, I don't know. . . ."

For God's sake, he thought, a lesson in The True Story. Of course, he listened.

"Well, he really wanted to marry me, he did, he did, no matter what I look like now. I remember to this day, I will never forget it, I did not appreciate its beauty. . . . We were rowing lazily in a boat out in the park; have you ever been out on the river there, Mr. Gest? It was all very proper, I was really (giggle-giggle) a nice girl.

"He put his hand on mine, and he said, 'Look into my eyes, Lucille, my own. Now how can you doubt me?'

"And I looked. He was a good man, a fine man, a wonderful man. . . .

"He said, very quietly, 'I want you to marry me, Lucille. I am strong and can forge my way, but when I come home of nights,

75

I want where to lay my head and a soft voice to speak to me. And perhaps' " (Lucille wept), " 'who knows, in the fullness of time, little ones to gladden our hearts with.'

"I remember every word. . . .

"But I wanted a career and while I listened to him with my eyes and my face turned down to the lilies floating by, oh, I was very proper and I think I made a very pretty picture, all clean soft lines and rosy cheeks, can you see that, Mr. Gest? I was really listening to something else.

"America had not yet answered the call, she had not yet gone into the war, but from Canada went up the cry, 'Serve! Serve!' and I'll tell you a little secret, Mr. Gest, if you won't think me too awful—it is really horrible—horrible, I was glad all the men were going to war. . . .

"I was awfully glad. I didn't mind if they'd kill each other at all. I thought of them wounded, their dark eyes, and they were desperately hurt, you know, wanting something, needing some-one, and I'd be there. Oh, the tears would rush to my eyes, the big wonderful words choking me inside, I would comfort them and such songs I'd write. . . .

"Hmm. So anyway, I was listening to him, a very proper young person with my head turned down to the water like a flower, like a lily myself, and I kept thinking of France.

"And I told him, 'Jim, you have honored me greatly, as any woman could not help but be honored. But I can't accept.' I made up my mind right then and there. 'Jim,' I said, 'I am going to France.' And I went to Canada. And they sent me to Egypt. And the first thing that happened when I got there, my face got burned!"

He had hardly been looking at her. Every time his eyes had come to rest, he had been driven off by the sight of the tight muscles working in that desperate sagging face. His attention was alternating between his secret thoughts of Elizabeth, brought on by Miss Turnbull's evocative words—how quaintly put—and the pennants for tonight's parade flying in the street. But her last words jerked him to attention. In spite of her True-Story method, he was finding himself affected.

"Hell," he said gruffly, "you can hardly see it on your face now."

Instantly, she placed her head on his shoulder. Her hands were about him. She sobbed. God, she was drunk! There they stood at the window like a silhouette. Mickey Mouse and the Ugly Duckling. She continued, clinging to him with her skinny paws.

"You can't understand, oh, you can't, you can't—a man is so free. . . . I spent eighteen months in a hospital. I was still there after everybody else had all gone somewhere else. I stayed there and I couldn't look at my face. I hated myself. I was hideous. Everybody hated me. Everybody wanted me to go home, everybody wanted everybody to go away. And I didn't have any romance. No notes. No poetry. I hadn't seen anything. And when I came back, nobody asked me about the war. They would look at me and they didn't ask me anything. And Jim mocked me. When he heard I was back, he rushed over to see me. And then he sat there. And then he said, 'Dear, I know I can't hope. I know you have given me your answer. You have your career and that is what you wanted.' And then he went away. And Mother cried and she said, 'Dear, let's forget you were ever away.' Oh, oh, oh!"

He didn't know what to say. What *do* you say? He patted her back. Christ, she was skinny, poor bitch, all bone and only half a yard wide. And had never even met one dark-eyed desperate-looking *poilu*. Not even a Turk, let alone a German. And she's completely without talent (he shuddered at the private thought, for he had his own fear for himself). Still a virgin too, unopened, like an egg still boiling after thirty-five years in the pot. While across the way, in State Hall, Jim Hudson blooms like a rose (such is life) and puts on weight. . . . And the door opened, and in came the rest of the company. Mr. Hohaley, under his hat. Matson, like Ichabod Crane in rehearsal for the Ziegfeld Follies. And lovely Helen O'Hara, sweet Rosie O'Grady.

Goggling, they advanced. They had all chanced to meet, downstairs. And now this! What a surprise, what a surprise! But Miss Turnbull remained in his arms.

"Ahem," said Miss O'Hara, no wiser than her years.

"Is this the National Authors' Project?" asked Matson, leering and winking like some blond gargoyle.

Only the director seemed composed, unperturbed, reflective.

"Don't, Lucille," he said, turning his cold eyes full on Charlie in a non-inquisitive encompassing gaze. "You'll spoil your afternoon complexion."

Miss Turnbull released Charlie's shoulders and, like a baby being transferred from one person to another, turned and put her head on Mr. Hohaley's.

"You are so good to me," she wept. "So good. So good."

She had an air of Now they are all about me, I shall be sustained. So they all stood, in fact. Like a tableau, thought Charlie, wiping his forehead.

Later, when they had grouped themselves about a table in a restaurant in the line of march of the Parade, he kept very silent.

"Liver 'n' onions," Mr. Hohaley ordered for himself, the homely old-fashioned dish accentuating his Southern accent.

"Martinis?" Matson asked, after they'd all ordered.

Nods all around.

"Martinis for everybody, I guess. Very dry."

"But *very,*" said Miss O'Hara, gaily.

"A toast," said Mr. Hohaley. "What shall it be?"

"To us," gallantly said Matson.

"To you," said Miss Turnbull. "So good, so kind."

"To many happy returns of the day," giggled Miss O'Hara.

"And you, Mister Gest?"

The words came hard. He felt foolish uttering them. Toasts

78

were just not his style, except in comic and conscious mimicry of those whose style it was. Much better just to smile enigmatically. "To dignity and labor," he said, all the same. Miss Turnbull's extended handclapping embarrassed him.

"Jesus," he thought, "we look freaky."

He looked at the people, the comfortable normal people at the other tables (some of whom were looking their way), with defiance.

It was a shock to him to think how much *charity* went into this job. He thought of workers he had known on other projects—how they hated to admit that they worked on projects. He wanted to think of the Project as a writers' job and himself a writer and the others writers. Fellow-craftsmen. And words and thoughts developing between them slowly and with care, and with dignity, as those things should. That's the way it was in his father's shop. All craftsmen, workers, and proud of it too.

AS IT DREW TOWARD EVENING, THE SCENE ON LOWER MONROE assumed an ever more frenzied form. Drums beat. Gangs of boys ran hooting through the confetti-strewn streets. Girls in tight sweaters, unescorted and in packs, fled before them screaming with laughter. Horns sounded off continuously. WELCOME PROSPERITY AND THREE-CHEERS-FOR-ROOSEVELT signs were everywhere. The Parade was to be made an incitement to laughter, to hysteria—an excuse for all the hell-raising that can be stored up in a year prosaic with scrubbing and cooking, or terrible with looking for work or over-working, as the case may be, with tales of domestic fury and the rising tides of wrath abroad or picking your nose over what will be the weather tomorrow. The square pegs came out of their round holes. The round pegs came out of their square holes.

South from Kenzie and from all the streets above came the Negroes in laughing clots of thousands, men, women, and children, like some army on the march. From Russian Dumps poured

79

in the Italians, the Greeks, the Portuguese, the Armenians, and all the dark peoples of the Balkans and the Mediterranean. The Germans came in from the North Side. The Irish. The Scotch. The Jews. The Russians. The old unhyphenated Americans. From behind the city's two commercial rivers, from the factory regions sucking labor from the South, came bus-load after bus-load of the drawling rubber-necked immigrants from the South, Missouri, Arkansas, Tennessee, Kentucky and from past even these. And in them all, under their faces, was the desire for faith. . . .

HE HAD A GREAT IDEA SUDDENLY. BY JESUS CHRIST, HE LIKED that idea. There was no idea he had ever had that he liked better.

"Say," he said, leaning over to Matson, "loan me two bucks."

Matson put a finger alongside his nose.

"Two bucks," he said solemnly. He shook the finger waggishly at Charlie. "You're a bad boy," he scowled, "and a spendthrift to boot. Yes, to boot. With the evening so young, and you with all these young ladies with you at this very table, why—?"

"No, you got me wrong. Lend me two bucks."

"Hmm, two bucks."

He rose and leaned over the table, swaying.

"Pleasant comp'ny, won'erful comp'ny, got to leave you now. Me and Mis'er Gest have both got to leave you. But not for long. Not for long. Phone call. Important business. Life 'n' death."

They were now at Kogan's. Mr. Hohaley, after dinner and more Martinis, had announced that he wanted to acquaint himself with the "artistic" life of the town. They were drinking Kogan's gin rickeys. Batiks of women deformed by labor looked down from the walls.

"You will be back?" Mr. Hohaley asked. "Me a stranger here."

"Life 'n' death. Positively. Back in a jiffy."

"Hue to the chalk-line," he cautioned.

"G'by now," shrilled Miss O'Hara. Liking the sound of this phrase, so gay, so blending the improbable future with the definite present, she repeated it: "G'by now. G'by now."

"The chalk-line, gen'men," Mr. Hohaley sped them, "earmark of a M'ssippi breedin'."

He raised his glass, blinked eyes above its rim, and tilted it.

"To Mississippi," Gest exclaimed.

"To Mississippi," Matson echoed.

"G'by now," Miss O'Hara repeated, having downed her glass.

All nudged Lucille, asleep with her head on her arms.

"I too was beautiful," Lucille sobbed, stirring.

Out went Matson, following his chalk-line. Gest, squinting the better to see his with, followed. Plunge! A snake-dance of college kids wrapped itself momentarily about them.

They approached a taxi-driver.

"Sir," said Matson, "this watch is worth fifteen dollars. I bought it s'afternoon."

"You crap," said the taxi-driver, using the short word as a verb.

"No crap," Gest protested, using it as a noun, "he's my brother. He's telling the truth."

"So what do you want me to do? Jump inna lake?"

"And this bill-fold," Matson continued. "See? Firs' I subtrac' a ten-cent piece from it, my total wealth at the moment. What is *it* worth?"

"With the dime in it, ten cents."

"And now this belt," Matson added, pulling it off, "fresh from Clemm's, also this af'ernoon, where earlier in the week it was a vital part of a contented cow. Now how much am I bid?"

Charlie could not allow Matson to become altogether denuded. He cast about himself wildly and finally came up with his yet unopened package of cigarettes. It was the only new thing he had. This too he tossed into the rapidly growing pot.

Matson began to pull off his tie.

The taxi-driver was impressed.

"Say, what is this? A Ann Corio or sumpin'?"

"I been trying to tell you," Matson said. "This man needs two bucks."

"Well," the driver brought up an objection, "it wouldn't do him no good anyhow. They aint a house open southeast of Lane. They're all down here to see the works!"

"You got me wrong," Charlie said. "'S to bring my folks down here too. Need the dough f'r taxi."

"What's the matter wit' streetcars? They're still runnin'."

"It has to be a taxi. 'S a special occasion. It's got to be in style."

The driver lifted his hat to scratch under it. "Well, wodda ya need two bucks for?"

"I told you. For a taxi!"

"Say, are you guys crazy? *This* is a taxi!"

"So it is!"

They stared at it with avarice. Then both lifted their eyes to the lucky owner. That worthy told himself that he had a soft streak, and gave in.

"Yez kin keep everyt'ing here but the watch," he said. "I'll keep that. Yez kin pay me the fare on your next payday and I'll give the watch to yez."

"Heaven will reward you!" Matson shouted.

"Heaven, yes!" Charlie cried. "But firs' I will. Not two but five bucks it'll be."

"If I hadda dollar for every dead-beat I thought was a live-wire when I first took him on—" the cabbie began.

"No, no, brother," Matson protested. "'S not a fair description."

"You're not talking about us."

"Okay," said the cabbie. "I aint doin' nuttin' anyhow. Now, what's the address?"

Charlie gave him instructions and his address for the passengers. Matson gave him the Martin Hotel address and arranged all necessary details in regard to the return of the watch.

"Look," Charlie said from the sidewalk, as the engine started up, "this's got to be put on with the dog. You're not a cabbie now, you're a chauffeur."

"I getcha, brother," the cabbie said.

The cabbie got to the Gests' front door as they were coming down the front steps. The Widow Cohen and Harry Goselkin were with them. Things looked promising between these two and Mrs. Gest made a point of having them along. The men were shaved to the bone. The women had put away their shawls and were wearing their "American" clothes. Janice and Clara were both very quiet. They had to be until they got to the Parade and knew that it was too late to be left behind. It was a most joyous procession, on the whole, although preparations had not been completed without friction and loud words. For now the Parade had great personal point, and seemed to be in their honor. Nussim had had to repeat his telephone conversation with Charlie at least a dozen times.

When the bell rang, Mrs. Gest screamed, "It's about Charlie. God, Good One! What can have happened!"

"Nothing has happened," Nussim shouted. "It's Charlie himself!"

"Charlie," Janice screamed.

"It's Charlie," Clara screamed, in her turn, "Charlie, Charlie!"

They all rushed down the stairs to be the first to open the door. They stared blankly at the pug-nosed face of Tom Carter, cabbie.

The "chauffeur" tipped his hat. His gold teeth gleamed like visiting cards. "Mr. Gest says to inform you that your car is waiting and I will take you to the Parade."

"Mr. Gest tells you— Who is Mr. Gest? *Charlie!*"

"Yes, Ma'am. This way, please."

"Oh, no. Go away, please. The cost is too much. Thank you, we cannot go in your car."

"There will be no charge, Ma'am. The cost is all taken care of."

"Charlie *paid?*"

"No, Ma'am. No pay was necessary. This car belongs to His Honor, the—the Alderman!"

Overcome, they all got in.

"Thank you very much, Mister."

They sank back in the cushions and let themselves be whirled off. The houses and evil-smelling blocks fell away on either side as though the car was on a treadway. If only the neighbors could see them now! White lumps on the sidewalks became faces at all the stop-signs, looking in on them wonder-eyed through the plate-glass. On the right side of the car, all manner of other cars were overtaken and passed. Not until they began to approach the immediate vicinity where the Parade would pass and the car began to go slower in the congested traffic, did they begin to catch their breaths and relax.

To hide his emotion, Harry said haughtily, "Is it permitted to smoke? Is this okay?"

"Go ahead," the driver said. "There's a ash-tray in the wall."

Harry could see no possible place for an ash-tray. The wall was solid. Rather than confess ignorance in the presence of a Jew-hater, he silently contrived to put his cigar back in his pocket.

"It will taste as well later," he informed the widow.

"Assuredly," she agreed.

And now they had entered the street of the Festival and Parade itself. A long brilliant street, with all its lights on, the people in the tall buildings leaning out of the windows and singing songs, the confetti and the torn toilet-papers falling and swirling in the wind like the ghosts of all the moths in the world, the policemen every ten paces with their fancy black capes and their special red canes, back of them the boiling, heaving, shouting sea of humanity on the pavements; and in the roadway, melting before the car and forming again, the running and singing children.

"This is as far as yez kin go," said a policeman at the next intersection. "To the right here, buddy."

"Well, here we are, folks," said Tom Carter.

"So soon," said Janice. "Gee!"

"Gosh," said Clara.

"Are you sure there is no cost, Mister?"

"No, Ma'am. Positive."

Mrs. Gest timidly placed a quarter in his hand.

"Maybe you like some candy sometimes. Yes?"

They got out of the cab.

"Is Roosevelt gonna speak?" Janice asked, her spirit hushed.

"Why of course not, silly," Clara answered scornfully.

They looked about them with wide eyes.

"What a land!" said Harry. "Is not anything possible here?"

The Widow Cohen said nothing, but she was obviously hoping so.

PART THREE

"Doorway to the right. Doorway to the right. Up two floors."

The elevator girls had been saying this all morning as load after load of ragged men and women piled into their cars and inquired for the Authors' Project. And they were getting sort of fed up with it.

"Ah declare," one of them said to another, in a lull, "Ah nevuh seen so many *mis'able*-lookin' white people in all my life!"

"Ah'm afraid they're here to stay," said another. "It's one of these *proe*-jects, I understand. The next thing you know, they'll be bringing shovels in here with them."

The lawyers and judges didn't like it much either.

"Are these people relatives of yours, Sadie?" Judge Daniels asked, as he came into the car. He was the noted pundit of City Court Number 3, famous for the wit with which he could give out twenty sentences in a day for similar traffic charges without once repeating a jest.

"They are no relatives of mine," Sadie said haughtily.

"Well," said Judge Daniels philosophically, "what's to be is to be. And I, for one, am resigned to it. Still and all, I may add the thought that if Mr. Roosevelt is just given enough rope . . ." He left the sentence unfinished. It occurred to him a moment later what he had done, and he laughed. "Do you know, Sadie," he said, "that's the first sentence I haven't finished *proe*-nouncing since I first got on the bench. Nevertheless, the verdict will be brought in. In '36."

Something in the Judge's words, *rope* perhaps, had caused Sadie to frown. Now she smiled.

"Judge, how you talk!"

Judge Williams got on the elevator.

"Mornin', Judge," Judge Daniels said, smiling sweetly, "I see where the forces of Democracy are up somewhat earlier this morning than usual, but are going to work instead of to court."

"True, true," Judge Williams answered smoothly, "but have you considered, Your Honor, how many dispossessed *Ree*-publicans have been allowed to profit by this change in the usual routine of the citizenry?"

"Touché," said Judge Daniels. Both men laughed, a suave laugh full of self-knowledge. The girl laughed too. She loved this kind of talk. She was tremendously and constantly impressed by the omnipotence and yet kindliness and democracy of these great men, at the very hub of things. Let her boy-friend get a ticket for having parked too long on one spot, she had but to

86

suggest it to Judge Bellin or Judge Maggis and he would fix it for her. The time her sister had come up from Alabama with her two orphaned children, Judge Daniels had procured her a position as housemaid with a lovely family out on Delancey. There her sister lived. Like that! And she, Sadie, knew people who could do such things for her. On the street, what was she? A nigger wench. And at home? She was one of fourteen children. The house she lived in was full of nigger-talk, nigger-fights, nigger-worries. But here, how different it all was. She loved her elevator. If it were up to her, she would have run it all day. She never wondered what the judges did in their spare time, what they were really like and how they had got that way. In a vague sort of a way, she saw them moving graciously and vaguely smiling through great gracious houses, something like the one her sister lived in. They never laughed out loud, they were never drunk, they never woke up in the morning with a hang-over, and certainly they never fought with their fists. . . . Nor did she ever feel it necessary to get any closer to them than this. That would have been sacrilege, like wondering what sort of underclothes the Virgin Mary wore. They were the only men to whom, on the elevator, the police tipped their hats and were respectful.

She had been on the elevators for six years and wanted to be on them always. The nicest thing she had ever heard was when old Judge Marrigate, who was now retired, had called her a "dark little lady-bird in a gilded cage." That's just how she felt about it.

"I just love to hear them talk," she thought.

Other judges and lawyers were getting on. She watched the starter in the middle of the vast marble floor, a black woman named Mrs. Givens. "Step back in the car, please," she said softly several times. She was wondering what the judges would have thought if they knew what sort of a woman Mrs. Givens really was. "Go," said Mrs. Givens. Sadie began to close her door. As it began to slip to, faster and faster, a form hurtled through the

87

narrowing crack. She didn't know it, but the figure was that of Lloyd Matson.

If she had known it, she might have observed quite a change in him since the day before. Matson, she might have seen, was now attired in a suit of those careless-looking baggy tweeds that accentuate one's British appearance if one happens to be a Britisher. Matson, with his lean, blond, and eager body, definitely looked British. In addition, he had acquired a pair of gold-rimmed glasses and they gave him years and a scholarly appearance. Across the front of his vest stretched a thin gold chain leading, presumably, to a gold watch.

"Almost didn't make it," he said genially, addressing everybody in the car.

Sadie gave him a venomous look. "Skinny son of a bitch," she said to herself. "Them heavy doors will *cut* you," she said aloud.

Matson looked about him more closely. Judge Williams was looking at him with amusement.

"Why, Judge," he said, "how you doing this morning?"

He stuck his hand out. The Judge shook it.

"And how are you, young man?"

"Second floor," Sadie called. Could she have made a mistake? The Judge's next words reassured her.

"Judge Daniels," said Judge Williams, "this is one of the—ah—young Democrats of the sixth floor we were discussing just a moment ago."

Matson chuckled and put his arm around Judge Williams' shoulder. He wanted the Judge to know that *he* was being kidded. "The Judge is putting you on," he said to Judge Daniels. "Republican's my ticket."

Both the judges burst into laughter at this.

"Second floor," Sadie said.

Judge Daniels got off. As Judge Williams began to say something, Sadie held the door open a moment to allow him to finish.

"Don't take any wooden alibis," he said heartily, "and don't go on record until you've cleared the courtroom."

The elevator closed on Judge Daniels shaking his head and hurrying off.

"Third floor."

"Well, my boy," Judge Williams said, "it's been nice. Give Mr. Hohaley my best, won't you?"

The elevator was now empty, save for Matson and Sadie.

"Four. All out."

"Nice fella, the Judge. Great kidder."

"Sure is," Sadie said. "All out, please."

"Well, be seeing you."

"Yassuh."

She studied his careless departing back a moment before slamming the door for the descent.

"White climbin' *nigger*," she said, "Ah know yo' kind."

MATSON HEARD THE HUM OF VOICES. HE ADJUSTED HIS GLASSES and threw open the door. As though he'd touched a switch, the voices stopped. The room was full of people, men and women. He was conscious of a turning of eyes on him, a focusing of attention. He heard a whisper. "Is that him?" He heard a woman say, "My, he's awfully *young*." Gathering himself together, he strode forward. All over the place people were straightening themselves up. Cigarettes were being put out. He went forward to the desk and set himself down. Opening one drawer after another, he made as though he were looking for something. "Damn!" He stared about him wildly. "Will somebody open a window?" A dozen men flew to do this. He went through his pockets. Finding a paper, he opened it. It was a bill from a dentist. "Uh-huh," he said. He slid a piece of paper into the typewriter and began to type with terrific rapidity. "Piss on you," he wrote. "Piss on you. Piss on you. Piss on your father. Piss on your mother. Piss on your whole family. I am Lloyd Matson. Piss

89

on the whole world." He surveyed this message frowningly, then added, "In the Year of Our Lord Matson, 10,000 B.C." and signed it "Matson the Almighty." After this, he withdrew the sheet and inserted an envelope into the typewriter. He thought for a moment, then addressed it, "Judge Williams, S.O.B., Supreme Court, U.S.A." He enclosed the sheet in the envelope, sealed it, tapped thoughtfully at his lower lip with the edge of the portentous missive, then put it carefully in an inside pocket of his suit, as though for future reference. . . . Then, quickly, he looked up—to see what? For a moment, he saw nothing. He had looked up *too* quickly and had tried to take in too much. Then the scene arranged itself, very satisfactorily. All about him he saw the sustaining eyes of hope, of anxiety, each pair of eyes trying to catch and hold on to his.

He smiled to himself, his assurance returning.

"I presume you are all applicants for jobs on the Authors' Project," he stated, rather than asked.

A dim growl of assent. "Yes, sir."

"You will please line up, five at a time. The others may be seated at the back of the hall."

The first one to face him was a motherly-looking middle-aged woman who turned out never to have had a job before at all.

"My husband," she began, "he is only working part-time at his trade. He is a painter and paper-hanger. I have got four children. . . ."

She spread the panorama of family life before him. Regular attendance at church. "But we just don't have *enough*—"

"I understand."

"And so we talked it over with the priest and he said *well,* under the *circumstances,* I don't see why—"

"And so you decided to go to work to supplement the family income."

"Yes, sir."

"Mhm. How long on relief?"

His pencil was poised.

"Why, we're not on relief. Of course," she added hastily, "it's not that we aint qualified, but you know how it is—"

"I understand."

He raised his voice.

"How many of you people are on relief?"

Not a hand was raised. They stared at him blankly. Now what? they seemed to say. Poor devils!

He stood up.

"Now I don't want to alarm you people. But I just want you to know one thing. This Project is outfitted to run six months. It has got so much money allotted to it for the period. After this, there is a good chance that it will be renewed, *but*—"

The excitable ones began to stand up to hear him better. One to every dozen, like a law in statistics, the angry men began to get up.

"But," he continued, "and I just want you to understand that I am just an official here, having no control over the rules that govern the life of this Project, just an *official,* you understand," he repeated, suddenly relishing the word, "this money—at least the part of it which goes for the personnel—must be divided between two categories: *non*-relief and relief—"

"It sure pays to be decent, don't it," a woman asserted suddenly, in a loud voice that carried. "All my neighbors are on relief and got good jobs on the side too, and me decent enough not to want to take that which I have never had to take before—"

"And what about me," a man said, "I *went* down to the relief. I tell this fella, he was some kind of a foreigner—"

"Jew most likely," somebody shouted.

"I tell this fella I can't afford no more decency. So he asks me a number of questions and I tell 'm my wife has still got some insurance. So he asks me how much loan-value is there on it. 'Wait a minute, Mister,' I said, 'You kin stop right there.' And I walked out. They have got my job, I told this fella, then they got my house. Then they got my own insurance. Now what the hell they want? I can't leave my kids *entire* without protection. Can I now? What do you advise me to do, I ask this fella. I am sorry, he told me, I must folla my instructions."

"Ladies and gentlemen," Matson shouted. He held up his hands and slowly the voices subsided. Some of the people sat down. They had said their say and felt justified. So the anger faded out of their faces. Now let's see what this young fella has to say. Matson wished to Christ he wasn't so blond. What he needed was a mustache.

"There is no cause for alarm," he said. "All I said was, the personnel, *arbitrarily,* must be divided in the two categories—"

"How much of each?" somebody asked.

"Yeah, get down to it!"

"There is a provision made that 90 per cent of the people must come off of the relief rolls, 10 per cent off the non-relief. This provision, I was going to say, was made in order that we should fulfill our two functions. First of all, we want to relieve people, so we take them off of relief. And I don't have to tell *you* that there's a depression on. Secondly, this is an *Authors'* Project. Where can we get our technical help? To assure ourselves *of* getting it, *if* we can't get it off the relief, we have arranged this proviso so that—"

A sort of apathy had taken hold of his listeners. The more he talked, the more he had them. A smile pulled hard at his lip and he had a hard time holding it in. The point was, he *knew* what he was talking about. And as he talked, he realized how well he knew what he was talking about. He wished that Mr. Hohaley were here now to hear him. The Judge. Charles Gest. The whole damn shebang. A tiny figure stood on a platinum-bright platform in his mind. That figure was Lloyd Matson, the cold-eyed Boy Orator. "I got nothing against the defendant, gentlemen," this little man said to the jury; "for all I know, he is good to his mother, a model of humanity, a gentleman, a scholar and an idealist. But—" and that's how it is.

For my part, he wanted to say to all these people, I would gladly give you all jobs. But am I to blame for the rules and regulations? And what do you expect me to do about them? And he wanted to tell them too that if it had been up to him they would not only have jobs and damn good pay but chicken in every pot and rainbows with all their electric lights. As it is, though, it's got to be Number 1, doesn't it?

"Well, one thing anyway," he said, "whoever can qualify has got as good a chance as the next fellow. All within the quota."

So ran his thoughts. So went his talk. He held a cabalistic celebration of his mastery of figures and facts, statistics and dull but vital information, and for pleasure paraded it all. He blamed Mr. Hohaley for today's fiasco, but he blessed him too, and it wasn't a question of getting mad either. He was glad that the director had shown his hand by putting in a requisition to the Employment Bureau when it should have been the Relief. He was glad that the Judge had snubbed him. He had Hohaley's number. He had everybody's number. The Judge, with his *position* in life. Mr. Hohaley, with his crap and his *past*. Charlie Gest, with his *questions*. People, with their *decency*. Cripples, all caught in their imperfections. Life is a darkroom, he reflected, and the thing to do is not to blunder about in the dark bewailing your blindness, or to sit in a chair on your dignity or to get mad, but to find the switch and turn it on. The minute you come into a room, thought Matson, aged twenty-one, "orphan," lonely in the world, "without kith or kin," find out where the light comes from.

He looked down at the woman before him to find her weeping.

"Your application will most certainly receive the most serious consideration," he began ardently, carried away by his eloquence.

"It just don't seem right," she sobbed.

He led her personally to the door, past the hostile faces of the others. "I mean it," he assured her. Hell of a nice woman, he told

93

himself, casting a fleeting and incurious glance at her battleship-broad beam.

He strode back to his desk.

"I'll tell you people one thing," he blazed. "Now I can't guarantee to do this for all of you. But that lady is gonna get a job, I don't care where, here or on some other project. I mean it! I guarantee it personally!"

Noses grew red in profound approval. What a fine young man!

"BE QUIET, HEART," SAID MRS. GEST, SCOLDING FONDLY. "LET mine Charlie talk. Today *he* is the guest. Not you, old everything-bad."

She put her left hand on her breast in a gesture of quieting the culprit.

"What is the word you use?" she asked Nussim.

The little man smiled.

"When the boss wants you should do something, he says *Continue!*"

"All right," said Mrs. Gest. "Continue."

She put soup on the table. It was a good soup. One of those recipes she had brought with her from Russia, from the old country, how many years ago! First you heat the water. Into it you put, no more, no less, three cloves of garlic. You need potatoes, peas, a dash of salt. . . . She put bread beside the plate, good aromatic black pumpernickel. Butter. And the coffee grumbled its little song on the stove.

"Nu?"

Charlie laughed. He picked up the pamphlet he'd been reading silently and continued aloud. It was Pamphlet Number 23, entitled *Consultants.*

He read from the text: *"There are two types of consultants we should wish you in the field to cultivate for your frames of reference in matters pertaining to your state—"*

The words didn't matter a damn to his mother, he knew that.

94

He also knew what she wanted to hear. Well, he felt reckless. The job was good, he believed that at last. The pamphlet, one of about fifteen he'd been given to take home from the office to study, proved that. Mr. Hohaley might still be a mystery to him (his seeming *unwillingness* to talk about the work), but the pamphlets were not. They had been compiled by Mr. Colon and his assistants, among whose names he recognized many renowned in the intellectual life of the times, and he could trace the line of their serious thought and inquiry in the questionnaires they presented for the "field" to investigate and assemble answers to.

"*The consultants are* (1), *your* involuntary *consultants*" (he stressed the word *involuntary,* looking amusedly at his mother), "*the men and women you will find in the street, the factory, in industry and in all the places that make up the contemporary structure* . . . Like *you,* old lady," he said. "Listen to this. *These will often be your best, because hitherto uncollected, consultants, proving themselves rich in folk-views and idiom. Your findings with these, for accuracy's sake, however, must then be checked with consultants of Type Number 2. They are your recognized, or established authorities, the leading men in each field in your community: the architects, the lawyers, the social workers, the newspapers, et cetera.*"

He read these words as though they were words in a poem, and walked solemnly back and forth, sawing the air with splendid gesture.

"In other words," he said, "they are talking about you, Ma. 'How do you breathe?' they tell me to ask you. 'I breathe with difficulty,' you answer, if I know you right. So I put it down in my little red book. Then I go to an authority—not that you're *not* an authority, you understand, but we have *two* types of authorities here, and you're the kind that speaks only for yourself. The other speaks for everybody, because they have the right to do it. So, for accuracy, I say, 'How does Mrs. Gest *breathe?*' and they take into consideration the peculiarities of the local climate, the peculiarities of the subject, and so forth, and they say, 'Well, as a worthy beginning to this question, we may say that, first of all, she breathes with her *lungs*—' "

"May his sins be expiated on the heads of our enemies," said Mrs. Gest, blinking with pride; "such a beautiful voice."

"And that's a good way to begin such an inquiry," Charlie continued, half-serious now. "So I come back to Mrs. Gest. 'Look here, old lady,' I say, 'there's a theory that you breathe with your *lungs*, not with *difficulty*, as you informed me. How do you explain this apparent contradiction?' So she asks me a question, which turns out to be so phrased that it's really a masterpiece of illiterate logic and down it goes into my little red book. In ages to come scholars will ponder over what Mrs. Gest said, and the light it threw on our civilization. 'With my lungs?' she says. 'What learned lunacy! And with what is *breathing* that is painted with smoke and stopped with trouble? Is it not with *difficulty?*' So we have both accurary and art."

"Accuracy and art," Nussim came in. "That's very good!"

Charlie stopped before his mother. His eyes danced.

"You understand me, do you not, my friend?"

"*Nu,* tell me then," she begged. "With God's help, tell me. Means it then after all something—you should not fool me—that a plain person can really understand?"

"She understands nothing of these matters," said Nussim complacently. "Only with *trouble* is she on an intellectual footing. I understand. And I say that it is a worthy thing. But I will say a word about the breathing."

This was one of his days off. It was the slack season for his line of work. As a rule, he confined his days off to keeping to himself and reading his old books, read many times since the days he had bought them, which was in another land and when his head was covered with hair. It was not safe to do otherwise. The poems of Lermontov. The wisdom of Spinoza. The dreams of Gorki. The various Commentaries. But today he could stand out in the open and his wife looked at him as first she did when he said to her, "Snub-nose, you can neither read nor write, not even your name, but I will get you into America and a President of the Golden and Fabled Land of America will be born from among your sons." Today it was safe.

"*He* understands," she said. To the cracks on the ceiling, old confidantes, "*What* does he understand!"

"No, no," said Nussim, smiling.

Charlie listened. He was curious to hear what his father would say. He had often wished he could sit down with his father and hear stories of his early life, of *his* father, of what he had thought on leaving him. He had wanted to know what his mother had looked like in her girlhood. There were a lot of things he wanted to know about his parents. Out of her belly I came and they cut the cord. Matthew Arnold's great poem of Sohrab and Rustum, read for the first time in grade school, had made him weep with its intolerable play on the source of a deep nostalgia in him, a poor kid playing in hostile city streets. "And we never lived in one place for more than a couple of months," he had written the next week in a composition for English. "Me and my Dad, we was like Sohrab and Rustum in the poem. I was Sohrab and my Dad was Rustum and one day I said to my Daddy, if you was to kill me accidental, would you take me back to Russia and bury me next to your Daddy? He cried just like Rustum and he said Russia is a long way from here, Charlie, and even there was not our first home. And why do you think I will kill you? Rustum's father was snow-haired Zal and he lived in Seistan. My Daddy's father has a long beard and he lives in Odessa."

A sense of delicacy had kept him from asking questions. Far from the open fields of the hills behind Odessa, his father's and mother's first abode here in the new city had been in the backyard of a Baker Avenue tenement block of buildings. In the winter you went outside to the toilet in the back and you lit matches to keep the rats away. And in the summer it rained in through the roof. Like a blotter, his expanding soul had absorbed the vast and complex disappointment of his parents, and he had often stood in silence and watched his mother scrubbing the clothes of strangers. Until Janice came, she had been strong, and how it had pleased them both when, on the days he accompanied her to the grocery stores to carry her bags for her, she had been mistaken for his sister. Then, with the coming of Janice, a mystery one with the mystery of why are the stars, where they are, and why do clouds pass from nowhere over the face of the sun and it rains, and winter follows summer and summer winter, she had become sick for life. Sentenced! The doctors had names for it, but he had none.

He himself could not remember further back than the tenements, much as he had tried. But, as he strained with intensity for news of his life, before the womb, he had at times, it seemed to him, heard tinklings of laughter and strangely ordered songs.

So he listened with curiosity to his father, as he always did when the quiet man chose to talk.

"There were two villages in a province of Russia," Nussim said, "and we will call them Bishik and Shishik."

Charlie smiled at his mother, and they both sat to eat their soup. Nussim went to the window and stood in profile, the little gray hairs playing gently with the movement of the lines of his face.

"As is natural," he continued, "in each one of these villages were Jews and in each were Cossacks. And the Jews and the Cossacks of each of these villages were friendly with one another. That is to say, the Cossacks had nothing against their Jews. 'Devil take it,' they would say to one another, 'in the whole world, no finer people than our Jews will you find.' But now what do you think?—"

Nussim stood before his wife and son and bent his intelligent kind eyes humorously on them.

"Is this the whole story?" he asked oratorically. "That the

98

Cossacks of Bishik and the Cossacks of Shishik loved their respective Jews and there is an end to it?"

"With God's help," said Mrs. Gest. "What then? What then?"

"Patience, woman," Nussim said. He resumed his walk. "So, the Cossacks of Bishik got together and held a conference. A conference such as the Cossacks can hold, in a room, with the faucets on the barrels running with vodka and on the agenda one point. And the question these gentlemen put themselves was, What kind of a world is it with no Jews to beat? So, after two days of talking over everything, they find themselves with an answer. How simple! We will go to the neighboring village of Shishik and we will beat *their* Jews. In this way, we honor our Jews, which is what they deserve, for they are honest folk, and still, we *beat* Jews, which is how God has willed it. And they went to Shishik and they beat the Jews there. And *how* they beat them!" Nussim leaned back and laughed until he had to clutch the side of the hot stove for support. "They cut beards! They tickled the maidens, the wives also, with their fingers, and with something else, too, you may know! They put a fire under the synagogue and ran around like firemen keeping those of their number who were drunk from falling into the flames! They took little boys and girls and beat their brains together like fists!"

"Well, say yourself," Mrs. Gest exploded, putting down her spoon in horror, "is this what you should laugh at in your foolish old age? Why do you laugh, fool?"

"Right! Wrong!" Nussim waved his hand to dismiss the thought. "Words, words! Besides, who laughs? We are talking about accuracy and art. Do you want to listen?"

"Go ahead," Charlie said. "I never heard *this* one before."

Nussim, flattered, went ahead. "So. The Cossacks, we can well imagine this, are now tired. Why shouldn't they be? A weariness overcomes them. 'Eh, brothers,' they say, 'it is time. Back to Bishik. Our wives wait for us to give us hell. The chil-

99

dren pine for their fathers. The bread stands on the table.' And back they went. *Nu,* is this all? Is there no more to the story?"

"As the truth is that we know you well," his wife said, "we also know there will be more."

"There will indeed be more," said Mr. Gest, "and, Charlie, I am telling it to you, for I wish you to know something at the end. . . . So, *aklol,* back they come and everything is fine. A story *could* end there. But we are not playing with checkers, my boy. Here come in the Cossacks of *Shishik.* Yes, of Shishik! Are not they people too? Have they no feelings? With tears in their eyes, the Cossacks of Shishik had watched the Cossacks from Bishik beating up *their* beloved Jews and had begged them, Stop, stop, to no more avail than when my own dear mother, hallowed be her name, begged my young face, when, with God's help, it was at last twelve years old, that hair should not begin growing on it and, in order that it should stop, wrapped a towel wet with my own (how shall I say it?) *urine* over it. . . . Yes, these good Cossacks of Shishik had begged the bad Cossacks of Bishik not to beat their Jews, but to no avail. 'Is it not written,' they had answered, 'that Jews must be beaten?' Incontestable (you must tell me what is the English word for this, Charlie). And to have fallen on their fellow-Cossacks would thus have been doubly wrong. And so, all through the beatings-up, they had stood by gloomily and wrung their hands or held their thoughts at home confined in the circles of their vodka-glasses or their wives' eyes. But now, they too came together for a conference. And they made up their minds, guess what! They would go, in retaliation, to Bishik, and beat up the Jews there. 'They beat our Jews,' they said in justification; 'we will beat theirs.' And this they did— only, as was right, twice as bad. And, of course, all that the Cossacks of Bishik could do was regret that they had given their fellows this opportunity. . . ."

He shook for a moment in glee at the ironic spectacle. "Yes, yes," he muttered. Then he stood silent for a while. "There was a point I wanted to make," he said, frowning. "What was it now?" While talking, his face had been animated, alive. Now it became again the face of a man who has spent forty-five years of his life in shoe shops, most of them of the "sweatshop" variety. "He was sitting cross-legged over the patches on an officer's boots when he was twelve," Charlie reflected. His father took off his glasses and began polishing them in an effort to remember his thought. His face had grown somewhat red with the attempt to disguise his embarrassment. The truth is, he had grown too absorbed in his story. The eyes, when he took the glasses off, were faded like woolens that have been through the wringer too many times.

"I was telling you how we were going to find our material," Charlie said. "How we were going to test it by submitting the findings to qualified consultants. . . . I had taken Ma's *breathing* as an example of—"

"Yes. Yes." His father, with a surging back of vitality, caught hold of the words. "Well, all I wanted to say is— You see, Charlie, I wish you luck. Work hard, it is a good chance. We, as you know, my boy, could never get enough on our feet to—how shall I say it?—" He spoke with averted eyes now. "Only, I wanted to say that *good, bad, right, wrong,* these are only words. Anybody can use them. And they have a right. They are human beings. . . . Don't be bitter, in short. Nor yet should you— because it is a good job and the consultants will be great men, powerful men—eat what your tongue rejects. The consultants— how shall I say it—think of our Cossacks. . . . The Cossacks were good men. No, no, I mean it. But the Jews, use your head, got beat up all the same—"

Mrs. Gest had been listening with growing indignation. Now, fearing that a plot was being laid, she entered passionately and shrilly into the fray.

"What kind of a devil's with dirty pants talk is this?" she screamed, her eyes rolling. "Old louse! The boy has a job! He—"

"The man (how do you say it? The *consultant?*) who speaks for everybody is a wise man," Nussim continued. "How can it be otherwise? He must think. He must be accurate. There are our own *filosofs!* But the man who speaks for himself, even if he is—forgive me—as mixed up as your mother, speaks from a *closer* place; his truth, in short, is (myself, I am not an unlearned man) a *truer,* a *finer,* truth, even if it is not accurate. Your mother"—he looked slyly at Charlie, blushing and avoiding Mrs. Gest's outraged countenance—"your mother, in short, even if we may laugh at her and she knows not what we laugh at, is wrong. But she is *right.* And if she says she breathes with *difficulty,* then this is how she breathes, even if the consultants write learned books on the business of the lungs."

He dearly loved a parable. "And if the Cossacks of Shishik and Bishik say that they respect and honor their Jews, remember not to laugh. Take down their words, they speak truth. This is strictly accurate. And God will remember that they were merciful and be kind to their children. But all the same, when the Jew comes to you and says, 'I have been beaten,' and names these same Cossacks, he is *speaking for himself* and it is a finer truth. It is Art."

Charlie stared at this strange man. What a pillar of strength and subtlety he was. How wise were his words, how full of knowledge of the mystery that life is. And yet, how simple. Without knowing his father too well, he nevertheless knew that his words were metaphors. He does not believe in a God who broods and weeps over his creatures. He is actually a man almost without hope. And, nevertheless, he is a prayerful man, remembering with sympathy even the "sorely beset" Cossacks of Shishik and Bishik.

But Mrs. Gest, utterly dumfounded at the strange turn of events that had led her husband to champion her supposed words, and say that she was right and the world wrong, could not find what to say.

"So I am right," she thought. "The world is wrong!" And finally she found speech. "My goodness," she said. "My goodness!" She felt as vindicated and as panic-stricken suddenly as a prophet might feel who, having for long predicted that the world would come to a bad end, goes out into the street one fine day and the finale is *happening*.

REALITY, A SENSE OF SUBSTANCE BROKE THROUGH THE VEIL of intangibility of the Project the next day when the office equipment began arriving. Up the passenger elevators (there were no others) came dozens of typewriters, desks, steel files and cabinets and scores of chairs, truck after truck backing up to the west side pavements to unload their cargoes and be off for more. Matson, in his element, sat at his desk interviewing a new batch of job applicants; this time, thanks to him, certified by the proper people and at the right place. Now and then a work foreman came up to him with a bill of lading. Matson would then arise, jauntily look over the goods the lading represented, then sign himself to the bill. He really had great talents for details of administration, and was supervising the installation of an architect's "shop" at the same time the interviews went on. Also, he found time to be at Mr. Hohaley's beck and call as that gentleman, sitting in the midst of the din and clamor attending the erection of a sumptuous private office about him, found need for him. The director was leaning back in his chair, blowing smoke rings into the air, and dictating endless letters to Miss O'Hara. These, inquiring after this one's family and that one's health, inviting this one to supper at the "town house," apprising that one that he expected to be in their town on such and such a date, were punctuated by telephone calls that arrived for him at regular intervals of half an hour throughout the day, of which at least half were long-distance, congratulating him on his appointment, offering all help within the callers' means and alluding gallantly to past friendships. Lucille Turnbull was out, presumably seeing people to whom her mission was still to "explain" the Project. Charlie Gest was installed at a desk near to Matson's, and was also interviewing applicants.

How changed was his lot! It was the first time in years that he had worn ties for more than one day in a row. With the exception of Lloyd Matson, people here called him Mr. Gest. He was getting into the habit, when he felt hungry, of ordering himself a thirty-five-cent meal at the corner restaurant rather than waiting until he got home to eat; or, when in funds, hopping a cup of coffee at a counter stand-up-and-gulp. Was this not wherein dignity resided, simply in a man's feeling that he had a job to do and therefore a place? The secret, now, of his father's peace and calm—no matter what had happened to the old man throughout his life—and plenty had happened: he'd been gypped, beaten, underpaid, you could add a line of *et ceteras* as long as a train— was that he had a job, a thing he could do and in which he excelled, and therefore, even if in a back seat, a place in the conference of humanity. To be on relief was shameful only because you gave nothing in return. A paradox here. The poor blame themselves not for poverty but because they cannot give more than they have. . . . "However," thinks Charlie, with the faintest touch of self-condescension, a touch which he notes and smiles wryly at, filing it for future reference, "no time for thought now. There is much to be done now." Tonight, he thinks, I am to take a train (I flash a government railroad pass) to Johnsburgh, the great sister-metropolis on the far side of the state, to set up a similar project there. Imagine!

I know that I know nothing. I know that the great roaring train of life has plunged forever past the crossings where I was always waiting, never able to catch on. But the people in that train, for all its power and glitter, are few, and if I know nothing of them, they know nothing of me and my kind. Homer, in ages past, laid down the Odyssey of Ulysses like a carpet over the fields of Greece and the people came out of their warm caves in the city and wept at its dark strange beauty. Mr. Roosevelt, we who were about to die, salute you. Lo and behold, the story of our people. And what's more, in goddam fine prose too.

In the busy buzz of voices, the scratching of pencils, the scraping of furnishings as they were heaved and rolled into place, the clangor of hammers, he sat at his desk and interviewed his fellowmen. On the other side of a large partition, in what Matson called the "city room," the new members of the Project were beginning to add up. They sat tensely over pamphlets, two and three to a man, and worked hard at acquainting themselves with the requirements of their new job. Five became six. Six became seven. There is true magic to be found in employment places.

The advent in the waiting line of Pete Cavagni brought Charlie's reverie up with a start. Until then, everything had been fairly easy going. He had hired three typists and two file clerks. You would need typists on a job such as this. They would keep the file clerks toiling like slaves of Egypt at the Pyramids. True, two of the girls had not typed since highschool. And then they'd only had a year of it. And Charlie knew how rusty they would be. But they would learn again. As he would learn to begin with. The new crew. The new destinations. But Pete—

The thin dark-faced youth slid into the chair before his desk and smiled at him. He smiled back. Mr. Gest, the father of his country! Why did the image of the motorman and the old drunken bum who wanted to ride without paying a fare flash through his mind? Perhaps it would always be there. Modern man's substitute for religion!

"Name, please?"

"Pete Cavagni."

The young fellow put his card down before Charlie. He looked at it. Pete Cavagni. Twenty-four. Banjoist. American citizen. *Three children.* Drives car or truck. Member of Musicians' Union.

Jesus! This kid! Three children?

"It says here," he said slowly, "that you're a musician. . . ."

Pete leaned forward eagerly. He had an open boy's face, the delicate transparent teeth of a child. Three youngsters call him father!

"Look, *Charlie*," he whispered. "Gimme a break, willya?" He looked down at the floor, looked up again. "I had a lot happen to me since we useta see each other."

So we know each other, eh? Charlie searched his mind. In the printing shop where he used to work evenings after high-school? In the shoe factory, banging out dies? Down on the playgrounds, boxing or playing baseball with the 36th Street crowd? Or maybe later, at the Greek's? He knew his memory for faces was poor. People walked up to him in the street. How's your family? Fine. How's yours? Okay. Mamie's had another baby. Well, so long. Give my regards to Mamie. . . . Who the hell is Mamie?

"I don't seem to remember—" he began hesitantly.

"I didn't t'ink you did, the way you acted. I knew *you* right away. Jeez, you're lookin' good. I bet you're in good shape. Don't you remember Gus Castoni? Moey Feinberg? Izzie the Stinkfinger?"

Grade school! 'Twas many and many a year ago, back in black time with the Raven itself and Edgar Allan Poe, but the grimy quadrangle swam now across his view, the boys and the girls he had known. Gus Castoni indeed. He hadn't thought of the burly Italian for twelve years, not since they'd moved out of the neighborhood. But now, of a sudden, evoked by Pete's words, he and Gus were boys again in a weird resurrection. Gus had held down the little Polish boy—what was *his* name?—and he, Charlie, the little hero, had swallowed the lump in his throat and stepped up to him.

"Let loose of him."

"Who's gonna make me?"

While little Dorothy Causland had stood on the girl's side of

106

the fence and watched him. *Dorothy,* suddenly! Think of having forgotten her! Snub-nose, twinkle-toes, a long red tongue forever on the stick-out. And she must be all of twenty-five now, for she was a year older than he. And where was she now, little Dorothy? . . . And shadows of the desperate fight that had followed flickered before him. Now he's up. Now he's down. Now he's up. "Blood on the saddle," sang little Izzie the Stinkfinger, "blood on the ground, blood in the air and blood all around."

"Jesus, yes. I remember Gus Castoni. What happened to the big son of a bitch?"

Pete's eyes poured gratitude at him for remembering. "He's doin' fine, Charlie. He's got'm a line o' trucks outta Quincy now. Been married fi' times. The las' time I seen 'm, it was down by the West Bridge, he was married to a German kid. Said he was gonna sample sumpin' of ever' nationality before he was t'rough."

He looked about him, then leaned forward as though to tell secrets that nobody else must hear. Then he told how Izzie had got it in the head in a hold-up in which his partners were Sammy Gorenson and Duke Boyle. "So den Horace Billings goes over to Izzie's house t' look at 'm fuh de las' time, even if he aint Jew hisself, and he sees Izzie's sis. You remember her, Charlie? She was da one fell onna ear offa Miss Cardinal's winda and like ta died. An' he gets a yen f'r 'er and the first thing you know, they are hitched up. He's a switchman now. Fuh de Union Pacific. They got two kids theirselves."

"What about Julie Ryan?" Charlie asked, Julie just popping up full-shape in his mind.

"You mean Dodger's sis, tha one wit' da pigtails?"

Charlie tried to remember Dodger. Dodger? Dodger? He couldn't make it. For that matter, he still had not placed Pete.

"Yeah," he temporized, still seeing Julie, "that's the one."

"The las' I seen o' her, she was hustlin' on 36th Street near Bailey. By Hymie's old man's drygoods store."

107

So she was hustling! Little twelve-year-old Julie!

"Say, you remember Dorothy Causland?" he asked shyly. "She was the—"

"Hell, I remember *her* all righ'." Pete laughed, as though in remembering her he was scoring an important triumph. "You had uh yen fuh her, di'n'cha, Charlie? Jeez, ever' time she dropped a pencil, yuh like ta bust a gut gettin' it fuh her. 'N' ever' time yuh did, she give yuh da thumb to da nose."

He gave Charlie a knowing wink.

"I guess she got married too, eventually, huh? Got a dozen kids by now. Fat as hell, huh?"

"Her wit' a dozen kids? Dat peacherino fat? Don't kid youself." Pete lowered his voice even more. "Dis'll kill yuh. She got married all righ', but she aint married now. She was Gus Castoni's t'ird wife. She stood up fuh two years, which is a longer stretch dan da others done. Gus was out ta tha place one night when I was still playin' regular at da tee-ay'er and he said she wuz da bes' wife he ever had. He said after he got aroun' all da nationalities and wuz ready to start in again, he would come back ta da Irish."

"I guess you knew Mike Fallon, talking about the Irish," Charlie said, to get off of the subject. "What happened to him?"

But Pete's memories here were blank, for a wonder.

"Mike Fallon?" he said. "Dat's one on me. I guess he musta been 'fore my time."

Pause.

"You know," Charlie said, "I guess I'm a rat, but I still can't place you, Pete."

"You can't?" Pete sobered. "I'll tell yuh. You wuz in da gradjiatin' class wit' Miss Marvin, dat's why yuh can't r'member me. I wuz two rooms below yuh. I was in Miss Magid's class at da time. You remember Miss Magid?"

"I remember her all right."

Pete's face cleared. "I knew you'd remember Miss Magid,"

he said. He waited. The fingers of his left hand started drumming.

"I don't know what to say," Charlie said, after a while. "You know, Pete, this is a writers' outfit." Pete began nodding his head rapidly, in rhythm to the words, yes. Yes. "We-e-ell, don't you see? It's not up to me. We're supposed to hire *writers. Newspapermen. Research students."*

Pete jerked his head in the direction of the successful applicants. Then he jerked it at the girl sitting at Matson's desk. The girl was seventeen or eighteen years of age. A dumb-looking girl with large breasts and a giggle. Nervous. As they looked over at her, she looked at them quickly. Looked away.

"You gonna tell me she's a *news*paper writer. *Re* what you said student?"

"No, I guess not. If she's hired, it'll be because she's a typist though. Or a steno. If you could only type, Pete. . . . Can you type?"

"No. Not me."

"Don't get me wrong, Pete. I've been sitting here, trying to think of something. I wish I could *do* something."

Pete smiled bitterly. The boy's face took on a kind of bravado. "Dat's all righ'," he muttered. "I t'ought, you 'n' me goin' t' da same school—" he left the thought unfinished.

Charlie couldn't let him go.

"How have you been, Pete," he said.

"Aw, I can't complain, I had my good times," he began. Then his bravado collapsed. "Da milkman quit leavin' milk at da house yesserday. My wife says, 'I gotta have dat milk, one o' my kids is sick.' Da milkman says, 'I been carryin' yuh t'ree weeks. I know yuh kid is sick. I been payin' f' dat milk outen my own pocket. I have got a fambly myself. I cannot afford to keep on givin' y' milk.' 'N' he didn't leave any milk yesserday or t'day." He tapped with his fingers, then he looked up. "Y'know," he said, "I got a sick kid."

109

"Jesus, Pete," Charlie said. "You look like a kid yourself."

"I don't feel like one," Pete said. "I look like one, but I don't feel like one. Y'know what I mean?"

Charlie nodded. "Yeah."

"I guess you bin ta collich, huh?"

Charlie laughed. "Yeah, that's right, Pete. I been to three of them. Last one was Cambridge. That's in England. I'm a graduate professor of literature."

"Yeah. I guess you learned all dat writin' and *re* what you said at collich, huh? I guess you got all dat ejication wit' yuhr old man's dough 'n' laid plen'y pipe too, huh? I guess y'aint fixed so bad right now, huh?" He took a slow look around the room. "Lissen," he whispered, a look of intense hatred suddenly flaring in his face, "I aint laid my woman f' six mont's. She got sick, see? So 'bout a mont' ago, I gets me a night out at a road-side joint I used ta play in da same band wit' dis guy, he's the boss. And I makes me t'ree bucks. So on de way home I stops in at a place. Y'know what I mean? I gets me a li'l piece. 'N' now I got me a dose. How y' like dat? My kids wit'out milk, my wife sick 'n' me wit' a dose!"

The thin face quivered. The eyes grew black and hollow and spiraled in and down, depth on depth. Charlie shuddered.

"Look, Pete," he whispered, in his turn, "why don't you give me your address. You know, something might turn up."

"When wouldja let me know?"

Pete didn't trust him, Charlie could see that.

"Tomorrow morning, at the latest. I'll have to go bat for you."

The little-boy look came back to Pete's face.

"Honest?"

"No kidding."

Pete insisted on writing out the address himself. In a large scrawl that covered the page. He stood up.

"If I see any of da gang," he said, "I'll tell 'm y' said hello."

CHARLIE WATCHED PETE LEAVE. CONSCIOUS THAT HE AND HIS old schoolmate had been watched all through the interview, a long one, by the other applicants patiently waiting, he sauntered over to Mr. Hohaley's desk. If we give Pete a job, somebody else, more qualified, as needy perhaps, goes without. When they gave me this job, somebody, less needy perhaps, more qualified, got left. Madness lies this way. He felt tense, as though he were expecting a blow in the stomach. But, characteristically, as he struggled with the problems involved, he savored fully the flavor of a situation whereby he could ask a job for another man.

"Sit down." He greeted him with a smile as though he were returning from far places. "Sit down, Mister. Long time no see."

"No, Mr. Hohaley. I—excuse me, I don't mean to take up your time. There was something I wanted to ask you—"

The fat man leaned back deliberately and blew a cloud of smoke. "Yes?"

If he let Hohaley look at him much longer like that, it would unnerve him. Christ, it was as though the man were always expecting to hear a certain thing. What? Could it be merely what he was about to ask for Pete? If so, he was lost—almost before he started. But he had to ask this thing.

"There's a fellow was just in here, used to go to school with me. He—"

As it began to occur to him what Charlie was asking, that look came off his face and he began to smile broadly.

"I think mebbe, Mister Gest, we can make arrangments fo' yo' friend."

"What I'm trying to say is, he's not a writer. I doubt he can sign his own name. He can't type . . ."

"Mister Matson, Sir."

Matson, who'd been looking over every few seconds to see what was going on, leaped over.

III

"Mister Matson. Do you have a janitor listed on our requisitions?"

Matson looked from Mr. Hohaley to Gest. Back again.

"No, sir, we don't."

"But, gen'lemen, don't y'all think we could *use* a janitor?"

Matson touched a finger to his tongue and then trailed it across the top of the desk. "There's going to be a lot of dusting needed around here."

"Well then, Mister Matson?"

"Well, I'll tell you, Mr. Hohaley. I can't very well put this bird down as a janitor." He began to explain how a certain rule read. The building in which the Project rents must furnish a janitor. The relief requisitions did not list janitors. "However—"

The director cut him off short. "Exactly, Mister Matson," he said smoothly, poker-faced, "however—"

"That's all I wanted to know," Matson shouted. "We'll put him down as a typist. *Now.* If I may have the name?"

Mr. Hohaley seemed annoyed.

"I b'lieve I can safely leave how 'he is put down' to my staff, don't you think so, sir? You will get the details from Mister Gest, Mister Matson. The gen'leman is a friend of Mister Gest's."

"Right," Matson said. He shook himself, that very odd gesture, like a dog, groaned. "Yes, sir, you sure can leave it to your staff."

"It's not just that he's a friend of mine—" Charlie began. But Mr. Hohaley was no more interested in what he might have had to say than he had been in how Matson listed Pete in the requisition.

"Exactly," he said coolly. "It's a question of loyalty. You have loyal eyes, Mister Gest." He turned suddenly toward Matson, who just had time to kill a chortle. "You made quite an impression on Judge Williams, Mister Matson," he said slowly.

Matson looked innocent, but an expression of gratification sprouted up out of his skin.

"Yes," Mr. Hohaley said, "the Judge said he b'lieves you to be a r'markable young man. Said he thought you would go far. I told him that I agreed with him. I told him that I *intended* you to go far." He smiled and turned to Charlie. "Don't you want to notify yo' friend?"

"Yes, I do." He wanted to thank him, but he found that the words would not come. He felt that Mr. Hohaley would consider them a presumption, because of the nature of the favor done, as though by innuendo he had accused him of something. And yet he felt also Hohaley's strange personal need of gratitudes. What an amazing person!

"Anything else, gen'lemen?"

"No, sir."

They returned to their desks.

"NAME, PLEASE?"

"Charles Petrie, sir."

"Profession?"

"Lawyer."

"A lawyer, eh? That's fine. I suppose you've had a lot of experiences writing briefs?"

"I wrote all the briefs for Simpson and Cawlins for three years."

"Why, that's fine." How the job was conditioning him. He certainly had never expected he'd be glad to meet a lawyer. "That makes you pretty literate, eh, Mr. Petrie?"

"I can make myself clear, sir, if that's what you mean."

"Fine. Fine. Now this job"—something occurred to him. "Excuse me just one moment, please."

He hurried over to Matson's desk.

"Say, Lloyd, I promised to let this fella Pete know by tomorrow morning. You better not write a letter. I'll go over to his house tonight myself to make sure he gets the message."

Matson shook his head and stifled sobs of delight.

"Why, you goddam dope, the *telegram's* already been sent. Just knocked it out over the telephone."

"Telegram!"

"Sure, a telegram. And you're not taking a train to Johnsburgh tonight either."

"No?" He felt disappointment.

"No. You're taking a plane."

"Why, you dog! How'd you fix that?"

"All you need do is *read*. Of course, not everybody's as smart as *me*—"

"I should say not. But listen, Lloyd. Thanks for the help on Pete. You helped me out of a tough one with that mutt."

"Think no more of it."

"You know, Lloyd, you're not a bad sort of s.o.b. at all. There's Pete. And the business with my folks and the taxicab. You're not at all a bad fellow."

"Hell, no, I'm not. But what about that s.o.b. business? Anybody say I am? I'll knock their left eye out."

He didn't seem the least bit sore though.

"Well, I think Mr. H. gets annoyed with you every so often. He was sore, I think, because you brought putting on Pete as a typist out into the open."

"He's just sore because I'm smart, that's all. I'm the smartest man in the world. If you stick with me, remember what I said, I'll train you. As for Mr. H., you'd better watch out yourself. He'll have his fingers in that hair before you know it."

"I don't think he's quite like *that*."

"He'd better be."

"Better? How's that."

"If he's not like that, then he'll be worse. A perverted pervert!"

114

This, however, was not yet the time and place.

"Well, see you some more, master-mind."

He went back to his desk.

"Mr. Petrie, I want you to know that we're glad to have you with us. I don't think we need beat about the bush, and I'm not going to ask you a lot of damn fool questions as to what schools you've attended, which hand you wipe yourself with, how many wives you have buried in your young life, how many cases you have won, lost, or drawn. You report for work tomorrow. I shall list you as a field worker. Skilled. Ninety-four dollars a month. I won't be here, but Matson there will assign you. He'll probably put you to work in the library going into law files. Which is what you're trained to do, and I hope you like it. Well, I guess that's all. Huh?"

Mr. Petrie took off his glasses and held them in a hand that shook.

"God bless you, sir," he said huskily. "God bless you. May God bless you very much, very very much."

"Not at all," said Charlie, affected by this response. "Not at all. However, an excellent plea. And well put. None better."

UP. UP. UP. THERE WAS THE STANDING AMONG THE CROWD AT the airport, the holiday crowd of everyday folk from the city who drive out at night to catch the cool clean air and a sight of the new wings in the sky, and the watching of the little red glows on the horizon. Then the roar of motors. Then the great flood spreading like calm silver fire across the black field. Let there be light. And the chariot came gliding down. The little clerks and factory workers allow their wives and children to huddle close and they stand and watch the great birds speechless. The gasoline trucks roll up. Long rubber lines feed the steel mouths. Then the mails are loaded on. Before you are admitted you discover that you remember your weight to be 145. No need to ask what sort of balance is being figured there. The pleasant bronze-faced men tip their hats in easy manly salute as you walk toward the gangplank, your overcoat negligent over one arm, your grip and portfolio full of Project business on the other.

He showed his pass.

"We're beginning to get a lot of government men nowadays. How was Washington when you left it?"

"Painted white, like a hospital."

"Sick house. Eh, sir?"

"Depends on the view. House of mercy. Either way."

The man laughed.

"We'll make Johnsburgh in two and a half hours. Get in at twelve."

"Nice flying weather?"

"The best. Ceiling like a lake."

"We'll be over land all the way though, won't we?"

"Ha, ha. Yes."

And they were off. The great motors roared, settled to a long steady drizzle of sounds, closer together than rain. The ship rose. Higher. Higher. The earth dropped down. The lights of the field went off. All the people down there. Ahead the black star-lit air. Man zooming on the great arc of earth on his own decks. It was his first flight.

"Stewardess!"

It was the man across the aisle. The shadow of a neck and he guessed at the rest of the face.

"Coffee," the neck said.

"I'll have some coffee too, please."

"Sugar and cream?"

He frowned. "No, just cream. Just a touch."

It was not the service that fascinated him, the clear-eyed kind girl who served him. It was the thought of the setting, the air deeper than anything known beneath them. Four miles above the earth we sat flying against the earth's orbit and they brought me coffee in a china cup. And I sat and drank it with my finger crooked.

"Have you been at this long?" he asked.

She tossed curls under her sky-veteran's cap. "Oh, yes. Five years."

"Five years! You can't be more than twenty."

"Twenty-three."

"You know," he said, "I didn't mean to be personal. I don't know whether you can understand this, but— Well, suppose my mother knew where I'm at just now. She thinks I took a train. She'd throw a fit."

"Air service," the girl began, "has passed its experimental stage. It's not generally known, but there are fewer, much fewer, accidents in the air than there are either on trains or on the highway." She seemed to be saying something now from rote, and he didn't like it. He didn't want to be reminded that men owned this airplane as they did everything else.

"No, no," he said. "I'm not interested in safety. That isn't it at all. There's something quite different involved."

"This is your first trip, isn't it?" she asked.

He decided to surrender. "Yes," he said curiously, "it is."

"That's sort of funny," she said. "I can always tell those who are making a maiden voyage." Did she hesitate over the *maiden?* "They ask questions. But they don't really want information. There's something they're trying to tell you."

"Do they succeed?"

"Well," she thought it over. "Not always. Did you know that this was the plane from which they caught Arno Shultis last year?"

"The gangster? No, I didn't. Wait a minute. I remember. Yes, I saw his picture in the paper. Now I know. I thought I'd seen you somewhere. You were in the picture with him."

She flushed. "I couldn't help being in the picture. I didn't want to be. Jimmy didn't either." Jimmy, apparently, was the

117

pilot. "None of us on the ship wanted to be in it" (of course not), "but the newspapermen insisted. . . . About Mr. Shultis. I knew it was his first time too, the way he sat and looked at everything and tried to see out of the window. Every time I passed by, he looked like he wanted to ask me something, or say something. But he didn't. I guess he was too shy."

Charlie grimaced.

She stopped, startled, then laughed.

"Uh-huh. Now here's the funny business. When we got ready to pull out again, he was back as a passenger. We try to be pleasant to our passengers, the company chooses us for our ability to be nice—"

"They chose wisely."

She smiled her thanks. "So I said, real pleasant-like, 'Nice to have you with us again, Mr. Martin'—that was the name he was traveling under, if you remember. He gave me a strange look. Then, when we landed, he only got off to get himself another ticket. Well, he should have known better. The newspapers cover us like they cover the police-stations and the city hall. This reporter asked Paddy Davis—he was the pilot on that particular trip—if there was anything interesting, and Paddy says there's a man flying with us has been on the ship for a week. So then, next time the plane came in, the reporter went to have a talk with this man and he recognized him. That's the time *Jimmy* was handling the stick. When the police nabbed him, it was a real scoop for this fellow's paper. Do you remember the interview they had with the gangster in jail?"

"I do now. He confessed three murders and half the holdups in the state."

"Well, there was something else. He said he was tired of running, that the Federals, the state and his own mob were after him. He—"

"I remember. He said, 'Why have a trial? Just put me back on that plane and halfway to hell just open the floor under me.'"

"Yes, that's it."

"So? . . ."

"Well, you'd think—them catching him on the *plane*—" she left the sentence unfinished.

"I don't suppose there's something else you'd rather be doing than this?" he asked, knowing what the answer would be.

"No, there isn't." She glanced at her watch. "Will there be something else, sir?" she asked, more formally.

"Uh, uh." Where had he read that if you ask a hostess for a date while she's on duty, she's got to turn you down.

He leaned back in his chair and inclined his head to one side, looking out. Black. All black. A star gleamed like a crack in the night. Ahead of him lay what? Johnsburgh, presumably. But that was only true up to a point. At the height of the relative (how can the relative have a height!) are, paradoxically, the outposts of the absolute. The future lay ahead, more tangible in the rush of the airplane than it could be found in city streets. The gangster must have felt this. The roads to Rome and suddenly the take-off, the one super highway, the speed canal. No wonder Shultis-Martin had not wanted to get off. Life on earth (earth!—there he went again) is so slow, even at its speediest, and there are so many oases by the way. . . . Here you had a sense of destination that grew even as the destination itself assumed less and less importance. And what of the passengers? Were they not more important than the destination itself? Or as important? A moot question. The plane and the night were a thing in itself. One thing! *Contact!* Most wonderful of all the words. Holy in its own right and not to be held responsible for consequences. There lay the whole secret. *Contact!*

The plane rushed on. He envied and shared what he felt must be the pilot's exultation, flying under sealed orders.

FAST AS WINGS ARE, THE VOICE, CARRIED ON WIRES, IS FASTER.

"Monroe calling Johnsburgh . . . Monroe calling Johnsburgh. Mr. Hohaley calling Mr. Henry Jevins. . . . Go ahead, Mr. Hohaley. . . ."

"Mister Jevins? How're things yo' way, Hank?"

"Fine, Billy, fine. What's on your mind?"

"Ever'thing under control, Hank. I think we'll get first-rate co-operation here. The Mayor's office has let us have two hundred chairs. I contacted Mister Molte, as you suggested, on the *Star-Globe*. He promises us the most favorable publicity. Ever'body's been just lovely. It's about the Johnsburgh situation I am calling, however."

"Yes? What about it?"

"Hank, there is a young man out of my office on his way to see you now. I have authorized him to set up a branch office there. Now, so far as the personnel of this office is concerned, I am certain there will be no trouble and I know that he will receive your suggestions most graciously. But on the subject of a supervisor for that office, I wanted to confer with you before our young man got there. Washington has given us the name of a man they want. Clyde Harkins—"

"He's out. Not in the running. Troublemaker."

"You understand, Hank, I could not question this selection. It came from Colon himself. I could but refer it to you."

"What about this fella comin' to see me. Who's he?"

"He's another of Colon's selections. He's native here. Seems harmless. A writer. Been without a job so long, he's scared of his own shadow. He's"—he was about to add that he thought him a radical; Jewish; but thought it over quickly and decided against it— "he's all right, I'm convinced."

"Okay, Billy, thanks for callin'. Take care of yourself now."

"Good-by, Hank. Give my regards all around."

He lay back in bed with a sigh. He felt a craving for coffee, pulled the cord by his side. Cordelia appeared. She was cleaning up, getting ready to go home for the night.

"You rang, Mistuh Billy?"

120

"Co'delia, fix some coffee. Make it black."

"Black as mah hide, Mistuh Billy."

He laughed. These colored folk!

"Co'delia."

"Yessuh?"

"How would you like to be a writer?"

"A which, Mistuh Billy?"

"A writer. How'd you like to go to work fo' me?"

"Ah's wukkin' fo' you now, Mistuh Billy. Aint I?"

"Yes, Co'delia, but this is a little bit different. You will continue to work fo' me, but you will also be an author."

"What will Ah need t' do, Mistuh Billy?"

"You will need to do nothing, Co'delia. You will stay on here as before and you will keep away from the Project. Except ever' two weeks, that is. Ever' two weeks, I'll tell you when, you will go to the Project and get your pay-check. How's that appeal to you?"

"Oh yessuh, that sho' do appeal t' me."

"One more thing, Co'delia. In this state, it is against the law for a colored woman to work in the same place as whites, so when you get yo' check you will bring it here. I will take care of the rest. . . . And—ever' week you will get two dollars more from me than what you are now gettin'."

"Yes, *suh!*"

"Bring me my writin' tablets, Co'delia." When they had come, he wrote:

Dear Mr. Charles:

I agree with you that Negroes are the last as a rule to be placed on white collar projects when they are set up. On this Project, however, this will not be so. We already have engaged Negroes and, in future, as our needs require, will doubtless engage more. I agree with you that a knowledge of the contribution the Negro community has made to the community as a whole is vital. I do not intend to overlook this fact. Always willing to discuss this further, I remain . . .

He surveyed this letter with cold satisfaction.

"That'll hold the black bastard."

The nerve! Calling him up, asking how many Negroes were at work!

He opened a drawer beside him and took out the late Mrs. Hohaley's picture. Now he smiled gaily, as though he faced a living woman. It was a just portrait. It showed a sweet-faced middle-aged woman, the eyes intelligent and brave and the mouth kind, although with faint lines at either side, as of some frustration that had settled in youth and nibbled slowly, humbly feeding on the lusciousness there . . .

His observation of the mouth was a mixture of amiability with a cruel irony.

"I declare, Madeline," he said, smiling, "if you don't *seem* younger every passing day."

He put the picture back, took out another picture. It showed two young women in gypsy costumes, about twenty years of age each. They stood, shyly, it seemed, beside each other, hand in hand, as though stopped by a photographer, a tourist, as they were on their way to a masked ball. The two young "women" were himself and Madeline, taken some fifteen years before, a bare three months before their marriage.

This picture, that he held responsible for the courtship which had followed, he regarded finally with even a greater irony. Here was the same Madeline as in the other picture, but a Madeline who had stood hand in hand with himself, and it was at himself that he looked. The picture had suggested an ideal solution—

"Sorry," he murmured to himself in this picture, "the masquerade gave me the wrong idea."

Cordelia interrupted his thoughts. Knowing her master's habits, she brought more coffee.

"Co'delia, girl," he said affectedly, "you know this is delicious coffee."

His eyes had returned to the hungry lines around his wife's mouth and he looked at them now with cruelty.

"Thank you, suh." Cordelia saw what he was looking at. She waited.

"What is it, Co'delia?"

"Gittin' late, Mistuh Billy," she said tonelessly.

"Well," he put his cup down, "back to work!" He lit a cigarette, puffed furiously for a moment. He put the pictures back in the drawer. His brain became occupied with its immediate plans, stratagems, maneuvers. He made himself busy. Lifting the telephone by his bed, he said, "Give me Western Union. . . . Western Union? This is Mr. Thornton C. Hohaley. Please take a message to Mr. Jonas B. Colon, Washington, D.C., to be delivered in the morning. Ready?

GREAT ENTHUSIASM HERE FOR PROJECT STOP ADVISE CAN YOU ATTEND BANQUET AM ARRANGING YOUR HONOR AT WHICH ALL STATE NOTABLES WILL BE IN ATTENDANCE STOP SPEAKERS WILL INCLUDE RABBIS PRIESTS BUSINESSMEN CLUBWOMEN PROFESSIONAL POLITICAL LEADERS STOP TO ARRANGE TO ATTEND WOULD BE SMART MOVE STOP.

He reached for the telephone directory and began turning the leaves. Every time he found a name he wanted, he put it down on a piece of paper. Just the name. The names after a while got mixed with his thoughts and eventually he fell asleep. Cordelia came in to remove the coffee cup and ash-tray and saw him with his mouth hanging open.

Cordelia had been with his family for a long time, ever since the little-known new wife of Mr. Hohaley had first blossomed out in Carlinsville as the lovely vivacious leader of the younger married and social set, and the Hohaley parties had become famous throughout the county. The colored woman looked at him now with sadness.

"You gittin' *stout*, man," she said, under her breath. Then she turned off the light and went out.

Mr. Hohaley lay awhile with his mouth open; then he began to snore. But he did not hear himself snore. In sleep his fancy, like his manners, found complete release. Now he not only seemed to be the director of the Authors' Project but the Governor of the state as well. But as Governor he was also, somehow, and it wasn't the least bit strange, Elizabeth, the Virgin Queen of England. He sat on a throne of green on a green lawn and past him came the court, curtsying. To each he extended his hand to be kissed. He threw his head back and laughed to see that polite thug, Henry Jevins, in knee breeches, with his great hairy legs showing. He laughed and laughed; he was vastly amused. Colon did not even come into the dream. Neither did Lloyd Matson. But Charlie Gest stood at his right hand and whispered witty things into his ears. Charlie was wearing tight trousers and the girls could not help but look at him as they passed by.

BOOK TWO

PART FOUR

Afterwards, when Charlie thought about Henry Jevins and tried to tell Matson about him, the thing he remembered most vividly about him was his voice. It was soft, it was gentle, it was mannered, but these in themselves did not compass its peculiar quality. It made you think of little children getting all tangled up under your feet, rain on the roof, and a nice warm fire to stretch yourself at. You thought of after-dinner speeches, wine at the club, and allowance-making affectionate laughter from the applauding members as you get up, pulling away your napkin, and there are crumbs on your chin. In the end, he found a word that described it most closely. It was a *puttering* voice.

The man was much like his voice and in that was fortunate, for he turned out to be a banker. Not that Charlie had had much experience with bankers, but he did not imagine that bankers had been very popular of late. He was of medium height, anywhere between fifty and sixty-five, and his white hair was as abundant as it had ever been. His rimless eyeglasses gave him a substantiality to balance his gentleman-farmer's appearance. Tweeds, a white shirt, and a brilliantly colored plaid tie helped along the general impression. All in all, he looked exactly like the kind of person Hollywood directors usually cast for the role of grandfather or guardian to chic society girls.

"Not bad, eh?" he chuckled, throwing his arm in a wide gesture around the combination office-den penthouse on top of the correct bank building in which Charlie found him. "Fixed it myself. Here, look."

He touched a button on his desk. A large section of a wall slid open, disclosing a mahogany bar and back of it a glittering array of bottles and glasses.

"What'll it be?" he asked, grinning with pleasure at the evident effect on his guest.

"Martini," Charlie said, naming Mr. Hohaley's drink, the first to come into his mind. "Dry."

"Martini it is."

He fussed about over the drinks (he had one of the same), humming a little tune. "You know," he said, "most people have the wrong idea about bankers. Think we're loafers. Oh, you can't blame them," he said hastily, not that Charlie had objected. "After all—the depression—people having all their money sunk on farms. The old mortgage comes due, you *know?* . . . Can hardly blame them if they think we live off them," he mumbled. "Good drink, eh? Everything I do I try to do good. . . . Yes, I built it all myself." Charlie was beginning to become used to his disjointed way of speaking. He could just see him in the movies. Grumpy. Lovable. His screen character would stick to him off stage. Old Fuss-Pot, his fellow-actors would call him respectfully. "Built everything but the bar. Got that from Jake Greidhalle when he sold out and went back to Germany. Would you like to see my collection of photos?"

"Yes, I would," Charlie said. "I'd like to very much."

Mr. Jevins shot him a keen good-humored look and put a hand briefly on his shoulder. "You'll do, son," he said, for some reason.

Seated side by side on a divan, Old Fuss-Pot (Charlie was beginning to think of him by that name) showed him through one of about two dozen picture albums that were stacked book-fashion on a specially-constructed shelf. ("Built it myself," Charlie expected to hear him say of it; he did.) The pictures were all of fish. Big fish. Sometimes the shot was of the fish itself. Sometimes Mr. Jevins, looking chubbier (they register about ten pounds heavier on the screen, Charlie remembered), posed proudly smiling beside his catch, taller than himself. Props on the pictures, interchangeable, were a bit of sloping sloop-deck, now tilted to the left, now to the right; wharf—upright; a bit of sail, hard to distinguish from the sky; twice a seagull, with wings spread soaring down from two different positions, and now and then a fellow-fisherman or a crew-member. The fish themselves, no matter what condition of haze the props were in, always came out clear.

As he turned the pages, Old Fuss-Pot kept up a running stream of chatter. He had caught all these fish off the coast of Florida, he said. Closer to Cuba, he should say, than to Florida. Went on vacation every summer there. For two months. Nothing like it. Sun. Fresh air. You can't imagine how fresh that air is. Have you ever seen the chests on natives of that region? Well, if they weren't the strongest things he'd ever seen, he didn't know what were! And the *trees,* the *fruit* there! Now this fish here . . .

He began telling the story of how he had caught *that* fish, a 520-pounder, and Charlie, who had not clearly understood why he was to see Mr. Jevins, a man without any connection with the Project so far as he could tell, now understood less than ever. Was it all a mistake? Imagine, if it were! But no, that simply couldn't be. His instructions from Mr. Hohaley had been, on this point, most explicit. He was to look in and see Mr. Henry Jevins, and his address is et cetera. Pay him a call, he is a good man to know. But only *after* he had been to the W.P.A. and to the relief people to get his set-up arranged. He remembered that instruction specifically.

Well, he had been to the relief people. To the W.P.A. He

had shown them his credentials and they had been most cordial. More than cordial, they had been co-operative in a degree he would not have imagined possible. Had delegated clerks to him (Mr. Sweeney at the W.P.A., Mr. Greeley at the relief), worked with him all morning, showing him lists, helping him make tentative selections. No time this trip, of course, he had told them glibly, for interviews. I am here mostly to get acquainted, to look over the field. Going back to Monroe to report, back again next week for interviews. At that time, will contact Mr. Clyde Harkins, of your city, gentlemen, whom we have selected to be the supervisor here. If you will put in his hands, gentlemen, what we have done here today, I will not need to bother you more.

"Mr. Clyde Harkins, huh?" Just the slightest emphasis perhaps?

"That's right. That's okay, isn't it?"

"Okay by us, Mr. Gest. Sure."

Outside on the street Clyde Harkins was at this moment waiting for him. He had called Harkins up on leaving Sweeney's office (no, he had called him *from* Sweeney's office) and they'd met at a point close to Mr. Jevins' place. Fine fellow, Harkins seemed. Quiet, courteous, co-operative, like Sweeney and (e-ley. So he was to be the new supervisor, eh? My God, Mr. Gest, that's fine. Starting now, eh? You'll be back next week to help me get started in the new place? Well that *is* wonderful. Meanwhile, I'm to see Greeley, Sweeney—hmm. Again that emphasis?

"That's satisfactory, isn't it?"

"So far as I'm concerned, Mr. Gest, perfectly satisfactory."

So he could claim to have had perfect co-operation all around, couldn't he? And now he was having an interesting talk with the friendliest and kindliest guy you'd ever think of meeting in a bank, of all places (he was at pains to underline the kindliness), or anywhere, for that matter. Why be prejudiced? And they were hitting it off fine. Like the airplane trip, it had gone off very fine. "I'll tell you, Lloyd, there's nothing like the right sort of living to make a pig fat. And there's nothing like a bath to make a man find out how superficial, after all, a lifetime's accumulation of even the weightiest dirt can be." It was going off fine, didn't he see! Like getting Pete a job. Like getting the lawyer a job. Like having one himself, for that matter. Like getting used to the idea that he not only had a job, one on which he could *work,* but that he was also a supervisor, a big shot, which was a status that never hurt a man's self-esteem since eternity began. Like beginning to take it for granted that you're a hero and an asset at home, *actually,* and not blushing and wondering when do you wake up every time somebody's nice to you. Like acquiring confidence; in brief, feeling a force entering you. Like looking forward to pay-day so you can go see your girl, "Elizabeth her name is, Lloyd," and knowing that pay-day will come. See? *See?*

And here came the beginning of the thing that derived its *horror* from the fact that Mr. Jevins had a *puttering* voice. Granted now that he, Charlie, was a hypochondriac, had lived in an atmosphere of illness, of hypochondria, *still* certain things in that life could happen, they were based on the *expected:* If a man's poor and can't afford a real house, he is not shocked to find rats in his basement, shock is not what he feels; if a man's undernourished, well, he knows why he feels weak; he knows why, call it hypochondria but the symptoms can even be reassuring, like *friends.* But this—!

He had been listening, for the last ten minutes or fifteen, without really hearing it, to Old Fuss-Pot telling about the fish he had caught. And giving him a drink. And a cigar. And him with his white hair. Understand? And now he heard a new note. When had it crept in? Things had been so pleasant, you see, he had not been watching. Never thought to. Just wondered, in a mild way, why he was here.

"Yes," Jevins was saying, "men like myself, like you too

131

maybe, but naturally you too. . . . I bet with you it's girls; I bet you could tell me something of the erotic. . . . Men like myself, at any rate, find that they need something besides the single-hearted goal, the *thing* in itself" (the picture of the airplane spearing through night had flashed through Charlie's mind). "We are corrupt. We go fishing. You maybe play, with girls. With *him* it's different. . . ."

(Him? Charlie thought. What have I missed?)

"Come now, isn't it true? Aren't we corrupt? Tell me, haven't you been in whorehouses?"

"Yes, I've been in them. I haven't always done anything."

"Ah, is that so? What did you do then? Don't you find it interesting that you didn't do anything? Did you *look?* You know, I'll tell you something. I have found that it is a great deal of fun to catch those fish. But I get more pleasure out of looking at my pictures and *thinking* about them—"

"I don't know."

". . . If you have time, you should go down to his office. See how simply it is furnished—why, it's almost a dive. Really, I feel ashamed of myself, all this splendor, the pride I have taken in it. The people come there, sit in the simple outer room, it's big, but there's nothing in it but a couple of dozen chairs, like the Salvation Army almost, and a desk for his reception secretary. . . . But you'd be surprised if you knew the sort of people who come to sit there and wait maybe hours before he is ready to talk to them. Not only poor people, laborers, women about to have babies and men out of work, kids just out of the penitentiary and trying to get a start; but senators; yes, persons like myself, who roll up in front in limousines, heads of banks and corporations—"

He was talking about Boss Joe, of course, but it sounded different than when you read about the Boss in the Monroe newspapers. And his voice was still kind. He was smiling. And he was looking at me. Like a father. Old Fuss-Pot leaned forward.

132

"There are thousands and thousands of most devoted men and women who serve him year after year, every day, in every fashion conceivable, and they deserve a reward. You know what it says in the Bible: Blessed are those who give, for the bread they cast upon the waters shall return a thousand-fold."

It didn't make sense. And the quotation was all mixed up.

The telephone rang.

"Yes? . . . What? . . . Yes, he's—been here."

He means me, Charlie had positively known. He knows I'm *still* here. But he means to say that what needs to be settled has been settled. As though I *was* here!

"No," Jevins said. "That's something certainly you're to *disregard*. Yes, that man's out. Why should we take recommendations from outside. We have men to fill that position ourselves. We want no Reds anyway."

Could it be that he was talking about him, Charlie had thought. No, that wasn't believable. Jevins' talk was shaping up to *some* kind of a sense, but that wouldn't have made any kind of sense. He meant Harkins, that's who. *Harkins* was the man who was out. That explained the overwhelming air of co-operation on Greeley's and Sweeney's parts. They were to show how co-operative they *could* be. They already had had their instructions. . . .

Jevins replaced the telephone. And now?

"Now, in regard to this Project that you're setting up. Of course, I have nothing to do with it, in any way. Am purely a well-wisher. Banking's my business. Mr. Hohaley has asked me to give you the value of my suggestions, such as they are. I will then. I say to you, Mr.—what is your name, by the way?"

"Gest, Mr. Jevins. Charles Gest."

"Are you—Spanish? You look rather Spanish."

"No. Swedish and Greek. People sometimes take me for—Spanish."

"Ah, I see. Well, as I was saying. We have dozens of deserving people here. Some of them are even college people, ex-news-

133

papermen. All kinds of people. I would suggest that you allow me to draw you up a list of these names. You could pick from among them. Whichever you choose from among them" (he dwelt on those last three words) "would be all right with *him*" (him again!).

"Most of these people would have to come from the relief rolls, you know," Charlie said, feeling cold. "Do the people you have in mind all find themselves on relief?"

"I think whatever arrangements would need to be made could —well, be made."

"If Mr. Hohaley has asked you," Charlie said, "I have no alternative but—"

He wanted to come out boldly with Harkins' name, but he had thought of something long ago: Harkins (you should have been there, Lloyd!) could be in terrible danger. He lived in that city.

"Friendly suggestions, that's all. No obligation."

Mr. Jevins stood up. Standing, he was much shorter than sitting. His age was emphasized, his white hair whiter.

"Come here to the window. Look. There lies a great city below you. Three hundred and fifty thousand souls. Each year for twenty-six years one man has organized it, made it possible for it to continue living with justice and bread for all. Given it its laws. . . . But do you think that all of us have proved grateful? Believe it or not, Mr. Gest, there are rats living here who would like nothing better than to undermine this city and this one man's work. For this reason"—he lowered his soft voice and his eyes grew merry behind the rimless spectacles—"we must be on our guard always to keep out those men who are not our friends."

He held up his left hand. A soft hand. Opened the palm. Placed it, the back of his hand, against the wall. It had the power of a rich symbol, like the fingers moving in the sign of the cross. Like hands outstretched. But different. . . . He lifted his right hand. Closed it in a half fist, as though it held something.

"What we should do with our enemies," said that puttering voice, "is put their faces against that wall. Like I put my hand. Like that. And then we should take half-bricks in the other hand (they're easy to handle). And drive them gradually through their faces until the brick meets the wall behind it. Like that." Crack! He laughed. "Won't you have another drink?"

Dismissed.

"No, thanks. I really must be going now."

"Well, good-by. Be sure to drop in to see me whenever you're in town. You people from Monroe come to Johnsburgh all too seldom anyway. Remember, even if Monroe is almost snooty about her place, Johnsburgh is still the older and closer to the capital. . . . Oh, just a moment." He slipped a card into Charlie's hand. "You'll find this place a pleasant one to spend an evening. In Johnsburgh we are far from being bluenoses and we believe in good times. You'll discover that Bud Cannon's boys are friends of mine. Just show them my card."

On the way down, Charlie had wondered why all the elaborate show. After all, who was he to have borne all Jevins' heavy artillery? He wanted Matson's opinion on a plausible answer that had occurred to him: Not he was being told, but *Colon.* He was Colon's appointment, was he not? Then Harkins must have been Colon's appointment too, not Mr. Hohaley's. And so, also, where does Mr. Hohaley come in here? And how far?

He breathed in the fresh air outside, but he still felt chilled from having heard a man who looked like a grandfather talk lovingly about murder.

CLYDE HARKINS HAD STEPPED OUT OF A DOORWAY HALFWAY down the block. Now Sweeney's and Greeley's politenesses were clear to Charlie; they had been laughing at him. Now Harkins' peculiar habit of wanting to wait outside everywhere and rejoining him from such a place as a doorway took on some sense. They walked side by side for minutes in silence.

135

"Who is Henry Jevins?" Charlie asked.

"He's a powerful man in this county."

"So you're a Red, huh?"

"You're telling me that I don't get the job?"

"I didn't say that at all."

"Well," Harkins said, "I'm a marked man. The bastards are out to get me. The healthiest thing you can do is just to forget all about me."

Charlie, surprised at the mildness of his tone, almost made the mistake of thinking that he'd meant it mildly. He looked sideways at him. He noted the interesting fact that Harkins bore a kind of resemblance to Jevins. Harkins was taller, a little balder. Two respectable-looking men, except that Jevins would have got a director's first nod to play Granddaddy. He could see them having adjoining pews in the same church.

"Are you really as resigned as you sound?" Charlie asked.

Was that amusement on Harkins' face? "What would you suggest? I call the police? Mr. Policeman, I demand my rights?"

"But you don't sound like a Red," Charlie said. He weighed what he was about to say, then said it. "I—er—know a few Reds here and there, mostly back in Monroe. Confronted by such a challenge to their—er—rights, they would hardly ask *me* what I suggest *they* do."

Harkins seemed to be weighing his own thoughts. There was a curious detachment to his words. Charlie had the queer feeling suddenly that he was walking with a ghost.

"In Johnsburgh," he said, "there are no Reds, no Democrats, no Republicans, no capitalists, no laboring men—"

"I don't wish to appear rude, Mr. Harkins," Charlie broke in. "I don't want you to think I'm defending the New Deal simply because I find myself at present to be one of its—in a modest way—officers, but there are Labor Rules and Regulations written into the instructions we have received for the conduct of the

136

Project. And the courts have teeth. Even if your name was Comrade Joe Stalin—"

"Please," Harkins said. With petulance. . . . "As I was saying" (he's as professorial as any Red, Charlie thought, gritting his teeth), "in Johnsburgh there are only two kinds of people. Sheep and Goats. And *both* these kinds of people are Democrats. The others don't exist. Republicans, you say? Foreigners— never heard of them. Socialists? The same. There is no question of Communists, you understand. . . . You say that I don't sound like a Red. I'll tell you something, Mr. Gest. I'm *not* a Red."

"You're not?"

"No, I'm not. I don't believe in the nationalization of women. I don't believe in the redistribution of the wealth. I think that niggers and whites are destined by God Almighty to be kept forever apart, unless they come together at the right ends of a whip. I think that the good old U.S.A. is the grandest country on the face of the globe and those who don't like it should go back where they come from."

Charlie felt Harkins to be further away than he had imagined. He felt angry, as though he'd been led into a trap. Had he? Was Harkins by any chance an agent of Jevins'? Harkins suddenly laughed. He tucked his arm into Charlie's.

"You *still* don't understand. The point is, what's all this stuff about the nationalization of women, capital and labor?" His eyes twinkled. "Who cares, who *cares?* Assert, refute, explain, define. Who's concerned with all this? . . . No, don't misunderstand me. Really, I'm *not* a Red. The point isn't there at all. 'Do you still beat your wife, yes or no?' That could just as well be the point. What's the difference? Your wife really has nothing to do with the cold bars behind which you will soon find yourself. And the same question, for that matter, would be just as effective if asked of men who have no wives. Single men, mind you. Widowers. 'Do you still beat your wife?' Or you could even ask this interesting question of a *woman*. Does *she* still beat her wife, yes or no? Nobody would even laugh. . . ."

He'll come around to it, Charlie thought. Now he knew wherein Harkins reminded him of a ghost. He was talking to a man who hadn't talked in many years. Like a man in solitary confinement groping his way through sudden sunlight. Let him talk, then. They were passing a lot where excavation was going on. At the back of his mind, Charlie had been wondering since he stepped off the airplane what there was about Johnsburgh that made it—different. The hills? Johnsburgh was built on slopes that barely escaped being mountains. A man driving his car through these streets needed, above all else, brakes that could hold him on a shoestring. No, that wasn't it. San Francisco is built on hills. There it was the bay you smelled everywhere—salt water. What was it here?

They were passing the excavating. Now he knew. It was the digging and building, the great holes in the earth that gave up smells that came from below grass, from below earth you could have grown on if it were farmland, from earth so deep that it begins to ooze. . . .

"What's all the digging?"

Harkins pointed silently to the trucks backed up to the hole. One of them had painted on the sides Joe Tremaine Concrete Already-Mixed Co. Another said Joe Tremaine Strong-as-Death Cement Co. A third said Joe Tremaine Contracting & Wrecking Co. Happening to look up at random, Charlie saw emblazoned across the whole block-long front of a department store: HELLO FROM JOE TREMAINE.

"Never heard of *him,* have you?"

"Yes, I believe I have," Charlie answered, with an affectation of the irony he heard in Harkins' voice, but Jevins' spirit brooded over him stronger than irony. "Jevins—Fuss-Pot was the name I gave him—mentioned him, I think. Back in Monroe the newspapers run an editorial on him now and then. In '25, I was just a kid then, when Mussolini came into power in Italy, the *Herald* had a cartoon of him and Musso giving each other a medal. When Hitler came in, they showed Tremaine and Musso on a seat and Hitler, smiling, saying, 'Pardon my northern accent, but won't you move over, gentlemen?' "

"Funny stuff, huh? The light touch, huh?"

"Well, yes, I guess you'd say that. The Communists during one of their parades in Monroe had a couple of cartoons showing—"

"Communists! Don't tell me about your Communists! I know all about your Communists. What were they talking about when Tremaine was swinging the State Legislature like it was a kiddy-car? They were talking about the coolies in China. When the big fight came up in '33 (I bet you don't even remember it) over the stuff Tremaine was pouring into the state highways, giving us the biggest automobile fatality list of any state in the Union, what were the Communists talking about? History will hold Goering responsible for the Reichstag fire, they were shouting. Who gave a damn about the coolies and the Reichstag? Who even knows where China is?"

Disappointment on Harkins' part? Sour grapes? No. More the contempt of the boxing fancier who had watched a likely boy get started and then seen the slugger try to box. Or the boxer slug. Or thought that he'd seen it?

He flushed. He had in mind an open forum of the Communist Party he'd attended in Monroe. District Organizer Chavin had spoken. "The workers in Spain are fighting our fight," he had said. He had spoken about the workers in Austria. In Germany. The underground movement against Hitler. "In every factory we have our comrades, organized in nuclei of five. In every platoon in every regiment in the army. In the Gestapo. The day Germany goes to war, she will explode." How brave these words had sounded. He wondered what he'd think now, hearing those words, after having known Jevins. And he wondered how much Chavin knew of Johnsburgh. "When will Johnsburgh explode?" he would like to ask. . . . Oddly enough, it was at one of those meetings that he'd first met Elizabeth. She had been collecting material for an essay to be delivered before her church on "Is Communism a Menace to Christianity?"

Charlie was curious to hear what more Harkins would say about the Communists. The poet Cummings had written that "the Communists have fine eyes." He wanted to pull that one on his companion, see what he'd say. He put his tongue in his cheek.

"The Communists—you know—they're poor people, after all. Volunteer workers. They don't necessarily get around, just because they read and *think* a lot" (he thought of Jevins' strange insinuation that the *lookers* and *thinkers* were corrupt. Malraux said this too, somewhere in one of his books; not quite the same thing. But he didn't say it about the Reds, and later he became a Red himself). "They're"—he faltered, caught in his own thoughts—"not necessarily up to the latest, but their *direction*—"

But Harkins had lost his interest in them.

"You know how we vote here?" he asked. He turned round to face Charlie, drilled him with a hard look. " 'Who you votin' fur, Buddy? Who? I don't getcha, pal. Woddya mean, you haven't looked at the ballots yet? There's only one decent set of people to vote for, aint they?' "

("And voting itself is therefore slurred as a corruption," Charlie would have put in, but this would have been stating the obvious.)

Harkins executed some pantomime. "At this point," he explained, "you take out a little book. You're standing at this man's door, you understand. Or maybe you've come into his house and you have your feet on his table. All right, you read in your little book. 'Your name is Joe Blow. You have got a wife and three kids.' And you *name* this wife and the three kids. First and middle names. 'You have got a little hardware business on Vermin Place.' See? You're *stripping* him. Take a man's privacy away and he's lost. No hiding place—he's finished. And by this time he knows *already* how he's going to vote. And you know that he knows that you haven't really got started."

("What do you think of that, Lloyd?")

He pointed to the excavation. "The hell of it is, this town is really well run. Every Christmas, these same trucks, loaded down with all kinds of toys, baskets of fruit, candy, chicken dinners, call on thousands of homes. 'With the Compliments of Joe Tremaine.' And the trains come in and go out on time. Not only that, but whenever there's any federal money floating around, this town gets its share of it. And more. And the people know it. We got congressmen in Washington, not just poker-players. And then the votes themselves. There's a lot of votes here, and when a man dies or moves away he doesn't quit serving his community; his ghost goes voting on. And in Washington they got to play ball with us, no matter what they say over the radio. . . . The only thing is, you can't get any books worth reading at the libraries here and the drugstores and department stores don't carry them either. You can't vote to take the graft out of government and you can't change a man, once he's elected, save death parts him and his job. Also, if you read where someone got bumped off by someone else, you want to find out who did the murdering before you raise a howl that justice be done. And if you're a workingman or businessman or a pimp or a whore or whatever the hell you are and you've got a beef with someone, you got to go to Joe Tremaine to settle it. And Joe has a lot of friends and a big organization to keep up, and for this service of settling your dispute you have naturally got to pay through the nose."

A couple of men passing by stared at them. Harkins lowered his voice.

"Like I said," he whispered, "I am not a Red. I'll tell you what I really am. Are you ready for a big surprise? Hold your breath now. I'm just a plain middle-class liberal small business-man kind of a Democrat who believes in the Constitution and the Bill of Rights. Yes, can you feature that? Just a plain Democrat. . . . You remember what I said about the Sheep and the Goats a minute ago? Well, here they call me a Goat. A Goat is a Democrat who is not owned by Joe Tremaine. The Sheep consist of the flock that follows him. And that is how the meek inherit the earth."

They were walking up the side of a hill and Harkins stopped talking until they had passed the crest.

"All I did," he said, more calmly, "was run a little weekly newspaper. This was about seven years ago. I only ran it for about six months. You know, I was with the *Post* here for over twenty years. Rewrite man. Reporter. At one time I was night city editor. Then I got let out. Depression. So I started me a little newspaper. It was a free-distribution sheet. All advertis-ing, you know. You get a bunch of merchants in one neighbor-hood together and they buy space. Then you write up their stores front-page as though it's news. And, of course, to them and their customers it is news. And then you throw a few thousand sheets into the homes of the neighborhood. And the idea is that when the people read your advertising in news form, they believe it more than if it was a straight ad. And then, besides, there's al-ways a picture of a local kid, and the church news and their names in black and white, who they had for supper. . . . Well, you know, Mr. Gest, I'm a newspaperman, so I thought I'd give the folks a run for their money and I start putting in a little editorial on the front page. Strictly local stuff. Such as: We need a boulevard stop on Cherokee, where the school kids have to make a crossing. Such as: The electric company ought to look into the possibilities of cheaper service in our new subdivisions; this will encourage people to move in here faster. Pretty harm-less stuff, eh? Reform, but constructive, wouldn't you say? But somebody didn't like it, and one day a fellow comes out to the plant.

" 'Hiya, Mr. Harkins. How you been?'

"I recognized him from when I was the police reporter on the *Post*. 'Hiya, Jim,' I said. It was Jim Dolan, one of the City Hall gorillas.

" 'Nice place you have here,' he said.

" 'Yes,' I said. 'Nice.'

" 'You want to keep it that way, don't you?' he says.

" 'Yes,' I said, 'I do.'

" 'All right,' he said. 'You will kindly sign this paper here.'

"I looked at the paper. It was to say that Jim Dolan was the new owner of the paper, that I had signed over the property to him for a consideration of three hundred and fifty dollars.

" 'Three hundred and fifty dollars isn't much money for a prosperous little paper like this,' I said.

"He laughed. 'Oh, you don't *get* three hundred and fifty. That's only what it says in the contract. All you get is fifty.'

"He took out fifty dollars and laid it on the counter. 'You furnish your own pen and ink.'

"I thought it over. After all, Mr. Gest, I have a wife and kids. But I kept on stalling.

" 'I didn't know you were interested in the newspaper business, Jim,' I said. 'In the old days, on the *Post,* you always seemed to be interested in other things, even if the police department never seemed to be able to find out what.'

" 'I am still interested in the same things I was then,' he answered. 'And I beg to remind you that not only was the police department unable to find out what this was, but the *Post* didn't do no better either.'

"These fellows are pretty sensitive, Mr. Gest. Jim was telling me that he was in the clear, that *his* position was not the one in question. He was doing it with a clear conscience too. As he said this, he looked as though he were on the verge of tears. By this I knew that I had almost made him mad. I didn't want any more trouble than I already had.

" 'Well,' I said, 'I don't know, Jim. I don't know if I'm *ready* to sell.'

" 'Okay,' he said, 'think it over, Mr. Harkins. I have a couple of teeth I must go pick now.'

"He came back the next day.

" 'Woddya say, Mr. Harkins?'

"I had meanwhile gone to see my old editor on the *Post*. He said there was nothing he could do. He had the grace to put it on the level of the news, though. 'I can't print what has not yet happened,' he said. 'If they do something to you, I will print it.' So I said to him, 'All right, I will keep you informed. But just in case I am not *able* to write the story after it happens, how will it be if I write it now and you file it anyway and use it *after* it happens?' So then he got sore in self-defense. He saw what I meant, all right. 'No,' he said, 'we cannot write the news before it happens.' 'All right,' I said, 'I will leave you with your sense of humor.' Well, anyway . . .

" 'No,' I said to Jim Dolan, 'I have thought it over and I have made up my mind not to sell.'

" 'This is a pity,' Jim said.

" 'A newspaperman,' I said, 'has ways of protecting himself.'

"I tried to look as though I had a few aces in the hole that he didn't know about.

" 'Well,' Jim said, 'it is none of my business, but for old times' sake, I will tell you that you are pissing against the wind. And it will land in your own face.'

"After he left I wrote a full story of what had happened so far and I said, solemnly swearing on the Bible, that I firmly believed that what *was* to happen had happened by the machinations of Jim Dolan and the men who stood behind him. And I named these men, ending up with Joe Tremaine, for whom they all worked. Then I mailed this letter to the Attorney-General in Washington and told him to stand by. And then I waited."

"And—" Charlie said.

"And, *nothing*. Nothing you could do anything about. The next week, on a Monday, I started to make the rounds to pick up my ads and not a one of the businessmen would give me any. They didn't give me any excuse or explanation, simply said they'd decided not to advertise any more in my paper. So I published an all-news issue. And the next week the same thing happened. The next week I printed an editorial, asking the public Why? And the week after that, I couldn't pay my printer, so I folded."

That was all he had to say. Charlie tried to ask him some more questions, but he shook his head and would say nothing.

"What's the use?" he said.

"Well, Monroe is not Johnsburgh," Charlie stuttered. "It's from Monroe that we're running the Project. This is the goddamnedest thing I ever heard of. I can't help the way your paper went bust, but the W.P.A. has labor laws and—"

"You too, my friend, are pissing up the wind," Harkins said. "All the same, you're very kind. I appreciate it. . . . Why don't you come home with me for dinner? My wife will be glad to have you. And my kids will be home after five."

"No," Charlie said, "I'd like to come. . . . But I've got to catch a train."

"We-e-ell—"

Charlie could see that Harkins now wanted to leave him.

"Well, good-by then, Mr. Harkins. I'll be seeing you."

"Yeah."

The hand he extended was as limp as his voice.

A little boy was passing on roller-skates. Charlie was startled to hear Harkins' voice, suddenly booming.

"Hey, *you*. Boy!"

The little boy came over, eyeing his interloper fearfully.

145

"Who is the greatest man in the world?"

"My daddy."

"You're wrong," Harkins boomed. "Guess again."

"My Uncle Elmer."

"Ha, ha! Don't be funny, little man. One more try."

"Mama says our Lord Jesus."

"No, no. *No.*" Harkins leaned down toward the little boy. *"Dat* don't get it, *Bub.* It's Joe Tremaine, isn't it? Isn't it? Joe Tremaine? Joe Tremaine? Joe Tremaine?"

The little boy picked at his nose to conceal the tremors that began to shake his body.

"Isn't it Joe Tremaine?"

"Y-yes, sir."

Harkins straightened up abruptly. "And he catches them young, too," he said, his face distorted. "Your witness!" Off he went, chuckling loudly.

The boy picked frantically at his nose but could not control his feelings any longer. He began to sob, his whole frame shaking as the sobs worked their way up from his stomach.

Charlie stroked his head with an awkward gesture.

"What would you do if I gave you a nickel?"

Gradually, the boy subsided.

"I would buy me an ice cream cone," he sniffled.

("So I put a dime down on the scales, Lloyd!")

"You go buy yourself two ice cream cones."

The little boy immediately drew a pistol out of his cowboy belt and rode off on his roller-skates, whooping and shooting caps into the air.

THE REST OF THE STORY OF HIS STAY IN JOHNSBURGH, HE DID not tell Matson. Mostly because he could not. There are difficulties in the transmission of the most vital experience that none but the great poets can successfully overcome, made up as they often are on re-examination of gossamer vaguenesses that strain

146

through no plot and are missed by the most exact camera. And, too, there are restraints. . . .

As though he were the one man left free to roam about a prison, Charlie spent the hours until plane-time going about the city. Not that Monroe was necessarily less a prison, but that here he had been made to feel man's limitations, man's servitudes, man's degradations, more dramatically. And this feeling came not so much from a contemplation of the job-hunger he had seen in Harkins, not only from the pity he had felt for the elderly ex-newspaperman who had been forced to make a living somehow for the last seven years (seven years!—*how?*) as it came from Harkins' statement (which he hardly dared doubt) that nobody cared. In Monroe, if nobody cared, that nobody spoke for himself alone (eh, Father?), but here nobody cared —*by order!* It was as though the people had one soul, although many bodies, and a document (a *spiritual* document) had been laid before this soul to sign; the terms on which it might have its bread. Harkins had refused to sign. . . .

And yet (of this he was sure), he (Charlie) was free only to roam about this prison. He was not free if the decision on Harkins stood. And if a man can be kept off the Project, then other men—for opposite reasons—may be put on. And what sort of freedom will it enjoy? And the work?

Flies in the ointment. Ointments are made by men like me. But who makes the flies?

The streets drew him to walk them. He went into a Chinese restaurant to eat. He was the only one in the whole huge expanse of floor and he took the seat in the exact center of the place, at a lily-white table. The manager served him and at every entrance stood a Chinese waiter in evening clothes. He ordered Chinese dishes, stabbing at them on the menu eeny-meeny-miney-mo. Later, he found himself in a hamburger joint. He ordered coffee and doughnuts. He let the doughnuts sit and ordered another cup of coffee. A bum came in and tried to mooch the boss. "Here," he said, "have my doughnuts," and told the boss to give the bum a cup of coffee and a plate of his chili-beans. Again and again, after minutes spent in drugstores looking at the titles of magazines, True this, True that, minutes spent on a shoeshine stand getting his ends polished, minutes watching fire engines chugging up over the hill and disappearing, hind ends high, over the tops, he found himself on the streets.

Wherein am I a free man, he kept asking himself. How is my giving Pete a job free, the act of a righteous man, and Jevins putting thumbs down on Harkins the act of a man who does not believe in freedom, a wrong act? Why three weeks ago was I ready to go on my hands and knees for the job I have and yet I was free; and now I have a job, self-respect (I *could* have it), and yet I do not feel free. What is freedom? What sort of light would a lamp have, turned up at high noon?

Look you, I follow a woman. She is an aged woman, should know much of life and men. What has she to fear from me (there is an old Russian proverb: Do not threaten a grandmother with the wrath of the penis)? What indeed, from me of all men, who am gentle, my soul knows it, and yet she fears me. She is aged, yet she is not free of sex. She is not free of fear ("The love of freedom ends in perversity," he could imagine Jevins saying), and she walks faster. Dusk has fallen on the city; she walks faster and faster, looks behind. See myself through her eyes: a Boris Karloff, a monster, a devourer of femininity. And why not? If she were the last woman on earth, would I hesitate to rape her? If she were possessed of the only loaf of bread in the city, would I not take it from her? Of a surety I would, she concludes, of a surety. Thus, triumphantly, she assures herself of bondage. Gladly.

But is not rape a matter of biology? The loaf of bread one of economics? . . . Man makes the ointments. Who makes the flies?

She stopped suddenly. He stopped too.

"Quit it, you little dago bastard," she shrilled; "if you don't quit following me I'll call the police."

"Are you Mrs. Susanna McGillicuddy?"

"No, I'm not. And you quit following me now."

"Sorry, Ma'am. I had a telegram for Mrs. McGillicuddy and they told me at the office you were she."

Suspicion hung on her nostrils like clothespins.

"How would they know I was Mrs. McGillicuddy?"

"They make it their business to know," he said darkly.

"But how—"

"Oh, then you are!"

She stared at him. Now a different sort of fear appeared in her face. "Are you crazy?" she quavered.

"I don't see that that follows," he answered, glaring at her angrily. "The point is, if you are Mrs. McGillicuddy, why in hell—if I may put it that way—don't you admit it and quit beating about the bush?"

She looked about her wildly. They were on a side-street and the closest help was at the corner and might be too far. He read her fears like the words in a book and, almost impersonally, admired the craftiness of her next statement.

"Well, I *am* Mrs. McGillicuddy. Now won't you walk down to the corner with me and read my telegram by the light of the lamps? You see, young man," she said ingratiatingly, "I'm not as clear-sighted as I used to be."

If he went to the corner with her, she would certainly get him nabbed. Would they lynch me, he wondered. At best, he would spend the night in the hoosegow and perhaps be given a good beating to go with it.

"Madam," he said simply, "I can't make it out."

He turned and quite calmly walked away. At the first hue and cry on the heels of her call, he was ready to run like hell. But she kept silent. And disappeared forever and forever and forever out of his life.

Later, he found himself walking ahead of a couple. He didn't know what they looked like. They were talking suddenly. First they were silent, then they were talking. He walked just ahead of them and listened.

"Say," the man said, "did you see who passed us back there by the hardware store?"

"No," the woman said, "who was it?"

"It was Teddy Johnson. *You* know, Mabel's brother. The one who married that Edith Jacobs. Didn't you *see* him?"

"No. *I* didn't see him."

"Well," a sudden spurt of rage sprang like fire into the man's voice, "where were you looking?"

Did she have to answer this question, Charlie wondered.

"I was looking in through the windows of the Plaza," the woman said.

"My God! What were you looking in *there* for?"

There was a meek note in her voice. "I don't know."

"Well," the man said (Christ, what passion!), "I don't know either. I certainly don't."

"And neither do I," Charlie thought.

And that was all, not one word more. Charlie kept on walking, not turning around once, the street wandered off and took a turn, the air was full of honks and sounds, and somewhere the strange pair were separated from him. At the end, he marveled, they were silent and spoke no more. For all he knew, they might never again speak to each other.

He passed a honky-tonk, one of dozens up and down the street. Couples, glued together, swayed to the musicians' rhythms. A smell of blended liquors spilled out into the street.

The mystery of the sum of many things had hold of him now. And if I ever write a book about it, and about all these people, and about myself and about Monroe and Johnsburgh, what will I say? Really, what can I say! For words are supposed to have meanings, but if you examine meanings ("To look too closely at

150

the meaning of words is corrupt too"). . . . Intently, yet absently, in the stress of his secret thoughts, he watched all the passing faces. A pair of radiant girls go by. Or lovers. A businessman with a saint's face. A beggar sometimes with a businessman's face. Sometimes, all too often, a girl with a girl's face. A businessman with a businessman's face. A beggar with a beggar's face. If some were apples, some oranges!

There was something in the Project that was right and it was being done wrong. He felt it with his instincts, his *rhythms*. There was something in his being on the Project that was right and still, unless certain others were on it too, his being on it, and the Project itself, was wrong. There was something in Harkins that was right, and his scaring the little boy, which was wrong, was not done for evil ends. But he wondered what Harkins had to say each day to his wife.

Had he been born in a mansion, he, Charlie Gest, what sort of a person would he have been? Or born Protestant, in or *out* of a mansion? Or in the sixth century, in China? He had once asked Elizabeth if, had he a hundred thousand dollars, would she marry him. He put the figure extravagantly high, instinctively, to forestall mutual reminder that the question, after all, had not as yet been put in any form. She had said yes, and he had nourished the cheap compliment, interpreting the sentiment as he chose. And yet how ridiculous all this inquiry was. If he had been born in a mansion, if he had had a hundred thousand dollars, then, assuredly, he would also not have been the son of his special father and mother. Then whose son would he have been?

Leave off! Leave off! I yam what I yam!

He happened to reach into his pocket for a cigarette and felt the card Jevins had given him. Cardon's Palace, it read simply, on the reverse side. And the address.

"Buddy, can you tell me where Cardon's Palace is?" he asked a bus-starter.

The starter jerked a thumb.

"Right across the street," he said. "There's the sign, bigger than the Chief Rabbi's nose."

"That's good," Charlie said. "The Chief Rabbi's nose. Didja ever hear the story about the Jewish whore and the Irish cop?"

"No," the starter said, his face preparing itself for pleasure, "I never did."

"Well, it's been a long time since I last told it. He meets up with her and says How's business? So she says Wrong again, that's my line."

He crossed the street. All men are gullible, he thought, as well as hostile.

He walked up a flight of stairs. He knocked at the door. A slot opened. A pair of eyes surveyed him. Who the hell were *they* afraid of? Charlie lifted the card and showed it.

"I'm a friend of Henry Jevins'. He told me to drop in here."

The door flew open.

"Come on in."

As he stepped over the threshold, the man frisked him. He did it so quickly and deftly, Charlie, through some acquired intelligence, had his hands up in the air to assist him before he realized just what he was doing. At the same time, the man did his job with such finesse and courtesy that he might have been helping him off with his overcoat or rushing to hold a match for his cigarette. Charlie almost said Thank you when he was finished.

It is a mistake to think of evil as unattractive. Only in its crude forms is it repellent. At its weakest, it takes the form of a mild curiosity that is satisfied by a respectable game of poker, the movies, or a mild flirtation with the curate's wife. Its modest historians are the police blotter, the bridge score, the bank book. At its strongest, it exerts a fascination like a whirlpool.

Charlie, since his talk with Harkins, had been greatly struck by the points of evil in which Johnsburgh and Monroe differed. The chief point was that here evil seemed organized, whereas in Monroe it was scattered, individualist, with all the virtues of

152

anarchy, democracy, call it what you would, but with all the faults too; poise that depended on personality where all too often there was only ego; gaiety that depended on spirit where all too often there were only spirits, and so on.

But Johnsburgh did not allow humanity to intrude on its fun. Human personality would have been bad form. Anonymous as people were in Monroe, here they were even more anonymous. The cult of the female form had not been left to the chance of a star performer in her sex; dozens of burlesque houses, "running wide open," as Harkins had observed and as he had verified at various times during his long afternoon, celebrated the female and proclaimed by innuendo that womanhood was dead. Dozens of gambling houses, also organized to the *n*th degree, asserted by limitation that the days of dreams and derring-do were finished and done with, if ever they existed, and only the spirit of gambling remained, to which the adventurers were ushered. It was not just the limit of money which in Monroe, he felt, was the chief limitation. Here in Johnsburgh the orgy, not the sentiment, et cetera, et cetera. . . .

And how attractive all this was; could be. Not to have a name, therefore not to be responsible. Not to think, not to dream, not to feel; not to know what these were; not to mourn their loss therefore. To have it all arranged for you; to be a part of everybody else and nobody yourself. Only to obey. . . . And to celebrate. . . .

And to hate. To run in the pack, yourself blind, all things the same to you, range-finders far above you acting as your eyes; to hold yourself like a gun, and to pull the trigger. . . .

He noted a shelf inside the door. It was covered with various items: umbrellas, packages (packages might contain anything, bombs, guns, and you could always unwrap them in the crappers), sticks—he knew what the packages might contain because he saw a naked revolver parked on the shelf. A Colt .44.

"No use taking chances, is there?" he said, jerking his head in the direction of the shelf.

"No, sir, there isn't," the doorman said. He was a burly, muscular fellow, his bulges belied by evening dress and a genteel bald dome. Concluding his examination of Charlie's person by a careful running of his hands down his trousers and then a palm grazed lightly over the back of the neck and halfway down the spine, he said, "We got worked last week for seventeen grand."

So the hi-jackers got hi-jacked too!

How amusing if Joe Tremaine and his police department got a rake-off both from Cardon's Palace and the hi-jackers who hi-jacked the hi-jackers.

"There's only one way to handle those kind of guys," Charlie said, putting down his hands. Welcome back, brothers, he told them silently.

"You're right there," said the guard grimly. "They won't catch us asleep."

Eyes looked down at him from peep-holes high in the wall. They didn't care what he said, that's not why they were watching him. They wanted to see what he would do.

It was the doorman's job to listen to what he said.

"Only one way," Charlie said. "The face to a brick wall and a brick through the face. Aint that right?"

"You said it. You can say it again."

He passed through a doorway in the lobby "cloak" room and came into the Palace proper. This was a series of huge rooms, connected by doorways from which the doors had long since been removed. Early as it still was, the spaces around roulette tables and other devices were packed with people. He was amazed to see the number of women present. Here and there a couple attired in evening clothes played. But most of the women wore cotton dresses, sometimes afternoon sort of jackets. It occurred to him that these had probably been here since morning and had not been able to tear themselves away. When Jevins was showing me his pictures of deep-sea fishing, they were already here, standing over the tables. While I talked and walked with Harkins, they were here. Their eyes were beginning to get hot but they didn't know they were tired, and I was walking around the streets by myself. When I got that first communication from Colon asking me if I was interested in getting onto the Project, these same people were perhaps spending their days here. How long ago all that was! The people here had a look between sleeping and waking. They were caught in a powerful grip, one he could understand, while it made him shudder.

A phonograph wailed in a garish voice:

> Ah caint give you anything but love, baby,
> That's the only thing I've plenty of, baby. . . .

Even the music was organized, and knew what it could and couldn't give.

He wandered from table to table. Some played pennies. On others he saw ten-dollar bills. The wheels went around for all.

"Number 33 was the winning number, ladies 'n' gen'lemen. Number 33. Number 33 it was."

It was a fifty-cent table.

He put two quarters down on Number 9.

The wheel goes round and round. Where it goes, nobody knows. The pin came to rest on Number 9.

"Nine it is, folks. Number 9 was the winning number." The croupier shoved a stack of coins at him. He put another fifty cents on Number 9. Faces hung about him in the smoky air, etched like acid medals under the green light of the lamp overhead.

"Nine again. Nine is the winning number."

"Fifty cents on Number 9 again."

. . . Round and round, like cockeyes in their sockets.

"Number 9 wins again."

The faces threw out speech that burst like bubbles on the hot air.

155

"That guy's got the sign on Number 9!"
"There's a run on Number 9!"
"Fifty cents on Number 9!"
"Fifty cents on Number 9!"
"Make it 9 fuh mine!"

Sneak away while the sneaking's good. . . . And the Israelites tore down His shrine in their hearts in the wilderness. Thou art a false god, they assured Him reproachfully, groping for Him at their throats. From behind him, as though from yesterday, from far away, he heard the croupier's unexcited announcement: "Nine again, folks. Nine wins. Get 9 while the sign's right. Get 9 while it's hot."

A row of pin-ball machines like Spanish caravels pointing toward the west. The billiards of the industrial age. Each ball has a hole. Shoot for the hole with the highest number as for the Spanish Main or the highest star. Hollow-eyed, the players stood under the westward-ho sky and prayed for rain. Around each machine stood a company, each man waiting for the player to fall, to take his place.

Moaning of voices before the public chapels.

"Papa needs new shoes, balls. . . . Git lucky, balls. . . . What do you hear me say, balls. You hear me, balls, don't you?"

Two thousand!

Two thousand and four hundred and one thousand and five thousand and three hundred and—

"Make it an even five thousand now, ball. Only two more of you left!"

Two thousand again!

And—nothing. . . .

Another player took his place.

He found himself staring into the eyes of a woman on the other side of a space. He would have taken his eyes away but then he saw that the woman did not see him. She was staring at nothing. So he kept on looking. And what if she were looking? And what if she saw him? They were unknown, he and she. They were simply part of the spell thrown up by Cardon's Palace. . . . Her eyes began to focus. She saw him. Oh, if you were Elizabeth and I was sure I was I! She was older than Elizabeth, thirty perhaps, darker. But there was a vague though strong resemblance. The faces of the dancers here are carefully masked, but their bodies and souls are nude. Elizabeth imagined in her nightgown? A powerful excitement began to rock his blood. He smiled. A Johnsburgh smile.

She started toward him and somehow he was not surprised.

"I've lost it all today," she said abruptly. Her voice had a husky weight, like her hair. She was smiling too. "Rent. Food-money. The children's savings. . . . If you have ten dollars—"

"Yes," he said, without hesitation, but also without eagerness, as though all this had been rehearsed. "Ten dollars won't be enough, though, will it?"

"No," she said. "It won't."

He waited to see what she would do. He almost knew what she would do. She swayed, her eyes glazing, then she walked away. He knew where she was going. She'll come back, he thought; it'll never occur to her that there's something else she could do. . . . He watched her walking among the players; oh, he kept a very close eye on her. She stopped to talk to this one, to that. But most of them wouldn't even look at her. They shook their heads No, some staring at her vacantly, as though they didn't know why she was interfering with their play. Only two said yes. He lost sight of her once and felt a fleeting overwhelming sense of anger, of frustration—as though he were Joe Tremaine facing a lapse in organization. Then she was back.

"Come on!"

He walked out awkwardly by her side, like husband and wife, he thought eerily. For one hundred thousand dollars, Elizabeth and he could have gone around the world in a super-de-luxe liner and in the newsreels they would have looked like Ginger Rogers

157

and William Powell with the steward serving them and the captain steering his ship with care. While the world watched and loved the lovers.

She walked swiftly through an alley, cut across a broad boulevard, plunged into an alley again.

"What about the others?" he asked.

"I gave 'em the address," she said. "I told each one when to come. You got nothing to be afraid of."

"I fear nothing," he said. "I'm a man without fear."

She glanced at him briefly, almost with a gleam of interest. Then he fell back into the gloom.

They came to the back of an apartment house. She led the way up the stairs. She swayed in the dark. To keep from touching her, he said, "The others will never find the way by themselves. You'll never see that rent-money."

"They'll come by the front," she said. "It's lighter in front."

There was something detached and impersonal in both of them. This was what the womb must have felt like, what eternity would be. Pale things moving to an appointed place. Another version than the airplane's of destination.

She opened the door.

"Shh, my kids are sleeping."

She turned and faced him in the dark room.

"Where's the money?"

He gave her some bills. He didn't count them. Neither did she. Might have been only two dollar bills he'd handed her, might have been ten or more. They seemed to have forgotten what the money was for, why she was doing this thing. She stood like a statue, except that her bosom heaved. Now what?

He put his hands out toward her. She led him to a sofa. Sleep walkers!

No, this was too easy! Too soft! Too anonymous. And something more obscure than these. He struck a shrewd blow.

"What about your husband?" he whispered.

"You got nothing to worry about, I told you," she whispered back. "He works nights. He won't be home for a long time yet." But her cold flesh shivered and he began to feel desire.

"I'm not worrying," he said, cruelly. "I love you. I think you're beautiful. If I were your husband, I'd kill you."

"You're not my husband," she said, holding her voice down. "You can take your money and go. . . ."

He caressed the shadows under her eyes. "You're beautiful," he said. "Do you know you're beautiful?"

"Don't," she said. "Don't say that! I won't be able to go through with this. You're making me feel so ashamed!"

"You *are* beautiful. I'm going to call you Elizabeth. . . . Isn't it funny? Elizabeth is my wife—but she'll never marry me. I could call you Elizabeth, and never miss her. . . ."

The window-curtains rustled with a vagrant breeze and a beam of starlight fell across her eyes, deep-set, deep and flickering like snake-tongues in the pale swollen flesh of her cheeks. Holding her eyes with his, he slowly put his hand under her skirt.

"No," she said. Her voice was savage. "Not now. You didn't pay to call me names."

"I didn't pay for anything," he said. "The money was stolen. I gave it to you as a gift. To help you pay the rent."

"I won't do it without you having paid for it," she whispered fiercely, struggling. "I don't want charity. . . . I don't love you, so I won't do it for nothing."

He held her. "It wasn't charity," he said desperately, as she strove to rise. "The money is nothing. If you don't keep it, I'll burn it. I'll throw it away."

"What do you want?" she asked.

"I want you to let me call you Elizabeth."

"My name *is* Elizabeth."

"I'll call you Elizabeth then. True love! Sweet darling!"

"What's—your name?"

"Charlie."

"*Charlie!*"

TAP . . . TAP-TAP. TAP.

"Tell him to go away," she whispered.

He winked at her, picked up a lamp-shade from the table, gently pulled the cord loose and wrapped it around his wrist. He went to the door and opened it. A man stood there, gaping at him.

"What do you want?" he growled, holding the lamp clutched tightly before him.

"I w-was l-l-looking for a man named R-Robinson," the man gasped.

"He don't live here any more," Charlie said. "Annie lives here. The MacIntosh Annies."

"E-excuse me, please."

She stroked his face.

"Will I see you again?"

"Maybe, honey. . . . If not, will you be sorry?"

"I don't know. My husband's twenty years older than me. He's been very good to me. He works nights. He's a night watchman. I started to go to C-Cardon's Palace. . . . Why won't I see you again?"

"Maybe we will see each other again. I'm going to Spain tomorrow. There's a war going on there. For liberty."

"What's that?"

"I don't know."

"What about—Elizabeth?"

"She won't care."

"Maybe she would. How can you tell? People don't always mean what they say. . . .'"

He was beginning to feel gloomy again. A little angry, as though he'd been cheated. And the conversation was beginning to bore him. She was turning into a woman with advice. A *hausfrau*.

First thing you know she'd be consulting him on what's good for a cold. Cooing over her children's pictures. Perhaps even ask him to come home tomorrow for supper. Tell her husband he was a cousin or something. He had no desire to play one of the corners in a triangle. He thought that he might not like her very much if she turned pedantic on him. She was sure to develop proprieties and attitudes. Above all, he did not want to stay long enough to be able to mock at himself. And what a Punchinello I could prove myself now to be, he thought.

All the same, he felt intensely grateful to her. He felt that he really loved her at the moment, and he had great tenderness for her. She had given him warmth and granted him name and dignity (and much more than that) and it pleased his vanity to think that he had done her a similar service. Through fancy and gesture we try to get at something more precious than the reality we know. He would remember her because something had come to pass between them that was not to be found in appearances.

But he felt restless and he wanted to get back to Monroe. Strength, at this moment, surged high in him. He did not exactly know what liberty was, as he had said, but exultation and eagerness, which are not things of knowledge, brought him to his feet.

"People never mean what they say," he answered her. "Elizabeth never *said* she didn't love me. It's—something else. It's always something else. . . . She's a bird of paradise. I'm an alley-rat. Does that make sense?"

"You're a gentleman," she said.

He kissed her. "You're beautiful. I really mean that. Listen. If we never meet again, I wish you well. Ships that pass in the night. You *know?* I salute you."

"I'd like you to look at the children," she said shyly. "I wouldn't ask you, but—"

"All right."

Two tots lay in the little bed. They seemed all chubby fists, tousled hair and blankets.

"How old are they?" he said, close to her ear.

"That's Mary Jane. She's three. The other one's John Henry. He's four and a half."

Now certainly he had to go. Before he stroked these youngsters' heads and made an utter fool of himself. And named them the names he might have named *Elizabeth's* children and his. . . . Before he asked her what she was going to do. . . . Well, how to say a difficult thing now? How to say that he'd driven her customers away and therefore—?

He emptied his pockets into her hands.

"There's enough there for the rent, I think," he stammered.

"No," she said, beginning to push it away. "How could you!"

"It's a gift," he said. "If this were Christmas, I could buy you something. A-and you still have the r-rent to pay."

"Wait a minute," she said. She rushed back into the room. He leaned against the wall. Closed his eyes, puzzled. He heard her rummaging in a drawer. In a minute she came back. She slipped something into his hands.

"I want you to wear it," she said.

Under a neon sign he looked at it. A medal. St. Christopher's medal, that keeps the traveler from harm. He propped his foot up on the fender of an automobile and took the shoelace out of one of his shoes. He slipped it through the hole of the medal and tied the ends in a sailor's knot. Then he put it around his neck and tucked it under his shirt, out of sight.

"OF COURSE," SAID CHARLIE SLOWLY IN CONCLUSION, "I KNOW that you *could* cut my throat with what I've told you. . . ."

The long chance is what he'd taken. He could have kept quiet, he told himself. All his life a man has been known to keep quiet. All *his* life, however, had been a sort of a stubborn resistance. No, he thought, as he said this to Matson, he could not keep quiet. The keeper can. The dead. Not the caged and taunted.

Matson flushed, his tension relaxing. Gest was a good storyteller, but, as he said—"I could cut his throat." It was possible. He liked Charlie. He liked himself more. And a nice thing about throats is that if you can avoid cutting them today they are usually still here tomorrow. Even more so. He had a lively curiosity to find out how strong in the pull the contending forces would prove. He was glad now that he knew that there would be contending forces. He liked the spice. Colon versus Tremaine. The New Deal, so to speak, versus the old practiced poker-players who had declared themselves in on the hand. And Mr. Hohaley? He'll try to play both sides, straddle the plunging mule with his coattails flying. But he'd need help. And that's where he came in. He'd help this Hohaley play both sides. But *Hohaley* was committed already to one side, and he wasn't. He could blow either way. Or both. With Hohaley or with Charlie-Colon. Or neither. He had independence of action, and he liked the feeling. Something like a girl in every port. . . . And for the first time in his life, a situation that he fully appreciated, he had a ship under his feet. And—ahem—the swift thickening of a juicy plot, Colon was coming to town Friday for a "housewarming" dinner.

"Yes," he said, smiling and winking, screwing his skin into wrinkles, "I could, couldn't I? I've been thinking that myself."

"I know you have. . . . After all, why not. I don't think you will though."

Matson found himself liking this fellow; he intended to know him better, much better.

"Maybe not. . . . You're either a prophet or a madman. . . . But I wouldn't tell Mr. Hohaley about it if I were you. To begin with, I think he already knows all that's happened. And Thursday's payday. Ha, ha. You want to get at least one more, don't you? And why not *many* more, huh? Whose Project is it anyway, eh? Question mark! And Colon isn't coming in until Friday. So why"—he quit beating about the bush—"wouldn't it be better, more *strategic,* if *Colon* were to talk to him? *You* know. Be talking about this and that, and then—in our presence,

163

natchally—say, 'And, oh, yes, before I forget it, how's things in Johnsburgh, how's Harkins panning out?' "

Charlie grinned, for the first time.

"You know why I don't think you'll cut my throat after all, Lloyd?" he baited him, slyly.

"Why?" Matson asked. He strove to hide his curiosity.

"Because there's nobody who appreciates your cleverness more than I do."

This statement was a master-stroke of strategy itself, as both young men immediately realized and appreciated, and together. The mocking glance they exchanged was full of respect.

"You're right," Matson said, gloomily now. "We'll have to talk more about *that.*"

"Of course we shall," said Charlie coolly. "It's a question of relative importances, isn't it?"

P A R T   F I V E

There was something he had dreamed of doing ever since eternity had begun for him, it seemed. Suddenly, one evening, soon after his return from Johnsburgh (by a process that will be made clear later), he knew that he was not going to quit his job after all. He felt happier at once. And he immediately made preparations to do the thing that he had dreamed of doing. . . .

It was early morning. He came to a house on Bethnal Street, opposite the synagogue. A red-brick house like all the other red-brick houses. And a number over the door. He looked at the scrap of paper given him by Harry Goselkin. This was it. He rang the bell. . . . Silence. He rang again.

A woman came to the door.

"Who you want?"

Harry had said that the woman would be white. This one was black. Of course, it didn't make any difference. But Harry had said . . .

"Mrs. Johnson live here?" he said doubtfully. "Emma Johnson?"

"You th' insu'ance man?"

"No, Ma'am. I just want to see Mrs. Johnson."

"Well, it haint no consahn o' mine. Ah jes' want you t' know, ef you *is* de insu'ance man, M's. Johnson haint got yo money foh dis week."

"No, Ma'am. I'm not the insurance man."

"All right," the woman grumbled. "Ah haint tellin' you yoh business. You go round t' the back. You won't have no trouble findin' M's. Johnson."

He went through a passageway dividing the houses and saw a line of washing in the back, fronting the alley that cuts diagonally across these Monroe streets and serves in the slum districts as a second street-front; a more intimate street-front, since there are no streetcars on it and automobiles venture on it but rarely, because of the dangers of punctured tires; and during the day women sit out in their back yards and gossip with one another and the barefoot children of the poor can play among the garbage-cans and in the alley-litter without fear of being run over.

As he approached the door, a little dog leaped from around the house and trotted along beside him, making small growling sounds and manifesting as much hostility as it could without coming to actual physical grips. Attracted by the sounds, a little black child playing in the yard first stared at Charlie and then put his hand over his mouth and by adroitly working the hand, first holding it tight, then loose, then wiggling it, produced a number of sounds somewhat like those of an exhaust or the pop-pop of rapidly bursting paper-bags of varying sizes. Mrs. Johnson opened her door and came out, wiping her hands on her apron, to which a smell of soapsuds clung.

"Mrs. Johnson?"

"Yes?"

She was a woman about forty-five, white, as Harry'd said. A rather small woman who looked as though she'd worked pretty hard all her life. He was in a mood to idealize her. She had the thin pursed-up-mouth appearance about her which makes so many middle-aged women appear unattractive and even haggling, and yet it is this look about them which is often an index to their characters—that of a day in, day out indomitability under crucifying odds and is at once the wounds and the medals they bear. A one-syllable person for whom all the syllables of heaven will never provide an adequate description, he thought.

"My name is Charlie Gest. . . . Harry Goselkin told me you might like to do housework."

"Yes, sir," she said, growing more cheerful and polite. "Harry, the Jew fella. Yes, sir, I could do housework."

"Well, this is for my mother. She's—uh—not very strong. You'd have to do all the washing for the family. And—"

"How many in the family?" she broke in professionally.

Funny. All the ways he had imagined this scene in ages past, he had never anticipated this particular question.

"There's five of us. Me, my mother, father, and two sisters. They go to school. Of course, the washing is only once a week mostly. Although there's a little washing every morning. Like the socks—"

"Why, sure. That don't sound hard. And do you want me to stay on the place?"

"Well, we don't have much room. We just have three rooms. And the bathroom. I guess the way my mother would want it, you would come in every morning and go home every night. Our place is only three blocks from here, so you wouldn't have to spend carfare—"

Was that a look of disappointment on her face, when he told her where they lived, as though she'd hoped it would be a West-End home? He hurried on:

"You'd have to help her each day with the cooking. Go to market for her, if she didn't feel good. Wash dishes. Wash and scrub the house once a week. And once every other week scrub the stairs leading down, which we share with the neighbors."

He hesitated, trying to think of all the things that his mother did, and that Mrs. Johnson would have to do. "I—I guess, if all this sounds okay to you, that you could find out more about it from my mother."

"Do yez have hot and cold water in your house to do the washing with?"

He thought a split moment. "Well, no. We got to heat the water."

"What kind of washing machine do yez have?"

He reddened. "We don't have a machine of any kind." He resisted the impulse to add "yet." What the hell! "My mother"— he paused, and then said the words deliberately, a slight unexpected choke in his throat making him speak slowly—"My mother washes in a big tub. She puts two chairs next to each other and then drags the tub onto them and balances the whole shebang. Then she heats up the water in a couple of buckets on the coal stove and drags them over and empties them into the tub. Then she puts in a hunk of soap and—naturally—the clothes as well and goes to work on the washboard. When she gets all through, she wrings out the wash by hand and hangs it up over what we call the 'summer' porch and over the kitchen and wherever she can find the room."

"Lawd-a-mercy, yez is just *poor* people!"

The simplicity and justness of this utterance made him smile at her. "That's right, Mrs. Johnson. Just poor people. I hear there's a lot of them."

His suddenly gay attempt at a joke fell on tone-deaf ears.

167

"You sure don't sound like a poor boy."

"It's my elocution," he said gravely.

"O-oh." She half-closed her eyes wisely, as though she understood exactly what he meant. "Well, Mister, I—always get three dollars a week f' that kind of a work."

"All right," he said. "We'll compromise. Will three-fifty a week be all right? And your food, *naturally*," he added, to show that he knew the ropes.

"Why, sure."

Her ready acquiescence was sober. He smiled at her.

"Look, Mrs. Johnson, there's something I want you to do for me. My mother—uh—has always done her own work, and she would continue—if it was left up to her—to do her own work. If she knew that I was going to pay you three-fifty a week, she would raise hell about it. So, since she'll be paying you, not me, I want you to tell her that we have agreed that you get *two-fifty* a week. I'll pay you the other dollar myself. Okay?"

She agreed to this also so soberly that he wondered if she had understood him. He repeated his instructions again. He explained in great—and for him gossipy—detail how hard money is to come by nowadays, and how loath his mother, "no offense to you, Mrs. Johnson," would be to pay such a price for help. "Even if she were at death's own door," he ended, with a flourish.

"Don't I know how it is?" she said. "You think me myself, I'd be goin' out to work, me with five children, if I didn't need every penny I kin make over what I get from the relief?"

"You got five children?" he said, shocked. Harry had said nothing of five children, only that the woman was a good worker.

But now it was she who grew anxious and hastened to assure him. Three of the children were with relatives in the city and the other two could "well-nigh tend for theirselves." Those two were the oldest, and were going to school (to the same school, he noted, as Janice and Clara). She had been out on jobs before, and she could fix their breakfasts for them before they left, and then they could eat lunch at the Jew confectionery outside the school at recess. And after school, why they could cook the meal when they got home and they would manage real well.

This conversation all took place in front of the shack she occupied with her family in the back of the house which bore the number Harry had given him. The little black baby had waddled ever closer to hear, and had been pop-popping his mouth every other word. Four other children, three of them white, of the neighborhood had congregated to hear what was going on. Attracted by the children, several dogs had appeared on the scene. A huge wistful-looking yellow cat stood on the shingled roof and mewed throatily for attention.

Charlie lowered his voice as he gazed at the stolid exterior of her house.

"But—can you take care of things over at our place and still take care of your own kids and place?"

She allowed that she could, with the help of Jesus Christ, and he—with inner qualms—called it a deal. Poor woman, she looked half-sick herself.

"Okay. When can you come?"

"I kin come today."

"How about in an hour?"

He would need time to convince his mother.

"That'll be all right, sir."

He wrote his mother's name and address on a piece of Project stationery and gave it to her. Silent, the several semi-circles of children and beasts watched him go, their blue, brown and black eyes following him wonderingly as he went.

BEREL THE SCHOLAR CLUTCHED AT HIS ARM AS HE CAME OUT of the yard. The old Galician, medieval in his skullcap, wild flowing sideburns and black long-coat, began at the exact word which had terminated their previous conversation, weeks before:

"What then—can they not be in the same person? Pharaoh-Moses?"

Charlie, though he now had to run, was feeling fine.

"I grant you Roosevelt, above all Presidents since Lincoln, may qualify for this duality. I grant you further that this may be a tragic situation."

"For all. For all. For him too," the Galician said, "him above all. We are the dusts of eternity that dribble like wet noses. We strive against rules granite as the fists of Jehovah."

The Galician's legs lengthened like shadows. He ran beside his hurrying audience like the wind.

"Pharaoh should be Pharaoh, Moses Moses. Those are the rules. But Pharaoh-Moses! How? The role of Pharaoh is to rule: to sit like Jehovah's bad conscience on the place of power; that of Moses—for Jehovah can be good too, although very seldom—is to smite at him who rules: to rebel, to give blows back. Is it not so?"

"It is indeed so, learned Berel."

"Today I shall write to the beloved and troubled President. He is a learned man. I will write him on the best paper, in pure Hebrew. I shall tell him to have courage: to reply to the Lord who will seek to try him with confusion. . . . Pharaoh-Moses! It is two in one to drive mad the greatest. For each smites the other, and the one takes the blows of both."

"You will not chide him," Charlie said gravely; "you will be gentle?"

"As my soul lives," Berel swore, "I will be gentle!" He perceived the jest. "I will not write. It is said that the chief weapon of the scoffers are the spears of mockery."

"No, no," Charlie said. "I scoff not. The words but hid the admiration I bear your great thought. I may even steal your thought and give it English words, so that millions of the uncircumcized may perceive the glories of the mind that are our common flowers."

"I will get a translator to watch my interests," Berel muttered. "You will pay me royalties in full." He strode off, singing a wild Chassidic song.

Pharaoh-Moses! What an interesting thought! He must catch the Galician by the beard some day, to pull him into the house so that he and Nussim may debate with each other. The thought of the failure that Pharaoh-Moses must suffer, according to Berel, was interesting too. One thought of Lincoln's face at the end. How sad it is! The faces of the Presidents who come after are not sad. Coolidge's watches for a bargain. Harding's is sunny. But, then, Berel would undoubtedly have claimed that theirs were the simple lives of Pharaohs. Lincoln's was the life of Pharaoh-Moses. So, says the Galician sage, is Roosevelt's. Will Roosevelt's face be sad at the end? According to Berel, the penniless dreamer of Bethnal Street, the greatest failures are those who tried greatest, for only the great know what might have been and was not grasped.

AND NOW HE APPROACHED HIS OWN, HIS NATIVE HOME. HE stood off and looked at it for a moment, as through another's eyes. How ugly the brick-red walls behind which are the rooms of my abode? How smiles the Camel Cigarette Girl, next week to be replaced by the Chesterfield Cigarette Girl!

Poor Bill was working with hammer and nails on a broken stair and he stopped to greet him.

"How goes it, William?"

Poor Bill, groping in his dark brain, drew out words and spread them aimlessly before him, as a child might spread his toys—an idiot child with no joy in his eyes, but with a child's prattle and the wonderful things all about him.

"I seen a rat in the basement," Poor Bill said. "He was a big rat. He had big eyes like plates. The boss said for me to fix this stair. He said somebody might fall. . . . I asked him to give me a dime for beer, and he said that somebody would break his neck on account of the stair. . . . I had me two glasses of beer yesterday. It was real good beer. It tasted good. It was cold. A man bought it for me. I fixed something for him."

"Weren't you afraid of the rat, Bill?"

The amnesiac stared at him wonderingly. His lip began to tremble, as though he were being bawled out.

"I was walking down the street one day and I seen a woman, she was my sister. So I went up to her and I said, 'You sure aint treated me right. You ought to be ashamed uh yourself, the way you have treated me.' And she run away. So then she got a copper after me."

"Jesus, Bill, was she your sister? Sure enough?"

"They give me a nice room with a Mexican fella and then the next day the judge said, 'Why did you frighten this woman?' And she was sitting between me and the judge. So I said she was my sister, but she didn't treat me right. And then they ast me a lot of questions and the woman says she is not my sister. But she didn't look like she was mad no more. And she was crying too. She give me some money and I had me a whole lot of beer. . . . There was a man, he got me some beer yesterday."

Poor Bill, what obscure urge prompted him to walk up to this strange woman? Was she like somebody with whom the gray-headed man had played as a baby? Each man is an island. There were no approaches to Bill's.

"Go get yourself some more beer, Bill."

He went past him and came into the house. By God, he must have got everything done in a hurry this morning, for the kids had not yet left for school. They were at the table, finishing their milk. Nussim, he saw, had left the house. His mother beheld him.

"Dark are my eyes," she lamented. "Why is he not at work yet!"

"Quit the histrionics," Charlie said. "You know damn well why I'm not at work. Thought I was bluffing last night, didn't you? Well, I wasn't. You are now a boss. A Mrs. Johnson will come calling on you and you're to give her employment."

"Charlie, I told you you shouldn't do it. All my life I have done my own work, I will do it now. What! Am I dead already, that you should find me housekeepers?"

"Do you really think that I went over and hired this Mrs. Johnson for you so that I could *argue* about it afterwards?"

She giggled like a little girl at the thought that the act was indeed done. And, while the thought that it had been done for her health's sake still left her resentful (as though a trick had been played on her, a trick in which she herself had been the chief conspirator), the thought that she—of all people—was now a "boss" began to tickle her.

"Airs I should give myself now," she said. "Paint I should smear on my face! Paint and powder too! And I should start smoking cigarettes and swinging my rumplets, like the betitted stars from Hollywood!"

She caught fire from this thought, once its full humor and audacity struck her.

"Fine clothes will I dull myself up in soon," she boomed. "Gloves" (she roared in English), "ho, boy! Enough of work and denying myself, let others work!"

"So it's all right, eh?" Charlie said.

He wanted to be quite sure that when Mrs. Johnson got there, she would not inform that lady that it was all a big mistake and that the boy is, God only help him, a good boy! but crazy.

But the old lady, her eyes shoe-shined suddenly, her cheeks bubbled-up and red, waddled out onto the "summer" porch and called loudly for Mrs. Cohen.

The widow, having heard everything anyway, appeared, her demeanor properly innocent.

"God be with you, what is it?"

"My Charlie is a foreman," screamed Mrs. Gest, "and I am now a foreman-*sha*. A *boss!*" She endowed the word with ex-

173

traordinary comic gusto. *"Goyim* with noses turned up like sweet potatoes will quail at my bidding, the policeman every night will guard the front door as though inside is the Queen of Rumania!"

"Well, what are *you* waiting for?" Charlie said. "Don't you know what time it is?"

The girls gave him a baleful look.

"Aw!"

"Beat it!" he growled.

At the door they turned. "You *stink,*" Janice screamed. Both ran. So engrossed was Mrs. Gest with the new game that she did not hear them go. On their porches now stood, not only Mrs. Cohen, but Mrs. Ptashnikoff, Mrs. Seller, and Mrs. Levy, the butcher's vegetarian wife. "The Vegetable" this last one was called.

"What first I should buy," Mrs. Gest coquetted with herself, "I don't know. An automobile? A new davenport for the living room. . . . I'll tell you the God's honest truth," she said, again reverting to English, but only for the oath, "if I buy an *uhftub-muhbeel,* bum around I will all day. So," she shouted, delighted with this problem, "when will I get time to look at my new furniture?"

"Good furniture is good furniture," shrilled Mrs. Ptashnikoff.

"Say," said Mrs. Seller piously, "why should she not enjoy both—the furniture and the *uhftubmuhbeel?*"

"But if I buy new furniture, I will not be able to afford a new *uhftubmuhbeel* right away," roared Mrs. Gest, sweet-cuckoo as the crow flies. "A boss from a woman in the house to wait on me hand and foot I must be too. And such a woman one must pay. Maybe it is better," she said, as though she had given the matter her most serious thought, "we should not yet get an *uhftubmuhbeel.* Besides, an *uhftubmuhbeel*—you know how these young boys are—!"

"Does one *not* know?" said Mrs. Levy gloomily.

174

"Young boys!" said Mrs. Ptashnikoff. "A joke?"

"One o'clock, not here yet. Oh," Mrs. Gest lamented, imagining herself seated in the window nights, waiting. "Two o'clock. Not here yet! Three o'clock! An accident perhaps, may the hour never come!" Heavy sighs of women rent the air above the various porches. "Four o'clock" (an authentic tremor in the voice). "Furniture I think I will get!"

Charlie shrunk from facing the avid battery of his mother's listeners. But he had to give her one last word. He came out onto the porch. Ignoring the women, he addressed her: "So be it. Furniture. The *uhftubmuhbeel* will wait. Yes? But remember, goofy, you are expecting a Mrs. Johnson. And you are not to send her away!" He waited for an answer. No answer. She was listening to something one of the magpies was shrilling. But her neck was red. "You heard me," he said. And went.

Realizing that it was now almost nine, he made a run for the streetcar. On the way to the corner he passed Mrs. Johnson going rapidly toward the house.

BY SOME FLUKE HE MANAGED TO GET TO THE PROJECT EXactly at nine. The clock must have been wrong, he thought. He made a silent resolution to get himself a watch this afternoon, after payday. A watch! By God, he *was* getting to be something or other!

"Good morning, Mr. Gest," Margaret Renny said, handing him his mail when he had seated himself.

"Good morning, Margaret. How are you, my good woman?"

"I'm fine." She laughed. "Didja have something to drink?"

"Nope. Nothing but ambrosia. Today—as they say in light opera—a dream came true!"

"A *dream,* huh? Blond or brunette?"

"Yeah." He noticed that the girl had marcelled her hair and was wearing a new dress. Obviously, these things should be noticed. The dress was a cheap one, and the marcel did not fit

175

her type of looks, none too bounteous in the first place. But if he said nothing, she would be hurt. "Say, you're all dolled up. Must've robbed a stage coach."

"How you talk, Mr. Gest," she said, pleased. "Stage coach! You know darn well that today is payday again. I get paid today."

"Get paid? Where? What for?"

"Why, here, Mr. Gest. So do you."

"So I do. That's absolutely right. And so do you, don't you?"

"That's what I been tryin' to tell you."

"What?"

"That we get paid again today, Mr. Gest," she laughed.

"Oh, yes, that's right. Well, you look nice all the same. Don't let me insult you to any other effect."

"Gee, you sure talk funny, Mr. Gest. You sound real excited too. I sure never know how to take you."

He was speaking into the telephone: "Then we may expect you, eh, Senator? That's fine. And don't forget, we don't care what your speech is about, or what you say, so long as it has something to do with the purposes for which the Project has been conceived. Any phase of it, according to the outline I've given you. Yes, sir. Well, good-by, Senator."

He hung up.

"Margaret, was your head properly uncovered? That was Senator Morris, the windbag from Marathon. He makes the fifteenth major speaker scheduled for Colon's banquet."

A STEADY HUM OF VOICES:

"That reminds me. There's this lawyer, he's been asking up and down the block for a Mrs. Simpkins. 'I got some money a aunt has left her,' he says. So everybody who *aint* Mrs. Simpkins goes around with him trying to help find her. So finally they find her. 'Your poor old Aunt Honey Lulu has left you a million dollars,' says this lawyer. So Mrs. Simpkins says, 'Okay, Mister. Lord knows I sure can use it.' So the lawyer says, 'Unfortunately,

176

it is all in pennies. Will you mind taking pennies, Madam?' So she purses up her lips and thinks a minute. 'You gotta make up your mind, Lady,' says the lawyer, looking at his watch. 'You are the third heiress I have met who don't like pennies. Are you superstitious? According to Aunt Honey's will, if you don't make up your mind by the time it takes a fair-sized eight-year-old boy to grow a beard, it all goes to the fund to keep pennies on dead men's eyes.' So Mrs. Simpkins says, 'Wa-a-all, I allays was uh-gin taking pennies, *but*—' "

"Push the door open a mite, Margaret," Charlie said, "I hear Matson exercising his wit before the rabble."

"Well, what *did* she do?"

Roars of laughter. People leaning up against the walls to laugh. Typists beating their heads symbolically against the tops of tables.

"Woddaya *think* she did?"

"To put it another way," came Francis' elegant drone, "what would *you* have done?"

"I would have took it, that's what *I* would have done."

"You would?"

"You hear that? *He* would have took it!"

"Mr. Gruenewalden says he would have took it!"

"Alla same, Mr. Matson," somebody broke in, "say-y-y, listen. It aint no joke. Them checks, where you gonna cash them downtown? I mean if you don't intend buying up half the store. You know somebody down here? I don't. The las' time, I hadda go alla way home. Me without a dime and a check in my pocket!"

"Boy, they kin load me down with checks," somebody else said.

"Me too."

"And don't leave me outta that, brother. Any time you got one of Uncle Sam's checks you trying to give away, let me in on taking a chance with you."

"Yes, *sir!*"

"Wait a minute," Matson said. "Who says you can't use a check downtown? Aint checks money? And don't you think the stores know it's money, even if you don't buy up half their wares? You think those guys are missing any bets? Listen, they will be only too glad to change them checks for you. And if they're not, just let me know. I'll be glad to take the matter up for you."

"That's right," Francis said. "Smuggs-Leventhal has got a sign on their fifth floor: 'W.P.A. Checks Honored Here.' "

"And they're not the only ones," MacGrover said. "You think the other department stores are gonna let Smuggs get away with it? Hell, no! They know when a man comes in to change a check, he will just naturally buy something if only to show his appreciation. And they will *all* change your check."

"Not all of them. Parrano's won't. Course, they voted Republican in the last elections, had a full-page ad in the papers, but at the same time—"

"And what do you think Smuggs-Leventhal voted! Didn't you see the ad *they* run? 'Grass will grow in a hundred cities if Roosevelt is elected.' "

"Ha, ha, ha."

"Yeah, that's right. So help me! 'Grass will grow!' That's what the bastards said."

"I know it."

"That's what the bastards said all right. No argument there."

"Hey, there's ladies present."

"Excuse it, Lady. I guess I forgot myself."

"That's all right, Mister. You're no worse than my husband and he says the same thing."

"Ha, ha, ha!"

"Three cheers for Mrs. Purvis' husband!"

Matson strolled into Charlie's office and sat down at the desk. He was smiling broadly: "I get a kick out of these guys," he said. "Get 'em hot, they'll skin beans!"

"Yes, sir, boy!" the conversation went on, "they will all take those checks. And, boy! they will honor them too. They will remind you who is the friend of the workingman, and they will not mean their competitors either."

"And if Parrano's won't honor us, why we won't honor them."

"That's telling them, friend."

"Boy, that's *gospel* truth."

"That old money *talks,* I aint fooling."

Newcomers caught the last words and came forward to agree. Each of them had a new word to add, and not one of them was one anybody else wished to quarrel with. Their agreement took indirect forms.

"Say, you know grocery stores still sell groceries?"

"They don't sell catalogues, man."

"You know duck dinner is not a Walt Disney invention?"

"It is a food, it is not a fairy tale, but there have been times when I thought it was."

"Well, gentlemen, this won't be like getting that old relief check, will it now?"

"No, *sir!*"

"You think I aint gonna miss them old relief gals coming into the house just as a man has gone to bed or to the toilet or is trying to tune in on the boxscores? You think I aint gonna miss that little uplifting chat she hands out before you get your four-fifty for the week?"

"Four-fifty! You were doing good. All we got was three-seventy-five."

"And *then* you had to wait for it."

"And suppose a week goes by and you don't get your check? You think those old gals make it up to you? You think they *honor* the debts you have accumulated while you were waiting for them to get around to you? And you think I aint gonna miss *that?*"

Francis coughed. "Is it not true that in spite of the fact, as you say, that we missed you last week, you did not starve to death,

179

even though we now find your belongings—and you too—out on the sidewalk instead of in the house where we last had the pleasure of conversing with you—?"

"Is it not true—?"

"Can you deny—?"

"Would you put yourself on record—?"

ON THE PRETEXT OF HAVING FORGOTTEN SOMETHING IMPORtant to his work, Charlie returned home at lunch-time. He had an uncontrollable desire to see his mother at rest. All morning, as he had listened to the excited voices of the workers waiting for their pay, other voices had been talking in him. All morning he had been smiling.

This, he knew, as he tiptoed up the stairs, was a great moment of dedication. This was a moment to which his heart had yearned ever since, as a child, he had begun to see that his parents were not infallible, invincible; that his father was not the mightiest man in the world, nor his mother the most beautiful and most omnipotent—the moment toward which he had daily and with despair plodded through dozens of employment offices, stretching like links from his fifteenth birthday on, through the want ads of thousands of dead newspapers, interviews with supercilious clerks, foremen, social workers. . . . To go forth into life and to return, and to lay gifts at the feet of the dearly beloved. To sustain those who have borne you, to shield them from evil.

"Well," he said, opening the door swiftly, "how's the baroness?"

Her blank and frightened look told him all he needed to know. "Oh."

He might have known that he would find her by herself.

"So you sent her home after all?"

"Charlie, she didn't come. I—I waited—"

"That's a lie. When I left here, she was coming down the street."

"Maybe she knocked at the wrong house, Charlie. What! Is this an only house on the street?"

"Do you think you're that unknown? She had the name, she had the number."

Not knowing what to say to this, she said nothing. Instead, she busied herself, running blindly. She passed nervously in front of the mirror over the sink, paused, and straightened her hair. A speck of dust on the mirror caught her eye. She grabbed up a dishcloth, wet it, washed the spot off. He watched her, seeing the essential obstinacy in her as a physical thing, something his fists wanted to strike at. She wandered to the "summer" porch, shooed vigorously at nothing in the air, muttered a curse at the race of flies. Taking up the duster, she started to work suddenly on the chairs, pulling them out from under the table and hitting at them with light expert strokes. He could see no dust arise. Avoiding his eye, she attempted to go past him into the middle room.

"Going to show me *you* can do the work, eh?"

She started guiltily.

"On my life, Charlie, I'm not going to do any work today. I was just going to fix myself a little. I—"

"Paint and powder. And a little ride in a *uhftuhmuhbeel!*"

She said pleadingly, with that little-girl manner: "No, no. The face. Just to wash it."

"You know that I'm going out now to bring her back, don't you?"

"Oh, Charlie! Take my advice! Better to save the money! We owe, we need, so much. Why should we waste the money on me! If I groan, as it happens, must you believe me that I am sick? A mother too can tell a lie. . . ."

He smiled to himself, but for discipline's sake wore a frown that (he let his mother see this) might easily turn to blazing and *righteous* anger. O Mother, Mother!

She sought the slightest trace of understanding in his countenance.

"Think, my boy," she said, whispering piously, "maybe she —I don't know how to say it—maybe she will not like the house. What then, is it a mansion? Is it really a place in which to invite servants?"

"Do you imagine this Mrs. Johnson comes as a critic?"

"Oh, my boy! *Think!*" her eyes widened. "The Christlike are haters of Jews. And what if she hates Jews. And one day, as your mother sleeps—"

"Worry not, Mother mine. She is of the Mohammedan Irish, those who are cursed in their own land as lovers of the Jew. And herself, she has confessed to me that she is partly a Jew. But only on her mother's and her father's sides."

She laughed. "Oh, Charlie, you make jokes. You got as much respect for your old mother as a—as a—dishpan!"

"A dishpan doesn't have a mother. Besides, you're not my old mother. You're just my goddam *kid* of a mother. Jesus Christ!"

He began pacing nervously up and down the kitchen. Somehow, he did not believe what he had just said to her. He knew that hers was a greater intuition than his, and that what she feared he feared too. But save, save, save for a rainy day! He could not endure that. *This* was the rainy day. Haunted as he was by what he had seen in Johnsburgh and by what was becoming evident to him here, he had need to be gratified in at least this one thing.

"Listen," he said at last, knowing that his mother was but waiting for the signal to plunge at her work, in which he had interrupted her, "you're not going to get out of this so easy. If it's not Mrs. Johnson, it'll have to be somebody else. I'll put an ad in the paper! By God, I'll make a door to door canvass (by God, but I will!) if it's the last thing I do on that lousy Project."

She was silent. It infuriated him to think that she felt trapped. "That's it," he shouted. "Feel trapped! Feel that I'm forcing something onto you! Oh, don't look innocent. Don't think I don't know you. You're just like Aunt Rifke used to be, by God if you're not."

"Charlie! Don't speak like that of Aunt Rifke!"

Aunt Rifke had died two years before. Complications was the name by which her disease had been known.

"You know what Aunt Rifke was thinking about when me and that silly bastard she married were taking her to the hospital for the last time?"

"Charlie!"

"That's right. Holler *Charlie!* Mustn't talk about Aunt Rifke! That dear downtrodden Aunt Rifke! Poor soul, how hard she worked all her life! *Oi,* Aunt Rifke! . . . Well, listen, I'll tell you the dope on Aunt Rifke, I'll tell you something about that two-faced old bitch. All her life she made everybody miserable, all her life she groaned about how hard everything was on her, but on Aunt Rifke's last ride, with the by God! *death* rattle in her voice—"

Mrs. Gest covered her face with her hands and swayed slightly from side to side. He shouted louder.

"—she gets into an argument with Wolf. You know what was the matter? She was worried about what hospital they were taking her to. 'Don't take me to a expensive hospital,' she groaned. By God, you had to lean down an inch over her mouth to hear her. 'It's too *expensive,*' she says. And she even tried to strike a bargain. 'Take me home,' she said. 'If you take me home, I will let you call a doctor' (she was doing Wolf a favor, do you understand!). A *favor!* And Wolf not knowing what to do and afraid to argue with her. AND SHE KNEW THAT HE WAS AFRAID TO ARGUE WITH HER! And she said, 'Take me home, don't aggravate me, *you know I can't afford to be aggravated!*' "

"Why do you hate me?" Mrs. Gest moaned. "Charlie, what did I do to you!"

"Hate you!" The injustice of this accusation made him tremble with added anger. *"Who* hates! What do you think this is for me, a joke? Do you think I came home on my lunch-hour to talk to you like this? But, Jesus, if I don't talk to you like this, don't you understand that I won't have anybody to talk to at all!"

"No, Charlie. By my life, I will not work. Go. I will rest all day."

"You see how you say that? You know that you don't mean it, don't you? You know you don't! You're just waiting for me to clear out! But look how you say it! Listen to yourself, my good mother!"

"All right, my breadwinner," she screamed, stung by the slur on her motherhood, "my *heavy* breadwinner. So I mean it not! How long then have you been adding wages to this miserable house?"

He stared at her.

"Listen, Ma. I am twenty-four years old. Is that right?"

"Nu?"

"When I was twelve years old, I already heard you groaning. I already knew that you were working too hard."

He saw how pale she was, but he could not stop.

"You call me your heavy breadwinner now. You're trying to make me ashamed because I want to help you." His tone was quiet, almost a whisper, but his outthrust head carried it forward. "But when I was twelve, could I help it that we were poor and you were already working yourself to death? You know, Ma, that I sold papers, but what was that!" He hated the theatrical sound of the words. "I've never been able to help you. Can't you imagine what that can do to a fellow?"

"Papers he sold! You went away when you were sixteen," she screamed. "I gave you the last ten dollars in the house, the money for food, to take with you because I could not bear you should go without a penny, a stitch to your bottom!"

He felt the impossibility of justifying himself.

"I went away because I couldn't do anything for you, and I hated every piece of bread you put on my plate. Just as I hate your obstinacy now in refusing to let somebody help you. . . . Do you know what I did with the ten dollars you forced on me?"

"I forced on you! God's orphan, with what would you have fed your miserable mouth?"

"I didn't spend a penny. I knew that I had to take it, that's why I took it. It was the least I could do for you! Yes, for you. Because I didn't want you to worry about me, even though I knew that if I didn't want you to worry about me, I would stay home. And a couple of fellows took it away from me in Arizona and beat me up for it."

Her eyes glazed with pain.

"You're trying to kill me."

"I can't go on like this," he shouted. "Why do you think I'm working! Why shouldn't I run away from this rotten place! I hate this house, myself, you—I tell you, I'll be damned if I go on with it!"

"Who's not taking this woman," she screamed. "Madman, what do you want of me!"

He quieted immediately. All this is ridiculous.

"All right. All right. I'll show you that I mean what I say. I'm not going to bring her back here. I'm not going to spy on you. She'll come here (if she'll still come, after you drove her away) and you'll put her to work. . . . But let me tell you this. It hasn't been fun for me to hear you at night, every night, when you didn't think anybody heard you and I pretended to be asleep. If you won't take this woman in to help you because I've convinced you with my arguments, then you'll have to do it for my sake. Ma, I need to know that I'm helping you. I won't try and explain it. . . . And this is just a beginning. The next thing is, we're going to move from this place. We're going to leave it as though it had the cholera in it."

"But suppose you lose the job?"

His vehemence overawed her at last. In this question, she stated the fear that had made her fight him.

"Then you fire Mrs. Johnson, for Christ's sake! That's all. And wherever we may be living, we'll move back from there. And if we owe money, we'll spit in everybody's eye that we owe it to and we'll move back. We'll get a band and a flag and we'll move back here. We'll have the cockroaches and the rats to welcome us. We'll have tears in our eyes and they'll have tears in theirs. And we'll come back here to die."

Mrs. Johnson stood at the door. She looked in and saw them talking.

"Hello," Charlie said.

He was dumfounded. Was it possible that his mother had been telling him the truth after all, and Mrs. Johnson had not come this morning as she had said she would?

He opened the door for her.

"I guess nobody was home this morning," Mrs. Johnson said, looking around the kitchen. "I knocked and knocked, but I guess nobody was home."

"Oh, you *knocked!*" He looked at his mother. "I guess that's when you went out to the market, huh?"

She nodded dumbly, begging him with her glance not to give her away. She had probably pulled all the curtains, stood in one of the other rooms holding her breath. With everything else that oppressed her, she was shy. And had not had the courage to come to the door and tell Mrs. Johnson to her face that her only son was mad. Not to say a spender.

HE BOLTED A SANDWICH AND A CUP OF COFFEE AT THE STATEN Grill and came up the elevator with the after-lunch crowd. Respectfully the workers crowded against one another and flat-

186

tened themselves against the walls, leaving a small significant space all about him. He had become again a symbol of power. Jerked thus from the world he had just left to the world he was entering, he was aware that the gesture deepened and complicated a growing state of mind. If he had seen all this in a play on the stage, he would have laughed, appreciating the irony. The elevator girl, of course, regarded all her passengers alike with equal contempt. Sadie, a grim pilot, was by way of being a realist in matters of the theater. . . .

SHE HAD NEVER HAD A SERVANT BEFORE. WHAT *does* ONE with a servant? Is it as if she, Mrs. Gest (let the truth be told!), is a *pritza,* to the manner born—a—a *government?* How, then, does one instruct a servant? If addressed too abruptly, would she not feel insulted? And, really, now, is she not after all a person, a living woman? How can you take a *living woman* and say, as to one's own, "Do this, do that!"

And another thing (resentfully, she marshaled reasons), so accustomed was she herself simply to do whatever was to be done, to drag herself methodically and unthinkingly from one job to another through the day, which never is long enough for all that is to be done, that she simply did not know how you make a beginning. And from where.

Besides (the thought filled her with anger at Charlie), who knows how this woman did her work? Plainly, from the looks of her, an *Irisher,* she was not to be trusted. Suppose she scrubbed too hard here, a little not enough there, that would be fine, would it not! And to let her "monki uhruhnd" with the food, what a thought too! Mrs. Gest had heard stories (don't ask her where, she had heard them) of these people. A sprinkle of poison dropped into the soup, a spit into the coffee—what then, is the Jew loved? A vision of Janice writhing on her back, poisoned, rose before her mind.

"Mother," Janice moaned. "You have killed me!"

187

She was filled with horror.

"God should only watch over us," she muttered.

Meanwhile the woman had taken off her coat. She had looked around the kitchen. A quick thrust of satisfaction in the proud breast of Mrs. Gest as she perceived, with woman's intuition and the instinctive knowledge of other women that transcends race, that Mrs. Johnson approved of what she saw. A house clean as a pin! A sink you could sleep on, so it shines! A quick one-act fantasy, one of those little plays that no playwright can match for utter and triumphant blending of the qualities of beauty and the ideal, was conceived, written and produced, witnessed and applauded in the fastidious theater of her mind, in a second. Mrs. Johnson, her face transfigured, stands in a circle of her friends in some unknown setting. They hang on her every word. And Mrs. Johnson talks.

"I'll tell you the God's honest truth," says Mrs. Johnson, "a house such as Mrs. Gest keeps I have never seen. So nice, so clean, it's a pleasure! I mean it. A pleasure! You would think," says Mrs. Johnson (not that the audience has objected on this score; far from it; for their faces beam and they murmur appreciatively among themselves), "you would think that she could not do it. After all, is Mrs. Gest a rich woman?"

"How does she do it?" say all the Irishers. "How does she manage?"

"It's the God's own miracle," says Mrs. Johnson helplessly. "She does it, that is all I know. *How,* don't ask me!"

Flash! The play had run its course. But Mrs. Gest had been warmed by it. Mrs. Johnson, after all—a woman, like herself— a woman—it was plain—who has worked so hard. And to have to go out to strangers! Tears filled her eyes. Later, she would modestly narrate to Nussim, to the Widow Cohen, to Charlie even, what Mrs. Johnson had said about her household. She would tell it as though Don't think this is my opinion, it is what Mrs. Johnson said. Nor would she be conscious of guile.

She warmed by the second to her visitor. It was nice to have somebody in the house with you through the long day. Actually, she could hardly think of her "visitor" as servant. With a sudden burst of energy, she set about bustling.

"A cup of coffee," she mumbled. "How can one go without a cup of coffee?"

Mrs. Johnson hung her coat over a chair.

"Yes, Ma'am," she said. "It's cold outside. I sure could do with a cup of coffee."

Before even Mrs. Gest could see the pattern of her motions, she had put coffee, bread, butter on the table. A lunge into the icebox produced her prize, the big jar that she kept carefully wrapped in a paper bag and toward the back of the lowest shelf for fear somebody would see it—a jar of herring and onions. A piece of cold garlic sausage came next, a little plate of tomatoes and black olives.

"Eat, eat," she urged. "For work one must have strength. . . . All right," she argued and conceded to herself, "I too will have a little something."

She looked searchingly at the other woman:

"Mrs. Johnson. *Please*. The herring and onions. You should not tell nobody. My family, they don't want me to have nothing. Only to know that there is herring in the house, Charlie would make noise to change the night into day. It's a disgrace for the neighbors."

She took a piece of herring in her fingers; quickly, with eager haste, she stripped it of as many bones as she could find, first ripping it deftly in two in order to get at the bones, and with a sigh put it between two slices of black pumpernickel bread, heavily buttered to exasperate the onions and bring out the full power of their flavor. Then, delicately, waiting until Mrs. Johnson too was ready for the assault, she put it to her mouth, one finger in the air, and took a huge slow long bite.

"Oh," she said, "how good that is!"

Mrs. Johnson, surprised at first by the nature of this beginning of her employment with Mrs. Gest, soon adapted herself. She ate what was placed before her, drank the contents of her cup as fast as it was filled (several times by the shy Mrs. Gest), and—in fact—began to gorge herself with an avidity even greater than her hostess'. The two looked at each other occasionally with the flushed gleeful expressions of conspirators. Finally, with a large sigh of repletion, they sat back. Mrs. Gest relieved the gas on her stomach by belching. Mrs. Johnson, who had been keeping it in out of a notion of refinement, belched. They looked at each other, both now at ease.

"Now you just sit there," Mrs. Johnson suddenly said, fussily, "I'll get the dishes cleaned before you know it."

Mrs. Gest, whose head was ringing from the effects of her totally unexpected and savage descent on the forbidden foodstuffs, allowed her to do this. She felt that she could do no other. Watching her, she saw that the job Mrs. Johnson was doing was a good job. The woman evidently knew how to wash dishes. She allowed herself the luxury of sitting a minute longer. Then, with a grunt, she got to her feet.

She went heavily toward the middle room. There, increasingly conscious that she had eaten too much, she began to make the beds. Why was it that the things she liked should be so fraught with poison for her! The herring, which had lain wistful in the icebox for days, haunting her disturbed and lustful dreams as a young maiden haunts the blood of aged monarchs, had, now that she had abandoned fear and eaten of it, begun to punish her. She could feel the little tell-tale lumps forming in the softest, the most tender parts of her stomach and breasts, the lumps that soon would be damming the blood-stream in its course, forcing the tributary torrents into her head where soon they would hammer, hammer. She bent over the pillows, shaking them, afraid to bend too far, for fear dizziness would assail her. And (she was immensely surprised, for she had forgotten that she was now a "boss") Mrs. Johnson had come to the other side of the bed.

"I'll do that," Mrs. Johnson said.

"Yes," she agreed weakly. "Thank you very much."

She found that she would have to sit down. Just for a moment. Yes, she had eaten too much herring, but even now she refused to believe that she should not have eaten it. All her days were full of the memory of what a strong capable woman she had always been (*always*), and she refused to admit how sick she was. Also, she did not know that she had eaten the herring as a way of telling Charlie that she did not need help, no matter how often she had asked for it. In fact, she blamed Charlie for her present debacle. *Nu,* suppose she complained, she kicked, it was her business. The way they stormed at her, you would think— you would think—she didn't know what you would think—

To hide her weakness, which would pass, which would have to pass, which had always passed, she invented the pretext of going into the kitchen to heat up some water for the wash to follow.

"You finish the beds, please, Mrs. Johnson," she said, "I will go put on the water."

She went into the next room and began to put on the water. She filled a bucket full from the faucet. As she lifted it, she got dizzy. She put it down gently on the floor, and moved to the table. She sat down. All this as quietly as she could, an immense concentration of will-power. She sat there and waited for the dizziness to pass. She just closed her eyes and endured the malignant passage of her beloved enemy, the herring. She opened her eyes, not able to stand being closed in with the thumping in her head. The huge empty jar stood before her, the mute symbol of the feast that had been here. She stared at it with no anger. Rather with puzzlement and pain that she should be so fond of it, and it so false to her. And suddenly, from the other room, where she had left Mrs. Johnson and could hear her moving about, she heard a heavy crash.

"My God!" she said, and came to her feet.

She rushed into the room.

Mrs. Johnson had fallen across the bed and from there had fallen to the floor. She lay there now, face down, moving her arms and legs feebly, like a fish that has been on land for some time but still moves itself in hope that, miracle of miracles, water will be its reward. And from Mrs. Johnson's throat came queer gasps, as though she were trying to cough and could not.

Horrified, Mrs. Gest went down on her knees beside her.

"Mrs. Johnson! For God's sake, pull yourself together. What is the matter, Mrs. Johnson! What is wrong with you!"

With infinite care, she put her hand on Mrs. Johnson's forehead. It was cold, covered with sweat. "God save us all," she muttered, and turned her over, putting a pillow under her head. She went to the sink, poured a glass of water, brought it back.

"Drink this," she urged.

Mrs. Johnson, her head lifted up level with the rim of the glass, opened her mouth. She drank a few sips. Her eyes returned to life.

"Lift me up," she breathed hoarsely.

This was easier asked than done. Mrs. Gest was no featherweight, but neither was Mrs. Johnson. Strange to think of two such women as fragile, to be handled with care. But, with a gentleness and patience that the sick know the sick require, she tried, shifting first her weight, then Mrs. Johnson's, engaging an arm here, a mass of flesh there, securing first this leverage, that fulcrum, until finally, after an apparent eternity of effort, the major part of Mrs. Johnson, the *decisive* part of her weight, had fallen across the bed, and a swing of the feet accomplished the rest of her. She lay, breathing heavily. And Mrs. Gest, her legs suddenly and completely faint and powerless with the effort, lay down beside her. . . .

So they lay, a quiet, even a peaceful sight, the two large women. And after a while the edge of the terrific thumping in Mrs. Gest's head wore off. The line of peril receded from her heart. Time beat again, and with the awakening of interest and vitality, a sense of the ridiculousness of the situation came upon her too.

She had a vivid picture, of a sudden, of Charlie's standing by the side of the bed looking at them speechlessly, the expression of his face.

"I laugh," she said aloud, between spasms of mirth, "but what is funny, let my enemies tell me!"

Mrs. Johnson groaned at hearing words, and tried struggling to a sitting position. Her "boss" rose.

"Ssh, *shuh,*" she said, as though she were addressing a child, "lay still. You must lay still. You mustn't move, Mrs. Johnson. It aint good for you."

"I aint et much for two days," Mrs. Johnson said, shamefaced and penitent. "I guess you give me too much to eat."

"Woe is me!" Mrs. Gest exclaimed.

"Just let me lay here a while. I get spells like this ever' now and then."

Mrs. Gest, overawed and contrite at the thought that she had helped bring on Mrs. Johnson's illness, got up and walked weakly into the kitchen. There she contrived to put the water onto the stove, as she had started to do, and lit the fire. She pulled out the tub, the washboard, and the chairs for the wash and got all in readiness. Then she sat down to wait for the water to heat. Hearing Mrs. Johnson begin to groan again, she realized how frightened she was.

"How you feel?" she asked, panic-stricken.

"I don't feel good," Mrs. Johnson said, in a plaintive voice. "I ate too much of that herring. I got a condition. I aint supposed to eat that kind of stuff. . . . I aint et nothing but bread and coffee for two days."

193

She closed her eyes and lay still, lines of suffering on her face. Mrs. Gest ran to the wall on the other side of which dwelt the Widow.

"Mrs. Cohen," she shouted. "Mrs. Cohen!"

No answer. When you didn't want the Widow to hear anything, she was there and heard all.

She went out on the "summer" porch and called Mrs. Seller to her window.

"Mrs. Seller, please, I beg you! do me a favor. Tell your boy he should make a telephone call for me."

"What's the matter, Mrs. Gest. Are you sick again, may it not be so?"

"It's a mad world, Mrs. Seller. When they say 'mad,' they should be believed. Not *I* am sick, it is my servant. My son, Charlie, the *philosopher,* he got me a servant. She gasps and goes out like a light!"

"One of ours?"

"A *goya!* But God is my witness, a *goya* is also, unfortunate person, a human being. What contains life can also suffer, Mrs. Seller."

"I will call my boy, if only he will deign to come."

But when the boy came to the window, Mrs. Gest discovered that she did not know where Charlie worked.

"It is for the Government," was all she could tell him. "He *writes*. He makes with a pencil. The Government pays him and he writes."

"Don't you know the name? Woddaya want *me* to do!"

"*W.P.A.!*" shrieked Mrs. Gest, seized with an inspiration. "He writes books for the Government."

Mrs. Seller suddenly drew back a large fist and slapped her son across the head.

"Ask her no questions, go telephone."

"Don't hit me, Ma. You think it don't hurt?"

"Hit him not, Mrs. Seller. An angel is he, not a boy!"

194

"Angel, go telephone! May the Devil, the Unmentionable One, seeing you, have mercy, and depart still alone!"

EVEN THOUGH THERE HAD BEEN SEVERAL PAYDAYS ON THE Project, the experience was still fraught with the same qualities of the unexpected and miraculous, and Mr. Hohaley—an elaborate showman—was making the most of the occasion, as always.

On each side of him, as he stood framed in the doorway of his office, the perfect and necessary complement without which he disliked to move, appeared the smiling faces of Lloyd Matson and Mr. Clarkson, the paymaster. Clarkson, a small whiskered man, still managed while smiling to look his harassed important part.

A hush. A perceptible drawing in and expulsion of the breath. Obviously, Mr. Hohaley was most convincing in his most favorite of roles, that of the grand seigneur. Has the Republican press been vituperative again of late, asking how long O Lord must the honest taxpayer be required to support armies of governmentally sponsored ne'er-do-wells? Has the New Deal, drawing in its horns temporarily, sent out feelers on the possibility of reducing work-relief rolls by a hundred thousand this winter? Is it implied that the President will move thus and thus? Is it averred that the Chamber of Commerce will protest such and such? And has the wife's cousin's cousin, who is in the know, darkly hinted at et cetera— There he stands, Mr. Hohaley, there in the middle of the floor, stands and smiles, smiles and bows, bows and waves, almost and imperceptibly and oh surely, surely his bearing a promise. And everybody burst out cheering and clapping hands (as it was becoming a custom to do on paydays). And, yes, there is that look on his face. He has the air of one who has come from far-off and important places where he has scored important yet personal triumphs—the look of Mercury, the Messenger, home from the wold. A modern Mercury, loaded down with the bacon.

He held up a hand. "Ssh," went the sharp whisper. Then complete silence. Charlie, though he felt that he was somewhat more privy to his campaign secrets, as it were, than most here, was as curious about what the director might say as any. Specifically, he was waiting to see how Hohaley would handle the matter of the banquet for Colon. The rest of his audience, with few exceptions, had no complicated feelings as they awaited the address; they only saw and felt the fat man's presence, and knew that he would have nothing but good to utter. He was far too elegant a gentleman.

"Howdy, all you folks," he said. "Glad to have you with us again. Th' same crowd. One or two new faces. Expect to see you around lots."

It was a perfect opening. Cheers again. Spontaneous hand-clapping. Beaming faces. The "newcomers" indicated who they were by looking modest and well-pleased, in a deprecatory sort of way. The "old-timers" all looked happy and proud, and glanced briefly at the "newcomers" with encouraging looks. He continued:

"I want you always t' feel as though you have a friend in me, a true friend. Someone t' whom you can come with yo' troubles and he will understand and help whatever he can . . ." and on in this vein. Finally: "And now, before the pay-clerk begins handing out those—ahem—" (laughter) *"checks,* I have some real news fo' you. I KNOW that this will please you."

Pollin stepped forward at this point. The ex-banker. The ex-teller, to be exact. Why do bankers all look alike? Had he read of a theory somewhere, Charlie wondered, that all cops get to look alike after a while? All social workers? All preachers? Party politicians? Widows? If so, then diversity was only to be found among the unclassified. Pollin, like Jevins of Johnsburgh, was past fifty and perhaps not quite sixty-five. Like Jevins, he was silver-haired, kindly in appearance; conservative by implication in the humorous expression he distilled inside for the out-

196

side to see. He wore glasses too. But he was a banker who had been on relief. Charlie, when he had assigned Pollin the job of compiling material on the Banks of the State, had been curious to see what Pollin's reactions would be to this (what might be) ironic task. It had turned out very well for Pollin. His contact with the bankers he had needed to interview had been completely without embarrassment to the genial man. In the back of his mind, as he had confided wistfully to Charlie, had been the thought that perhaps he was at the beginning of a comeback.

He stepped forward now, a respectable humble old wreck of a man in his ill-fitting clothes of a former and fatter day.

"May I speak?" he asked huskily.

Mr. Hohaley (the slightest steadying on him of his watchful eyes) gave the required permission: "My news can wait."

"Mr. Hohaley," he said, and cleared his throat, "I have been asked— I have been asked"—he paused, overcome momentarily. Encouraging cries went up of "Go on, go on!" In the background hovered the delighted face of Lucille Turnbull (a power on the Project in such enterprises as the collection of funds for presents to the ill, the engaged, the dead, the illustrious—one obsessed with testimonial literature). Pollin looked back at her. All about him were the people he was representing. He gathered strength.

"Yes, Mister Pollin?" Mr. Hohaley said softly.

Pollin pulled himself together. He mopped his brows with a large handkerchief. Then he smiled, a gracious confident smile.

"How silly it is of me to find this welcome task so difficult," he jibed roguishly at himself, "I should have a silver tongue at this moment, for this auspicious occasion." The white head leaned forward and the old eyes rolled. "Mr. Hohaley, I have been delegated to read to you a token of our appreciation and gratitude, a small offering indeed for all you have done for us." He put a piece of paper up before his nose. "This is a poem, Mr. Hohaley. I wrote it myself." Quickly Charlie looked at

Lucille. He had thought that the poem would be hers. He saw the smile tremble on her lips. "I believe that it accurately reflects the feeling that each and every one of us have toward you, our dear benefactor." He read:

Here's to Mr. Hohaley,
A vision of kindliness.
He is more friendly than a Quaker,
And we hope that him will God bless.

He has done so much for us,
That none can repay, none can repay.
He joins with us to wish that soon
Will dawn another day.

Now that he had started, he read on and on. There were perhaps fifteen stanzas in all. Mr. Hohaley stood and bowed and smiled as he heard the lines and the workers all gazed at him. Finally Pollin was finished, catching everybody, including himself, by surprise.

"How wonderful," said Mr. Hohaley.

The workers, led by Pollin, began to clap hands.

"And now for my news," Mr. Hohaley was saying. His look was all triumph. "We are to be privileged to entertain Mr. Colon in our own city as our personal guest. The plans are complete and the banquet—"

The applause was overwhelming.

"Natch'lly, I would not like to ask you to stand the cost of all this. I would much rather make all this my own treat, as it is and must firmly remain my own idea, the bill of goods that has been sold mine, but—"

Into the breach of his pause leaped Pollin, as deftly as though he were taking a cue: "Oh, no, sir. It is for us that you strive, dear sir; so you must allow us all the privilege of sharing the expenses of this highminded endeavor."

And he was abundantly seconded.

"Thatsa right," Costello shouted. "We pay. We pay. Is privilege all right. Thatsa what. And we *insis'* we pay."

"Yes, sir! Our treat, Mr. Hohaley!"

"I'm ready with two!"

"Put me down for five!"

"Me too!"

"That's too much," Mr. Hohaley said. "I b'lieve we can swing it fo' two dollars apiece. At least fo' a start. And then, if it happens that this is not enough, the next payday will be soon enough to take up anothah collection."

"What about the workers in the district offices, who probably won't be here for the banquet? Don't you think, Mr. Hohaley, that we should make them chip in too, seeing as how this is for their good as well as ours?"

"The out-state workers will be invited to contribute, if that is what you mean," Mr. Hohaley amended, smiling.

"All right," Mr. Clarkson piped nervously, "if you'll line up for your checks now. And will you please carry your identifications ready with you, as I have not had the opportunity of becoming acquainted as yet with each and every one of you."

"You'll get the chance," somebody shouted.

A rush ensued toward the desk at which Mr. Clarkson seated himself. There was a great deal of excited laughter and loud talking now, but those in the front of the line suddenly grew very quiet. They had caught sight of the thick pile of little blue checks on the desk, one of which each of them was to receive. The sight was something they could not get over, or quite used to, and it took all their attention.

Charlie, meanwhile, just before Mr. Hohaley had come to the end of his speech, had been called to the telephone.

"This is Adolph Seller, Charlie. They told me how to get in touch with you through the W.P.A. There is somebody sick at your house and you should get a doctor. Your old lady told me to call you up."

"*Who* told you?"

"Your old lady. Betcha surprised. She told me to be sure and tell you it aint her who is sick. She said you would think it was her, so I should be sure and tell you it aint her so you don't have to bother me and waste no time. She says you should call a doctor."

HIS MOTHER HAVING ADOLPH CALL UP TO SAY THAT SOMEBODY *else* was sick, not she, was too novel not to have a touch of questionable mystery attached to it. Softly, for some reason, he came up the stairs. Softly, without knocking, he opened the door. The first thing he saw was his mother standing over the washtub and scrubbing away as hard as she could. There was a scared and anxious expression on her face, but also (as she looked up and saw him) an unmistakable air of having her own way after all, chalk-white though this air was. In her excitement, however, she had forgot to wash and get rid of the herring-jar and he smelled it. She smelled it at the same time he did, but at once—considering Mrs. Johnson's illness to prove that there were weaker ones than she in this wide world—determined to brazen it through. He could almost see her defenses forming, obstinate, gloating (just now) cat-like little instruments of war.

"What did you do?" he asked. "Knock her out?"

She spoke with scorn.

"A helper he got me. Three times already she has vomited on the floor."

"And you? How many times did you vomit?"

"None of your business."

He went in to take a look at Mrs. Johnson. His mother had drawn the shade in that room, and the sick woman lay in darkness, only the glint on her dry lips and the open teeth showing. He went back into the kitchen.

"She looks pretty sick. What happened?"

Mrs. Gest tried to look as though her good offices had been

exhausted in vain. "She ate too much, that is all. I said, 'Please, Mrs. Johnson, don't eat so much.' "

"And the herring—all gone between the two of you, huh?" She burst into tears. "Nothing he lets me eat. Bread, vegetables, who can live on bread and vegetables. Who *wants* to live on bread and vegetables! No meat, no herring, no nothing. This is too rich, this has got too much I don't know what, this hasn't got enough, my troubles alone can understand them. And don't go to the show, it is bad for your eyes, it draws the blood, it makes your head hurt, and when your head hurts, you are in danger. And a blood vessel you will burst maybe. Don't worry, don't laugh, don't, don't, don't! And wash not, the doctor tells me. Ten years ago he tells me and all the time I keep on washing. Now my son gets a job. Two months he has a job. Stop everything, he says. And brings me a cadaver, she falls from her feet!"

Her crying had the quality in it that distressed him more than any other form of weeping or displeasure she possessed (and after half a lifetime of practice, she was a virtuoso). It was that of a child, a forlorn child (he always imagined), sitting in a corner and watching the other kids play. There was in it none of that artifice he could at any other time expect from her.

"Don't cry, Ma," he said gently. "That isn't what I meant."

He walked to and fro in front of her, wishing he could touch her, say something. Alas, years of the extremes of experience build up a seeming hardness that is difficult to break through and the expression of which is never conventional. People who seldom suffer can, in moments of grief or need, fly to each other. To an outside observer, to the God of churches perhaps, such immediate and complete demonstration may seem the height of true affection, but affection (like courage) is easy to exercise when no great drains on it are required, and for this reason the greatest shows of affection are invariably shown (so it would seem) among the untroubled. Soldiers watching each other die try to say all that they can no longer say—or even imagine—with the apparently irrelevant proffer of a cigarette.

"Ma," he said with difficulty, "I got nothing against you eating herring. If I could fix it, I would make you eat a ton of herring a day. But—" A gesture completed what he could not find words for. "You're awfully pale, Ma. Why don't you go lie down." Feeling that it might bring a laugh, he added, "The boss and her helper. What a boss! . . . I'll do the wash."

It did. "The *boss,*" she said. "Has anybody in all the history seen such a boss!"

Groaning and laughing, she made her way to the bed.

"Mrs. Johnson," he heard her say, "I will keep you company."

He heard her lie down.

"Oh," from the Jewish woman.

"Oh," from the Irish.

He could not deny himself: "You never let anybody help you unless you drop," he said bitterly. "How does it happen that you relax, even then?"

"Canst thou wipe thine own nose?" she returned languidly.

"A female Jehovah!" he taunted. "The great she-God Gest!"

No answer. . . . He waited for one, gritting his teeth and yet hoping that she would not be drawn into another quarrel. Then he put on an apron and began to scrub. For five minutes he scrubbed as though he had to be through in five minutes. Then the unaccustomed muscles in his back began to ache and he realized that he'd have to time himself. He stood up, stretched, shadow-boxed a moment to loosen up, and went back to the work at a steadier tempo. He found himself digging down on his mother's "Oh," coming up on the Irishwoman's.

After a while he began to smile less grimly. Capital and labor were in that bed, taking their ease in a queer siesta. . . . Once upon a time, and a silly time it was—let's tell silly fables— there was a boss, the silliest boss that ever lived—and she was my own dear mother. And the National Association of Manu-

202

facturers had a meeting and to the great hall came Mr. Henry Ford, riding in one of his brand-new Fords, and Mr. Chrysler, driving a Chrysler, and Mr. Tom Girdler, riding a human girdler, and Mr. J. Pierpont Morgan, floating in on the ballooning House of Morgan, and oh so many others, look in the noble and Christian Almanach de Gotha for the soul-stirring details, and also my mother came there, for she was a boss too, in her way now also one of the masters and rulers of mankind . . .

The doctor stared ironically at his apron and the sweat on his forehead.

"Well," he said sourly, "where's the patient?"

"There's two of them," Charlie said coldly. "Capital and labor. They're in conference in the next room."

The eyebrows lifted. "Two?"

"Yeah. We rose in the world. My mother got a helper. It was the first rung on the ladder which was toughest."

"Hmm."

From long practice Charlie stayed out of the room. He heard the doctor's gruff tones, his mother's defiant yet wheedling answers. Mrs. Johnson, amazed that anybody should care this much about her, was saying something too, protesting her astonishment; he could get her mood from the crescendos and diminuendos in her voice. The doctor finally came out, closing the sliding door behind him.

Charlie continued to scrub.

"Well," the doctor said, "these two old girls really had them a bat, didn't they? . . . Can you fix to keep the other one here overnight?"

"Sure. We always take care of workers' compensation. Never wreck a worker without observing the Golden Rule. This establishment follows the principle of collective bargaining."

The doctor looked at him with distaste and wrote out a prescription. "I gave them a needle apiece too. They'll be asleep shortly."

"Fine. Fine. I want nothing but the best care. Specialists. Everything."

"Yes, naturally," the doctor said dryly. He motioned Charlie to the far corner of the room. "Let me tell you something. Your mother's sicker than you think. She should be in the hospital."

"My mother will like that."

"They always do. Well, that's how it is."

"What about the other one?"

"She's in the same fix. Same malady."

He had not taken off his coat and hat. He picked up his bag and went toward the door. Charlie followed him.

"Don't you want to get paid?"

The doctor turned, his hand on the knob, and looked at him with a dour mocking expression.

"*Paid?* I'm afraid you couldn't pay what I am in the habit of asking."

"Come now, Doc," Charlie said, drawling his voice familiarly, "those were the *old* days. This is a new era. Haven't you heard? I'm a big shot now. Got a big job."

"Well, my regular fee is ten dollars. Which of course is out of the question for you," Glaser said slowly, looking at him speculatively. "Isn't it? Why do you put on these airs? Suppose we settle for a dollar. Hmm?"

Charlie pulled out a thick wad of bills, turned over several fives from his newly changed check, and peeled off a one-dollar bill. "How right you are, Doctor. I really should settle down, *mature*, now that I too have a vested interest to live for. Well, thanks again, Doc." He put the bill in the doctor's hand. "Thanks a thousand. Particularly for not asking the full amount of the regular fee. You've been like a second mother to all of us, including my mother."

No sooner had the doctor (clearing his throat and purpling

with rage) started down the stairs than Mrs. Gest called him in.

"Charlie."

"Yes?"

"What did he say?"

"He said you're all right. He said I could give you herring for supper. First you have to sleep a bit."

"On my life, Charlie. Don't joke. What did he say?"

"Well, let's see. Well, he said, 'Charlie, your mother's in pretty good shape considering that she doesn't follow her diet as she should.' Then he asked me what I was doing nowadays and I told him I was a supervisor of an Authors' Project and still doing some writing on the side, maybe more nowadays because I don't have to worry about my bread and butter so much. And he thought that was fine. So then he got an idea and he says, 'Say, come to think of it, if you're doing so well, why don't you have the old lady come into the hospital for a couple of days, just for observation, maybe we can correct her diet,' fix it so maybe you can get something you like now and then without hurting you. Like a leg of chicken on Sunday. And I thought it was a hell of a good idea. So I said, 'Okay by me, Doc, but the old lady's kind of nutty and it may need a bit of fixing.' We-e-ell, he laughed and said, 'Well, see if you can fix it. It's a swell chance for her, seeing as how you're making dough now.' "

He turned his attention casually but quickly to Mrs. Johnson, before his mother could say a word.

"Well, Mrs. Johnson. Doctor's orders are for you to be our guest for tonight, so you'd better keep the old lady company right on. If you like, I'll ask your kids to come over and see you later in the afternoon. How's that?"

"I don't know what to say. If—if—"

Mrs. Gest felt that she should have a say too.

"Not a word," she said warmly. "You stay. You are welcome. You shouldn't even open your mouth."

She made as though to get up, on the instinctive notion that, as the woman of the house, she should be bustling about.

"Lie still," Charlie said, putting his hand on her shoulder. "Relax. Just lie there. I'll go over to Mrs. Johnson's. Then I'll stop off at the drugstore and fill the prescription. I'll bring home a delicatessen supper and some canned soup."

"Aint you going back to work?"

"Yes, I'll do that too—after Janice and Clara get here."

The "Supervisor" took off his apron, washed his face and hands, and went to run his errands. The "boss" left alone with her "force," felt shy again and began to make conversation.

"And how many children, long may they live, Mrs. Johnson, have you got?" she asked brightly. She still felt, somehow, that she should get up. She should *run*, she felt, *do, be!* But (emanations of the drug in the needle began to rise to her brain) the God's honest truth it was that she could not only not have lifted an arm, she could not even have given a *squeeze.*

PART SIX

But what does a man do while he waits? He did not know for sure. How can you be certain of disinterestedness anyway where there's a personal stake involved? Meanwhile day succeeds day, the insoluble questions present themselves . . .

Most insoluble of the difficulties was that of the personnel, and he always found himself coming back to it: "The trick is to take the arbitrary and to adapt it in a usable pattern. . . . And here, all of a sudden, are almost two hundred people—of whom only the merest handful are capable of adaptation to the special requirements of this work."

Like horses dragging a partially seated but stubborn rider, his thoughts always brought him back: to the relief and the non-relief people on the Project with whom he must work—to the rank-and-file.

As he grew more acquainted with them and they began to focus in his mind, coming out of the red-tape and the "facts" that surrounded their applications, the mass of data through which he must dig, but cautiously, never knowing when the pick will strike raw nerves, he found his mind taken off Clyde Harkins. . . .

There was, for instance, George Marvell. George was old, a tall frail stoopshouldered man of just under seventy, with white hair like a halo of years, glasses almost as thick as the tomb that would soon hide those horribly faded eyes, ears that heard as though eternity was already pressing on them. George (it was heartbreaking to think of this) had once been the editor of a great metropolitan daily—which *thirty-five* years ago had merged with the *Planet* to form the present *Sentinel-Planet*—a crack newspaperman. George sat at his desk for hours, bent and smiling and seeming to wait, as though expecting the sun to enter him again, and from time to time he would awake momentarily. Then his voice would fill with tears as he told the "youngsters" stories of the old days. In such moments pride returned; one had to be careful with Old George; he knew that he did little to earn his pay. . . .

How anxious everybody was to *earn* the money he received, to avert the cry "charity!"

And then, on the other hand, there was another newspaperman, MacGrover, the fellow with one eye brown, the other blue. Charlie had to smile, recalling Matson's account of the hiring of this man.

"There he sat, this multi-colored MacGrover. So I looks down at his recommendations. On private stationery, no less. And from Jim Hudson's own pen. Yeah, from Lucille Turnbull's own little alphabet of dreams of a cool generation and a half ago. So I say, 'Now, ahem, Mr. MacGrover, old sport, let's see now. What paper did you say you worked on?'

"So he tells me. 'De *Sentinel-Planet,* dat's who. I worked for de *Sentinel-Planet* t'ree-four years. Yes, sir.'

"And I say to myself, 'Watch it, Matson, old fruit, there's a woodpile in that Ethiopian.' 'Come again,' I say, 'De *Sentinel-Planet?* What kind of work did you do for de *Sentinel-Planet?*'

" 'I druv a delivery-wagon for de *Sentinel-Planet,*' says he."

And then there was Mrs. Cardozo (Charlie was looking at the file of application blanks filled out, going over them not once or twice, but many times, trying to fit the words to the person, the person to the words inscribed here, the information to the information from Washington on the exact outlines of the job, the job to the man). . . . Mrs. Stephanie Cardozo— what a wonderful name!—an Irishwoman who'd married a Sephardic Jew—a great scholar (of a race of scholars) with just enough inherited dough. Enough to get by on, and Mrs. Cardozo, who—to use her own words—had worshiped the ground he walked, left with three kids after his death and the money cut off somehow (there are always kids mixed up with people, Charlie thought, kids in fact or kids in frustration, either way), and here it was twenty years since she'd been a schoolmarm. And out of practice. And (this had its own interest) with an inferiority complex her husband, without meaning to and without her becoming aware of it while he was still with her, had gradually conferred on her. She thought she wasn't brainy enough for the world any more, and the dependent kids made her anxious. Poor old gal, what a prima donna she was now, how careful you had to be of her feelings! But the "world," as she called all contacts necessary to her work, was not over-careful of her and hardly a day passed that she did not come to him in tears, forcing compliments and blandishments from him. . . .

And there was Ruth Minn (picking up these files at random),

the sole seventeen-year-old support of an aged mother and father (if it isn't kids people are mixed up with, it's parents). She was the child of a couple who had married for warmth in their forties and fifties, but the child of that marriage was cold. And then there was Johnny Stephens, another newspaperman. The Guild had recommended Johnny. Johnny was fifty. Still handsome, debonair. He too, like Old George, had once been a crack newspaperman. George had been a plodder, and steady as the seasons. Johnny had been a bum with the girls, a swell dresser and a two-bottle man. Like the old lady in the joke, who would have made a fine match, even at her age, only that she was "a little bit pregnant," Johnny was a little bit insane. He was a paretic. (Nobody knew this at first, and when they did they never spoke of it.) Lovable Johnny. Yesterday he had come into the office. Charlie was at his desk, but Johnny went to Matson's desk, thinking it Charlie's. Johnny sat there an hour, then wrote a note:

Dear Mr. Gest: Please read this when you come in. I'm of the opinion that there's a good future [he must have meant *feature*] to be found on the ferry-boats. I'm going to stay on one tomorrow and help them pass the time. Toodle-doo.
P.S. There was a fellow sitting at your desk while I was in the office who looked exactly like you.

And today, sure enough, he had brought in the article. A strange document, beautifully lucid in spots. Over it all, the atmosphere of clouds. And a youthfulness and unawareness that would have seemed cheerful if you did not know it to be tragic. Johnny, shipwrecked, and going down. With a manicured hand waving good-by.

Yes, there are all these people (let's for a moment not think of the work—how *can* one continue to think of the work!). On the file-cards they are just names. So-and-so; sole support, etc.; skilled, semi-skilled, etc.; good personality; needy; needy; deserving; undeserving; drinks; doesn't drink; needy; etc. When you first meet them, they are a haze. Later, they emerge from cards, from filing systems. Jesus, they're people. A stab of anguish suddenly (and at any time): This is humanity! And I'm a man with them (they've got me on file-cards too, for that matter. If not here, then in Washington. What do they say of *me?* Author of *Her Lips, Her Hands* perhaps, for Christ's tortured sake!). There are more delicate problems here, Compadre, than that this one is incompetent, that one insane. . . .

They are the girls who, chances are, will never get married, because their old folks will never die or their kid sisters and brothers will never cease growing up. They are the old men and the mad men (like George and Johnny) who have gone down the far side of the mountain but there was no rest and they are driven back, back up the slopes that are impossible in nature to scale again and that they are required in man's society to scale all the same. And you mustn't laugh. You mustn't scold. You can expect nothing except as a gift, the most precious and costliest ever given. "The fox of the field has his hole, the birds of the air have their nests, but the sons of men have not where to lay their heads." And then there are the people who once upon a time were somebodies, and still expect to be. There's the ex-banker, the ex-housewife (ex-lover too!), the ex-millionaire-rags-chain-peddler, the ex-jeweler ("a touch of ice at the wrist will cool the whole body and the mind can be at peace, even in July"), the ex-tailor, ex-sailor, always ex, ex, ex. All of them with the signs they carry over the empty shelves of their scattered lives: TEMPORARILY VACANT. CLOSED FOR REPAIRS.

And yet there's the work. We come back to it, Charlie thinks. *I* come back to it. Because of my own needs, I am driven back to it. As to a destination. But how much more pleasant to sit around at the Greek's, anonymous with the other fellows—not too anonymous, for in one's pockets are copies of Blake and Babel. To dream of Elizabeth, to touch her sometimes. And to be proud, to know that in one is a gathering, a great multitude, and that some day the power to speak will come. And to know that Elizabeth then will know why you were proud, and would not take her (the dearly beloved, oh believe me, Elizabeth—oh believe that the harsh and discordant words were all camouflage) in the road that Nussim took Sarah. In that day she'll read the words you were too shy and savage to say, and will know that the greatest love in the mad world we live in today is *not* to touch, *not* to harm. . . .

You lying bastard, you word-mongering fool, that's no dream at all. If it's a dream, it's the most dangerous dream you ever dreamed. For right now you know that the work is not, and can't be, a destination, an end, in itself. Man's still tied to himself, every Prometheus his own rock, and that's why you're working: because it's 150 bucks in your jeans every month, because it's swell to have all that money with all that goes with it, and because you want to keep on getting it. And under that circumstance you'd take your Elizabeth, *on her own terms.* And that's why you haven't been seeing her of late, because you want this very much, and it would break your heart to know that all this is a mirage.

And only then, if it *is* a mirage, will you go back to the other dream, to the depths that you wish to fool yourself are the heights.

And now (as he read in the pamphlets of Washington's beautiful plans) he wished that he had never been sent to Johnsburgh. But even if he had not known of Clyde Harkins, he would still have known that this house was built on sand. For while two-thirds of the Project workers were either illiterate or totally incompetent for the work to be done, there were now—just one instance, he thought gloomily—exactly eighty applications in the files from Negroes and not one of them would be used, he was sure. Forty of these Negroes were college graduates; twelve of them were Ph.D.'s.

HYSTERIA, IN SUCH SOIL, IS AT BEST ONLY TEMPORARILY SUPpressed. For some time after his return from Johnsburgh, Charlie wavered between the impulse to quit and the desire to surrender, to give in to forces which were in possession. To come in with the gang, boy. To take it slow and easy. As Mr. Hohaley often put it, and the saying seemed sinister to Charlie, "Administrations in Washington come and go, but we continue to live in the state and anybody who doesn't expect to die or move soon has a long lifetime of having to live next door with the same neighbors."

Matson almost persuaded him to this latter course. Not by words, but by example. Our brave young hero was gallivanting through the most luscious days he had ever lived. His room at the Martin Hotel was, almost nightly, the scene of gay parties. Or, rather, the beginning and the end of such parties. In between, he rolled up an ever-expanding acquaintanceship in the city's nightclubs and taverns. He was a great favorite with all who knew him. But, somewhat to Charlie's surprise, Matson, instead of withdrawing from him as his possibilities for entertainment grew, became more and more insistent on his company, and hardly a night went by that Matson did not call him up from wherever he might happen to be to tell him to "Come on over."

Matson was, to use his own phrase, living "high, wide and handsome, treating or owing everyone." More than once Charlie had seen him walk into a saloon and invite all present to line up for a drink. He had been known, on one occasion, to give his overcoat to a shivering Mexican on Kenzie Street. And, on another, when Matson had left his table at Kogan's saying that he'd be back in a few minutes, Charlie had gone outside to look for him, only to find that Matson had set up business across the street from a legless beggar and was pretending to be sightless. This, however, was not to compete with, but to help the beggar. He had collected fifteen cents by the time Charlie came out, and he gave the legless one two-thirds of his take. As he explained to Charlie, the beggar had not done well that day and Matson, on being appealed to, had discovered that he was out of funds.

"It's just as goddam blessed to take as it is to give," Matson said. "Another thing: I don't think much of a man who will insult a beggar by giving him something that he wouldn't beg for himself."

Toward the middle of the month (when funds were running low) the two friends would find themselves at Kogan's or some such place where Charlie was known and where they could "get away" with a beer apiece for the evening. And they would talk. Charlie, who sometimes found himself disliking or even hating Matson because of a callousness and indifference that he imagined he found in his friend, would try to get under his skin by assaults on his intellectual and emotional processes, the former of which he found more advanced than the latter. "You remind me," he said once, "of a prodigious linguist who has mastered the Chinese language and can talk it perfectly except that he doesn't know what a single goddam word means." Matson, enjoying himself vastly, would seem to agree to everything. "You don't care what anybody says about you," Charlie said, baffled and angry, "so long as what they do say is about you. . . . You knew that I'd be out looking for you, so you begged for your friend the beggar. You would have begged for a millionaire if you could have got a laugh out of it."

He didn't know why he lammed into Matson the way he did. The Project was no good, why should he think it ever would be? If blood could be shed in Spain, and for no reasons other than men's blindness, greed, and cruelty, then why not understand that ink could be spilled wastefully here? And men deprived of the right to work, i.e., *rights?* Negroes, for instance, are not allowed to eat in restaurants with white men in this town. But since when have I quit eating in restaurants? Where do you make a beginning? And so on, the old weary round. He ended up by trying to avoid Matson, as he avoided Elizabeth, quarreling with him deliberately. Every drink he took he grudged, every moment he spent lightly was a nail in the coffin of his self-esteem. Although he had often thought of how pleasant it would be to have a little "folding" money to spend, he derived no joy from it, for he had assumed that it would be money "well earned." Where he really wanted to be now every working minute was on the Project, *making* it work against all the odds. He was haunted by the days slipping by, the days and the days, and nothing getting younger, stronger—not people, not the work, not hope—and whenever his mother asked him how the work was, he said "Fine" and shut up completely after that.

It was at this time that he came to the decision that he had no alternative but to stick with the job. . . . And then, when Mrs. Johnson and his mother both became ill, he became certain that he would not change his mind. As a matter of fact (and this final point best illustrated the mutability of his mood, which in turn illustrated best the hysterical undertones of the Project), his mother's sickness shocked him out of the extremes of exaltation and despair into a state of mind wherein it seemed to him that holding onto the job (at any price) was the only reality that he dared entertain. He thought that he felt relieved. Of course, as he soon discovered, this latest stage left him in as unstable and troubled a condition as any that preceded it. And so he was when, unexpectedly—a day ahead of his schedule—Jonas B. Colon came into the office.

A LARGE CRAGGY FACE WAS WHAT CHARLIE SAW; EYEBROWS whose bushiness emphasized the man's almost total baldness and the deep studious eyes; tie and shirt that harmonized perfectly and gave the man (who was tall as well as thin) an exotic elegance; and a precise diction, coupled with a tendency to stuttering; in the Midwest, Charlie considered, before he even knew who the man was, you say *project* with the *o* hard and short, but where is it that you say *proe*-ject? In the East?

214

The man had waved his hand with a quick gracious gesture and brushed past Margaret Renny, Charlie's secretary, as she began to ask him whom he wished to see and what his business was. He walked into the office and asked if "the Proe-ject director, Mr. Hohaley," were in.

Charlie had said "No." Then he had looked up, seen the man, noted his appearance, which he concluded was what might be described as distinguished, and asked if there were anything he might do.

"Who are you?"

Charlie smiled in answer to this question, smilingly put. He thought the man some sort of a distinguished crackpot, an out-of-town friend of Mr. Hohaley's, perhaps. For a wild delirious moment he even thought that it might be a projection of Mr. Hohaley's image of James Branch Cabell, come to pay its respects and explain how it had all happened.

"I'm Charles Gest. Assistant to Mr. Hohaley. Anything I can do?"

"Oh, *C*. Gest."

C. Gest was the name under which Charlie wrote.

"Yes, I am." He looked his question. His pulse beat a bit faster. It seemed odd to be recognized as a writer in a place like this.

"I've read several of your short stories lately. Nice command of idiom."

The stranger walked leisurely to the window, looked out. He walked over to the door and observed the typists at their seats, listened to the clack-clack-clack of typewriters, not quite so even as they were at the Bell Telephone Company, for instance, but clack-clacking nevertheless. Charlie waited until he returned. Now how had he known about Charlie's stories!

"It's damn seldom that I've met a man who's read stories of mine," Charlie said. "Makes a fella feel good. *Damn* good."

The man seemed to be enjoying himself.

"You're far too modest," he said. "That letter of particulars on yourself you sent me some time ago, one would think you were apologizing for your stuff. Onigo dug some of it up for me. Not very commercial sort of style, of course, but much better than you'd led me to think."

Onigo was the chap they called "Colon's traveling salesman," Charlie remembered. Colon! That's who it must be.

"I wanted that job very much," Charlie said. "Most jobs are commercial, aren't they? I thought maybe my stories weren't commercial enough for it. I always feel apologetic—well, not apologetic, but *tired*—when I have to explain about my stories *in re* employment. When you tell people you're a story-writer, they ask you where you've published. If you don't say *Saturday Evening Post* or *Liberty*, something like that, they're disappointed. They get that blank look, and I get awfully tired. It seems easier not to give names."

It was Colon. "Do you know," he said, "I've never been west of Washington. I was born in New York State. I know every hamlet in Europe. How many languages do you think I can speak?"

What a dandy! Charlie felt some surprise. He discovered that he had not altogether expected Colon to turn out to be so agreeable. He did not know whether he was quite pleased. He could not help but think of the steel under Jevins' soft exterior. The frustrated and mortified figure of Clyde Harkins, he imagined, would have stared at this man. Colon did not seem like the sort of a man who could pin anybody's ears back.

And yet, it was a relief to meet a man of Colon's caliber.

"A lot of languages, if I can judge from the way you ask that."

Colon smiled mysteriously and pulled at the long lobe of his ear—an habitual gesture that he resorted to quite frequently. Charlie noticed that his fingernails were torn. That made him feel better. The man was not all of one pattern. Impressions (first

216

ones at any rate) might be wrong here. Dandies don't tear their nails.

"I have the ripe command of seven. Count 'em. English, of course. French. Spanish. German. Russian. Greek. Latin. The partial use of two others. Turkish and Hebrew. Quite a duke's mixture, eh? And now, do you know what impressed me most as I came west from Washington?"

"No, sir, I can't imagine."

The man's charm was infectious and Charlie, smiling broadly, noticed that Margaret Renny was smiling too. As a rule she was indifferent to what went on conversationally in this office, burying herself in a *True Story* magazine at any moment's leisure.

"That I can't speak American. It's a fact. In Chicago—I stopped off in Chicago before coming on here—I went into a tavern for a glass of beer. I heard two truckdrivers talking about a ball they had been to the night before. It seems that it had been quite an affair. There was talk of somebody who had anticipated trouble and brought a *difference* with him. At first I thought that a difference might be a girl. You know. Girl, boy. *Different*. But then it developed that he had used this difference to hit a man in the head with. Obviously he would not have hit the chap with a *girl*. So I asked the waitress to ask these fellows if they'd have a beer with me and they sent back word that they'd be delighted. We had a beer and I asked them what a difference was. Can you imagine what they told me?"

"Yes, sir," Charlie grinned.

Colon looked surprised for a moment, then he brightened.

"Of course. You would know. Do you know, young woman?"

"Yes, sir," Margaret recited. "A difference is a wee-pon which is carried for in a time of need."

"Remarkable. You both know. You really do. But have you thought how graphic our language is? Mind you how original the expression is, and how apt. A little man has reason to fear a bigger or a more formidable man. So he carries a *difference*. Judiciously

217

used, it represents the balance of power in their respective weights."

"There are a lot more phrases," Charlie said. "You take an adjective and turn it into a verb. *To cruel* is one. If you have a grudge against a fellow and want to do him dirt, you *cruel* him."

Colon pulled at his ear. "My word! That's wonderful!"

He seemed to like walking about the place, peering into this corner and that.

"We didn't expect you in until tomorrow," Charlie said, to be saying something.

"Well, Mr. Hohaley made everything appear so very jolly. As long as I was coming in, I thought I'd make it a bit of a holiday. I've been working rather long hours. Was getting to feel awfully tired. That's all right with the home guard, but meeting a lot of new faces. . . . Well, a chap wants to look his best, don't you know."

"Yes," Charlie said, thinking of some of those new faces. Added, "That's true."

Colon went to the door of the "City Room" and beckoned the first man whose eye he caught. That man was Johnny Stephens.

"Me?" said Johnny.

"If you please."

Johnny came in. He walked straight to Charlie and shook hands with him. Then he leaned over Margaret's desk.

"What you got on tonight, kid?"

Margaret gave a guilty laugh, looked quickly at Colon.

"Same thing I got on now, what do *you* think?"

The picture this formed in Johnny's beclouded mind must have been pleasant. He laughed as though this were the hugest joke.

"Wait till I tell the boys down at the corner," he said. "It'll kill 'em."

Charlie didn't know what he'd say next, so he said, "Oh, Johnny, this is Mr. Colon. Mr. Jonas B. Colon. This is Johnny Stephens. Johnny used to be a great newspaperman."

"How do you do, Johnny?" Colon said.

"This is the Authors' Project, isn't it?" Johnny asked. He held Colon's hand in his.

"Yes, it is," Colon said.

"How do you know? I never seen you around."

Colon looked puzzled. Johnny retained his hand.

"This is Mr. *Colon,* Johnny," Charlie said. "He's the big boss. He came in for the banquet. Remember?"

"Well, glad I met you," Johnny said, his curiosity satisfied. He dropped Colon's hand, waved gently to all, and went out.

"I was going to ask him something," Colon stuttered, his eyes popping.

"He's nuts," Margaret said. "He sure is. I don't know what he was thinking."

"Hmm." The large thin face looked distressed. "I wanted to ask him how he likes the Project. . . . Is he dangerous? Does he get violent?"

"No, sir. Johnny's a very nice fellow."

"He's on the supervisory staff," Margaret blurted out, sorry that she had said what she had about Johnny, whom she liked, and trying to make up for it.

"Supervisory staff!" Colon exclaimed. He looked around quickly at Charlie, seeking his eyes questioningly. Then as Charlie, who was flushing deeply, steeled himself to answer and not to burst out laughing: *"Stephens!* Yes, of course. I remember the name from the breakdown of personnel you sent me. But on the supervisory staff!"

"Gee, Mr. Colon," Margaret burst out, "I didn't mean to j-j—"

"Jimmy the works for Johnny?" Colon asked. "Was that what you were going to say?"

"Yes, sir," Margaret said faintly. "Then I—I guess I must have realized how f-funny that w-w-w—"

"Would sound?" Colon tore at his ear. "It would have sounded funny at that. 'Jimmy the works for Johnny!' The language has limits, it seems. You can 'jimmy' the works for anybody but Johnny—or Jimmy. Those are forbidden."

He seemed to relapse into a brown study. Now Charlie saw how he tore at his fingernails. He put the nail of his thumb against the nail of his index finger and rapidly, as though he were wielding a miniature scythe, began slicing. A gentleman farmer.

To add to his entertainment, a clapping of hands was heard outside in the main office. Cries arose of "Three cheers for Mr. Hohaley." Several cheers, in fact, were tried out, but it is hard to cheer spontaneously in a large office situated in a legal building in the heart of a bustling downtown business section. Mr. Hohaley was merely walking through on his return from afternoon cocktails with a group of Lucille Turnbull's "contacts."

"That's Mr. Hohaley," Charlie said, somewhat superfluously.

News somehow had got abroad that Colon was in Gest's office. Perhaps Johnny had spread some wild tale that a man who said he was Colon had arrived in town to uproot this happy little heaven of employment in a jobless world. Perhaps that is why the Project workers cheered Mr. Hohaley as he passed. It may be that they saw him, at this critical time, as a sort of St. George, off to meet the dragon. At any rate, he made straight for Charlie's office. And in a minute a new atmosphere had entered. Greetings and salutations. Laughter. One story following another. Exchange of overly-enthusiastic bits of information on mutual friends and acquaintances. How odd that Jerry Blake, the big shoe executive, should have gone to school with Jonas B. Colon and yet should be one of Mr. Hohaley's most valued advisers now, a consultant on state government and business statistics! Et cetera.

How glad he was that Mr. Colon had found it possible to come in a day earlier! There was so much he wanted Mr. Colon to see here, so much there was to enjoy in our fair metropolis. The art museum this afternoon. There is a symphony concert this evening. Tchaikovsky! He wasn't sure whether the "Maestro" himself (Tchaikovsky!) would play with the orchestra, but it would certainly be worth hearing all the same. These Russians! And talking of Russians, there was a Bulgarian restaurant he had discovered (in the company of Pat Jarvis: "He's the Streets and Sewers Commissioner, Sir," Hohaley dropped casually); it is *the* place for visiting firemen! And the gypsy music is ravishing.

Off they went, Charlie with them, on what Mr. Hohaley was to refer to, even weeks later, as "a madcap round of cultural pleasures." A gigantic exhibition of Picasso paintings and concoctions was current at the museum at the time, and the city's intelligentsia and lovers of art were wandering through the galleries, making intelligent and art-loving remarks. In addition, there were hordes of school-children being led from picture to picture by their teachers, and their remarks, while conditioned by their guides' ideas of discipline and appreciation, were invariably derisive and incredulous. The pictures aroused their deepest antagonisms, and Mr. Hohaley, too, stared with abhorrence and disgust at these four-eyed ugly pre-Africans and other monstrosities that were supposed to be art. But Colon, who said that he knew Picasso personally, stopped long at each canvas, even at the things that were not painted but were pieces of wood and string put together like toys or models for machines, and explained them all in terms of the contemporary European consciousness, which (he reiterated with gloomy enthusiasm) was the sickest and the most sophisticated the world had ever known. And soon Charlie was amused and irritated to hear Mr. Hohaley join with Colon in denouncing the ill-mannered brats who were allowed to speak so loudly.

They went from there to the Bulgarian restaurant, and, strangely, the place was Bulgarian. And a gypsy orchestra did play. And the food was good. Satisfied that he was selling his guest the ever-present "bill of goods," Mr. Hohaley was actually enjoying himself. Charlie, who was beginning to understand at least the top layers of Hohaley's nature, saw that the habitual watchfulness had melted somewhat. He had long ago sensed that Hohaley thought he and Colon were old friends, acquainted long before there had ever been a Project. But it was part of the queer and almost insane atmosphere of the place that Hohaley had never asked Charlie the direct question on this point. He understood that Hohaley's impression must be derived from the fact that he was the only person in the state who had been hired through the Washington office rather than through him. And Hohaley's treatment now of Colon made sense in that light. He had Charlie down as an "artistic type" and therefore, since he was Colon's friend, Colon must be one of the same breed. Like Matson, he subscribed to the theory that *if, pull,* and *in* were the three mightiest words in the language. Charlie had never believed that this truly represented Matson's views, but he suddenly saw that Mr. Hohaley was compelled to believe in such a dispensation because of an inherent inability to conceive of man as being able and conquering in himself. While he ate his ice cream and the gypsies got hot under Carpathian woods, he examined the ramifications of this thought and the light it threw on the Project.

The concert too was very good. Unfortunately it was an all-Beethoven affair. Tchaikovsky's music was not even mentioned, let alone the news that the dead composer might be present. But, as Mr. Hohaley said, with a fine show of that petulance which cultured people often exhibit when deprived of their spiritual meat, one has to make the best of it—undoubtedly, later in the season, the proper compensation for the unforgivable switch would be made. It always was, he concluded philosophically, in Monroe. Which was a bit slow on its feet, but got there all the same.

During intermission they took a few turns around the lobby. Mr. Hohaley, who seemed convinced that he was making a great success with Colon, and also apparently fascinated with the unwonted abundance of cultural items in the conversational menu this afternoon and evening, drawled (drooled?) on in his fashion, commenting on this author, then that, going from one topic to another, interlarding the whole with sage comments on the state

222

of the theater in general, and conspicuously—by this time—avoiding all specific mention of the Project. Colon, who had all day seemed to be fascinated for reasons of his own, beginning with his encounter with Johnny Stephens, now began to sink beneath some load. Or so it seemed to Charlie. He suppressed a yawn once or twice. After intermission, while Artur Schnabel pounded the keyboard, he even looked at his watch several times. Charlie wondered if Colon considered Hohaley a "pansy." Once or twice, by a sudden startled look in Colon's eyes, Charlie thought that he did. But he himself was not so sure as yet. He was beginning to think Matson might be uncommonly right in guessing Hohaley to be a "perverted pervert." Sexless while wrongly sexed.

THE NEXT TIME CHARLIE SAW COLON WAS AFTER THE BANQUET the next afternoon. Because people are more or less the creatures of habit and have disciplined their appetites and dreams to different times and seasons, there are forms of madness that belong to the day and forms that belong to the night. But the madness of the banquet was no relief from the madness of the night before. It was indeed a logical continuation of it.

It was all the more madness because of the ritual manner in which the banquet was conducted. An insane associational idea in Charlie's mind: a miscarriage is being baptized, given a name!

One thing leads to another. . . . Ritual has meaning only in that it perpetuates in fixed forms truths of which it is symbolical. As the speeches lap over the mouths and lave the ritually filled plates, the question naturally presents itself: To whom and of what are the speakers speaking? At one set of tables sat the "hosts," at another set sat the "guests," the latter having come, presumably, to honor the former. But the "hosts" were too humble to lift their eyes and ate hurriedly and ill at ease, and the "guests" spoke only to each other, and exchanged verbal visiting cards during their speeches. The insurance broker says he approves of literature and takes a crack at President Roosevelt for something he did in the fiscal year last. The Mayor's representative admits that he neither approves nor disapproves of literature, literature not being in his line, but says that the Mayor stands four-square back of Roosevelt, and then—growing heated for a moment—tells how the organization went down the line in '32 and will do so again, God grant us more Democrats, in 1936. The rabbi recalls the religion of reciprocal goodness that flowered in Israel and soulfully passes on a few maxims. The Women's Club, through one of its many representatives, speaks feelingly for twenty-five minutes of Edgar Allan Poe and Longfellow and ends up with a twittering plea that we finally declare ourselves free of England. Speech follows speech. And finally, when all's said and done, nobody really knows what it's all been about.

Mr. Hohaley, of course, was immensely satisfied with the proceedings, and said as much each time he introduced a speaker. But Colon, whose own speech consisted of ten minutes of uninterrupted stuttering and interrupted audibility, sought Charlie out soon afterward.

"HOW MANY WRITERS WILL YOU NEED TO INSURE A BOOK IN a reasonable length of time?" he asked abruptly.

"At least six," Charlie answered.

"You'll have them. . . . Tell me, why is there only one Negro employed on the Project?"

"I don't know."

"You must know." His tone was sharp. "After all, you're Mr. Hohaley's assistant. Your name is signed with his to the reports you send me."

Charlie flushed. "The report you probably refer to states that there are not enough qualified Negroes in the city."

"Is that your personal opinion?"

224

"My personal opinion, since you mention it," Charlie said slowly, "does not necessarily coincide with my official one."

"I'd like to speak to you *personally*," Colon said. He flashed Charlie one of his smiles.

"All right."

"I don't suppose I need tell you how important it is that the Project nationally make a good showing before the next congressional appropriations?"

"No, sir."

"I thought not. Er, do I need tell you the real reason for my having come into town a day ahead of the schedule?"

Charlie looked at his troubled face. "No, sir. I think I can guess."

"There is something I may as well tell you now." Colon ran his fingers over his bald head and dropped them to his ear. "Mr. Hohaley is not exactly—how shall I say it?—a choice of my own for the position he occupies. He—" He saw that Charlie was smiling faintly. "You guess that too, don't you?"

"Yes, sir, I'm afraid I do."

Colon grew red. The sharpness came back to his voice.

"You're not a bad guesser, are you, Gest? . . . Well, my reasons again for coming into town earlier than I'd expected. Gest, I've been getting a series of complaining letters on this Project from all sorts of people. A Mr. Charles of the Racial League—do you know him?—"

"Yes, sir."

"—has been complaining that Negroes are not being employed on the Project. He says that there are many well-qualified members of his race available. But Mr. Hohaley (and your signature is on the reports too, of course) says that there are none. Now, are there or aren't there?"

"Speaking personally, as you've asked me to do," Charlie said, "I think there must be many qualified Negroes. I've taken a number of their applications myself. Matson has taken a number of others. I suppose you recall—in my own application—that I did not complete high school. Well, many of these Negroes were university graduates. It's kind of funny."

"Also, there was a man in Johnsburgh named Harkins. For some reason he was never employed. Mr. Hohaley informed me privately that he was some sort of troublemaker, non-acceptable to Johnsburgh people. I wrote Harkins myself subsequently for a report, and he never answered me. What about that?"

"It's a long story, Mr. Colon. If you like, I'll tell you all about it. I've been wanting to reopen that case for a long time. Harkins was no trouble-maker. They called him a Red. But his trouble really was that he tried being a democrat, *liberal,* in Johnsburgh."

"Would you be willing to send me a written report on Harkins?"

Charlie hesitated the briefest moment. "Yes, I would."

"You looked doubtful for a moment."

Charlie said nothing. Then: "That wasn't why I hesitated. I was thinking that—I'd hate to see the thing stop at a report."

"I see. Well, I don't blame you for feeling that way. From what I've seen of the Project so far, there's a thoroughly unhealthy atmosphere about it. . . . Now, for what I've been coming to. I want you to see one thing, Gest. I cannot promise that Harkins will be reinstated." He saw Charlie's face harden. "I can't answer for anything so far as Johnsburgh is concerned. After all, the President had to draw some parts of even *his* support from that city" ("That's what Harkins said too," Charlie thought), "and I am not the President. *But*—I must and shall see to it that—"

Charlie listened to what Colon said he must and would see to. It sounded nice. But Charlie had been over the ground too much in himself to be impressed until Colon said something specific.

"How would it be if—making the best of what is now a bad

bargain—the, shall we say, executive and editorial ends of the Project were to be completely divorced, except for the nominal control that Mr. Hohaley will continue to exert as Director, and you—as Assistant—be put in charge of the editorial end, answerable only to me?"

Charlie thought about it: "No, it wouldn't work out. As things are, the responsibility falls on Mr. Hohaley. If I'm sole Editor, the responsibility is mine. I can't guarantee any sort of a book with the kind of a non-relief staff we now have."

"I'll give you six writers. That's agreed. Yes? I'll expand your non-relief quota by that many."

Now Charlie began to look at him with some interest. This was specific. "Could we put them on right away?" he tested.

"Why not? . . . Look," Colon said, happy himself that things were going to turn out all right, "tell you what. I'm going to call a meeting this afternoon on the Project. I'll handle the whole thing. Just as though we haven't already talked this over. So don't be surprised at anything I say. You understand?"

(He's a bit batty too, Charlie thought. He suppressed some troubled misgivings.) "Yes."

"Now," Colon exclaimed. He struck his hands together with a conclusive gesture. "What suggestions do you have for the additional personnel?"

"Well"—Charlie hesitated, feeling vaguely uncomfortable— "I would—well, I would certainly suggest that, of the six, three Negroes be taken on. As to the other three, well, there's—to begin with—Hennessey to consider, in Swanseaville."

"He's the novelist, isn't he? Pulitzer Prize winner. Hmm. Do you know, Hennessey would have been my choice for Director if—well. . . . Who else, besides?"

Charlie did not welcome this confidential, almost off-hand, reflection on the novelist. The *if* that Colon propounded had nothing to do with him.

"I want you to know that Hennessey's a friend of mine. I

don't want you to think that I'm any more disinterested than Mr. Hohaley is—" This was foolish. He went on abruptly. "Then there's Mrs. Van Fern. One of the Four Hundred. She's contributed to several of the national mags. She can write. If she's interested in working on the Project, there's none better. And she"—he smiled—"is not a friend of mine. . . ."

"Mrs. Van Fern." Colon took the name down.

"And then there's George Folinger. He's an unemployed member of the Guild, writes book reviews. Helped Professor Blakey at the state university on research for a couple of books in social studies of some kind."

"George Folinger."

"Among the Negroes, I can't think of three of them off-hand, but there's Georgette Wilson." He stared at Colon. "She's a Ph.D. Used to be an editor of a Negro newspaper. A first-rate person. Came up to the Project once, asking for a job. I took her application. When I got through, I told her the usual mumbo-jumbo: 'We are well pleased . . . when the quotas are loosened up (I didn't tell her what had happened to the first quotas in the first place),' etc. . . . She just looked at me. Then she says, 'What percentage of your Project personnel at present are Negroes?' I could have lied to her. But I didn't see that I had to do that. I looked right back at her, and said 'a fraction of one per cent.' My telling her that was an act of friendship, strange as it seems, and she took it that way. I knew we were friends when she got up and left."

Colon's hand shook. He avoided looking at Charlie.

"Miss Georgette Wilson. Miss or Mrs.?"

"Miss, I think."

"Fine. . . . Er," Colon said, "about people like Johnny Stephens. You'll have to continue to put up with them. As editor, though, you'll be able to give them jobs where they won't interfere too much with the work."

"I'm glad," Charlie said simply. "I'd hate to see Johnny go—

228

even if it were to another Project. And putting up with him isn't hard at all. He's not a bad fellow, as I told you."

"I suppose you have others on the job who aren't, well—"

Charlie finished it for him. "Yes, a few. But one doesn't mind them at all, strange as it sounds." That had more of a patronizing than a strange sound, it seemed to him. "Every man has a right to live like a human being," he said. "Johnny has as much a right as I have. I don't set up as a judge. Cast the first stone. I mean that. But looking at the matter from the narrow point of view of a job that needs to be done, you get burned up over the people you can't get put on."

This also did not express the matter fully.

"I do set up as a judge," he muttered. "I judge myself when a person like Clyde Harkins"—Colon fidgeted—"or Georgette Wilson doesn't work, and I continue to do so."

Colon himself was in a mood for confession, now that the matter had been settled. "You have a wonderful thing like this Project put in your hands," he said. "You sit up nights, working out the finest thing that ever came to America. This isn't the only Project, you know. There are thousands. America will have, for always, things now that it never could afford: Hospitals, schools, roads, books, theater, most of all, a research, a consciousness and a possession of culture, of—" he broke off. "Paradoxical, isn't it? In the midst of a depression we are allowed to hand ourselves riches we could never *afford*. And then," he made an expressive gesture. "Politicians," he said, with a look of fastidious disgust. "Special interests. Corrupt business combines."

The persisting image of Clyde Harkins. Clyde was lost; Charlie was sure of it. Clyde had been so sure of it too. Colon had plainly sidestepped him, as out of his province and strength. Something occurred to Charlie that had been in the back of his mind, but which he had not been able to remember to ask.

"About that new arrangement," he said slowly. "Suppose,

after you leave, Mr. Hohaley decides not to like somebody's work, or the way he's getting 'co-operation'?"

"He can't 'dislike' it fatally without authorization from me," Colon replied. "Of course, you're referring to yourself?"

"To all members of the administrative and editorial staff to be. Negroes, for instance. He dislikes them almost as much as he dislikes a lack of co-operation."

Colon laughed. "One thing Europe taught me. One thing only, and that is: We can't let it happen here."

"How did it happen there?"

But Colon was suddenly moody.

"Let's not talk about it," he said.

BOOK THREE

PART SEVEN

On a day some three months later Mr. Hohaley called Charlie into his office, presumably for a conference on phases of a joint report on the work to be sent to Mr. Colon. Actually it was to sound him out on his attitude toward Matson. Charlie had known, almost from the beginning of the Project, that Hohaley disliked his friend, but this was the first time that he had actually brought this dislike into the open. It happened that Matson had lately been active in openly advocating that Project workers join a union that had been started; and Hohaley's hostility to the union, while veiled, could not be doubted. And so, was this an attempted killing of two birds with one stone?

"How do you figure Mr. Matson?" Hohaley asked, with all his casualness. He blew a ring of tobacco smoke. Watched it. Charlie saw Helen O'Hara watching it. As the ring began to dissolve, he blew a hard thin drill of smoke through it. As often before, Charlie wondered whether Hohaley had ever been on the stage.

"Well," he said. He found that he could be casual too. "He's a crack man, of course. He's only twenty-one, you know. A good reporter. As well as executive."

He looked at his cigarette. Frowned. It was as though he were thinking hard what there was to say bad about Matson, but holding back as yet. Your turn now, so to speak.

Actually, though, he was thinking. No, it couldn't be that Hohaley was trying to get at the union through Matson. Why not through him, for that matter? Hohaley knew that he had been among the first joiners. None of them had made any bones about it. Everything open and aboveboard, they had decided. Perhaps Hohaley would try getting at the union through both of them, one against the other. Charlie knew that "divide and rule" was a motto that Hohaley had translated into action before now. But, as he thought this, he knew that he was wrong. Regardless of how he felt about the union, Hohaley really was after Matson. And something had happened to make this the time. What?

Hohaley was thinking too. He had listened to Charlie's little summary of the subject under discussion with a bright look, the kind that makes itself smile to further the impression it seeks to convey that all this is really unimportant and one hardly knows why one is talking about it. As soon as something more interesting turns up to talk about, this look says, we will talk about that.

"I know about his record," he murmured.

He was really watching Charlie very closely.

"As to how I figure *him*—" Charlie began again. He was improvising as hard as he could. His peril, he felt, lay in this, that by Hohaley's silence and bright regard he was being forced to talk. The social game was being used to do business with here. He wants me to hit into Matson, Charlie was certain. And suddenly (he was not altogether sure of this, but he felt tremendously excited) he had an insight into Hohaley. It was not, however, he told himself, an insight that disposed of whatever thoughts he, Matson, and the others had had on the director. Rather, it pulled them all together and gave them a sort of coherence. Assume Hohaley to be—as they all did—an abnormal man, a womanish man, but a womanish man without womanly feelings or desires; in short, a perverted pervert (Charlie rather

234

liked Matson's phrase) or, to be perhaps even more exact, a perverted invert, then his mistake in sizing up the director had followed from his having thought of these "facts" in connection only with the director's sex life.

Good lord! The director had no sex life! The Project therefore had to be his sex life!

How simple when you thought of him that way! Imagine a man without talents or sympathy but—and this was important—a man also without sex, and then think of this man as one who conceives of himself as—you might say—a girl surrounded by her (would-be) lovers. But a girl who can never really take a lover, no matter how much she shops around—who for that matter can't possibly imagine what a lover is, and therefore can't imagine the various goals of love. Such a man (empty, empty—empty as an animated empty sack that strives to fill itself!) would have to be forever on the *play*, always playing one unhappy lover—in situations not of their own choosing, of course—against the other. And for what ends? Hohaley himself would never know. But as a sign to himself, he would never, could never, permit any to remain cold to him. *The play's the thing* in a way that Shakespeare never could have intended! As reward and punishment (this must be his sole political-sexual platform), he would favor only the ones who had been attentive. And so he could be, had been, fickle, cruel, capricious, exacting, irresponsible, and cunning—qualities you'd expect from a slut who was out to get and never to give, but hardly qualities you expected to find—even when they were shoved in your face, if you didn't have the key to the code—from an administrator, a *representative*.

So suddenly did this explanation of the vague, indirect, and arbitrary man strike him and so true (after the characteristic doubts of his own theories) did it seem on the instant, in the light of all that had happened on the Project, that Charlie could have laughed out loud in relief. God, how many times, in the

235

days and the months, had he wondered about Hohaley, investing his slightest nod, his most trivial aside, with the consequence and the gravity that his position *must* confer! Even after Colon had come and gone, and Hohaley had already revealed himself in a thousand instances, how Charlie had contrived—somehow, against all the facts—to imagine qualities in his superior that he could not as yet grasp. How he had tried to discern visions and plans that after all (even if he might not approve of them) must exist, disguising his growing suspicion that perhaps there was very little after all to grasp (as he just as suddenly remembered Matson had been prophesying all along). How he had sought to find in the ambiguous situation some subtlety superior to his own, sheltered and imprisoned as he had always considered himself to have been in mean streets and circumstances with tricky fancy as his only confidant and playmate! And now— God save the mark, the pound sterling, and the Turkish lira!— this *coyness,* this playfulness and—*sterility.*

So that's why the "division of authority" had not worked out —there had been nothing for it to work out against! Day in, day out, in a thousand ways that could not even be defined, Hohaley had made it impossible to work out. Even his attachment to Tremaine rather than to Colon and Washington was an instinct of self-preservation, not a knowledge and a plan. And no wonder then that Charlie—and through him Colon and the whole deliberate design—was defeated and frustrated. He could have fought Hohaley—he and the others had fought him, all along— but it was too hopeless a task; he was too conscious of defeat when it happened, but Hohaley was never conscious of it. Therefore, in the end, not so much by an exercise of will or of conscious guile but by the natural indulgence of natural instincts, Hohaley always got back what *words* had seemed to deprive him of. Charlie thought (or, rather, the scene flashed through his mind as a series of pictures) of Miss Wilson's complaint to him that here she was an editor of the Project, in charge of

Essays on Minorities and Folklore, and not allowed *to sit* at a desk on the Project! How could Mr. Hohaley know what such a denial meant for Miss Wilson? What to him could be her deep desire? Her passion? Her will to live? What did Hohaley know, what could he know, of desire, of true humiliation? From which, and many another thing, Charlie had come to understand that only force may successfully meet force. But Colon did not as yet seem to understand this. That is why, he told himself, he, Charlie, had joined the union, with his clearest conviction so far. Because in Hohaley's *position* was all of his strength. And Charlie had grown convinced of the futility of pitting *qualities* against that position. Let the union speak now.

Only in the light of the rot that his coyness covered did Hohaley's evident wish to find fault with Matson make any sense. It could have been nothing, after all, Charlie reasoned, that Matson had *done* that offended Hohaley. Matson (Charlie marshaled that insouciant worthy's rather solid abilities), for all his eccentricities and mannerisms, his spendthrift habits and his moocher's ease, was a most efficient person and a hard worker. His contact with the Project did not base itself on the same hopes as Charlie's, but that he had contact was undoubted. He knew more about some aspects of the Project by instinct than Charlie or anybody else would know after six months of study. And the workers had confidence in him, his sunny presence and general democracy being an office fixture that their morale needed.

No, not in anything that Matson had done resided Hohaley's grievance, for Matson was the best assistant he could have had. It was rather in what he had *not* done that Hohaley found fault. Matson was, perhaps, too "independent." He was willing to work sixteen hours a day for Hohaley, but not to "worship" him, even for a minute, nor to give him a millionaire's blank check of approval. He would not kowtow, unless it were a wide mocking bow, and mockery was death to Hohaley. Hohaley's prime requirement of his subordinates (if Charlie's theory was true) was flattery, and Matson did not fill the bill.

All this flashed through Charlie's mind as he groped for what to say, not knowing for a long instant what that would be. But his theory provided him with a cue. Hohaley did not want Matson's record. He wanted reassurance. If he could not get that, then he would want Matson's scalp. . . . So, then, draw a long bow and play the gentleman a love song.

"As to how I figure him—" He paused. Then continued, as though he had most seriously considered the unfortunate, who, plainly, had fallen from high grace. "To begin with, he's—at heart—very shy" ("at heart" and "very shy" were good platitudes to start off with, and you could go almost anywhere from there). "He's an orphan, you know. I imagine that he must have had a very tough time of it as a boy. Psychically, you understand. And—uh—you develop defense mechanisms. What can a little boy do who has no mother or father to run to when he's been hurt? And then an argument starts up with another kid, say. 'My old man kin lick your old man.' That stuff. Everything's been going fine until then. And here's the little boy, all of a sudden. The cat has his tongue. He has no father to lick anybody else's father. One imagines," he said, as though he and Mr. Hohaley were disinterested denizens of another, serener world, "that he learns to keep his own counsel. But you pay some sort of price for this. It all depends on the affliction, I suppose, what sort of cure you get in its place. At first you look as though you don't care that you don't have a father, and it follows that you act with your fellow-boys as though it doesn't matter that they do have them. Then, after a while, because the life of your emotions grows in and doesn't get expressed by all the thousand and one ways that the others have access to, one—the little boy— begins to imagine that there is no other sort of life. You see, there's a sort of atrophy happens to the boy. He gets to the point—after a while, of course—where he sees the relationship of what we call normal lives going on all around him, but they don't make sense. He's never had it himself. So he doesn't believe in them. It's make-believe. It doesn't exist."

Now that he was talking, simply talking, which is what Hohaley had been willing him to do, he kept on talking. As long as he kept on talking, he held Hohaley's little tricks on a leash and he protected Matson. At the same time, by his manner, he made it seem that he might be on Hohaley's side. And, in a minute, if Hohaley wished to carry this thing further, it would have to be his turn again to talk.

"What I'm getting at is" (if his theory about Hohaley was correct, it would show now in his reaction to this next statement) "that here is Matson, willing to serve, willing" (yes, he would say it, even if it went past what he'd intended) "to give his best, because he's been on the defensive all his life and giving his best is the only way he can prove his worth and show that he's equal to the others—in the mind of an orphan there is always an algebraic symbol which is called 'the others'— But, remember his background, he was never one to carry his heart on the outside of his shirt—"

As he shoveled all this nonsense at that smile that was still smiling brightly, he began to catch some fire from his own words. The bathetic little fiction he was erecting around his raucous egotistic jeering friend, he began to discover, to his eye-widening amazement, was actually credible. He smelled in it the odor—the not always very pleasant one—of truth. And also he saw that the hidden way he was taking to defend Matson's right to what might be salvaged and remodeled of an original purity of purpose was also a defense of his own. He grew self-conscious.

"And another thing. . . . A very important thing," he rushed on, "remember that he's been watching this world of 'the others' from the outside—or, if you like"—he played with the words, with the old protective desire to conceal—"looking *out* at it from his insides—and he only half-believes in it. Out there they make all the gestures of love, affection, sincerity, so forth. Okay, it's their privilege. But let them show these things exist. Let them come and prove it."

He wanted to add that if these things are proved, then the orphan comes rushing, melting with an ardor of love. That is what he had been leading up to, but the words stuck in his throat. . . .

And in a moment, when Hohaley saw that Charlie was through speaking, he spoke again. The bright hard smile had at no time softened.

"He's a strange young man," he said, as though musingly. Charlie saw that he was in the condition known in polite fiction as "foiled." But he did not grit his teeth.

Hohaley smiled sweetly: "Is there anything else to take up, Sir?"

By this Charlie knew that the "lovesong" had not been received. This did not change his theory of Hohaley. But it turned his thought back to Matson. That Hohaley was still after Matson's scalp was obvious. So it must be that the matter was more serious than he had thought. And something had been *done* after all. And now (and, as a matter of fact, even while he had been explaining his friend to Hohaley) little things about Matson—particularly of late—began to be remembered: The lad, as well as being precociously canny, was reckless. Add this to his love for intrigue, plus his dramatic flair (which gave him a tendency to "spring" things suddenly), plus his long-time opinion of the director, plus his feeling that Colon needed to be stirred up anew. . . . And?

"The signatures remain to be signed," Charlie said.

He watched the strong yet blurred profile bend over the pages of the report. In a page by-lining some of the work done by individual writers, Hohaley saw Johnny Stephens' name.

"Nice writer," he said indifferently. "Very nice."

240

"Yes, sir," Charlie said.

"How is Johnny, by the way? Haven't seen that gen'man in a coon's age."

Hohaley turned the pages, peering very carefully down paragraph headings. Let him look. The lies concerning the state of the work were all Hohaley's lies, and all here as he wanted them presented to Washington. The truth, according to Charlie's understanding of the truth and in keeping with the "division of authority," would be contained in another report. And it was up to Colon, not him, to do what he wished about these lies.

"Johnny's fine," he said. "Very nice fellow all right. He often speaks of you."

Hohaley affixed his signature to the end of the long communication. "Wonder why Johnny didn't keep up with the newspaper game," he murmured. "There was a newspaperman!"

Friend, now your teeth are showing. "He's a bit paretic," Charlie said calmly. "I thought you knew."

"Oh, is that why?" Hohaley recovered in an instant. "That's kinda dangerous, isn't it?" he asked, with that bright smile.

"No, not any more. Not when he gets to the stage he's in. . . . Unless the danger is to himself."

"Hmm. He never told me about that. . . . Well, he didn't need to tell me. I *knew*." He shot Charlie a keen sudden glance. "We live in a wonderful country, Mister Gest. Don't you think so?" ("Yes, I do," he wanted to say). "Which proves what I have always contended—that goin' off the deep end is not always a timely matter."

Charlie stared at him.

"For pareticism," Hohaley concluded, "which yesterday was considered dangerous and advanced, today is accepted."

MATSON HOWLED AND HOWLED. THE LAUGHING MUSCLES IN his long lean body went spasmodic and flapped him like a pancake.

"*Machiavelli* of the twentieth century! The intellect like a keen potato that put James Branch Cabell in his place!"

"I was supposed to start beating your breast in proxy and scream '*Mea culpa!*' "

Matson grinned, appreciating the form in which Charlie had put the question. "Your glass is empty. Phyllis, two more beers."

"Coming up. Two malt juleps."

"Man does not live on beer alone," Charlie said resentfully.

"He can try, can't he?"

"I knew a man once who went insane," Charlie said. "He thought he was a joke that had been laughed to death. He lay around in his padded cell all day long waiting for Eddie Cantor to resurrect him."

"You're a Jew, aren't you?" Matson said, seeming to change the subject.

"Yes. Why?"

The confirmation came out easily. He felt disinterested. At the same time, a shock of surprise at the question. It served to show how little—after all—even two such close friends as they had become could be sure of in each other.

"Tell me some more. Would you turn the other cheek if the first got smitten?"

"That's for Christians, isn't it?"

"Well, elucidate on one more. Would you sleep with a woman the second time who had laughed at you the first time?"

"I don't know." He watched the foam practicing the right of secession from the beer. He wasn't so sure now that Matson *had* changed the subject. "Men in glass houses, you know."

Matson was still smiling.

"Everybody has his own brand of ego. I bet you would sleep with her though. Act of queer charity. . . . But the point is, do you think I would?"

Charlie watched him affectionately, smiling now in his turn. Did such a question really ask for an answer? Was it intended as a question anyway? He guessed it was not. His interest in this conversation had awakened now with intensity. All he knew of Matson, he reflected, was what he had got from stray and quite accidental asides. Born in the coal area, from his accent. An orphan all right. He had seized on that last. It seemed to him that that fact was rather important in understanding him. Then, too, he remembered the squalid room in the Mexican quarter in which he had beheld Matson's first home here. . . .

"You know," Matson said suddenly, "it's amazing how close you came to hitting the nail on the head in explaining me to the boss. You turned on all the proper dials. There's a lot to you, old fruit. Not everything inside that skull is hair-roots. But you got the wrong station, all the same."

"I was just trying to kid him along. I wasn't really trying to get the right station. I just started turning the dials, as you put it, by mistake. And then I couldn't stop."

Besides, he wanted to add, you know best why I got the wrong station. Assuming that I did get the wrong station.

He shrugged his shoulders: "I'm a hit-and-miss driver without a car."

"Yes, but all the same. . . . Well, let me tell you something, my analytical friend. You weren't really talking about me, even if you came close. You were talking about yourself."

"That occurred to me too. There's more than one who wears the same size shoe. And everybody eats with his mouth."

"Did you really believe that this orphan Fauntleroy you were describing is just aching to be admitted to the happy family life, but is waiting for the tribal buggy to come and get him?"

"In a way, yes. Look how people can get you to do anything for them if only they ask you to. I think if they didn't ask you, you'd let them sit. Even if it was in open sea and a shark about to nibble on their butts."

"That's egotism. Not a high standard of love, as you're trying to imply. Everything I do is for myself. People are simply audience."

"Am I audience?"

"You're not me."

Charlie stirred uncomfortably. "I went through all that, if you don't mind my pulling the grandfather act. I ran away from home several times. It gets to be an old story. I don't know why I'm talking about it. There were times I wished I were dead, simply because the rest of the world was alive. I didn't see it that way at the time."

"You had a family. Let's switch to *real* families. That's why you were always coming back."

"That may be it. I'm denying nothing. You have no family."

"So you really think I'm an orphan. Boy, you got some distance to go yet. . . . That's where you went wrong. . . . I've got everything you made this little orphan boy *not* have. Parents. Cousins. Aunts. Uncles. I got the ugliest old man ever seen outside of a Neanderthal art collection."

"You're not making this up, are you?"

"Hell, no."

"Then why did you say a minute ago that the reason I always came back was that I have a family after all to come back to. Wouldn't that have worked for you as well?"

"No, it would not."

"Why not?"

"You'll grant that there are families and families—I think I'm being pretty specific?"

"If I begin to glimpse what you're driving at," Charlie said stiffly, "I'd suggest that perhaps you should be careful what you take for granted."

"Should I? Look. Underneath whatever might have ailed you —I take it you know what going without food means, and no coal in the house, and so forth—with all the natural quarreling and ill feeling that can come from that sort of conditions, you still *approved* of your family. You *liked* them. You liked the *kind* of people they were. The old man was all right with you and so was the old lady. . . . Your folks are still living, both of them, aren't they?"

"Yes."

"Well, I *didn't* like my—family. Do you know what that means? To live in a house with people who make you sick of being a human being?"

He gave Charlie a wild look. Then let out a guffaw and downed his beer.

"Hey, Phyllis, what's the matter with this glass?"

"It was full a minute ago."

"It's empty now."

"Another round?"

"This one's on me," Charlie said. "Give me a shot of bar liquor with mine."

"Beer coming up. Two malt juleps and half an inch of tonsilitis remedy."

"It's a language," Charlie said.

"Yeah," Matson jumped up and put a nickel in the phonograph. "You see, it's not the same thing as just being an orphan."

"Well," Charlie said, after a minute or two, "you did go *inside* —underground, so to speak, didn't you?"

"So far, so good. Yes. Sure. I told you, didn't I, that you did pretty well with what you had to work on. But I wanted you to get the rest of it clear. I'm not standing outside of anybody's door, waiting to be let in. I mean *anybody's*. There's nothing for me to see inside."

This was not as hard for Charlie to understand as Matson thought it was. "Well, you're as woefully honest as I thought you were."

"That's just a word."

True to form, though, Matson was still smiling. "I'll tell you something. Really, I despise our Reverend Hohaley. I've always despised him, from the minute I laid eyes on him. I despise Judge Williams. I shake hands with swine every day that I'd yank past me into a fire if I could." He drank his beer, grinning from ear to ear. "Well, what about you?"

"I find it hard to despise people," Charlie said. "It's a constant tragedy to know that you can only get at things (many of which I do despise) through people."

"Aha. I thought so. That's where I have the advantage of you. The war against the abstract will crucify you yet. Every time you get ready to plunge the knife at some concept of evil you'll see the whining human face and get full of pity. Then the whining little face will borrow the knife from you and give it back, right up to the hilt."

"There is no such thing as an argument," Charlie said. "When people grow intimate enough or are sufficiently tormented by each other, they exchange views, more or less impassioned. The argument itself is silent, and goes on ceaselessly in the individual between himself. Reasons are private things, like pimples on the back."

Matson laughed: "My state of orphanage is my soap to cleanse me. Ninety-nine and forty-four hundredths per cent pure. Good old orphanage. Good clean simple old orphanage."

Charlie remembered how the conversation had opened.

"There was something you asked about whether I'd sleep with a woman the second time who had laughed at me the first time," he suggested. "Were you using that as an—*abstraction,* or did it—?"

"Happen? No, it hasn't. But I still have my own brand of nightmare. I dream that I go to bed with a beautiful woman and I'm impotent. Then I roam around the street—it's always at night—wondering if I have the courage to go back. I've dreamed it so often that sometimes I believe it's actually happened. I want to ask people what *they* would do. You're the first one I've really asked. As you know," Matson said slowly, "I don't believe in asking questions."

"I'm not a psychiatrist. I have nightmares myself. Who doesn't, I suppose."

"I bet there's a knife mixed up in yours."

Charlie stared. He thought of his recurring vision of his mother standing over him while he slept, with a knife raised in her hand, her bloodshot eyes waiting for his to open so that she might let her hand fall. He kept quiet.

"You know what Caesar said," Matson whispered, in a hoarse stage voice that he purposely let carry all around the drab little saloon in which they found themselves, " 'Yon Cassius hath a lean and hungry look. Such men are dangerous.' That's me. Cassius Matson. And Brother Hohaley—he's my Caesar, actual and abstract."

The waitress was looking over. A couple at a far table, looking up, met Matson's gaze. Confused, they grinned foolishly.

"Not that I hold a brief for Caesar," Charlie said, "but that I find it necessary to remind you what happened to Cassius. But not only to Cassius. Seriously, don't you think that Cassius was a bit of a stinker?"

"I guess you think that Brutus was noble. Surrounded by evil men, huh? As well as warring with them. Sure you do. I almost forgot that you're one of those guys who tilt at *things*."

He looked over at the couple, hoping to annoy the man by catching his girl's glance. They were both looking down.

"Ye Gods, Phyllis," he roared. "I *told* you there's something the matter with these glasses."

"Two more coming up," she said, wearily.

"It occurs to me," Charlie said coolly, "that 'Brother' Hohaley is not so much your Caesar as he's your 'beautiful woman.' A version, anyway," as Matson began a violent derisive gesture. "Yes. Really. How the great man would be flattered to know that he inspires such feelings—even if only in dreams. Don't you think?"

247

"That bag of fat? That continent of pus?"

"*That* bag. *That* continent. . . . Listen. Don't you think we've come to where we ought to have some pretty plain talk on the subject?"

Matson, after the initial gesture of disgust, seemed to be thinking very hard. Now his face lit up with a delighted smile. He seemed very pleased of a sudden.

"Hell, Charlie, that's not bad! You're full of noodles, but I like how you talk. He stretched himself, with imperial instancy. "I feel fine. Jesus, let's get out of here. Let's walk."

"You goddam exhibitionist."

Matson, outside, put his arm around Charlie's shoulder. Because of the difference in their heights, their steps were disproportionate and their sides jarred briefly before they had made the necessary and mechanical adjustments in their gaits. In that moment of shifting balances, Charlie got a sensation from his companion of exposed ribs. An association flashed in his mind of a picture he'd once seen of starving war-babies staring out of the print at the well-fed faces of those—an ocean apart—who stared back at them. The hungry fellow! The contact had given him more understanding of Matson than hours of conversation would. In helpless comradeship, his eyes filled with tears.

"As to *hunger*—I believe you understand me—" he muttered, " 'family' or no 'family,' we all have our hungers. . . . As I've told you, I thought at first that Mr. H. was gunning for you because you're active in the union. But, I don't know, maybe I'm wrong. Your telling me about the 'beautiful woman' gives me a clue I've needed" (he began to smile again) "in getting your full number. Matson, listen, you're really a disgraceful dog. If you could have made it with him, the flesh-pots he stands for, you'd be the biggest reactionary on the Project today. At that, I knew what you were trying to do all along, clue or no clue—"

Matson swaggered as he walked and talked. "Go on, you bastard, say it!" he roared. "I tried to lick in with Hohaley and

248

Judge Williams and Jim Hudson and Henry Jevins—by telepathy, that one—and you're right. I did. You knew it all along. And you also knew that I wouldn't make it. How did you know that?"

"I've told you before." Charlie smiled. "You're too fastidious —really—to go where you're not truly appreciated and honored. See, I haven't said that you were too noble. . . . As to your 'beautiful woman,' all joking aside—let's say that that image stands for your—uh—boyhood, which was awful, for it returned blows for kisses. Since which—I've found you out, my bold buc- caneer—you've, to say the platitudinous, shrunk from life every time you've had to come in contact with it again, seeing in it— under the appearances—the beautiful, cruel, laughing woman. . . . Don't tell me I'm talking about myself again," he con- cluded. "Of course I am. I'm doing that too. I only hope that I haven't overtipped the balance too much that separates us and talked a little more about myself than about you."

"Grant that Hohaley's my Caesar—may this tongue be wrenched from its place for such blasphemy—and I'll allow that you've been talking—or trying to—about me. But there are still one or two points in addition to that."

"Yes?"

"First of all, you do have a family. You're anchored. I'm not. That's not a virtue in either one of us, but each of us has to make it a virtue. Secondly, and maybe because of this first, maybe not, you have a faith in Colon and in ultimate rightness (not that the two are necessarily to go together) which I don't have. Thirdly, you think of us as a Work Project and I think that it must be a Relief Project. All those make for real differences. Fourthly— and don't shake your head and get modest about this—you're an artist and I'm not; because of it, you're basically calm and sure of yourself; only circumstances can be wrong for you. Whereas me—"

Charlie smiled bitterly. He wasn't sure whether he admired or hated Matson: "I'm getting a little tired of this. I mean *tired,* literally. Tell me one thing now, no more. Why did you join the union?"

"You're a bit behind the times. I've also joined the Communist Party."

"Why?"

"You had something to do with it. So did Hennessey. Hohaley too."

"All right. Now the real reason. Why did you join?"

"Revenge on the 'beautiful woman' for making it impossible for me to live without blindfolding my ears."

"*Revenge* is a word you're going to have difficulty with in the Party."

"Chavin, over at Party Headquarters, said the same thing. Shall I tell you what I told him?"

Charlie was silent.

"I told him that each of us has his *true* reason for joining, regardless of what *sounds* good. Chavin himself talks about the masses, but he also talks just as much about the drabness of *living*, the way he had wasted his life up until he changed it. Well, I ask you. Then there's the case of George Dobbington, a colored fellow. Say, that one's right up your alley. You want to hear it?"

"If you want to tell it."

"Well, he *thought* that he had two kids. He really had *one* kid. George, before he joined the Party, was a Catholic. And the first kid that he was *going* to have, he couldn't afford it, so he had his wife get an abortion. So then he gets a job and his wife tells him she's going to have a second kid and he says Okay, go ahead. So she has this kid, and they go have it baptized. So that involves conversation with the priest.

"So, one thing and another, the priest gets a hold of them and they start going to church again. And then—now this is where you're going to find it interesting—this young fellow, when the kid comes along, loses his job and his wife gets one, and he stays home to take care of the kid. And he takes care

250

of this kid for about six months and all this time he's brooding over why doesn't *he* have the job and his wife stay home to take care of the kid. And, at the same time, he is getting very fond of the kid and getting so that he wants to stay home and take care of him. But they continue going to church and the priest talks of this and that, and one day he comes onto the subject of abortions and he says that abortion is murder. The Catholics, you know, believe that when a man drops it in, he should mean it. Can't say I disagree with them on this point. Not exactly—

"Anyway, the priest says abortion is murder and this young fellow (remember, he's out of work and doesn't like it, but at the same time it's given him the opportunity of growing fond of his kid), he starts thinking about it, and he starts to wondering what this other kid would have looked like if, instead of being aborted, it had been allowed to live. *Allowed* to live! Get it? And he finds himself giving the kid that was not allowed to live a *name,* and a *sex,* and fixing him up with all the details that go to make a person alive and not *just* a name. But the matter doesn't rest there.

"Dobbington comes to the priest, and he tells him, 'Father, here's how it is with me. Every time I give Marvin'—that's his *living* kid's name—'his food, I wonder whether *Johnny* (Johnny!) is hungry. Every time I change Marvin's diapers, I wonder whether Johnny's diapers are wet. And one time I let Marvin go unchanged and he started crying. And I let him cry, because *I wanted to imagine how it was with Johnny,* unchanged and unfed, just lying around somewhere, my baby, and with no one to look after him. No one to take care of him, you understand, and his immortal soul perishing for lack of love.' "

Charlie accepted the cigarette thrust at him.

"Ask George the reason he joined the Party," Matson said, "he'll tell you it's to lift the masses. That sounds good. But the real reason is that he's taking revenge on a loving Church that calls him a murderer."

251

"Somebody's going to pay for that lost kid of his," Charlie said.

"So you agree with me," Matson said.

"I didn't disagree with you in the first place. Not on your reason for joining." The story, which had fascinated him, left him unnerved, and he felt that the victory was with Matson. "What revenge are you taking on Hohaley?" he asked. "You see, we're back at the beginning again."

"I can't tell you," Matson said, with his old smile. "You're not a Party member. You'll just have to wait until the union meeting and hear it at the same time everybody else does."

"I take it that you've told Chavin."

"Yep."

"You didn't join for revenge. You joined out of a frustrated dramatic instinct." He tried a shot in the dark. "Have you told the whole story of your revenge to Chavin?"

Matson's triumphant smile answered him.

"I thought not. Comrade Lone Wolf No-Collaborator Matson. . . . Oh, yes, why did you—ask if I'm a Jew?"

"Because I like you, fella."

"Come again?"

"Well, I was raised in a community that hated Jews. I thought I'd hate Jews myself if I ever met them, along with hating everybody else. So when I met you, I looked to see if I'd hate you. I didn't. By which I knew—my grinning and skeptical gargoyle—that I was at last free of the abstract."

THAT NIGHT AT THE MARTIN HOTEL, WHERE MATSON'S ROOM was being used for the union's third meeting, was a different sort of a scene.

Lucille Turnbull stood at one door to the hotel and a man named Regan, obscure and silent until this night, stood at the other. They warned Project workers against entering.

Charlie came in from the side that Regan occupied.

252

"Hello, Regan."

"You're making a mistake going in there, Mr. Gest."

In his hand Regan held a notebook. A pencil was stuck between an ear and his head.

"What're you doing with all the stationery?"

"We're taking down the names of everybody that comes through here after I have wasted my good breath in warning them to stay away."

"That wouldn't be part of your Project duties, would it?"

"This aint on the Project, Mr. Gest. This is an entire different thing."

"It is? How?"

"Well, sir, the way I figure it—it's the decent element on the Project against a bunch of Reds and troublemakers who are trying to cause trouble for it through the union."

Charlie had the peculiar feeling for a moment that all this was the weird re-enactment of something that had happened before. Like a neon sign which has come to the end of its insanity and, in a flash, has gone back to repeat itself. Then he remembered that he had read just such conversations in magazines, in articles describing the formation of other unions.

"You were at the meeting at the Project today, weren't you?" he asked.

"Sure I was. Everybody was."

"Did it seem to you—really seem to you—that Francis was a troublemaker?"

"He's in the union, isn't he?"

"Mrs. Van Fern is in the union. She's in the Social Register. Is she a troublemaker?"

"If she's in the union, she is."

"And Hennessey. Do you realize that he's one of the most distinguished men in this state? And Matson's in the union. He's Assistant to Mr. Hohaley."

Regan compressed his lips.

"And I'm in the union. Do you really intend to take my name down when I walk past you?"

"Them's my orders."

"Who gave you your orders?"

Regan stared. Familiarly, he allowed a jeer to appear on his face.

"You heard Mr. Hohaley speak at that meeting at the Project. You heard him say that anybody wanted to join the union had a right to do so. Didn't you?"

"You ain't fazing me," Regan said, with apparent irrelevance.

"Did you know that Jonas B. Colon is a member, a *dues*-paying member, of the Civil Workers Union?"

"If he was to walk past this door, I'd take his name down too."

"And Franklin Delano Roosevelt, who's the Father of the New Deal like Washington was the Father of our country, and who wrote into the New Deal labor's right to join unions, suppose he walked through these doors?"

"It would get my name in the paper to take *his* name down."

Charlie saw that he was being laughed at. But there was no doubt of it, Regan was in dead earnest all the same. Charlie walked through the door and crossed the lobby. Lucille Turnbull turned at his approach.

"Hello, Mr. Gest."

"Hello, Lucille."

Her eyes were as shiningful as when he had first met her, and she was as anxious and meek. Little lamb, who made thee?

"Doing business, Lucille?"

"Well," she said, "we can't allow this to happen to dear Mr. Hohaley. After he has shown us how good and kind he is."

At this point, Alice Menenbaum came in through the door. Lucille's face turned red. Alice was the only Jewish girl on the Project. She was a typist.

"Don't go in there," Lucille screamed.

The sudden transition from meekness to hysteria and screaming startled Charlie more than anything else could have done. He stared. Alice gave them a scared look.

"Go jump in the lake," she said, gulping.

"I'm taking your name down. You'll lose your job for this."

"Can they do that, Mr. Gest?" Alice asked.

"I don't think they'll be damn fools enough to try it."

"Yes, she will lose her job," Lucille screamed. As she encountered Charlie's eyes, she smiled at him and immediately her face got red again. "I'll see to it that she loses her job. She won't get away with it, she won't get away with it."

"Go jump in the lake," Alice said, and ran past her.

Bellhops stood about, gaping. Guests were starting up out of their seats in the lobby.

"She's a Red," Lucille announced loudly to them and to the lobby in general. "Don't let her get on the elevators. She's a Red."

By this time, Matson (who had been upstairs in his room), had received the report of those who had already arrived, and had gone to see the manager. With him, he appeared in the lobby. The manager was very much disturbed.

"You'll have to clear out of here, Miss," he told Lucille. "We can't have this sort of thing going on in the hotel."

"Beat it, for Christ's sake," Matson said savagely. "Don't make a damn fool of yourself."

To Charlie's surprise, Lucille—at the words of command— burst into tears and immediately left.

They all crossed the lobby to where Regan stood.

Regan was talking to Mrs. Van Fern and Hennessey, who had just entered on his side. Or, rather, Mrs. Van Fern was talking to Regan.

"Aren't you ashamed, a grown man like you, playing peek-a-boo when you should be attending to your own business?"

255

Regan was saying loudly that he wasn't going to argue with a lady. Hennessey stepped up close to him.

"My name is Hennessey. Yours is Regan. So you'll understand me. How would you like to find a Mickey Finn parked in your left eye?"

He wasn't really angered. The statement asking Regan how he would like a Mickey Finn in his left eye was a steal from one of his own novels, *In Streets of Home.* He was having as much fun as he could out of the situation, considering his real horror at the intimidation being employed here.

But Regan didn't know this. He saw Hennessey advancing on him, and threw himself into an attitude of self-defense. As Hennessey concluded his remarks, Regan—to everybody's amazement but his own, for he had calculated his distance carefully— threw his right hand at Hennessey's chin with all his force. Hennessey, a gentle soul who was always surprised to know that there are fists in the world, received the full charge of it, and fell flat on his face. The victorious Regan, seized then by the manager and a bellhop, allowed himself to be escorted outside.

"I never seen a Jew yet could fight," he asserted loudly and maintained his ground after the hotel men had released him.

Matson approached him.

"My name is Ginsburg," he said. "Take this."

He landed a haymaker on Regan's chin, but Regan did not fall. Matson, though tall, was too light for his punch to be really effective. Regan staggered and, recovering, advanced toward this new foe. Charlie and the manager hurtled forward and grabbed him.

"You bunch of kikes," Regan howled, striving to release himself.

Matson hit him again. Charlie, feeling that this wasn't fair, released his hold on Regan so that he could hit Regan too. In a minute the sidewalk was the center of flailing fists. In the end Regan went down. A stubborn and serious-minded fighter,

256

he was simply outnumbered and could not withstand the multiple assault. He got up, breathing heavily and holding his nose.

"You busted it," he said.

"Let's see," Matson said.

Regan obediently took his hand away. Matson hit him, square on his nose. Regan went down. Matson yanked him to his feet and hit him again. Charlie grabbed Matson.

"For Christ's sake, Lloyd, leave him alone."

"Let me get at him."

"You'll have to fight me then," Charlie said.

For a moment, the two friends faced each other. Then Matson laughed. "Okay." He went back into the hotel, and Charlie, after a glance at Regan, followed him. The glass door swung to behind him on a sea of gaping awed inhuman faces.

"NO USE WAITING FOR ANY MORE PEOPLE, IS THERE?" MRS. VAN Fern asked. Her voice shook slightly. She spoke to nobody in particular.

Matson glanced briefly at his watch. "No, I don't think so," he said. Decisively then: "Shall we get on with it?"

"God, yes!"

There was a general gravity in the air, as though a momentous thing were about to happen. Here we go, was the secret feeling. Conspiracy! The dark word! The recent conflict gave sharp edge to the electric mood which vivified them all, yet kept them stern-faced, thin-lipped, almost apprehensive. None of them could have any doubt as to the true author of Lucille's and Regan's presences outside the hotel this evening. The dejected figure of Hennessey, sitting on the edge of the bed, still dazed, was an uncanny and somewhat comical reminder. . . .

"I suggest then," Matson said, "that we get the necessary business out of the way. After that," he grinned broadly, "one of our members will have a startling set of photostated letters to lay be-

257

fore the union which will be of the deepest interest and will indicate where one of our first major tasks will lie."

"Well"—Charlie had a very good idea who that member would be—Matson said, "first then, nominations."

"Gest for president," George Folinger said.

It was an ironic circumstance that the six non-relief people hired at Colon's instigation three months ago were among the first union members.

"Second," said Mrs. Van Fern.

"That ought to be out," Matson said. "The head of the union ought to come from humbler beginnings."

Laughter. Charlie would have joined in the laughter, but he was thinking of those certain photostated letters to be presented to the union after the preliminary business had been gotten over. What those letters were about, he had no idea; would they mark the beginning of Matson's "revenge"?

"I'm chairman tonight," Miss Wilson said, "but, if I may be permitted to nominate, I'd suggest Francis." Dan Francis was the only field worker present, as Alice was the only typist. "Electing a field worker is a good symbol. It'll serve to remind you that this is not a union of editors and supervisors, in spite of the ten editors and supervisors present tonight, but of all the workers."

In this, all concurred. It glossed over the fact that the union had failed to attract the rank-and-file workers so far.

Francis rose to the acclamation. He was a tall handsome chap, about forty-five years old. A bit of a mystery. Why should he have been alive enough to "issues" that the overwhelming majority of the workers did not even see? (To say that they were all kept away from the union by fear was evading the question, Charlie thought.) You did get the idea though that Francis knew what was going on.

"Thank you very much," he said. "I'll do my best to make a good president."

He sat down. Charlie caught his eye. Both smiled. Francis had the look of one who never fails to see the humor in a situation. It took nothing from the quiet manliness with which he confronted one.

"For vice-president?"

They were all unanimous for Folinger. And unanimous again for Mrs. Van Fern for secretary-treasurer. She declined. Unanimity again, then, for Georgette Wilson. This, with a brief report on dues, a union constitution, and dues-books concluded the business.

Everybody was glad. The fist fight, the unspoken things in the general air, made them unfit just now for details.

"And now," Miss Wilson said, "the main item. I know you've been waiting to learn what it is. I was hoping there'd be more of us. Matson?"

Matson, who had been waiting for this call, took a stand in front of his desk. Flourished with a key. Opened a drawer, drawing attention to the fact that it had been locked. Then, with a sheaf of papers in his hand, made his way to the bed. "Gangway here," he ordered.

Expecting they knew not what, everybody cluttered close to see what he had to disclose.

"As a fortifier," he held back, "don't you think I ought to order up some drinks first?"

"Oh, come now," Mrs. Van Fern shrilled, "let's have it, for goodness sake!" Her nerves were on edge. "Don't act like a silly pup!"

Matson gave her a look full of malice. It reminded Charlie how a common action can draw together the most diverse sorts of people, giving their action the outer aspect of harmony and mutual purpose. He knew that the two detested each other. They differed on practically all things. Mrs. Van Fern, when she didn't like the coffee or food served her in a restaurant, had been known to march back to the kitchen and tell the chef how it should be made. Matson, who kidded waitresses mercilessly, considered such an action intolerably vulgar and brazen, "just what you might expect of well-bred people!" Mrs. Van Fern had her opinion of anything Matson might do.

It's a moral universe, no doubt of it. Every man his own Jehovah on small matters. On the big jobs, they choose sides and pick a big Jehovah.

"I am very sorry, Mrs. Van Fern," Matson said, his tone icy, while he winked—in the lady's full sight—at all the others, "I forget that while others take nine months to get born in, you were in a hurry and did it all in three days."

Before Mrs. Van Fern's mouth, which had instantly opened, could close and deliver fitting words in answer to this, and while her flush was still on the mount but had not reached its peak, from which it must recede before she could find speech, Matson divulged the contents of the letters and, in an instant, interest was solidly with him and the quarrel had passed.

"I have here the photostated evidence," he pronounced, "that Mr. Hohaley, after having collected divers sums of money from the Project workers—including some of the do-nothing and nondescript crowd here assembled—and not once, you may recall, but thrice, three times, to the tune of two dollars apiece each time, did, with or without malice, complainant stateth not, put the sums of money to his own use, and did not pay the hotel for the repast for Brother Colon and the half hundred parasitic notabilities who were our guests, for which purpose the lucre had been collected in the first place."

He put the first document down neatly in the center of the bed. "Read," he commanded. No further urging was necessary. They read in a state of dull incredulity, and yet—as it had struck them what Matson was saying—they knew they believed it implicitly. It was a letter to the hotel. An answer, it was instantly apparent, to a dunning note.

Dear Sirs: Your letter of the 14th received and wish to state that there will be some necessary delay before the obligation of our Project to your hotel can be consummated. As you are no doubt aware, we are a Government agency and must comply with many Government regulations before sums of money for special purposes can be released. Our debt to your hotel is a sum of money for a special purpose, according to the Government treasury. Sincerely,

Here followed the signature and title of Mr. Hohaley in typing, and under it the facsimile of his handwritten signature.

"Observe the date on that letter," Matson said. "It corresponds to a date soon after he had made the *second* collection—when he said the first collection hadn't been large enough. The obvious implication is that he was spending the dough as fast as he was collecting it."

Mrs. Van Fern was the first to speak.

"A crook!"

The word hit Charlie with the force of a blow. His first reaction amazed him. He felt an urge to jump to Mr. Hohaley's defense. At the same time, he was sharing in the generally festive atmosphere that instantly developed.

"We've got him," Folinger shouted, passing a verdict. "Of all the hypocrisy—

"That money was our 'job insurance,' " Matson said gravely. "A smart bit of business."

"We ought to march right up to his house and confront him with this," Mrs. Van Fern said.

As wildly excited as any of these angry and frustrated people who suddenly found themselves, by a turn of events they could not instantly comprehend, to be in possession of an offensive weapon, Charlie still—at Mrs. Van Fern's last words—found himself disliking her for what seemed the smugness they revealed. Was smugness called for? Not that he had hoped that the fight would be on what some might call a "noble" plane, but that the misuse of the money simply seemed to him pathetic

261

rather than anything else. No, *pathetic* was not the word. A word somewhat grosser and less "sympathetic" than that was needed. The revelation showed a *fallibility* on Mr. Hohaley's part that was almost sickening, even while it remained the most satisfying and dramatic proof of what Charlie had long suspected in him. In sight of victory, Charlie felt revulsion. He was troubled with the thought that Mr. Hohaley might be a human being after all.

But, immediately, and at the same time, he turned his anger on himself. What a weak little bastard he was, to be sure! For what—after all—had he expected the breach in the director's *front* would look like? Even the mighty and all-powerful Tremaine—what would his downfall, when and if it came, look like? A rotten tale, no doubt, of income-tax evasions on dollars made up of the pitiful nickels and dimes of old men and orphans!

What difference, then, that Mrs. Van Fern was smug, even that Matson was smug, Matson more than she? Matson's owing money was not the same thing as Hohaley's owing money. It's all in the circumstance, he told himself, and what he had thought was instinctive sympathy for Hohaley as a human being was nothing but the last and capping stage, finally, of disillusionment, *disgust!*

He looked at Matson almost humbly. Matson's remark that he, Charlie, warred with the abstract but would always withhold the knife at the sight, close up, of the "weak pitiful face" came back to him. How right Matson had been!

"That's only Exhibit A," Matson was saying. "Please note the date on this subsequent entry. From the hotel, three weeks later."

It read:

Dear Mr. Hohaley: We feel that we have been most patient in regards to the unsettled bill for $210 which exists between us. We should appreciate immediate receipt, etc., etc., etc.

"And here," Matson said, "is his answer to it." He flourished another letter, and immediately put it aside and showed the last in his pack. "Now, mark this well. This one's the pay-off. It's dated just one week ago. Still from the hotel. The bill—after a third collection was made for it—is still unpaid."

"Well," Hennessey said, getting up suddenly and walking nervously to and fro, "what are we waiting for? Let's go out and crucify him."

There was a miserable and angry undertone to his voice. It brought everybody up short. Charlie then realized that scruples such as he'd been having had been passing through other minds. But Matson took the statement as a personal attack. Charlie saw him in one of his rare angry moods.

"Excuse me, I thought the idea was to get him!"

Silence. Crudely put, that was the idea.

"What's wrong with crucifixion?" Matson asked. "Crucifixion —after all—isn't it just a form of execution? And when we formed ourselves into a union, wasn't that in effect a sentence that we'd passed like a vote—to turn a man out of office?"

"To put it more simply," Georgette Wilson said, "isn't it a question of us 'getting' him or him getting us?"

She didn't have to, of course, but she gave a ten-minute resume of conditions on the Project to prove that it was just a question of time, if Hohaley were unchecked, before he'd be sniping them off, one at a time, beginning with those of them he didn't like for personal reasons.

"You know all this," she kept saying every other sentence, getting more excited as she went along. "Who was it said that the price of liberty is eternal vigilance?" Without pausing for an answer, she went on: "Elections have come off already. Roosevelt has come in again. We're the ones who brought him in. But like in '32, the 'state gang' came in with him. Landslide stuff. And there's where the danger is. But this time, the Tremaine boys have another whole four years ahead of them, instead of—as just before elections—a few measly and insecure months. And they won't be satisfied this time with only Johnsburgh and half the state capital as their bailiwick. Look at the newspapers. They are

263

reaching out for Monroe, and they'll get it too perhaps. And everything in between. And they are more than getting the Projects. So far as *this* Project is concerned, Mr. Hohaley is still going through the motions of consulting Washington—"

"I've heard it rumored that they're going to move the Project to Johnsburgh," Folinger said.

"Down at Racial League there is proof that layoffs nationally are coming," Georgette said.

"Hohaley is still plowing his plantation the same way, sleet or snow!"

Matson broke in, through a rising tide of feeling against Hohaley. The lean fellow still rankled at the word *crucifixion*.

"You're a bunch of simpletons. All of you. One side arguing about crucifixion. The other about the rightness of crucifixion. And giving yourselves 'character-testimonials!' I don't see the matter either way. It's not a moral question at all. Squeamishness in this case is plain stupidity. Shows a deficient intellect, not a fine thirst for either justice or vengefulness. As I see it, there's a war on between two sides. And we're on the side our bread is buttered on. The bread of our bodies, but also the bread of our self-esteem. Do I really have to keep on talking?"

You know all this, do I have to keep on talking! Both Matson and Georgette kept on saying this, Charlie thought. Right. No need for anybody to talk. Move, Charlie thought, savagely of a sudden, get the bastard out!

Francis had lifted his hand, diffidently, in the manner of a schoolboy.

"Yes?" Matson said.

"I aint—am not—a writer," Francis said, smiling, looking around pleasantly from one to the other, "so maybe I shouldn't be talking here at all—"

"Go ahead," Matson shouted. "Go ahead. Go ahead." He sensed that the matter was swinging his way. "For Christ's sake," he roared, "you don't have to be a writer to talk. I'm not a writer either. I'm a low scoundrel."

"All right, Matson," Miss Wilson said soothingly, as though she were his champion and saw eye to eye with him and would protect his point of view. "Yes. Let's hear it, Mr. Francis."

Everybody made ready to listen to Francis, who had said nothing before or after his short speech of acceptance of the union presidency. They were prepared to give his words a maximum importance. He was a rank-and-filer, a sort of Project worker few of these editors and supervisors flattered themselves they really knew.

"Well, I'm not a good speaker either," Francis continued. "I won't make a speech. There's just several things was occurring to me. I'll just sort of pass them on. . . . First of all, I got nothing against Mr. Hohaley *personally*. But if he had on us what we got on him, he would certainly use it—"

"That's true!"

"If you don't think he's gunning for us anyway, just look at Mr. Hennessey's face where Regan—excuse me, Mr. Hennessey —landed on it. . . . If not for Hohaley, Regan would have been at home tonight instead of out front. Another thing. I aint heard nothing on *this* point. Who *is* going to pay the hotel bill? Will we have to pay for it all over again? Well, I don't think so. He wouldn't have an excuse any more to ask for money. Well, will the Government pay it, like he tells the hotel?"

He stopped and smiled around at everybody.

"It's my guess that nobody is paying this bill until somebody is forced to pay it. I don't know how well you have figured out this Mr. Hohaley. I have been doing a bit of figuring out myself. It seems to me that he is the sort of a person who will always delay a thing until it is too late. But we have got a obligation to protect ourselves. He is the sort of a person whom I used to meet now and then when I was a traveling salesman. There was one fella, had a store on the road, he was always out of this and that and always *going* to order it the next time. But when a customer came in, he never had it. He wasn't a bad fella, and I aint saying that Mr. Hohaley is a bad person. Let's say he is a *careless* person. After this fella went broke that I'm telling you about, they found out that he owed everybody money. He was always going to pay it back too, but he never did. And naturally, over a length of time, his *personal* credit suffered."

"But if he never paid his bills, he should have had lots of money," Mrs. Van Fern objected, "even if he didn't have any customers."

"Well, you see, Ma'm," a dimple appeared incongruously in Francis' handsome face, "it would seem so. But that's the trouble with careless people. He didn't have any money either because he had spent it all on a little blonde girl in the next town." (A suppressed snicker from several people as they thought of Hohaley and a girl.) "You got to take such a thing into account. . . . Well, what I'm trying to get at is, that we don't have to think is he a crook or just careless, or whether we are being Christians or otherwise in this matter. *We're* not the ones who reneged on the hotel, *he* is. And we're not the ones who are going to make trouble, the *hotel* is. The way I see it is, if a man was working for me and he was no good along the lines I have indicated, then regardless of what I thought of him personally, I would fire him. Let's say Mr. Hohaley is working for us. All right. He ought to be fired."

Modestly he stepped back to his chair and sat down. Mrs. Van Fern clapped her hands. Everybody clapped. Francis' speech had relieved the tension. His analogy was well liked, and it did much, with its commonsense approach, to dispel a paralyzing disgust. As for Hennessey, he shrugged his shoulders.

Matson advanced to the center of the floor. "I'm indebted to Brother Francis," he said, with a deep bow, "for his suggestion that Mr. Hohaley should be fired. At last the dread word is out. That is exactly what the union should and will strive for. The

Detective Agency of Matson, Matson, Ginsburg, and Matson—which is giving its services free to the union—is now working on a further set of revelations that will, with the present one, bring about this end."

"By what means?" Charlie asked. "If the Project blows up with Hohaley, what good will it do anybody?"

"It won't blow up," Matson said. He smiled. "There won't even be a fuss. When the second bomb blows off, Mr. Hohaley will simply—resign. Colon will thank us for having done something he should have done himself long ago—and appoint another director."

"You won't say by what means?"

Matson turned to Miss Wilson. "I ask for a vote of confidence."

"What's your pleasure?" the chairman asked.

"Oh, he has my vote," Charlie said. "Why go through all this."

He knew that he was deeply distressed, deeply troubled, all his instincts and knowledge telling him that Matson was dragging the union—and with it the Project—along with him to an action which was necessary to him, and to him alone. But he could not speak. If only Colon would act like a man—but what was the use of wishing! All Colon would guarantee was that no administrative members would be fired on a whim of Mr. Hohaley's. Which—suddenly—brought up the question of whether Matson were staying within his administrative immunity. Well, never mind, never mind—the matter was now out of his hands. Better so, better so. He told himself this for the thousandth time. He wanted it to be out of his hands. He told himself—his own confessor—that he was not to be trusted. Matson's right: I have a family, am rooted. I dream of Elizabeth. What don't I dream of and (there's the question) still don't dare? But Matson's untrammeled. He belongs with Horatio Alger and Paul Bunyan—free spirits, unhampered by flesh. Not for nothing are priests allowed to live only with themselves.

All of this because of a Mr. What-the-hell Hohalcy! A Tremaine! Christ, what a joke! . . . The further set of "revelations" that Matson promised, Charlie knew, was the second part of the "revenge" they had discussed. Chavin had known about the photostats. But what would this second part be? Charlie was content now to travel with this broad stream, beginning to roar and thunder, that had gathered from many tributaries, going back to invisible and unknown sources.

As the meeting began to break up, with optimistic promises from each that he'd bring two new members to the next meeting, something occurred simultaneously to several of them.

"By the way, Matson, how did you happen to come across these interesting letters?"

"Yes, and how come they are photostated? Are you truly a detective agency?"

Matson gave out a proud pale perfect sneer. "Hiss," he said, "don't tell anybody. I jimmied his desk!"

IN ANOTHER HOTEL ROOM, A LITTLE LATER THAT EVENING, A man sat at his typewriter, staring with a furious concentration at the keys. He was Dan Francis, the newly elected president of the National Authors' Project Union, Monroe Chapter.

He had rushed to his room immediately on leaving the meeting, and while the exact details of what had happened there were still fresh in his memory. In some room across the hall a man and a woman were having a violent quarrel, the sound of which had gradually started strange reflections in Francis' mind. What this loud quarrel between husband and wife had made Francis think was: Suppose a young man were to achieve baldness overnight, literally, with all the other physical characteristics that are associated with the condition, wouldn't he go mad instantly? Here was this man and his wife, the two of them always quarreling. Suppose, when this man and his wife had been young, in the first flush of their health and ardor, they had gone to bed one night and waked up the next morning, *to see in each other what these two had seen this morning!* The woman spare and anemic, her face a bitter history of all the battles she had won; the man tall and fat and shaking as he walked. Francis could imagine them twenty years ago.

The details of the union meeting were still fresh in Francis' mind. He had stopped at the corner restaurant only long enough to eat a sandwich and gulp two cups of coffee before rushing home to get at his typewriter to write a report of this meeting, a copy of which (in duplicate) he planned to send Mr. Hohaley. And then this man and his wife had started quarreling, and the thought (which had been taking clearer form for weeks) now sprang up in his mind in full outline.

The picture threw him off the track for a moment. He paused to collect himself. He had already put down the names of all those who had attended the meeting and was beginning on a description of the general business preceding the meeting.

A man begins as a baby. A baby grows to be a man. There he stands, strong, erect and as full of beauty as a panther is full of pee. Then, all of a sudden, the man looks at himself again. He is fat, bald, bowed down. In one crushing instant. Everything's behind him. The thing is intolerable.

Francis winced before the picture. Something remote and tremendously reluctant was going on in him. . . . He had started out in life as the son of an average middle-class family, one generation removed from Europe. His father had been a grocer during the day and a preacher on Sunday. A good normal life, and he had gone through grade school and then high school and had then gone to work because he did not see any reason for going to college. His father, who had not had any education himself, would have been glad to send him. And his mother urged him for a while. And then had come years of average jobs, mostly as a salesman for various concerns, for he had a glib tongue and a good personality, and salesmen made good money in those days. The crash of 1929 had ended what he had thought, without thinking, would be "that sort of a life" from now on. He was a bachelor, having seen many women he had desired but none he wanted to marry.

Then had followed years of precarious employment, dwindling commissions, and hopes that had never soared high but were always present at the end of the day as a pleasant leaven for the seemingly endless sameness (not altogether unpleasant, either). His parents had both died during one of his trips from home, and one day he found himself in Chicago without a job and with no idea of where to get one. It was cold that day, in the dead of winter, and he saw an ad in the paper asking for men—preferably those who were personable and had had some experience as salesmen—to work in a department store. He went and applied and got on, walking through a picket line, for the place was on strike. The job was that of a "spotter." He bought things and made out reports on the clerks' "attitudes." After a year he had outlived his usefulness, for the clerks get to recognize spotters, and he moved on. But meanwhile his bearing and manner had attracted the attention of Slim Harvey, who was the head of the "fink" agency that supplied the stores with their "protection," and Harvey proposed that he come to work for him as a labor spy. He worked for Harvey for three months, being active on three "jobs" in that time. Then he had received a letter from a friend in the home town telling him that, if he wanted it, there was a job he could have at Timmy Simmons' Wholesale Liquors. He had taken the job, which had lasted another two months. Then Timmy Simmons had closed his doors for keeps, going back to Ireland to retire.

A strange lethargy began to come over him. (In this lethargy was the first symptom of the spiritual disease which was later to give him ideas about young men waking up to find that they had become bald overnight.) He did not go back to look up Slim Harvey. (He didn't have the money for the bus fare and he found that he couldn't muster up enough energy to write a simple letter asking for the advance loan.) He drifted from one mooch to another and finally, having exhausted the hometown friends he happened by chance to meet on the streets, he began to drift from town to town and, six months later, quite unrecognizable, he found himself in Johnsburgh on the eve of a municipal election. A procession of bums was passing, walking along the sidewalks, and from their general air of gayety—one or two of them were chewing toothpicks and he could smell the traces of a meaty stew and of liquor on their breaths—he surmised that they were being marshaled to vote. Johnsburgh's reputation was known far and wide. He fell in line with them and voted as Donald Armand, a truckdriver residing at 1302 Hammers Avenue. For this he received a dollar. As he stood on the sidewalk outside the polling place looking at his dollar, one of the wardheelers asked him if he wanted more "work." He said yes. By the end of the evening he had voted seven times.

The next day, after a shave and a haircut and a square meal, he had gone around to see Betsy Mueller. He had laid his history of labor spying before Betsy, and Betsy sent him to Henry Jevins. Jevins, eventually, had placed him with the Authors' Project in Monroe with instructions to keep his eyes open and to report weekly to Mr. Hohaley. And Francis had come to work, registering under his right name as unemployed and on relief and residing at the Homeless Men's Bureau.

He had often wondered why he had gone to see Betsy that day, and concluded easily that he was hard up and knew who Betsy was, but the truth was—as he knew without admitting it—that he was becoming pretty scared. After all, he was no longer young; he was forty-three, and no longer strong; there was the beginning of a kind of a cough that he'd never had before. Of course, he had been hard up before. Why had he not then taken measures to rehabilitate himself? This is a legitimate question. There was, for instance, the writing to Slim Harvey which he had shirked. The answer was that there may come a time in a man's descent from the living when the sudden sight of a horrible and eventual destination acts as a momentary shock which gives him, for that moment, as a reaction, the appearance and capacity of great energy. He had experienced that moment in Johnsburgh and had acted on it.

There was no moral feeling in connection with the work he did. Certainly he had had no conscious questioning of the ethics of spying on twelve-dollar-a-week girls in dime stores, department stores, and drugstores. He knew how it was with them. He knew that their lives were not always pleasant. He knew that things might go pretty tough with some of them after his reports were turned in. But if he thought about it at all, it was to the effect that they would have done the same thing if they were in his shoes. If he had thought it necessary to carry this thought to a conclusion, he would have considered the girls hypocrites for the contempt they would undoubtedly have had for him if they had known who he was.

But he had no real need of such thoughts. The life of salesmen —of any kind of businessmen—is not altogether the model of rectitude that the future salesmen are given as a guide to life in their schools, boy scout movements, homes, and Sunday schools. They get to know what cutting a corner now and then is. In a less respectable business, they just cut a few more corners.

The vision that came to Francis as he listened to the quarrel of the husband and wife—the vision of senility rushing on youth with the speed of a train—came to him this evening with especial force. It was the final cap to the thinking he had been doing about the unionists since almost the beginning of his acquaintance with Charlie Gest and Matson and the others.

This acquaintanceship, which he had cultivated for "business" purposes, had begun at the banquet for Colon when he had had a drink at a near-by bar with Charlie Gest. At this time there had been no questions in his mind about the kind of work he was engaged in. He had a "job" to do and, as a first step, he was making the acquaintance of Charlie Gest. With the instincts of a detective he had sensed, from the very beginning, that there was an antagonism of purpose between Mr. Hohaley and his staff. Gest's friendliness had offered him a good point at which to start.

Never overstepping bounds, he had worked well. In public, on meeting Gest—or Matson, to whom Gest had introduced him as a friend—he always tipped his hat and addressed them formally with the mister in front of their names. Sent out on assignments he never presumed on this friendship to bring in anything but the best work. He had even suggested assignments for himself, going to some trouble to think them up.

The trouble was that after he had known Gest and Matson for a very short time, he had begun to admire them. This admiration had progressed, the more he knew them, to the point where— as at this moment, while he was trying to concentrate on his latest report to Mr. Hohaley on the organization of the union—he was having serious difficulty in "exposing" them. It was not as though there had been a sudden conversion on his part to what the victims of labor-spying might have called decency. No travail of conscience was involved. His motto was still, so far as his conscious thought on the subject was concerned, a contemporary variation on the Golden Rule: "Do unto others as you *think* they would do unto you." Something altogether different was involved in his hesitation.

Without his having realized it, there had always been a strong desire for adventure in his make-up. That was why he had stopped his education after having completed high school. It had vaguely seemed to him that working would be a shorter cut to adventure. This same obscure urge had also led him to adopt the calling of a traveling salesman, in the belief that, in this day and age, adventure lay along the nation's highways. It was this governing and partially unrecognized desire that had kept him from marriage. The sort of adventure that all his married friends said marriage represented did not appeal to him at all. So long as he was free, there was hope that something would show up around the corner. But, as has been shown, by the time he had come onto the Project, he was pretty well licked.

In his encounter with Charlie and Matson and—through them —Hennessey, Folinger, and the others, he sensed a type of adventurer he had never encountered before. The shopgirls on whom he had spied, the businessmen along the road with whom he had matched wits, the other salesmen—all their motives were clearly understood. Their arena was a common one with his. But these people were "different." He had never been able to detect a point of view in them that stemmed from the possibility of personal gain, even when they thought it did, and it puzzled him. All their ideas seemed idealistic. Their goals were along no maps that Francis knew; their gains were not such as you could put on your back or in your stomach. The idealisms he remembered of his youth were placid by comparison. Those idealisms had not represented adventure, but the reverse.

If Francis had met these boys five years before, as he said to himself, he would have passed them by as crackpots—the kind you read about in books or see in the movies now and then. Meeting them at this time had proved to be a heady experience. He had had his gutful of good clothes, easy times, dollar motivations. His disease of the spirit had grown from the defeat of his spirit before phantoms. Gradually he had really grown humble before these adventurers of a type never before encountered, and he tried his hardest to understand them.

The one he admired most, and for whom he had developed a real fondness, was Lloyd Matson. Watching the great skinny bundle of energy and gestures that Matson was, he was reminded in a thrilling way of himself, but of himself only as he might have been. In Matson was that fullness and debonair quality that he had had; also (he suspected) a background much like his own. And Matson was a man of action. Francis really did not understand the others; he only admired them. But Matson's arrant egotism, the sheer sharp steel of his youth, was like wine to Francis' beaten spirit.

It was not solely an unsupported admiration of their personalities, however, that had made Francis' task increasingly difficult. His view here would certainly have surprised his friends. For he thought of them as men of affairs, successful, acclaimed, newspaper men of prominence and brilliance, creative writers. This view was based mostly on their position. Where had he been at their age? Traveling on the road. At their age he had been a dummy. Here they were, so young, and already had written books. (To his mind, the short stories that he'd been told Charlie had written became "books," of which he stood in awe as of the unknown; and the newspaper articles, unsigned, written by Matson, existed on the same level as the newspaper article of the most famous and highly paid foreign correspondents and lovelorn columnists of the day.) And Hennessey (he went without saying) and Folinger and Mrs. Van Fern—each had such distinction in his degree. He had seen them hobnob with Colon who, again in his mind, was in the "Government," one of President Roosevelt's "braintrusters." Those things counted. And despite this, they were essentially modest, without the sort of side that in his world the slightest prosperity induced in a man. He knew that Matson and Charlie, for instance, thought differently on many things, but the differences did not interest him. What did interest him was that they lived on a "level" which was unknown to him.

All the same, a spy was what he was and a spy's work was what he had to do. Each week since he had been put on the Project, he had sent in his reports. Most of them had started with the words, "Nothing in particular to report." He had seen the union coming on three weeks ago, and this had changed the tenor of his reports. "There is talk of a union being started," he had reported. "I will check on it." And now there was this report, and he could certainly spread himself on it. His habits made him lick his mental chops at the thought of the scandal Matson had uncovered. But an accumulation and complexity of things held his hand.

He listened to the man and the woman quarreling in the room across the corridor. The man was banging away at his typewriter. Again Francis wondered, What in the hell does he knock out on the typewriter every time he begins to lose the argument. The woman was talking steadily: "Why, you yella son of a bitch, if you'd uh had the guts a dog is born with, why—"

Francis listened, his nerves trembling with the itch in his fingers to get out the necessary story, the complicated feelings he had toward his co-unionists, and that sense of sickness in his head that came on him with the vision of the baldheaded man and his ancient wife. Round and round went the vision in his mind: Strong and beautiful, with their bodies full of life and desire, the two creep passionately to bed. . . . And in the morning the two awake and look at each other. And they shriek—*they shrie-ie-ie-iek!*

He closed his eyes, fighting down the desire to throw his head back and shriek. Shriek! And from somewhere came the memory of one Sunday morning when he had gone to church with his mother and father, the three of them walking down the sunlit street nodding hello to the other groups slowly and happily making their way toward the church. And he was in the church and the preacher was speaking. He did not see the preacher. He saw shadows and heard an organ-sound, and he heard the preacher's voice, something he had said: "The greatest and the highest adventure is the search for God." Where it came from, this memory, he didn't know. As it flashed through his mind, he thought of the tall, laughing, reckless Matson. "He is seeking God," he whispered to himself.

The sound of his own voice, suddenly heard in the forefront of the phantasmagoria of his mind, was strangely comforting. He opened his eyes quickly. Nothing there, of course. Nothing but the room and him in front of his typewriter and across the room the dresser with its mirror in which, at an angle, he saw his pale thin middle-aged still youthful and strangely smiling face and across from this room the other room. But he felt calmer, warmer. He sat without thought for a while, but feeling better, better, better all the time. Under his smile, he was a very lonely man, and it did him much good to feel better than he usually did.

Then he began to type again. He was smiling. He told his correspondent that a union was being started. He already knew that, of course. That he had attended its first formative meeting, and was pleased to tell that he had been elected president of the local, which put him in a good position to learn more and that another meeting was scheduled for the day after tomorrow—a meeting to which Mr. Hohaley was to be invited again. He named the persons who had attended this meeting, and stated that during the course of the conversation it had been mentioned that Colon himself was a member of a union, a national union of government employees with headquarters in Washington, and that the unionists had stated their views openly and without any thought but what they were doing something of which Mr. Hohaley and any concerned parties would approve. He carefully omitted any mention of the bill Hohaley owed the hotel, or of the photostated copies of the correspondence. He sealed this communication, a three-page paper, in an envelope, and stretched himself lazily over a job well done.

After this, he proceeded to shave himself, looking meanwhile at the headlines of the newspaper propped up in front of him. The foreign news did not interest him and neither did the editorial section. For some reason, he did not want to look at the funnies just now. He came across the movie section. When he got through shaving, he looked at this section more carefully. Was it not too late for a movie? He decided on a picture at the Crown which was featuring Ginger Rogers and Fred Astaire. Hell, even if he got to see only part of it—! The companion picture was *Stella Dallas,* a "throbbing heart drama" of a woman's great love, featuring Barbara Stanwyck. He didn't like throbbing heart dramas, all that woman mush, and he didn't like Barbara Stanwyck, having a theory that as an actress she could be said to put it on too much. He hoped this was the picture that went on first and he'd miss it. But he cast about for another program. He could find nothing to top Ginger Rogers and Fred Astaire. If there was one thing he loved to see, it was a really fine team taking each other around the floor as though it was easy. Like they were made of coils and india rubber. So that's where he went, to the Crown, walking into the theater an hour late.

PART EIGHT

News of the fight, by the next day, had spread all over the Project and smiles were covered as Matson approached.

"They think I'm supposed to be sore," he told Charlie. "Can you beat these lunkheads?"

A minute later, after he'd been to his desk and looked at his mail, he came back smiling. "Look at this."

It was an inter-office communication from Mr. Hohaley:

Mr. Matson: This is to advise you that effective as of now, I would prefer you to devote your full activities to map-making and to details of administration other than financial. I have instructed all department heads that in future I will handle the finances myself.

"I think you ought to go and see him and ask for an explanation," Charlie said. "At a time like this, with everybody knowing that you're active in the union, you can't have them thinking that—"

He stopped, puzzled at the smile on Matson's face.

"What the hell are you smiling at?"

"Yes, I guess I'll go see him. Want to come along?"

"It'll look like a delegation."

"Come on in, this may be good."

The typists and stenos looked up to see them walking across the office space towards Mr. Hohaley's room. There was a neutral hush about them. Lucille Turnbull sat at her desk and tried to glare and smile at the same time. Her face was ghastly. Here and there was an openly hostile look or a friendly grin. The whole atmosphere of the Project had changed. It seemed stripped for battle.

They entered the sanctum sanctorum. Mr. Hohaley, leaning over some correspondence, heard them come in and Helen O'Hara greet them. He kept them waiting.

Helen scanned Matson's face, looking for scars of battle. Matson shook his head, grinning, and nodded No. For all his manner, he was pretty white. Charlie thought that he seemed a bit nervous too, which surprised him. It always surprised him to see emotions in Matson. It was a measure of his admiration that he conceived of Matson as being a perfect gladiator, poker-faced.

They waited a minute or two, Charlie feeling awkward. They really did seem like a delegation.

Matson was the one to speak first.

"I got your inter-office communication," he said bluntly. Mr. Hohaley flushed at the rudeness. He looked from one to the other, his lips tightening, then back at Matson.

"Yes, Mister Matson?"

"I don't understand it. Isn't my work satisfactory?"

"Perfectly."

"Then—?"

"I have decided that you are more necessary at this stage of the game in the editorial end of it."

"Two weeks ago the Project financial affairs were in an awful

279

mess. Clarkson couldn't handle them. He said so. So did you. I came in and am straightening it out. All this was by your invitation. What the editorial end needs is not me. Gest would have asked for me if I were necessary, I think."

Charlie had perked up at Matson's first words. All this was new to him. The situation was even more complicated than he had thought; he had not suspected that the finances were in a bad way. He felt as though he were beginning to understand Mr. Hohaley's hostility to Matson. Goddam the heroics-worshiping son of a bitch. It would never have occurred to him, when he asked Charlie to come in here with him, to give him an idea of the set-up first. That would have been too simple. Same for the photostats. Tell it to the union all of a sudden. Watch them keeling over, left and right. . . .

He listened avidly.

"Who is the director here, Mister Matson, you or me?"

This was double-talk, Charlie saw. The kind he gave me when he was asking my opinion of our poor "defenseless" hero. Only difference is, the protagonists this time *both* understand what it's all about.

"If you want to make a point of it, Mr. Hohaley, *you* are."

"What do you mean by that, Sir?"

"I mean you are the *director*. I was just called in to straighten out the finances. It was at your invitation."

"And now I invite you to attend to your map-making and to the editorial end."

"Mr. Gest hasn't asked for my services. According to the chart of various authorities that Mr. Colon supervised the drawing up of when he was here, Mr. Gest has the say-so on who is to be in his department. We were talking just before we came in here. He asked me why the change? I asked him to come in with me and find out."

Charlie was embarrassed. He did much better with imagined than with real scenes. It would have relieved him to know what this was all about. But Matson, he guessed, under his manner, was enjoying himself thoroughly.

"Mr. Gest?"

Hohaley's gaze was a complex of all the moods Charlie had ever seen in him. He, too, seemed amused. He was also curious, cold. He surveyed Charlie long.

"Yes, Mr. Hohaley?"

"You will accept Mr. Matson in your department in whatever supervisory or editorial capacity you think him best suited to and the necessity requires."

"I'm sorry, Mr. Hohaley." He listened to himself with amazement. He was glad now that he had come in with Matson. They complemented each other. He had always felt that they did. "I can't accept him."

The Director's brilliant eyes narrowed.

"And why not?"

First of all, he wanted to say, there is the division of authority made by Colon that Matson mentioned. Second, there is the injustice to Matson, who is obviously being punished unjustly for something. He ran out of arguments. But above all, he thought, Matson's demotion at this time would undoubtedly be interpreted as a blow at the union. The union's prestige was involved. Of that, he was positive. He had to act as a "company" official but also as a union man.

"I'm waiting," Hohaley said, sensing an advantage in his hesitation.

"I must abide by what you and I agreed to in Mr. Colon's presence, at his request." He fell back on that.

"So," Hohaley said, "you must abide." He looked at Helen O'Hara.

Helen immediately came over. "You're due at the Historical Society in fifteen minutes, Mr. Hohaley," she said, staring at Matson and Gest.

They were used to his habit of being due somewhere.

281

"I want to talk about this some more, gentlemen," Mr. Hohaley said.

He allowed Helen to bring him his hat and coat. Charlie, out of habit, helped him on with his coat.

"Meanwhile, Mister Matson, one point. You are relieved of financial matters effective this day. I will appoint a successor to assist Mr. Clarkson."

Matson shrugged his shoulders. "I'll go out into the county and make maps," he said rudely. "Seeing the town by day, since I've been *assisting* Mr. Clarkson, will be a novelty."

Hohaley went out.

"What's the big idea?" Helen asked.

"What's what big idea, baby?"

"You know something, Matson?" Helen asked.

"*Matson,* huh? No more Lloydy-Woidy, kiddo?"

"You're on your way out," she pronounced solemnly. "You too, Gest."

"On my way out of what?" Matson asked.

"Yeah, out of what, strawberry bush?" Charlie echoed.

"All right, I told you. And it's your own fault.'

They leaned over her desk. "How do you figure that, kiddo?"

Her young face was youthful and prim. She busied herself at her typewriter. It would have been more effective if she had been able to type.

"You missed your chances, that's all I got to say," she said. "You have thrown away your own future."

"I ADMIRE THE WAY YOU PULLED IT OFF," CHARLIE SAID. "I admire the way you pull anything off. But I'm afraid that the little lady was right. With your own little hands you done it."

Hennessey, who was wearing a piece of steak over his left eye and had been protesting proudly all morning how he had got it, sent over an inter-office communication by Rose Feeney, his typist. It read:

They can't do nothing to you, Matson. You're too big. Tell 'em to go soak their heads.

Matson looked over at Hennessey and grinned. They waved at each other. The whole office watched the interchange of greetings.

"So I done it with my own little hands, huh? Man, I don't know which is dumber, you or Helen O'Hara."

"The point is, what *did* you do. I know what *I've* done, but what did *you* do? If it's a long story, suppose we scram out of here."

"It's a long story all right, but maybe we'd better stay here. Listen, there are two fellows coming in from the State Treasury Department to make an investigation of our finances tomorrow. That's what the whole thing is about. Hohaley's scared to death."

"Holy Jesus! You *sent* for them!"

"Not exactly. . . . We'll go back to the beginning. Are you ready, Subconscious?"

"I'm ready."

"Good. I don't really think you are, but let it pass. . . . Well, it was about three months ago, and I happen to be passing Clarkson's desk and I notice that he looks even sicker than usual. So I stop to pass the time of the day and maybe help him select some medicine. And while I'm there, I happen to look at what *he's* looking at."

"One minute. Is this the beginning of your second set of revelations?"

"Yep. Inter-related with the first."

"Go ahead."

"Thanks. Because Clarkson doesn't understand the proper titling of payrolls, all of our payrolls from the beginning of the Project, with the exception of those that I handled personally, were mistitled. . . . Now, we're going to jump about considerably. I'll have to go back and forth on this. I showed Clarkson his error, and showed him how to correct it. So now he knows. You got it so far?"

"Yes."

"Well, now the self-sufficient Mr. Hohaley had given him strict orders that he was not to take orders or suggestions from anyone but himself in regard to the payrolls. So Clarkson asks me please won't I talk to the boss and ask him if he may make the corrections I have indicated that he should. So I say I'll be glad to and in I goes to see him. I give him the dope. Clarkson will have to remake face sheets. He'll have to make out Form Numbers such-and-such, which are mandatory under Replies to Notices of Exceptions, et cetera, et cetera. I guess I don't have to tell you the details, do I?"

"I'll take your word for them. So?"

"Yeah. So, here we go back a bit. Cast your mind over Hohaley's rule in regard to mail addressed to him. I'll give you half a second out."

This rule was that when the director was out of the office (which was most of the time), mail addressed to him was not to be opened. Since most of the mail to department heads was also addressed to him, the inconvenience had often been considerable.

"Well?" And as Charlie prompted him, he realized why Matson had paused. "Say!" He grabbed at Matson's sleeve. "He put in that rule about not opening *any* of the mail addressed to him just about the time that he must have begun receiving those dun letters from the hotel?"

Matson grinned. "That he did, little one, that he did. But that's another detail. To go on with *this:* So, as I said, I give him the dope. I tell him what's wrong with the requisitions. And that's that. I suggest that he give Clarkson instructions accordingly. And he thanks me kindly, tells me he likes my spirit. It's nice to have men about him who are alert, not such as drink of nights."

284

"So? For Christ's sake, so?"

"So (for whatever reason: inefficiency, lack of realization, maybe these plus mad-at-me for knowing more than he) he does *not* instruct Clarkson. That mouse is afraid for his job, and he does the bills over again, but does them *wrong,* throws out what I'd helped him on, as he *thought* Hohaley wanted them. And the requisitions continue to go out the way I saw them. And, about a month ago roughly, the first of them finally gets through to the end of the trail, to Washington to the Accounts Office, and they promptly take exception to it (hell, of *course!*) and notify the State Treasury, who in turn notify our Mr. H. Well, it's the old story. He's out of town. Gone a week. So Washington doesn't receive the urgent reply asked for in this first notice of exception, so they write him another. Still no answer. He got back to town eventually, but by that time the first notice seemed old and unimportant (he judged it by its date and forgot what had caused it to age), and the second one had not yet arrived. And, to make a long story short, they wrote him five times in two weeks and no answer, so they—the big chief of the department this time—write him—pretty strongly—that if *he* doesn't care, he should think of the workers on the Project and their suffering if the payrolls are held up and to do something about it, for sure as hell and high water, the payrolls will be held up.

"At this time, Clarkson (I expect he was telling the truth on the whole) takes sick and is forced to ask for sick leave. So Mr. H. calls me in, 'since I know more about the finances than anybody else,'—them's his words, so help me—to straighten out the mess. Then I discover that this isn't the only beef the different agencies have against us. Trenton, the Procurement Officer, has been asking (also without an answer) why hasn't he been getting any contract requisitions of late for rental of our new space and extra furniture, telephones, etc., since I quit handling it, and he too is getting pretty tough about it. Tougher than the others. Trenton says that if he doesn't get the proper requisitions in a week, the Treasury Department will be instructed to inform all parties concerned that they are no longer responsible for our bills. Shut off our funds, and that's the end of the Project.

"So I go to work. I dig into Clarkson's desk and find three of Washington's letters and this last one from Trenton. So I write them both. Tell them I'm in charge (hell, the boss had *told* me to straighten out the mess) and ask them for all past correspondence. They both sent it on down pronto and I went to work."

He paused. "It was a mess."

"That's where the joker comes in?" Charlie said.

"Yes," Matson said, looking at him slyly. "That's where it certainly does."

"So what did you do?" Charlie asked, the premonition forming itself as Matson spoke.

"Exactly what it's beginning to dawn on you that I did do. I called up Franks in Washington long-distance and I said, 'Look here, old man, this here Project is in a hell of a shape. It has run out of all sensible excuses, so you better send around a couple of your best stink-men, for I'm telling you right now, I'm not going to be responsible. This is not my job, and I don't want it. As soon as I have cleaned up this mess, there will be another one along just as bad.' "

"And that's how they're coming in. And Mr. Hohaley knows who did him the favor."

"Right."

"But, Jesus, Matson, don't you know the consequence so far as he is concerned? He'll can you for this. Sooner or later, he'll fix you for it."

"No, he won't. I have reason to believe that before the day is over he will know that I have the originals and the photostats of his hotel correspondence on the banquet business. They're my protection."

"I see. And when he tried to pump me about you, he was missing those letters."

"Yep, I'm afraid so."

"And now, you're going to tell him yourself."

"No, *I* don't have to."

"*You* don't have to."

"No," Matson said, enjoying Charlie's mystification, "*I* don't have to. The only way to fight dirt is with dirt. Jevins and Johnsburgh should have taught you that."

"Just a minute. Why am I hearing all this for the first time now? Why didn't you report on this financial situation to the union at the same time that you told us about the photostats?"

Matson laughed. "Good. You're a bright boy. I was waiting for you to ask me just that. I'll tell you why." He put on his stage-whispering act. "Because I didn't want the members of the union to know about the financial condition of the Project. After all, you and I are *officers* of the Project as well as union members. But I did want the matter of the photostats to get back to Hohaley."

Charlie got up, wildly excited of a sudden, and sat down again.

"You mean there's a spy in the union!"

"Ha, ha. How bright you are. And I even know who he is."

"Who?"

"Wouldn't you first like to know how I found out?"

"Yes, I would," Charlie said weakly.

"Once upon a time, I thought there might be a good chance of me getting into the second-story business. Silky O'Matson. So I got myself a master-key. And when I got into Mr. H.'s desk— if I remember correctly, I took pains to mention *that* at the union—I not only found the letters on the hotel business, but I also found this spy's reports. Now get this. The reports weren't signed, but you know the old saying—a criminal always betrays himself by some clue, no matter how apparently slight. So I

287

noticed that while there was no signature to them—an XX stood for his name—there was this one report where he had run out of paper and he used a piece of hotel stationery in the pinch. So I hike down to the hotel advertised, and tell the manager I'm a lawyer looking for a transient to whom his Aunt has left a quarter of a million dollars and may I look at his register and any other registers he may have on the premises. So I look and find the name."

"A crappy trick."

"But it worked. That's the beauty of the crappy trick genus. Most people reject it because it's so crappy. But it takes the really *smart* man. . . ."

The rebuff, even while it annoyed Charlie, impressed him as having enough truth in it. . . . The trick is to look at a new situation without prejudice, he paraphrased Matson in his mind. "But this bastard, whoever he is"—he faltered, going over the names of the union members in his mind; who could the stool-pigeon be?—"shouldn't he be exposed?"

"What for?" Matson looked at him puzzled. "At least, why right now, before he has served his dirty purpose?"

"I don't know. But—"

"Sure. *But.* Well, don't worry. We'll kick his butt soon enough. . . ." In a good humor again, he laughed. "This thing has got to be timed. A fighter who goes all out in the first round is going to whip himself before the half-way mark. Don't you worry about our little stool-pigeon. When we're ready for him, we'll whip up a virtuous public indignation you'll be able to shave on."

Charlie had to let himself be led. And the guy is only twenty-one!

"Well, who was it?"

Matson was looking toward the door. "This is too good to be true. I should have been a dramatist. Here he comes now."

Charlie looked, and of course saw—Francis. The president of

the union was smiling amiably at Mrs. Van Fern. When she beckoned to him, he stopped at her desk to talk to her.

"He'll be coming over here in a second to report on his assignment," Matson said. "When he does, control yourself. Look absolutely natural. Huh?"

"He heard everything that went on!"

"Sure. Why not? There were no secrets. I *wanted* him to report on the photostats business. The only way to keep these guys in line is to have something on them. I wish to Christ I had something on Colon so we could make him finally make up his mind and do something."

Charlie stared in fascination at Francis talking to Mrs. Van Fern. "You said that a criminal always makes some sort of a slip," he said shakily. "You made one, you know."

"How's that?"

"If Hohaley decides to call your bluff, and if Jevins decides to back him up. Jevins will blow and your whole house will come tumbling down."

"He won't call my bluff. He won't call on Jevins either. He'll be afraid to."

"So then what?"

"The Treasury Investigation finds him inefficient. Then the union—through me—asks him to resign. Otherwise we publish the letters. He resigns. Afterwards, let the hotel sue."

Charlie felt that he was losing his mind. He shook his head. "You're going to end up on the gallows, my friend. Everything looks airtight, but there are too many beautiful coincidences to be quite true."

"That's because you're a fatalist and believe things to be predestined. But life is like that. It's real, but who can call it earnest?" Francis started over, and Matson again cautioned Gest. "Remember. Smiles and roses. We're going to play with him like—like—"

"The mice with the cat."

"Catnip will do it though."

Francis stopped in front of them.

"Gentlemen."

His manner was courteous as ever, his smile urbane. But there were circles under his eyes. Charlie lifted his right hand and said, "Heil, Hitler." Matson put his hand to his forehead, lips, and heart. "Salaam."

Francis' smile, if they could have seen, was wistful, as well as urbane. "I bring you greetings and salutations," he said, unconsciously complimenting the manner of speech of his friends. "I beg that you join me at the Grill for a cup of coffee at lunch time. And"—he looked at his wrist-watch—"it is now ten minutes to twelve."

"Won't you join us?" Matson asked.

"I'll be glad to," Charlie mumbled.

Hennessey sent over another inter-office communication.

In re respiration: Gentlemen, from where I sit, hot air seems to circulate about you like a halo of smoke around the beautiful but sweaty and damned. I suggest that you loosen your collars as I have my own. And remember, beer is the best mother that a poor man ever had.

Matson shrieked with laughter, and in a minute so did Charlie and, in a slightly puzzled and more subdued sort of way, so did Francis. Everybody in the office immediately stopped whatever he was doing and looked over. Matson and Hennessey and Gest were waving at each other.

"What on earth is going on there?" Mrs. Van Fern shrilled in her patrician voice. "Your fun is just too revolting for any use."

Helen O'Hara came out of her office and stared bleakly at them for a moment and went back in. Charlie tried to think of flaws in Matson's story and meanwhile, with a sense of impending catastrophe on him, laughed and laughed. The first act curtain, he thought, half-hysterically.

THE FLAW, THE SLIP-UP IN MATSON'S PERFECT CRIME EXISTED,
of course, as we know, in Francis' conscience. And, because of
it, Hohaley thought his path to be clear. This was to make Clarkson the scapegoat when the crisis developed—to pretend ignorance of the true state that the Project affairs had fallen into, and
to say, with every sign of anger, that Clarkson, whose application
blank had stated that he was a graduate of the University of
Illinois and a certified public accountant, had deceived him.

He had already taken the preliminary steps. Clarkson, a really
sick man, had, through a lifetime of heart disease, acquired a
fear of asking for time off, for with him it was not a matter of
a couple of days or even a week, as is proper for a sickness, but
of a long time, months maybe, even years, and he couldn't afford
to indulge himself and to start a habit which, while it led away
from the grave, led but to the poorhouse, as he saw it. When,
therefore, Hohaley suggested that he take some time off, he was
profoundly grateful. He was not really a certified public accountant. He had been a bookkeeper. The Project affairs gave
him a headache and worried him terribly. Also, his heart was
acting up. So was his liver. He took Mr. Hohaley's "suggestion"
of a two weeks' vacation with pay. After the investigation Hohaley planned, when the investigators would have told him
what he presumably did not know, to fire Clarkson.

The real business on hand was to get rid of Matson. Logically
enough, Hohaley put the blame of the union on Matson's shoulders. If not for Matson, everything would be all right. Everybody
would be satisfied. All this would not have occurred.

But getting rid of Matson at this time presented certain difficulties. Hazards, even. To begin with, he did not want it said
that he was anti-union. The CIO had just begun a great organiza-
tional drive. The whole town was labor-conscious, and it seemed
to be a stupid fashion nowadays to be pro-labor. Matson, the
bastard, would be certain to make the most of that.

Secondly, Matson had been recommended by the news editor

of the *Star-Globe*. And the one thing that Hohaley had imbibed with his political milk was the axiom never to offend the press if possible. In addition to Matson's having an in with an editor, he was a member of the Newspaper Guild. Certainly the Guild would have something to say on the matter, unless the dismissal were carefully engineered.

Thirdly, there was the personnel of the union, one of the most bothersome imaginable. Hennessey, a three-time novelist and a Pulitzer Prizewinner, sure to have access to many pens and avenues beside his own. Mrs. Van Fern, one of the city's Four Hundred, with innumerable connections just where they might hurt most. Charlie Gest, important chiefly because he had been Colon's own recommendation for the job. And Hohaley already knew which side Colon would be on.

Charlie Gest, he thought bitterly, and imagined scene after scene in which Charlie approached him, begging forgiveness. . . .

For several days Hohaley pondered the angles in the case and all his chances to come out of the mess with his colors flying. Meanwhile, awaiting the opportune time, he continued his apparently cordial relations with members of the union and watched them organizing the others. His own people—Lucille Turnbull, Regan, old man Pollin—came in from time to time to give him glowing accounts of how the workers felt toward him, and even Johnny Stephens came in one day absently to inform him that somebody had told him there was a union being formed on the Project and did Mr. Hohaley want him to cover it.

Hohaley graciously allowed his supporters to foster the idea on the Project that it was not a matter of his opposing the union at all, but a question of trust in so far as the workers were concerned. In this way, quite a feeling was built up among the workers as a whole against those of the unionists who were in a supervisory capacity. They were particularly wroth when it came to the part of the argument where the pay of the supervisors was compared to that of the common herd. "It's easy to get hifalutin' and high-and-mighty," went the talk, "when you're getting a hundred and fifty a month. What would they do if all they was getting was eighty-five?" And the answers to this rhetorical question ranged from murder to revolution.

And then the investigators, a Mr. George Pretzel and a Mr. Carl Wilberg, two very carefully clad and tight-lipped men, appeared on the Project.

This was on a Friday. By a coincidence, this was also a payday. The office was full of people going in and out. The word went around that a couple of guys were in Mr. Hohaley's office making an investigation at the union's behest. A feeling of resentment grew.

Mr. Hohaley, who had no desire to be in the office to answer embarrassing questions, told the investigators that he didn't want them to think that they were not entirely free to make whatever investigations they found necessary and so he would leave them at their leisure. He indicated the various files in which they would find what they wanted and told them Helen O'Hara would be at their service, if they needed her. Then he went home.

Driving behind Pete Cavagni in the clear cold sunlight, he thought what a fine day it was. His spirits, which had been uncomfortable until he had got out of the office, rose now; and as he absorbed the tiny and various sights of the city streets, his mind evolved plans.

When he got home, he called up Henry Jevins long-distance. He had it all planned out. "Sorry to disturb you, Hank, I know how busy you are just now, but on the question of this union, a serious business has come up. . . . A Mr. Wilberg and a Mr. Pretzel from Franks' office are in town to look over my books. Nothing serious in itself; I have nothing to hide. But pretty serious is the rumor-mongering that can go with it. . . . To come down to cases, it developed like this. . . ."

293

A grunt at the other end of the wire. Jevins knew when to listen. Hohaley knew that Jevins was not fooled by his apparent levity. Jevins, however, had got where he was not by judging people but by using them. And he would not ask embarrassing questions about expense accounts.

". . . So this man Matson, who was so promising that even Judge Williams told me that he would go far—this Matson, when I put him in, as a mark of my trust, to supervise Clarkson in his handling of the finances (remember, Clarkson is a sick man), he deliberately misled him and got him to make the wrong requisition numbers, to use contradictory dates on travel-expense sheets, and in short, so to confuse, delay and entangle him, that finally Franks, who himself had passed these accounts, was told by Washington to investigate. Having no other alternative, this is what he's doing."

Jevins coughed. "I'm not worried about Franks. You don't know that *he* is, but he knows that *you* are one of our people. Our boys don't fight among themselves. The Party doesn't allow it. But tell me, does this Matson have anything special on you that he could use in the newspapers?"

Hohaley hesitated, thinking. The only thing he was worried about was the matter of his hotel bills and letters, which were missing. But impossible that Matson or anybody else should have them. If Matson had had them, certainly he would have let him know. . . . The bastard would have played his cards to the limit. And, again, if he or anybody else in the union had them, *Francis* would have got wind of it and let him know. So, double-check. No, they must be at home, somewhere in one of his trunks or in his own desk. These were in such a mess. That damn fat old Cordelia!

Thus circumstance, which is the instrument of irony, meets itself coming around the corner and lifts the hat to itself.

"No. Nothing."

"No letters? Bills?"

"Nothing."

"Good. . . . Now don't worry. Go ahead and get rid of him. I'll back you."

"But—"

"Oh, yes. That's right. . . . All right. I'll handle it through Washington. That ought to do it. You may expect an order for his release by tomorrow. From Colon."

"That's all I wanted to know."

But Jevins was not entirely satisfied.

"You've still got a lot to learn about this business of ours"— Hohaley smiled to himself. He had no fears now. The serious talk was over. —"I don't care about this mess you got yourself into. I don't know whether Matson did all this you say or not. It isn't important. But the union has to be broken sooner or later, and this is our chance. Now listen."

"But Matson *did*—"

"I'm not interested. Franks passed your requisitions, so he didn't know his business either. Well, we don't put a man into office solely because he knows his business. You understand? That's what men in office have clerks for. But *control* has to be exercised. That's something that a clerk can't handle for you. . . . Now about the union. It'll fight you. Maybe strike. Remember: *Colon* fired Matson, not you. Therefore at the first sign of trouble, you can follow Colon's lead. Fire them as fast as they raise their heads. Be firm. That's the first rule in politics. Meanwhile give a story to the papers about Matson same time you fire him. This gives you the jump."

He had to accept the censure. "I understand, Hank."

At that, he had got off well. What if he had had to tell Jevins about the hotel bill! He shivered in relief.

THE MILLS OF THE GODS GRIND SLOWLY, PROBABLY BECAUSE (as has been noted earlier) they have all eternity in which to work. But Jevins was a pretty busy man who knew the value of time. He got right to work. He called up his representative in Washington.

"Si?" he said. "Hank speaking. Look. I want you to do me a favor. There's a fellow named Lloyd Matson on the Author's Project in Monroe. I want him fired. I don't care what story you use. Call him a troublemaker. Say that he peddles dirty pictures to the stenos and it's getting to be a public disgrace, but the Project can't be embarrassed, so it has to be kept on the q.t. Say this is a tip from a pretty influential source who wants to keep out of it, as a friend of the Project."

One final call. It was an old gag, but it always worked. "Hello, Fixer? You remember the set of pictures you worked up for me on the Sterling case? Okay. I want you to fix me up another batch. No. Not the same pictures. Send them to Mr. Thornton C. Hohaley in Monroe. And—ah—let me have a set of clear prints for myself."

The call finished, he forgot all about it and Matson and Mr. Hohaley, and went to work on another problem, absolutely unimportant here. His mind was a set of connections, and he himself an engine that he put to its service.

The representative went to his go-between in Washington and asked him to do him the favor of getting Matson off the Project. This man got in touch with Colon. . . .

"You'll have to play ball, Jonas. I don't think you have an alternative."

Colon tore at his ear. "But I have nothing against the man."

"I told you the report. He's been peddling postcards."

"I CAN'T BELIEVE IT," MATSON SAID. HE WAS UTTERLY FLABBER-gasted. "It doesn't make sense."

Charlie read the dismissal form.

Owing to necessary reductions in the non-relief quotas, imposed on executive orders from our Washington office, we are forced to advise you of a termination of employment effective as of today.

"Doesn't it mean anything to him that I have photostatic copies of his correspondence with the hotel and that I can blow him sky-high?"

It didn't make sense to Charlie either. He read and re-read the communication in silence.

"He should have been afraid to do this to me," Matson said. "It's arithmetic, isn't it? He gets rid of me, but in getting rid of me he does away with Billy as well. What do you make of it?"

Charlie didn't know what to make of it. Matson's scheme had seemed to him too slick to really work. But he had to admit that he could not see where the flaw had come in.

"Well, what do you expect him to do," he asked sarcastically, "call you in and say 'I surrender, old man?' Maybe he's just going to make a deal with you, that's all. Maybe you're not supposed to take this seriously. He may want you to come to him and then he'll give you terms. If you do this, then I'll do that. And so on. It's just bait, most likely. If you don't come in to see him so he can make the arrangements for you to be a good little boy in the future, why he's liable to be disappointed."

Matson made an impatient wave of the hand.

"But I'm fired," he said, "that's no bluff. Well, only one way to find out—"

But when he went to ask Hohaley what was the meaning of the dismissal, prepared for the sort of thing that Charlie had suggested (after all, though Charlie's suggestion might not in itself make sense, there was no other explanation that he could think of), he found that this could not possibly be it. Hohaley was cool and arrogant. There was a gleam of triumph in his eye.

"It means just what it says, Mister Matson. We have had orders to reduce the non-relief personnel and somebody had to go. It was you, on the basis that your work can be divided among the effective personnel still remaining."

Matson looked for the slightest sign that Hohaley might be

bluffing. Not a sign of it. His composure and pleasure were unmistakable.

"May I see the order calling for a non-relief reduction?"

"I'm afraid not, Mister Matson. You see, such orders do not concern you any longer."

"I see." He did not see. He couldn't understand it at all. That the investigation had fizzled on the protective rocks of Hohaley's connections was unthinkable. That couldn't happen—not with the photostats in existence. . . . Perhaps, he thought, he's already settled the bill and doesn't quite allow himself to believe that the photostats are damaging enough in themselves.

He couldn't be that stupid! Or could he? Anyway, nothing to lose. Let's fire away.

"You don't think I'm going to take this sitting down, do you, Mr. Hohaley?"

Hohaley shrugged. "Your actions are up to you. It's a free country, Mister."

"Quite right. You're free to fire me for having done my duty. But I *still* have my duty, you know. And I'm free to take the necessary actions."

He smiled. "You don't scare me, Mister. I've seen your kind before. And I expect I'll continue to see them. But I keep on going just the same."

A momentary doubt of himself assailed Matson. Perhaps he was dreaming. No. Hohaley had to be afraid. Hell, he held the whip. Hohaley must know it.

"You know," Matson said grimly, "if things had turned out differently, I might have admired you very much. You have certain qualities that I like in a person. You're hard. You're a good bluffer. You know that I'm hep to you, but you play on like none of it is true. But it *is* true. So help me Jehoshaphat, Mr. Hohaley, I'm—in some ways—just like you, I'll go the distance on it. What do you think those hotel letters will look like if they're plastered across the front page of a newspaper?"

He faltered, assailed by a sudden suspicion. Up until the time that he had finished summing up Hohaley's qualities, Hohaley had kept on smiling, but as Matson came to the hotel letters, his face began to undergo a change; the smile seemed to start crumbling and flaking off, as though it had been plastered on.

Before Matson's suspicion could crystallize and form a clear pattern, he had already gone on: "The hotel correspondence, even if, as I imagine, you have already paid the bill, tell the—tell the—" (he was watching the crumbling face; the abject fear) — "By God!" he shouted. In a violent reaction, he smashed a fist into the palm of his hand. What a fool he had been! Hohaley didn't know he had the photostats! But *Francis—?* To hell with that right now. The situation, of a sudden, presented entirely fresh angles that he hadn't thought of.

"What hotel letters?" Hohaley whispered. He turned to Helen O'Hara, who had been watching Matson with a triumphant little-girl, didn't-I-tell-you look and was still holding this look, uncomprehendingly. "Miss O'Hara, will you please mail what you have ready now!"

"They're not ready yet, Mr. Hohaley."

"Mail what you have. *Now!*"

"B-but—" She wanted to say that she hadn't even pasted down the envelopes yet, but the look on her superior's face astonished her.

"Do as I say!"

The girl, on the verge of tears, began to gather up letters helterskelter, dropping some, stooping to pick them up, dropping one or two again. Tucking them all into her hat and slinging her coat over her shoulder, she grabbed her purse with the other hand and ran from the room. At the door, smitten, she turned to look. Matson had waited while all this was going on, assembling the new picture that presented itself in his mind. He smiled at the girl, a new assurance in his face. But the girl was looking at Hohaley now, whose dry burning eyes were on her, thrusting her from the room.

The door closed behind her.

"What bill are you referring to, Sir?"

He was still trying to keep up the pretense, but now things were assuming the shape that Matson had thought they would from the beginning. But what a fool he was, he told himself, even in his triumph. For now it was quite clear what had happened. And without knowing of his "protection," what sort of a damn fool must first Hohaley and then Jevins have thought him. And then Jevins had ordered him fired. How and through what channels was at the moment unimportant. The point was, not Hohaley but Jevins was responsible. And now a trump card was lost. For it was Jevins with whom he was now dealing. Not Hohaley but Jevins must get him reinstated. And would Jevins be willing to swallow his pride of power to do this, even to save Hohaley?

Well, he would let Hohaley do his own pleading with Jevins.

"The hotel bill, of course, for the banquet. Perhaps you would like to know what banquet?"

"I don't know what you're talking about."

This sounded like a movie. Matson pulled one of the several copies of one of the letters out of his pocket and put it before Hohaley. Hohaley stared at it, then made a gesture to snatch it. Then he seemed to realize that it was only a copy.

"This is blackmail, Mister Matson."

"Blackmail?"

He knew that he didn't need to debate that point. Hohaley was playing for time. All right. That was his privilege. He knew what Hohaley must try to do in the end. That was all that concerned him.

"Blackmail's just a word, Mr. Hohaley," he said, to give him the little time he needed. "The point is, what do you intend doing about it?"

Hohaley's answer confirmed his hunch that he would have to get Jevins' okay.

"Give me until tomorrow."

"Okay. Tomorrow is fine. Say, in the morning? Before lunchtime—and the—uh—home editions?"

Hohaley nodded, unable to speak.

"And—uh—meanwhile—I continue at my duties as though nothing has happened?"

Hohaley nodded again.

"Perhaps I should tell you in parting," Matson said, smiling, "that I have taken the precaution of burying my several bones in widely separated places. It may be, of course, that I've been to too many movies lately."

Outside, catching Charlie's anxious eye, he gave him the all-clear signal, the thumb-and-index finger held aloft in an O. He strolled down to his desk, exchanging banter with the girls as he passed them.

But his words were not quite so optimistic.

"Francis *didn't* tell him. The bastard doublecrossed us all. Well, we'll see. . . ."

"IRREVOCABLE," MATSON SAID HEAVILY, "THAT WAS HIS VERY word."

Charlie stared. He reached into his desk. Brought out some sheets of paper.

"Petitions for your reinstatement," he said expressionlessly, "Hennessey and I drew them up last night."

Matson's face was red.

"You didn't have much faith in my coming through."

Charlie smiled. "I don't want to see you not come through."

Matson tried to laugh his old way. "So sweet of you." It didn't go. "Let's see one of those."

Hennessey came over as he read. . . . "Grossly unfair. Union threatened. Labor spy. We humbly but firmly petition . . ."

301

Mrs. Van Fern came over. Then others. There was a little clump of unionists around Matson. All began talking at the same time. Charlie was aware of the office workers looking over, his own beating heart. A smile of triumph on Lucille Turnbull's face, in the far corner of the room. Dean of virgin whores, he thought savagely, mixing his metaphors. . . .

"Well, here goes," he said. "Here's one for each of you."

He went over to Margaret Renny first.

"Margaret, there's a petition I have here I would like you to sign."

As she looked at it, he began to tell her what it was all about. He saw her looking at it and looking at it. She turned it around to see what was on the other side. She turned it back. He saw a trickle of red on her lip where she was biting it. His voice was trailing off. He stared at her, not able to understand all at once that she was not going to sign it.

"I'm s-sorry, but—"

"It's for *Matson*," he said. "Lloyd *Matson*."

"Mr. Gest, I can't."

He looked around him, confused. Who next? Pete!

"I can't do it," Pete said doggedly.

Charlie exhausted all his arguments.

"For God's sake, Pete, why?"

"I got a wife and t'ree kids, Charlie."

"I *know* you got a wife and three kids, Pete. Jesus, I know *that*. But what's it got to do with respectfully urging the reinstatement of a man who—"

"I wouldn't sign it if it was for my old man," Pete said. His voice was low, his eyes evaded. "Lloyd Matson is not feedin' my kids."

The words burst from him. "But he *is* feeding your kids. He made it possible for you to get onto the Project. Don't you remember that day you came up to see me? I couldn't have put you on without his help!"

302

There were deep inflamed spots on the musician's cheeks. " 'N' I thank you, I thank Matson too."

"Thanks!" But now it was Pete who was looking at him steadily, his own eyes that had difficulty maintaining their gaze. He's right, Charlie thought. What has he to do with me or Matson? What has Matson's action to do with *him?* But then it seemed to him that there was more to this than simply an action by Matson which had misfired and brought about certain consequences. For if it were not more than that, then why would he and the others be concerned as they were! But all this would be hard to say in so many words. "It's just a *petition,* Pete," was all he could say. "You don't even have to be a member of the union to sign it. You don't have to even want to be a member of the union. But if you think a worker shouldn't be cut off from his *livelihood* without at least a fair trial, then you should sign it."

He was dumfounded by the expression now on Pete's face.

"You must t'ink I'm a hoosier, huh, Charlie?"

A cunning smile, a *trader's* smile. Pete was taking refuge in familiarity. What are you trying to sell me? That sort of a smile. With one foot firmly wedged against the door.

"Sell you?" he said, as though Pete had said it.

He walked away a few steps, looked around to see whom to talk to next. It seemed to him that Mrs. Van Fern, leaning over the broad back of Claude Johnson, was about to make a "sale." Doggedly, into the very teeth of the enemy, he walked over to where Pollin sat.

THE AIR WAS A DIRTY SCREEN THROUGH WHICH THE SNOW FELL. As yet, even as they walked (Charlie and Hennessey), it fell softly, almost imperceptibly, and the air still looked black with all the factory smoke in it. But, as they watched, the snow grew thicker and thicker. It fell softly and thickly, but you could see through it to where people on the other side of the street leaned against it, their blackness emphasized by the general effect of whitening air. As they watched, the snow changed its character and all that it touched before their eyes. The street became different, the way it does. The parked cars, even the telegraph wires, looked like cartoons, black underneath, white on the top and sides. In a while, everything was white.

At Pershing Street they stopped a while to watch Leo the cop. Majestic as the Metro-Goldwyn-Mayer lion, whom he resembled, Leo stood in the middle of the street queuing the traffic that crept warily along on its individual bellies.

"I predict Leo's going to be embarrassed the first time he has to help break up our picket line," Charlie said.

"He'll get used to it, I can predict you that," Hennessey said grimly.

After the traffic signal had changed, they remained standing there until the next change. The wind the newspapers had been talking about all week had come up at last, and it was a sight to watch the snow going around Leo like the stripes around a barber's pole.

"We-e-ell," Charlie said.

They crossed the street.

"Afternoon, gentlemen," Leo hollered. He had been written up as the city's handsomest and most polite downtown cop and he was proud of the distinction. He was never so handsome and polite as when he was speaking to writing folks. Of course, he preferred speaking to newspapermen who were working at it.

Hennessey and Charlie waved back.

"The best to the boss," Leo hollered.

"She'll get the message."

A bloodcurdling sound on the next corner. A streetcar banging *bong, bong, bong* slid back on its spine trying to stop. Will it, won't it—it didn't! *Bong, bong, bong,* it crashed into the smoking Chevrolet stalled in front of it on the tracks. The driver of the car got out. Gloomily, Hennessey and Charlie watched him. He had a slow bent way of getting out of the car and walking around it to talk to the conductor of the streetcar, who had also gotten out.

"Nobody killed," Hennessey said, "let's go."

Charlie laughed. A more pacific and gentle person than Hennessey he had never met. The big fellow burlesqued pugnacity by the command of a robust and blasphemous vocabulary and often an ultra-menacing attitude. He fooled people with this mannerism sometimes, occasionally to his cost. As for instance, when he had tried to fool Regan.

"Look," Charlie said. "What do you think? Are we really in for it?"

"Certainly. A strike will be voted as sure as Four-Star is named after me and I've evaded its curse by cleaving to Seagram's."

"But what do you think yourself? Do you think we ought to strike?"

"Well, you heard what the 'experts' said." He put a certain emphasis on the word *experts*. " 'Hohaley's refusal to reinstate Matson,' they say, 'leaves you no alternative but to strike.' " He laughed. "Why shouldn't they say that! They go up to see Hohaley in committee. They represent important and well-rooted unions themselves. They're important men. Just to be sure that nothing is done under cover of darkness, they notify the newspapers and the pencil-boys all show up. Then Hohaley turns them down. The fat fruity bastard is shaking like a leaf, and they can see it, but he turns them down. 'Why?' they want to know. Hohaley can't convince them why. First he says Orders from Washington. But he won't say whose orders. Then, when the committee asks him if he'll take it on himself to put Matson back on pending investigation, he says Matson's no good anyway. Deserved to be fired. Passes out a few dirty pictures for the boys to look at. Well, what the hell. Then the experts get mad. They can't make head or tail of this prick. So then they come back to talk to us. We're smart, intelligent, the right is on our side. Right makes might, see?

305

'Nothing to do but strike! Less than that, under the circumstances, would fall short of militancy.' "

Charlie knew all this, what the 'experts' had said.

"But what do *you* think?" he persisted.

Hennessey shrugged his shoulders. "I wish you could get in touch with that bastard Colon. I won't justify Matson's craving for the spectacular, but after all, we wouldn't have got into this mess if Colon and his stooge inspector from Washington hadn't encouraged us to resist Hohaley's encroachments and promised us support in so many words if it came to the pinch."

"I'm going to try again all right. It'll make the fifth time this week."

"In here?" Hennessey suggested.

"Huh?"

They went into a place and had a beer.

"It just now comes to me," Hennessey suddenly laughed. "I have been in three strikes and as it happened, we lost them all. I have written three novels and each one was about a strike which the workers lost. The critics criticize me for defeatism. Screw the facts, say the critics, in effect, give the workers something they can pin some hopes to. At the same time, they stroke my tail by 'admitting' that I'm an honest writer. 'It takes Hennessey, almost alone among the writers of our time, to portray the factory worker as he is, *but. . . .*' So I made up my mind that the next book I write, I would pick me a strike where the workers would help me out and win." His face was gloomy now. "How do the critics have the nerve to *prove,* on *paper,* where a man is wrong!"

Charlie saw that Hennessey, in his way, had answered his question. He turned his glass. Unfortunately, it looked the same from all sides.

"They'll do it though, every time. The first book I wrote, they practically killed themselves jumping on my bandwagon. 'The workers almost made it,' they said, 'but the author is young and promising. His style is vigorous, and we're sure he'll come through with them next time.' Just to show me their hearts were in the right place, they talked me into the Pulitzer Prize. Then it happened a second time. 'Not bad,' they said, 'not bad. Architecture good. Interior scheme and taste excellent, but Mother of God, what in hell kind of *people* has he moved into this abode! Do these people *live,* or do they merely reflect what's going on in our author's head?' It's the third time that did it though. By this time they weren't watching my typewriter any more. They were busy looking into the inside of my head. And boy, don't think they didn't hit the jackpot that time. That's the time they really hit it for good. 'Hennessey's in a rut.' Yeah. *'Rut!'* Those bastards have lived on speed highways so long they wouldn't know a rut any more from a hole in the ground."

The bartender had been trying to hear some of this. "Still bad outside, huh, gentlemen?" he said.

"Yeah. Tough on ruts," Hennessey said.

"You mean rats?"

"Yeah. Rats."

"Rats is smart," the bartender said. "Don't think they aint. Them sons of bitches aint sticking *their* noses out in this kind uh weather."

"Yeah. Smart bastards. Ruts."

"You said it. Smart as a whip." The bartender stared.

"That's rats for you. Smartest bastards in the world," Charlie put in. He just didn't feel like getting run out just yet.

"You can't beat a rut," Hennessey said. "A rut is ten times bigger than a house. A house is smarter than the biggest hoose who ever farted his way through a novel by Ernest Hemingway. A hoose is a dumb heroic bastard. He's out in the cold all day. Maybe he's too dumb to do otherwise. His antlers is maybe too big. A house lives down in the basement and travels through the cracks. You know what the house is doing while that hoose is out in the cold!"

The bartender was getting a bit tired of all this. There's such a thing as too much of a good thing. Such a thing as an abuse of hospitality. Not that this wasn't a friendly bar. It was the friendliest bar on Kenzie Street, and he would tell the same to any son of a bitch who expressed an interest to find out about the same. But just because this was a friendly bar, some bastards thought they were entitled to a test for sound. . . .

"Yeah?" he said. "What?"

There was just a touch of coolness in his voice.

"Holing up," Hennessey said. "Holing up, like the smart little bastard that a house is. And a rut is ten times bigger than a house. And ten times as smart."

"Look, Four-Star," Charlie interrupted, his mouth twitching. "*If* I may be so presumptuous while you're on an important subject."

"Go ahead," Hennessey said. He was smiling himself. "Under this clown's mask festers a frown that would make the Grand Canyon imagine itself a pin-scratch."

"I can understand your not thinking that we'll win the strike. But what makes you so goddam certain that there's not a chance, not even a *chance,* of winning? After all, isn't it true that—"

Hennessey had lifted his eyebrows, and his forehead was red from the effort of lifting them even higher. He was trying to give an impression of the blandest and most supercilious surprise at such naïveté.

Charlie faltered. "Well, if you don't think we'll win, and you're so sure we won't, why in hell don't you open your trap sometime and tell the rest of us about it? We might listen to you."

" 'Beware the Ides of March!' I'm always saying that."

"Hennessey. Shakespeare's butt-boy. That's a hell of a comedown for an Irishman."

"Well, hell, Charlie, it should be clear enough why we won't win. Mainly because the Project is a non-profit-making organization. That's the chief point the 'experts' left out of consideration. And you can't strike against the hand that's feeding you. You can only strike against the hand that you are *feeding*. You take an industrial plant. You strike a day even. The company loses in orders. It's big dough for them, and you strike until either you starve or the stockholders lose their shirts. Or their vacations in Florida. It's all the same thing. A matter of attrition. But in this strike, who's going to lose money? Only us. The Government saves the money. The state balances its budget. The reactionary press hollers, 'Look at the dirty bastards! They won't even take relief, let alone work!' "

"What about the three strikes you were in, if it's that simple? They were industrial strikes."

"Nothing's simple. *Clear* and *simple* are two different things. We got to starving before the bosses got to lose their shirts."

Charlie's tone was casual. "If you don't think we'll win the strike, you ought to talk up and say so at the vote."

"Why don't *you* talk up? We don't seem to be in disagreement."

"Well." Charlie threw the whisky down and sipped the beer. "I had a sort of a row with Matson. I've been kind of rowing with Matson for a long time. There was a time once, right after I'd got back from Johnsburgh—it's a long story—when I asked Matson if he was going to doublecross me on a certain matter. He said no, and I believed him. If I hadn't believed him, I wouldn't have asked him. But the funny thing is, I couldn't get rid of an idea that he was *capable* of doublecross. In an almost mystic sense. Why I thought so, I couldn't be sure at the time. Well, when he broke the story of the photostats, I knew that he had pulled a doublecross. Only he hadn't doublecrossed just me, he had doublecrossed the whole union. By pulling it along with him, sink or swim. It was my idea that the Project's the thing. Matson thought otherwise."

"Shakespeare," Hennessey said, "—pardon me for quoting an Englishman—said the world is full of actors. He was wrong. It's full of playwrights. Matson wrote the play one way. With himself the hero of the Project. Fate wrote otherwise. Jevins and Hohaley rewrite the scenario. *They* are the heroes of the Project. Matson becomes their Crown Prince only."

Charlie flushed. "I don't know much about strategy. I don't know a goddam thing. It seems to me, all the same, that we should have been more patient to begin with. . . . I wanted to quit at first, when I first found out how things were going to be around here, but you've still got to keep on living. I've still got my folks to keep help feeding. And it's the same with everybody else here. . . . Suppose we do boondoggle. That's the way they seem to want us to do. Sooner or later Colon's got to do something about it. Sooner or later Hohaley is bound to give himself away for good. Things like the hotel bills, and the financial mess. Meanwhile, there's a book I've been wanting to write for a long time. At home, before the job, I could never afford to do it. The old lady would see me at the table trying to get started, and chase me out of the house. I don't blame her. We couldn't afford it. Why shouldn't I spend the time on the Project getting paid for nothing and writing my book? I've even got a secretary and a telephone. I'd've been a fool to do otherwise."

Hennessey rubbed nervously at his face. "I feel the same way about it," he muttered, "but it's too late now. The thing got away from us. It got out in the open too soon. Everybody's watching it. That's the way it is in a war too. Everybody sick and mad as hell and at the same time hoping it'll be done with human reason and brains and then some son of a bitch at the top who's in the middle of things slips on a banana peel while pulling a fast shortcut and nobody can back out."

All this, as they both knew, was somewhat beside the point.

"The sensible thing to do," Hennessey said, "if this were a scientific laboratory and everybody walking about with white sanitary masks across their faces, and gloves on their hands, would be to vote a strike down, because people don't go on strike to prove something, or to gain an experience, but to *win*—unless they're independent and don't have to give a damn. As to Matson, the union would say that they discovered he was a pederast or something and let him go. He's just one man. He took his chances, on his own, regardless how it would have benefited the Project as a whole if he had won out. He's willing to do that too. He's told everybody that even if he's reinstated, he's going to quit. That ought to be enough. . . . Besides, we've only got sixteen members. . . . And the whole photostatic business would be turned over quietly to Colon. Meanwhile the union is allowed to exist and the workers can get educated at a proper pace. . . . But it isn't a lab. We're not a bunch of scientists in a laboratory either. We're—we're more like an army of the kind that Christ spoke of: the halt, the lame, and the blind. There I go—writing my next novel. The only thing is, the army has nobody to lead them, except themselves. Who the hell wants anything to do with them except themselves?

"Here's Matson. The quixotic son of a bitch. That's how it is. We haven't got the universities to polish us up, the large fortunes to help us out. I was talking to a woman-refugee who had seen Hitler come into power. You'd be surprised what she told me. I mean about how on the inside and comfortably, in absolute security and scientific accuracy, the forces of fascism worked. Everything in absolute order. With their formulas and plans arranged with labels on the shelves. And three meals a day. And Strength-Through-Joy bitching parties every Sunday. While the radicals, like an unbandaged wound, were all on the outside, on the street, noisier than a pack of dogs. I guess that's how it is, Charlie—" He broke off awkwardly. "We live and learn, kiddo."

They kept drinking straight whiskies with beer chasers. These were working hours. To hell with the work. What work? There wasn't any work being done on the Project these days. Hennessey was beginning to get tight faster than Charlie. The anger and frustration still lay between them, and now inhibition began to vanish.

"It's a funny thing," Hennessey said, "every time I ever went on strike, I had the feeling that I have now. I always get blue as hell. I won't back out of it, but I know we're going to have a hell of a time and I start pitying myself and everybody else. But I always think we're going to win. This time I know we're going to lose. I'm going to have a crying jag after a while. I always do. I don't believe in starting on a strike except with a head that's so bad that I can't think what I've gone and done. Not on the first day, anyway."

"We're wound up like Dorothy Lamour," Charlie muttered. "It's funny as hell. Let 'er rip!"

Of all the unionists, he admired Hennessey most. He felt for Hennessey a deep undemonstrative, but unvarying, untroubled admiration, such as he felt for Nussim but never could feel for, say, even Matson. Nor was Hennessey unlike Nussim in spirit, in many ways. An unflinching goodness and a way of thinking and seeing straight, regardless of temptation, and yet a non-controversial and even yielding manner in speech and action, in spite of his belligerent pose, which lured the unwary or the hostile into confusing the man's profound amiability and kindness with placidity and even indifference. A long-distance guy. Like Nussim. "I always get blue as hell, but I won't back out." That's where you found the real guts. To be there in the fifteenth round as well as in the first, there's the trick. . . . And an associational thought passed through Charlie's brain: "The first-round boys stake everything on a knockout, and that's where the second-round boys have the advantage."

"Nothing else *but* wound up," Hennessey was saying. "Not a chance to back out. Only chance is if Colon comes through. We're in it up to our necks now, kiddo. All the forces are conspired to that end now. If and when I write my fourth book on how we lost this strike, you can read it and see what I mean. I haven't got the heart to explain now."

"You're nothing but a defeatist. A nothing but a nothing. A

lousy Irish disgrace to the international and fraternal cause of pure unmitigated hope."

"I'll make you the villain, Gest. How you masqueraded as a saint—alias Saint Patrick on the police blotters of half a dozen continents—while all the time you were really the International Jewish Banker, Sebastian J. Handlebar himself, all seven of the infamous brothers at the same time

> With a yo-yo for every yum-yum
> And a concubine, booo-jous and dumb

"But what else have you on the other side?" he broke into himself. "Is Hohaley's flesh truly the same as mine? Does he bleed when he's pricked, as I do, or does he only bear? Is he of the same flesh as Matson even?"

"Poor old Myrtle. Well, back she goes into the factory. You know, it's a funny thing, Charlie. Every time I go on strike, my wife goes to work in a factory. She comes into the place and they say, 'What's the matter, Four-Star on strike again?' That's how it is. Poor old girl, she sure hasn't had an easy time of it with me. Slaves in a tobacco factory while I'm on strike. Then after I get through, I'm blacklisted in another place. . . . Would you believe it, there isn't a factory or newspaper in the state that'll hire me? And not because I've worked for all of them. Hell, no. Because I'm *famous!* That's right. Because I'm famous, God bless the critics. I repeat myself. When it's learned that Hennessey has gone on strike somewhere, then fifty college-graduated employers all over the state look at the news and say, 'Hmm, a very interesting author, I must make a special note of it that he is not allowed to come to work for me.' Me," he suddenly shouted, "the author of four books, three novels and one book of short stories, in spite of hell and high water, and I don't know what in hell I'm going to do for rent two weeks after I'm out."

"I've never met your wife," Charlie said, somberly.

They were still drinking drink for drink. They didn't always

313

drink them down at exactly the same moment, but they were staying abreast of each other all the same.

"She don't look the least bit like an author's wife, any more than I look like an author."

His face blazed like a huge red sun. "If I pass out before you do, Charlie, you'll have to carry me. I weigh two twenty. What do you weigh?"

"One forty-five. That's because I stopped growing before you did."

"That's funny. I was born before you were. How could you stop growing sooner?"

"I don't know. It's too ideological for me."

"Jesus. This is one contest I got to win. Act of mercy. I can carry you a lot easier than you can carry me."

"It'll be me does the carrying this trip. You got a start on me and your stomach's bigger. You been exercising it longer."

Hennessey began to weep. He'd been drinking steadily for three days.

"I feel so sorry for everybody. So goddam sorry. We got to go through so much before we amount to anything. First we got to have every goddam fool who calls himself a revolutionary experiment with us. Matson, the ten-day Communist! The workers got to take everything, from both sides. My poor old girl hates the very sight of me and my books."

Charlie leaned his head back against the back of his seat to hold it steady and tried to focus his eyes. "Jesus, Hennessey," he said inarticulately, "don't cry." He tried to find the one, the true Hennessey, but before him swam a swamp of many Irishmen, Hennessey and the repetitions of him, all huge, all red, with skyblue blurred eyes, and all of them weeping.

STRANGELY, IT SEEMED, THE ONE TO SPEAK UP AGAINST THE strike finally was Matson himself. It was obvious to the unionists what this speech was costing him in pride.

314

"I've told you," he stammered, "that even if I'm reinstated I'll quit. . . ." He flushed. "I'm single. Unattached. The job doesn't mean anything to me now." Honesty before these white tense faces compelled him: "Maybe it never meant anything to me. I don't know. I feel a lot differently toward all of you than I ever did. You're—real people. . . ."

It was no use. The main thing would be relief at last from tension. Every time they looked at Folinger in his role of president they thought of Francis, the *stool-pigeon*. There were currents of hatred in the room. Matson's words should have given them release, but to what would they return? Surely not peace. Surely not security. Behind the tempting offer of withdrawal they could still see the face of Hohaley and the vengeance waiting for each of them behind those cold brilliant eyes. And the taunts or even worse, the silent sneers, of Hohaley's supporters on the Project already filled them, in anticipation, with fury and added repression. . . .

All the plans had been made. Leaflets drawn up. Requests for support.

"What is your pleasure?" Georgette Wilson asked.

"I call for a vote," Folinger said steadily.

"Before we vote," Georgette said, "I would suggest that we make one more attempt to call Colon."

This was unanimously passed. The call was put in.

"Who's gonna pay for this call?"

"The strike fund," somebody shouted.

There was a passionate darkness in the room, as though everybody was looking and *seeing* with his eyes closed.

While they waited, they exchanged small-talk. What do you suppose happened to Francis anyway? The fellow has disappeared. Taken a total walk-out powder. On the Project too, as well as on the union. Wouldn't put it past Hohaley to have fired his own fink. No, Francis probably just quit, walked out. Couldn't face the exposure. . . . Everybody was smoking hard.

315

The call came through. "Washington office on the line. Are you ready?"

"Let me handle this," Folinger whispered. "Hello? . . . Authors' Project? Let me talk to Mr. Colon."

The answer he received was reflected in his face. He hung up. "Not in," he said briefly. "Don't know when he'll be in."

"The strike will bring him in, the swine!"

The vote was taken. A unanimous decision. The reinstatement of Lloyd Matson was the first and main point. Can we afford to ask for the dismissal of Hohaley? Can we afford to expose the complete inadequacy and inefficiency of the Project? Publicize the hotel bills, reproduce the photostatic copies, demand a public investigation of the total financial set-up? No. None of these. Not yet. Let's wait, at least. There were their scruples, the strikers' *loyalties* even, to the workers who had not as yet come out and to the Project nationally. Let's not give anybody a chance to blow this thing up on all of us. After the reinstatement of Lloyd Matson came the point of recognition of the union as bargaining agent. Then the abandonment of discrimination against Negroes as an employment policy of the Project. Everything modest. Simple. The demands decent and reasonable. The various committees were appointed, plans of procedure to gain support reviewed again. It was five minutes to one. Solemnly now, the workers went back to the Project to get their belongings. As they came up the elevators, they encountered their erstwhile mates returning to work from their lunchtime.

Left behind to get at the newspapers immediately, George Folinger got in touch with the *Star-Globe* and asked for the news-room.

"News-room."

"Will you take a story?"

"Shoot."

"I'm calling from the Musicians' Hall, in the Grove Building . . . temporary headquarters . . . at one o'clock today, sixteen workers of the Authors' Project, following the dismissal of Lloyd Matson, a member of the supervisory staff, went on strike to . . ."

CHARLIE, THE NEXT MORNING, SUDDENLY REALIZED THAT they were on strike, out of a job. It was an emotional realization entirely, all in his guts. The intensity with which this realization came to him made him understand that he had not realized this before. He had not really felt what this would be like. He had read the afternoon papers. Only the *Star-Globe* carried the story so far. The sight of it in print made a terrific impression. He was at the strike office at the time. Matson was drawing up the contents of a pamphlet to be printed at once. Alice Menenbaum, one of the four women strikers, was typing some letters. Charlie smashed his fist down on the table before him and jumped up.

"By God," he yelled, "I'm going to get hold of Colon."

In silence they watched him dial for long-distance.

"I don't think Colon quite realizes how unpleasant we can make it for him," he said, more quietly.

Folinger got up and stood near him, while he waited for the call.

Again, the Washington office. . . .

"This is Mr. Gest calling. . . . *Gest.* . . . Let me talk to our Field Supervisor, Mr. Fred Onigo. Important Project business."

"Just one moment, Mr. Gest."

Charlie turned to the others. "They're getting him." He motioned for quiet. "Hullo, Onigo? Listen, Fred, I'm not going to waste any time. This phone is costing dough, and it isn't Project money now. We're on strike. Yes, we finally went on strike. Did you know that we'd been trying to get Colon all week and that I sent him a registered letter that he didn't answer?"

"No, I didn't, Charlie. For God's sake, when did you go on strike?"

"Today. But I can't take too long in explaining now. If you

like, I'll send you a letter tonight with the full particulars. But right now, I want to say something for you to tell Colon. Can you hear me?"

"Yes. Go ahead."

"Tell him that I personally think he has doublecrossed us. That I think he's been in his office all the time, but wouldn't take our calls" (Onigo was silent). "Tell him he doesn't get out of it that easy."

"Wait a minute, Charlie. Aren't you flying off at this half-cocked?"

Charlie spoke quietly. "You want to hear a funny thing, Fred? This'll interest you, since psychology is a hobby of yours. Get this. We voted a strike at one o'clock yesterday. And we've been thinking about it for three weeks. But it wasn't until just about five minutes ago, when I decided to call you, that I *realized* that we were on strike. Do you know what that means? We're on strike, Fred! We're out of jobs. We've gone *out*. I just now realized it. And I'll give Colon the benefit of thinking that he couldn't be expected to realize it any faster than I have. But he's got to realize it now. And you've got to impress him with it. He's tied up with this besides the obvious connections, as you know. He's bound morally to support us. If he doesn't, then sixteen people may never go back to work here because of their hopes based on what he has wanted them to do all along."

Charlie let Onigo interrupt.

"I'm sure there has been some mistake. Colon is not like that. He's really a squareshooter. I'm certain he'll support you all he can."

"Okay, Fred. Let him reinstate Lloyd Matson, as he can do, and we call the strike off. We're not even demanding Hohaley's dismissal. But I don't know if I can agree with you on Colon being a squareshooter. Tell him for me that we have damaging letters on Hohaley's Project affairs—he can call me to find out just what they are—and we'll have to use them if we have to.

318

And also there's correspondence between Colon and myself, in which he says a number of things that will be embarrassing to him for us to divulge."

"I'll tell him, Charlie. I'll make it a personal matter to get in touch with him. And I'll see that he calls you."

"Okay. Thanks. I'd better hang up now. This costs us money."

"Wait a minute. Hello, hello?"

"Yeah?"

"What's your number?"

"Number? Oh. What's the number here, Matson?"

Matson thought a minute. He couldn't remember off-hand, and there was some wild scurrying for a moment to find where it had been written on the walls.

HARDLY TEN MINUTES HAD PASSED WHEN THE TELEPHONE rang. Charlie, at the moment, was standing at the window, watching the picket line in front of the Project across the street one block down. After his talk with Onigo, almost the entire union had gone down to get in the line. A vein was still beating hard in his temple and his throat felt as though it were being choked. He did not think of the telephone call as for him. Alice took the call.

"Washington calling," she screamed. "Mr. Colon on the line!"

"Give it to him!" Folinger growled.

The two came around Charlie as he took the receiver. After a moment of drawing a deep breath and composing himself, he spoke into it.

"Hello, Mr. Colon?"

"Yes. Gest?"

Charlie recognized the pleasant voice. In his mind's eye he saw the civilized face of the man at the other end of the wire. At the greeting, he felt immeasurably calmer instantly. At this moment, so reassuring was that familiar voice (contact at last!), he was

319

ready to believe, as Onigo had said, that Colon was entirely innocent of indifference and betrayal. That it was all some sort of
a mistake now to be cleared up.

At the sound and meaning of his own words, though, he
began to have doubts of this hope: "I—I've been trying to get
in touch with you, Mr. Colon. I—I called you five times this
week. I sent you a registered letter."

"Onigo tells me that you have certain documents that—"

He broke off abruptly. Each of us speaks what's on his own
mind, Charlie thought.

"We have documents—photostats—of pending bills between
Mr. Hohaley and the hotel where they had the banquet for you,"
he said coldly. "The documents, if you recall the circumstances
of the banquet—"

"For God's sake, I recall nothing. Do you think I have nothing to do but—"

"I sent you reports all along. This was by your request,
whether you've had time to look at them or not. This week I
tried to get in touch with you five times. I sent you a registered
letter."

"I'm a busy man," Colon shrieked. "I didn't get your calls.
I haven't read your letter. I've been out of town."

"Let me talk to him," Folinger shouted, as the thin pipe of
the angry voice pierced and went past the receiver. "Jesus, let
me tell him."

Charlie motioned him off. "Look, Mr. Colon," he said softly,
"we're on strike. They fired Matson. We—"

"You shouldn't have gone on strike. I don't know that
Federal employees have the right to strike."

"Perhaps you refer to civil service workers. Federal people.
Our status is very uncertain. There's a lot to be defined." He
felt that they were talking at cross-purposes. "The strike is not
important, Mr. Colon. It's just a symptom, like a running nose.
I don't have to tell you that. Remove the cause of the cold, and

the symptoms will disappear. The point is, *they've fired Matson.*
You could reinstate him so easily. If I had been able to get in
touch with you before, we wouldn't have had to go on strike."

"But the point is," Colon shrieked, louder than before, "you
have gone on strike. You were in a hurry. You couldn't wait to
get in touch with me—" it must have occurred to him that he
had given the order to fire Matson; he faltered, but continued
and finished the sentence he had already begun—"to intervene
for him."

"Why won't you let me talk to him?" Folinger demanded.
"Are you the assistant director of the strike too, for Christ's
sake?"

"You've put me in a spot," Colon was shouting. "What do
you expect me to do—stick my neck out?"

"Folinger wants to talk to you."

"Wait a minute. I'm talking to you. Put him on and I'll
hang up."

Charlie handed the receiver to Folinger.

"Colon, this is Folinger speaking. What kind of a dirty deal
are you trying to put over on us?"

"I've got nothing to say to you."

Charlie could hear the voice. He could still recognize it as
Colon's, but now that he was away from the telephone it was
somehow not Colon's. It was just a sort of a tinny record that
was coming over—a record that had been transcribed long
ago. . . .

"You've got to have something to say to me. What do you
think you helped start here—a tea-party?"

"I can't talk to you over the telephone!"

"You can't answer our letters either, it seems."

So that's it, Charlie thought. Letters are in black and white.
Telephone conversations may be recorded and witnessed on ex-
tension wires. What a cautious bastard! The strike's on, then.
Not a demonstration strike as he had hoped against hope it

would be. But the real thing. The McCoy. The Strike, "last weapon of the workers." He thought of how Matson had jumped the gun, maneuvered the situation to run into a pre-conceived and inevitable end. He thought of Colon, running for cover. So it's to be the *strike,* last weapon of the workers when they've been shoved around, lied to, driven from corner to corner like dogs in the house. . . .

War! The beating of conclusive drums! How exciting to read about!

"They found pictures in Matson's desk—" Colon was shouting. "You think I want them to publicize *that?*"

He realized his mistake too late, and stopped.

"Well, then, if you knew they had found pictures, then they must have informed you that Matson had been dismissed—even if you were out of town for *us.*"

Ears in the office perked up—

"I can't talk to you over the telephone," Colon shouted.

"Okay, Colon. We'll say it with picket lines. And not only here. We'll say it in Washington. In New York. We'll publicize this thing until you'll wish that you had seen sense. And I'll give you one guess right now all the things we will have to say —and what's more, that we'll find it possible—with the support of thousands to listen to us—to *prove.*"

"Let me talk to Gest, will you? There's something I want to say to him."

There was a note of pleading in his voice that impressed Folinger.

"Okay," he said. "But remember. We didn't call *you* up this time. You called us."

Charlie picked up the receiver.

"Yes?"

He felt apathetic.

"Look here, old man. I can't discuss the merits of this case over

322

the telephone. It's too complicated anyway, as I'm sure you will agree."

"I'll agree to that," Charlie said.

"I promise you that I'll do the level best I can in the matter. I have already instructed my representative to come to Monroe to investigate the whole matter. He's taking an airplane this afternoon. Meanwhile, why don't you fellows go back to work?"

"No, no," Folinger whispered. He shook his head No.

"—It's the best way out of this mess for all of us."

Charlie remembered something Hennessey had once said: "A storm has been gathered. . . ." It had been Hennessey, hadn't it?

"Why don't you put Matson back to work provisionally—or on probation—I don't know the technical terms for this," Charlie countered, "while your investigator collects his evidence and makes his findings? I really don't think the union would consent to any other arrangement than that," he added, to soften the flat contradiction to Colon's offer.

"But I can't do that. Can't you see that, Gest? I've got to be fair to all sides. I've got to get a report from my man first."

Fair to all sides! Coming from Colon, what kind of crap was that!

"It'll be at least a week before your man will have all his evidence. He'll have to talk to a number of people here in Monroe. He'll have to go to Marathon, to see the Treasury people. He'll have to go to Johnsburgh. . . . There'll be sixteen of us out of work meanwhile. We can't afford it."

"But you don't have to be out of work. You can go back, pending the inquiry."

"Suppose we go back, and Mr. Hohaley then fires somebody else? For reasons that won't need to look as though they have a connection. What then? Will you guarantee now that if we go back, there'll be no more dismissals?"

"I can't guarantee anything. I'm not *negotiating* the strike now with you. This conversation is strictly *off the record*. I called you up to talk to you man to man."

Charlie felt that it was not necessary to mention that this was an ambiguous explanation, at best, of the real reason for the call.

"I see," Charlie said. "You tell us to go back, but you don't even guarantee our own safety, let alone Matson's. . . . Let me ask you: Do you believe in unions?"

"Of course I do."

"Do you believe in collective bargaining between the duly elected union of a plant and the employers?"

"Of course."

("He's not afraid to admit *that* over the phone," Folinger said to Alice bitterly.)

"Well, now, look. If you'll read the letter I sent you you'll see that before we went on strike, we sent committee after committee to see Hohaley to ask him to do just what you now suggest—to let an independent jury of representatives of various unions (this included *your* union, the Guild) investigate and pass judgment, this judgment—if it declared for our side—then to be submitted to you for arbitration. He refused all this. He preferred to force us either to strike or abandon Matson. We are on strike now. And we'll have to stay on strike until a decision is reached. . . . His actions go contrary to your own statements just now on the rights of unions to collective bargaining. And besides, there was your own promise that no administrative officer could be fired without your okay. You'll remember, from when you were in Monroe, that we thought that a necessary condition. So I think you would be within your powers to reinstate Matson temporarily. If you do this, we'll go back. If you then find that Matson should be dismissed, we'll let him go and accept the decision."

324

"The best I can do is send an investigator," Colon repeated, in a low voice.

"Okay. But since you won't admit that what's going on between us now is collective bargaining, then the union is left free meanwhile to do what it feels best."

He waited politely for Colon to say good-bye first. Colon was having a difficult time expressing himself in his next statement.

"You'll have to hold up using those d-documents you wrote me about," he stuttered, so low that Charlie could hardly hear him. "Y-you can't jeopardize the Project."

"All right. I'll promise you that. Until the investigator gets here."

Johnson and Hennessey came into the room. Johnson was one of the three Negroes. They were carrying their placards, Hennessey with his still across his front and back.

"Nice feeling," Hennessey commented, puffing on his ever-present pipe. "Walked through the streets coming back. People stopped to look what restaurant was being advertised. One fellow walked around me, read front and back. 'Where's this joint located,' he says, 'and why don't you have any prices?' "

Alice laughed. The front of Hennessey's contraption read, in bold black letters, AUTHORS' PROJECT ON STRIKE. The back read REINSTATE LLOYD MATSON.

"I don't know how they could mistake you for a restaurant advertisement," she said.

"The man was a WPA politician," Hennessey said, "he couldn't read."

Folinger asked why weren't they on the picket line.

"A trifle," Hennessey said. "Tell him, Johnson."

"They arrested eight of us," Johnson said. "They left four. They said two's all they would allow to picket at one time. So we left Mrs. Van Fern and Georgette down there and came up here to report."

325

"There you are," Folinger said, looking triumphantly at Charlie. "And Colon wanted us to be nice boys and call off the strike."

"Oh, did Colon call?"

"Yes," Folinger laughed. "He called. Boy did we get him told! He's gonna send an investigator."

"What's there to investigate?" Hennessey said. He removed his placard. "Well, got to start raising bail." He went to the telephone.

While he was looking up a number, Johnson addressed himself to Charlie.

"What's he mean, an investigator? Isn't he going to bat for us?"

"I don't know," Charlie said, "it might be a doublecross."

"I thought you said that Colon would be sure to—to—back us up, if only we could get in touch with him."

Charlie winced. Then laughed. "Sure I did. And Matson had a scheme that was sure to work—only he didn't say for whom. And Colon told me last time he was in Monroe that he intended to see that the Authors' Project lived up to its name, and he pinned a deputy's rose on me. . . . It looks like we all say something which isn't true. Don't you ever say things you don't mean?"

Johnson thought Charlie was sore at him or something. He didn't know what about, and got sensitive. "My mistake," he said, his eyebrows raising. "I didn't know I was stepping into something."

Folinger pretended not to hear what Charlie had said, but his neck reddened. He himself had lost his temper earlier. He went to the typewriter and began working out a letter.

"Well," Charlie said, "you want to take a turn in front of the old brothel, Alice?"

He picked up Hennessey's posters and put them over his

326

shoulders. The girl ran to the mirror over the washbowl and began powdering her nose.

"How do I look?" she said, at last, her voice tremulous.

PART NINE

He was waiting to take his turn on the picket line. Hennessey and Johnson were out there now. It was a quarter to eleven and Georgette and Mrs. Van Fern were busily engaged making coffee and sandwiches. Folinger was explaining the strike to a couple of musicians whose hall had been put "for the duration" at the strikers' service.

"It's like a symphonic arrangement, gentlemen. See what I mean? From the beginning, you heard that one note that made the end inevitable."

The musicians were not symphony players. One was a saxophonist; the other beat the drums when he was working.

"I guess so, if you say so."

The telephone rang. Charlie answered it. It was Margaret Renny.

"Lemme talk to Mr. Gest, please."

"That's me."

"Gee, Charlie, I got to speak to you. There's something going on here. I think you ought to know about it."

"Sure. How about Sloppy Nell's?"

"Swell. That's a couple of blocks away from the Project, and they won't see me. How about a quarter past eleven?"

"I thought you didn't go to lunch until twelve."

"They changed our hours. There's a lot of changes around here. The place don't seem the same."

She seemed nervous. As though she were looking over her shoulder. He cut it short.

"All right, kid. A quarter past eleven."

He looked up to see everybody looking at him. Under the banter and the gaiety that had characterized them since the strike had begun, there was great anxiety. They were always expecting to hear that something was breaking in their favor.

"That was Margaret Renny. She wants me to meet her in half an hour. Says it's important. She couldn't tell me over the phone."

"Do you suppose it has to do with the investigator?"

"I don't know. She just said that something was happening over at the Project."

"I bet it's the investigator. He's been in the state now for almost a week. By God, he's seen everybody here but the opening of the baseball season. Why in hell doesn't he show up around here?"

"I don't know," Charlie said. "No use speculating."

The street was being systematically covered with a fresh layer of snow. The snow that had fallen earlier in the week had now impacted and the sidewalks all seemed a foot higher, bringing walkers that much closer to the rooftops and the free sweep of the wind. At least, it seemed colder because of it. Buildings seemed to shove their way out of the hard white earth like monuments of buried men. He walked into the restaurant and scraped his feet on the doormat. The insides of the windows were frosted over. Margaret was sitting in a booth at the back of the place.

"Jesus," he said, "it's cold outside."

She seemed thinner than when he had seen her last. Her eyes, normally large, were bulging out of her head, and there were specks of red on the balls. Her face, reddened by the wind, emphasized the tiny blotches on her skin.

"Well?" he said. "What's the big news?"

She was looking at him hungrily.

"Gee, Charlie, I bet it's cold on that picket line. I used to try and see the picketers from Rodolfi's window. We all used to get together up there and watch youse. But Regan stopped it. Mr. Hohaley has made a supervisor out of Regan."

He remembered that she had called him Charlie over the telephone. Well, times change. The era of Mr. Gest was over. He was Charlie again. He liked it better that way. At the same time it emphasized the fact that he was through.

"Regan," he said bitterly, "a supervisor. Why, that son of a bitch can't spell his name."

"Yeah. The place aint the same. All we do is just sit around and read the newspapers. And we talk to each other. But there aint no work being done. You don't hardly hear even a typewriter. Mr. Hohaley brought in several people from Johnsburgh to show that we don't need you, but they don't do nothing neither."

"You think we got a chance of winning?"

"I don't know." She twisted her lips and bit at them, a nervous habit that he disliked. He turned his eyes away. "That's what I wanted to talk to you about," she said. "You know Lucille Turnbull?"

"Sure, I know Lucille. Go ahead."

"Well, she has done an awful thing to herself. This morning —it only happened just this morning, well—gee, I don't know how to tell you!"

He lit a cigarette, leaned back in his seat. She was sitting with her back to the window, and he looked past her at the street. All the people hurrying by. He tried to imagine Lucille outside the window. She presented herself holding a tin cup.

"What about Lucille?"

"She—she *cut* herself. She had a razor with her and she didn't even go into the bathroom to do it. She was sitting at her desk a-and she just went ahead and cut herself. Somebody looked over and there she was. Sitting in a pool of blood."

He kept looking out of the window. Somehow he wasn't surprised. He felt as though nothing would surprise him.

"Was she dead?"

He heard his voice asking this. He wanted to yawn. As he watched the black-clad figures rushing past the window, he wondered how he would look himself going by. He began to see himself. He was rushing by. No sooner did he get out of his own line of vision than he was back where he started and was rushing by again.

"No, she wasn't dead. Listen, Charlie, she cut her wrists a-and she cut herself in another p-place."

"Another place?"

His eyes came back to her. The girl was furiously red and tears stood in her eyes. She began to cry softly, without making a sound.

"What other place?"

"She—she, it's hard for a woman to say it. . . . She *cut* herself"—she was looking down, trying to make him understand—"in—in—"

Suddenly he understood. A wave of cold horror, beginning in his sexual organs, spread through his body.

"She cut herself—down *there?*"

"She di-didn't cut herself bad. She'll be all right. Th-they took her out. That isn't what I wanted to tell you."

"No?"

He sensed a threat to the union in her last remark, and jerked himself free of the web of thoughts and memories of the skinny woman that Margaret's words had thrown him into.

"What else is there?"

"There was a reporter up there right after it happened. Mr. Hohaley gave him some kind of a story and then he was telephoning and then Mr. Hudson came in. Mr. Onigo from Washington was also with him. They came in together. And then they began to—to—"

"For Christ's sake, Margaret. Go ahead!"

"They was calling the girls in, one at a time. First they called in Constance Rinaldi and then they called in Florence Hartzig. Then they called me in. They asked me if—if—anybody had b-bothered us at work. They wanted to know if you or Lloyd Matson. Or Hennessey."

"I see. What did they ask you, Margaret?"

"Well"—the girl looked up and smiled—"Mr. Hudson was doing the questioning—"

"The great lover!"

"What?"

"Nothing. . . . Go ahead."

"Mr. Hohaley was just sitting at his desk. Smoking and looking. *You* know. Like you say he does. And Mr. Onigo was standing by the window. He had his back to me, but he looked kind of disgusted. Mr. Hudson was sitting at the desk with a piece of paper and a pencil in his hand and he says, 'You was Mr. Gest's secretary?' and I says, 'Yes.' So then he—well, he just *asked* me! He said, 'Did Mr. Gest, in any way, shape or form ever make a pass at you which you, as a lady, would be inclined to resent?' He said that whatever I answered him, he would hold it in the strictest of confidence. He said that it was a terrible thing what had happened to Miss Turnbull and he wanted to impress on me that it was my duty, like everybody else at this time, to co-operate with him."

Could this be himself talking? Could this be a girl named Margaret Renny? Maybe, as the popular joke had it, they were two other people.

"What did you say?"

"Well, what do you *think* I said! I got up and said, 'I don't know what has happened to Miss Turnbull and I also don't know why you think Mr. Gest or any of the others have done anything

331

to bother us girls.' Then I drew myself up to my full height—"
Charlie chuckled at the picture.

"And I said, 'I want you to know that Mr. Gest has always been a perfect gentleman in every way, shape or form to me, and I will certainly welcome any other investigation questions you may have to put to me.' "

"Then what happened?" Charlie grinned.

"Well, Mr. Onigo turned around then. He was grinning too. Just like you, Charlie. I didn't see what was funny. If somebody had said about *me*—"

"What did Hudson say?"

"Well, he was sore. He didn't say nothing, but I could see he was plenty sore. I don't know what Mr. Hohaley thought. He just kept looking at me."

Charlie stood up. "We-ell." Something occurred to him. "Say, what about the others? I guess they asked *all* the women those questions."

"They was asking them when I left there. They was calling them in one at a time." She remained seated. "I'm on my lunch-hour, Charlie," she said shyly.

"Jesus. Excuse *me!*" He sat down again. *"Waitress!* . . . I don't suppose you know what the others said?"

"Well, gee, Charlie! What would *any* woman say? Any real woman. . . . I know Constance said the same thing I did."

The waitress came over.

"What'll you have, Maggie?"

She flushed with pleasure at the diminutive of her name.

"I'll have a beef on bun. A piece of apple pie, if you got it."

"Yes, Ma'am. What'll you have, sir?"

"Cup of coffee. Hot."

"You ought to have something else, Charlie. You can't live on a cup of coffee."

"What makes you think I live on coffee?"

"I just thought—"

"Well, I ate just before I came over. Two delicious ham sandwiches from the aristocratic hands of Mrs. Van Fern herself."

"Well, I feel funny, me ordering and you . . ."

He watched her eat. She tried to offer him half her sandwich. He shook his head silently No.

"Well, this'll be dutch, huh, Charlie? Please!"

"Okay," he agreed. "Dutch. I'll pay the sales tax."

She seemed nervous, and kept on talking while she ate. She babbled on how different the place now was, what with all the empty desks and what had happened this morning and Mr. Hudson now always in and out of the place and she didn't know what-all. Finally: "Charlie, there's something I want to ask you. You don't hold it against me that I didn't come out on strike with youse?"

He flushed. At one time he had been so foolish as to hope that the whole Project would come out. "No, why should I? You've got to *want* to come out first. You've got to know why you're coming out."

Tears were in her eyes again.

"Gee, Charlie. You don't know how tough things have been with us at home. I just *couldn't* come out with you."

He thought of his own home.

"My old lady has been sick, Charlie. I got little brothers and sisters. And—"

"Yes," he said, "I understand. My old lady just come back from Europe. My kid sisters are making their debut next year. The only problem my old lady's got is keeping the young ones from drinking up all the liquor in the house."

She didn't know whether he was kidding her or not. Her eyes dropped, and she bit her lips nervously.

"Listen," he said, immensely ashamed, "I'm—kind of *nervous*. I either find that I don't know what to say, or I start chattering. It's all right about you not coming out. I understand."

333

"Well, what I wanted to say was, I'll come out now, if you want me to. Gee, Charlie, it's so *cold* out there. Us girls, when Regan aint in the office, we stand at the window and watch youse walking up and down in front of the building. I think George Folinger ought to get himself a heavier coat—"

"No," Charlie said. "There's absolutely no reason why you should come out." He knew perfectly well why she made this offer. It touched and angered him at the same time. . . . "You never did know why we went on strike, did you?"

Her lowered head answered him.

"You don't know now, do you?"

"No," she said in a soft voice. "I can't understand it."

He didn't know what else to say.

"Come on," he said, "I'll walk you part way back."

He watched silently when, at the cash register, she fumbled desperately in her purse to be on time to help him pay the bill. He let her do it.

"Gee," she said, as they emerged, "it's gettin' *awful* cold!"

They walked down Pershing Street instead of taking the direct route. Leo the Cop started to wave as they crossed the intersection at his beat. Charlie began to wave too. Then Leo seemed to remember that Charlie was a striker now, and withheld the gesture before it was completed. Charlie had already begun his wave, and felt angry as he withdrew it. A bastard. But Leo, he knew, looked more puzzled than illegitimate.

"One more question before I forget it: wasn't there some sort of note Lucille left? People usually leave notes."

"Yeah, I wanted to tell you about that too, only I forgot. She left a note and she said that she was doing this because the—it was something about the strike. . . . I don't know just how she said it. They was talking about it at the office. Helen O'Hara was telling us girls that she seen it."

Just before they parted, Margaret—in crossing a street— slipped her arm inside his and let it remain there. He felt that

334

she was waiting for him to give it a pressure, but he couldn't bring himself to it. Life is fully as unreasonable as it seems, he was thinking. More so. Here was Margaret. She would—as she herself would have put it—work her fingers to the bone for him, if he'd only say the word. He just didn't like her though. She had bad skin and she was too skinny and, anyway, he wouldn't have liked her anyway. . . . One likes, one doesn't like. O Elizabeth! Oh, you heavenly bitch!

HE WENT STRAIGHT TO THE PICKET LINE AND TOOK HIS PLACE, relieving Hennessey. Mrs. Van Fern had already relieved Johnson. The big Irishman limped off, leaving the plump aristocratic woman laughing helplessly for several minutes. It was really amazing how well these two apparently opposite and ill-sorted people got along. His background was an unrelieved story of drab life in a midwestern factory town, punctuated by a year in the trenches in France; hers included Vassar, trips to Europe, and relatives who had married into Viennese nobility. All his jokes and stories were—or should have been to her—vulgar, but she swore that if left on a desert island, she could be content with two things: a set of Shakespeare and Hennessey to read them to her. Charlie joined in her laughter, watching Hennessey limping off, a broad red hand supporting his back to indicate that he was on the verge of lumbago, if not worse; he felt a mild surprise when, a second later, Margaret walked past him and he realized that he had actually got there before she had. She must have walked around the viaduct, for Christ's sake. She walked in stiffly through the door, not greeting him.

Mrs. Van Fern began telling him the story Hennessey had been telling her, but he didn't listen. He suddenly wanted to get a paper.

"Look, Olivia, do you mind if I leave you for a moment?"

She was startled. "Of course not," she said, a bit stiffly.

He came back with a paper. As they walked up and down, he turned the pages. A passerby said, "Pretty soft, aint it?"

"You said it," he answered, without looking up.

At last he found it. On the fifth page. He read it. Without a word, he turned it over to his companion.

"Look at this."

She read:

STRANGE SUICIDE ATTEMPT
AT AUTHORS' PROJECT

Miss Lucille Turnbull, a member of the supervisory staff of the Monroe Authors' Project, made an attempt at suicide this morning when she slashed her wrists with a dull razor while seated at her desk at work.

She inflicted other wounds on herself, and an investigation is pending, according to the police and Project officials.

A note was found in which, police say, she blames a strike in progress for her action. The Project has been struck since Wednesday last. The strike was precipitated, [etc.]

While she read, Charlie saw Onigo and Hudson emerge from the building. They all looked at each other, Mrs. Van Fern's face flushing with anger. Hudson's face was grim and scowling. Onigo looked at Charlie blankly. He stared back. Then he saw, as the two men passed in silence, the tiniest drooping of Onigo's eyelid. It was the first gesture he had seen since the strike had started that made sense. He had the certain feeling that Onigo, all other phases of his investigation completed by now, surely would drop in at strike headquarters. He felt that he could hardly wait for that moment. He had a wild sense of exultation in the thought that by tomorrow the strike would have been settled, and Matson back at work again. And the work would begin again. But this time everything would go off all right.

WHEN FOLINGER AND MATSON CAME TO RELIEVE THEM, THEY said that Onigo had called up to arrange a meeting at his hotel room for that night. They were both extremely excited and all four walked up and down the picket line as Folinger kept giving them further details of the argument he had had with Onigo as to whether he should come to strike headquarters or they should come to his room. Charlie kept silent. He was thinking that it was ominous that Onigo had refused to come to the headquarters. After all, he had gone to the Project. Mrs. Van Fern was thinking the same thing. She too was silent. But Folinger was inclined to pass over this aspect of the matter. He told how he had asked Onigo if he had heard of Lucille's suicide attempt and how Onigo had laughed.

All four were startled when the solitary policeman stationed at the scene of the picketing (he spent his time seated at the lunch-counter across the street, where he could be seen gazing their way for hours on end, a cup of cold coffee before him and a mournful expression on his face) came up to inform them that it was against his orders to allow four of them on the line to walk at the same time.

"I'm sorry, friends, you'll have to break it up. There's a law against tracking up the snow around here."

He made his joke rather wistfully. He was a young probationary policeman and still at a stage where he worried over how his orders would be received. It was not a physical reception that he feared. He would know how to take care of that. Rather, he feared the thoughts of those forced to obey his orders. Later, of course—it was his consolation to think—he would get over such sensitiveness.

In this case, his joke was received rather well. Folinger laughed, and Matson positively almost doubled up, so did the jest tickle him.

The officer blinked, gratified.

"I don't like to ask you people to do this," he explained. "Youse have always conducted yourselves without no cause of trouble to nobody, but it's my orders. And you wouldn't want to see me get in wrong, would you now?"

"No bother at all," Mrs. Van Fern said shrilly, catching up Matson's and Folinger's mood. She put on her most gracious hostess manner. "Oh, officer, I wonder if you'd do something for me."

"Why, sure, lady—if it aint against my orders now."

"I'm sure it's not. My cousin will be leaving the bank in a few minutes and he'll be missing me here. I wonder if you'd mind telling him that I send him my love and regards and not to come to tea this evening, as I shan't be home."

"Your cousin, lady?"

"Yes." She pointed to a long sleek limousine parked along the other side of the street, in front of the bank. "That's his car. I'm sure you can see it quite clearly from the hamburger stand." Before the officer could say anything, she turned to the others. "Why don't we sort of celebrate a bit, eh? Let's all take off this afternoon, and deceive everybody no end."

"Right you are," Matson shouted immediately. Although, normally, he and she did not like each other, he took her arm now. "Come along, all," he whined, with an affectation of her drawl.

They started off, gaily. Folinger was about to protest, but Charlie took his arm now and began to propel him in the direction of the others. "Come on, my God, the Kingdoms of the Earth await us."

Off they all went now. The officer stared first at their retreating figures, then at the Project, which was now left unpicketed and somehow empty-looking and incomplete, and then at the limousine. He didn't exactly follow this up by scratching his head, but his head felt as though it had been scratched all the same. Not wishing to appear conspicuous at this time, he went across the street and re-entered the hamburger stand. He sat down at the counter. His cup of cold coffee, by his orders, had been left standing there. He let it sit. He watched, in a sort of thoughtless daze, for somebody to get into the limousine. In a few minutes, somebody did. It was a colored chauffeur.

"Don't touch this coffee," the officer commanded.

He went out and approached the limousine. The chauffeur, after having arranged himself comfortably at the wheel, had allowed his head to fall back until it fitted snugly against the upholstery at the back of his neck, and with a sigh was beginning to close his eyes.

"This car belong to somebody works here in the bank?" the officer asked. He made his request somewhat gruffly, for it seemed to him that he—being a policeman—should have known whose car this was. He avoided the chauffeur's startled, then scornful eyes. He had an idea just what the chauffeur was thinking.

"It belong to Mr. Ellory Hornsbrook Van Fern," the chauffeur informed him bleakly, after which (after a moment of unwavering scrutiny) he closed his eyes again.

The officer pondered the astounding name he had heard. He hated to stick his chin out again, but the man had not answered his question. He had to stick his chin out.

"I didn't ask you who it belonged to. I asked you did it belong to somebody in the bank."

"It do," said the chauffeur, once more opening his eyes. He cleared his throat. "It belong to the president of the bank. Mr. Ellory Hornsbrook Van Fern is de name of the president of the bank."

The officer went back to the hamburger stand. He looked across at the Project building. Not a picket in sight. A couple of judges came out. They looked like judges. He watched them as they apparently also noticed that there were no pickets on duty; he saw them smile and say something to each other, and he felt uncomfortable, as though there was something that he should be doing about this. He hoped the sergeant would not come along just now. A man came out of the bank and entered the limousine. The patrolman leaped from his seat.

339

As the chauffeur was about to start off, he stuck his head in at his window. He addressed the president of the bank.

"You a cousin of a lady who is a picket across the street here?" He had a shaky feeling that he was getting himself into trouble.

"Yes, I am," the president admitted. "Is she under arrest?"

"No, sir. She left word with me that you was not to come to her house tonight. She will not be home."

"Hmm. Thank you very much. You're sure she's not under arrest?"

"No, sir. She went off with three pick—three gentlemen. I heard them say something about a celebration."

He watched the car roll off. His forehead, he discovered, was cold with sweat. He wiped it off.

"What happened to the picket line?" the sergeant asked.

He whirled on the sergeant. He wondered what the sergeant would say if he told him about the bank president and the lady picket. He could just imagine what the sergeant would *think*. So he didn't tell him.

"I dunno," he said. "I dunno what happened to the goddamn thing."

"You dunno!"

"They just went off. That's all I know."

The sergeant looked up at the Project building. He could see no changes in that structure to explain the inexplicable happening. It was a mystery. A sure-enough mystery.

"Gone off," he said, "just like that. Some people," he said bitterly, "think it's easy being a copper."

The patrolman, grateful for the observation, which was his thought exactly, and feeling now that the sergeant would not be thinking secret things about *him,* suggested that they go back to the hamburger joint to sort of figure out what was the matter here.

"Hamburger joint!" the sergeant said, turning his gaze on him.

"Maybe we ought to go back to headquarters," the patrolman said, thinking perhaps he had said the wrong thing.

"Headquarters," the sergeant said. "That's a good one! You think we kin leave like that? These bastards kin leave their picketing if they feel like it, but we got to stay on our line of duty."

He led the way back to the hamburger joint.

"What happened to my cup of coffee?"

"You didn't say to hold it for you, so I poured it out. It was cold."

JUDAS TO JONAS, ONIGO THOUGHT GRIMLY:

"Yes, Jonas, I've seen everybody, done everything that was necessary. There will be no explosion here. The Project will continue. Jevins consented to force Hohaley to pay the hotel bill and advanced a check to take care of the hotel immediately. . . . Don't ask me how Hohaley will raise the money to repay Jevins. Your guess is as good as mine, and I won't tell you what my guess is. . . . I also presented the check to the hotel, and in my presence they destroyed the copies of their correspondence and I impressed upon them the fact that they might have to make a public denial of the whole affair. Naturally, they consented to do this. . . . Nobody, you see, now knows anything about the affair except our poor heroes, the strikers, and they're going to find that their mistake was that they played around too long with a time-bomb. . . . They're divided too on the question of using the hotel's letters. . . . As to the financial mess, two men from the Treasury have been working day and night. It's now cleaned and covered up. From now on, the financial department of the State WPA will take direct control of the finances. I hated to give in to them on this, but it was absolutely necessary. Their request for control, in view of the mess Hohaley

341

has put the thing in, was not unreasonable. And, naturally, they will deny anything if it comes to a public accusation by the strikers. . . . Finally I went up and had a lengthy chat with the editor of the *Star-Globe*. It's the only paper in the city worth considering. The others are Democratic and will not—all other things being equal—take a chance on impairing the President's chance of cutting out his critics' tongues locally. Nor will the *Star-Globe* handle the matter. I placed information in their hands showing that the national union, of which the Monroe chapter is a new local, is not interested in the strike. That its national policy is one of co-operation with the Administration. Incidentally, the president of the union has deserted, a chap named Francis; left town, rather mysteriously, and this adds to the generally unsavory looks of the whole thing."

"You've done a good job. What about the union?"

"Well, I don't know what the union will decide to do. I don't see that they have any alternative. Jevins has decided to allow eight of them to go back to work—he's not an unreasonable sort of a beast—he understands that *Washington's* prestige must not be allowed to suffer too much. Matson, however, is out. He insists on that."

"Did he specify which eight are to go back?"

"Yes, he did. Gest is out. Hennessey is out. Folinger is out. Van Fern is out. He has no objection to any of the others, but insists that no more than eight be admitted back. And none of the supervisors are to return in their former capacities."

Colon groaned. "Hennessey *must* go back. Do you realize that he's a national figure? The Project can't afford not to take him back. It'll be a scandal."

"There's just a chance he'll allow Hennessey to go back. For personal reasons, I also insisted on Gest. The point I made was that two *writers*—at least—must go back. And Negroes—one *Negro* at least must go back. I think that if you agree on his main

342

points, he will agree on these—but I'm certain that he won't allow anybody's return in a supervisory capacity."

A long pause. "Anything else?"

"Nothing else. Just my own recommendations."

"What are those?"

"I suggest that you accept none of Jevins' terms."

"You know we can't afford that."

"We've got to afford it. . . . Listen, Jonas. Ask yourself a question without prejudice. What would happen if you were to dismiss this Hohaley? Charge: incompetency (he would never dare dispute that). Reappoint Matson. Call back the strikers. Put in Hennessey as head of the Project. He's the logical one—and was, in the first place. Or, if he is not acceptable, appoint some college professor in the state. A man of experience and integrity, a man above reproach or criticism."

"Jevins would put his forces here in motion. They'd blow us up."

"He would not dare, Jonas. Don't you realize that these fellows' stock-in-trade is *fear?* Don't you realize that our case is air-tight? Jonas, for God's sake, we would be doing our duty!"

"Roosevelt had to accept Tremaine's aid in '32 and this year too. *Twice!* So must we."

"Roosevelt was elected by millions of people who would stand back of him if he decided to get rid of Tremaine. The same people would stand back of us."

"But, Fred, you've lost your mind out there. In the first place, how can you compare the one with the other? This is small stuff, Fred. Roosevelt came in on a great hope—"

"Our Project is part of that hope."

"But we've got to produce," Colon shrieked. "It's too early, too soon. We don't dare. We've got to wait. In a couple of months now New York and Pennsylvania will have published their books. California is rounding into shape. Minnesota and Florida and Illinois—they're all rounding into shape. But nobody knows

343

it but us. We've got to protect them, Fred. We've got to give them a chance to come out first—be published. Afterwards, with shelves filled with our books, we can crack down. We can say, *Look here*—"

"But, meanwhile, there's the *situation* here. Jonas, this Project is *through,* if we say the word. And the people on it are through. I've seen Jevins' dossiers on them. They're blacklisted. And think of their morale. They're not figures in a plan, after all. They're *people.* That's what I think we forgot out there in Washington, when we encouraged them to work for ideals that we only *dreamed* of. You encouraged them yourself, Jonas."

"I encouraged them to work, yes. To resist, even. I didn't tell that fool Matson to take affairs into his own hands and start something that we weren't ready for as yet."

"But he didn't take affairs into his own hands, Jonas. The Project would not have been able to continue if he hadn't straightened out a mess. You've got to allow for his inexperience—remember the main things. The *strikers* did. And then, again, if in the *first* place—but why go on? You *know* all this! The point is, that he resisted too well."

"He wasn't thinking of us—if he *had*—"

"That makes no difference, as I see it. It was our fight that he was waging."

"Well, then, I repeat: We're not ready to take up the challenge. These people—yes, I'll say it brutally—must go overboard. For the sake of the others. That's final, Fred, and I want you to go ahead now and take the next plane back."

"All right, Jonas. I'll go ahead. After all, there's nothing *I* can do. I'm simply your representative. But an interesting parallel occurs to me. I've been thinking of Spain all the time I've been here in Monroe, Jonas. Spain, like this Project, is a small thing. Hardly worth the upsetting of things and notions as they are in the great, the big countries of the world, ourselves as well as in England and France. And yet I think that it's in Spain right

344

now that the fate of the big countries is being decided as well. You would fight, would you not, if Tremaine were in Washington right now, demanding his way on the *whole* Project? So would the British and the French, so would we, if Hitler were invading them and us. And yet, to return to Monroe, Tremaine's forces are invading us just as surely there as here. And we'll *never* be ready. For the time to resist is when the need to resist first becomes apparent.

"In Monroe we are casting sixteen people adrift and we're putting our okay on the degradation of a Project involving two hundred people. That's a small matter, compared to the Project as a whole, I agree with you. But it's not a small matter to the *people* on the Project and in the long run it won't be a small matter to any of us. For we're all degraded and brutalized by their abandonment. And we *could* win, if we only made up our mind to take the chances that go with the fight."

To which Colon answered: "I have thought over everything you have just said, and it remains a difference of opinion between us on the chances of winning. I can't take those chances before the other Projects have backed me up with their books."

Nevertheless, the parallel with the Spanish situation had shaken him. He did not want to think of Europe, but of America. This is *America,* he thought angrily. Still a pioneer land, still waiting to be discovered, still to be built up and *colonized.* The pun startled him as he thought it, and added to his essential discomfort. For emphasis, he repeated his instructions. But he felt harassed, interrupted, all the same. How do you keep out the traitor questions? He felt somewhat as the preacher of a fashionable congregation might who is giving a sermon on the Kingdom of Heaven and is by way of proving his points rather well when, all of a sudden, the church begins filling up with lepers, whores, wild orphan children, the hopelessly maimed and wounded, the smoke and the smell of ravage, and he knows that he should fit them into his argument, forcing them down the throats of the

345

congregation, but he sees that the scented and hitherto appreciative ladies and gentlemen are beginning to fidget and get ready to take up headquarters for religious instruction and inspiration elsewhere, and so he decides that his argument is best served by keeping the congregation and he has to ask the visitors to leave. . . . The decision is righteous but uneasy.

And there the conversation ended. It was a quarter to eight. The committee would be here almost any minute. Onigo began to arrange chairs, glasses, and drinks. How meaningless—to listen to "evidence" for a cause the verdict for which is already in! He was wondering if he dared take it on himself to fire Hohaley, reinstate the strikers, give all this out to the press as an accomplished fact and thus force Colon to take the offensive on this basis. No, he immediately concluded, this was impossible. Hohaley would not accept the decision, Colon most certainly would not back him up, he himself would be more isolated than the strikers themselves were, and it would all come to naught. He smiled to himself. Would Matson, in his place, have done what he was suggesting to himself? He had an idea that he would. Gest, no. Hennessey, no. But Matson, yes. He had met Matson twice on earlier visits to Monroe and had formed a great opinion of the lad. Gest and he had discussed Matson on one occasion— long before all this had happened—and Gest had said that he thought of Matson as a sort of Horatio Alger. Horatio Alger? Paul Bunyan as well. Paul Bunyan, John Henry. The G-man. Little Caesar. Frank Merriwell and Billy the Kid. The complete type of the American hero and legend. He was inclined to agree with Charlie on this. Well, let the foul plot work itself out. I myself am no hero and have done my civilized best to stop it. In vain. Let heroes take the stage.

WHEN CHARLIE RETURNED HOME THAT NIGHT AFTER THE meeting of the committee with Onigo, it was with a heavy heart. Onigo's hospitality had not fooled him. Nor had his erstwhile friend's ready agreement with the strikers that "this" Hohaley (it was obvious where Onigo's sympathies were) had certainly acted like a fool in not taking Matson back, thus forcing a strike. He knew that Onigo had thought Hohaley a fool long before. So had Colon. And nothing had been done to prevent the fiasco that had resulted in the present situation. And tonight Onigo had said nothing to make him believe that anything would be done.

He had told Folinger, the official chairman of the committee, that his investigation was now completed, and that they should know the results within a couple of days. He himself was not authorized to divulge them.

The girls were already in bed, where they could be heard talking softly before dropping off to sleep. Nussim was dozing over his newspaper and did not notice him come in. His mother was sitting at the bedroom window, looking out at the street.

"Letters somebody is sending you," she said.

Three letters! He had to go down to the front steps to get them. He saw that his mother must have been feeling bad all day. Obviously, if she hadn't, she would have got them herself. She had a great curiosity about mail. Sometimes her curiosity was so great that when he did not get home soon enough, she would have the girls open his mail so she could see what was in them. She had not even sent Janice or Clara downstairs to get them this time.

This last thought filled him with alarm. That she had been too sick to descend and climb the flight of stairs was understandable. She had been growing progressively weaker for months now, as he knew, ever since the operation on her spleen. But not to care to send the kids downstairs when she knew there were letters there!

He went into the "living" room to open the letters, but she was not watching him, nor did she ask whom the letters were from. Surreptitiously, for a moment, he watched her as she sat at the bedroom window, looking out into the street. Seen thus in

347

profile, with the lines of her face softened and petted by the evening shadows, it seemed as though he were looking at a feminine double of himself. He waited for her to ask him whom the letters were from. Even after he had opened them and was immersed in their contents, he still waited to hear from her. It troubled him deeply that she was silent, and he tried to understand why this should be strange. Then he remembered an old horse he had seen on a country road once. He had been a boy then, a boy scout (for God's sake!), and the troop was on a hike. They had come across an old mare lying in her tracks and the farmer sitting disconsolately in his seat, staring down at her.

"It's no good," he had said, when the boys—shouting because of the chance to do their good deed—had come running up to help. "She won't take neither the sugar nor the whip!"

Charlie trembled violently, but remained still. Automatically he had opened his letters. How different all this was from the day he had received that first letter from Colon. Yet it seemed to him that the pattern was the same, and a cycle was being completed.

The first letter was from Clyde Harkins. The handwriting was unknown to him, and he had to think before he could remember who Clyde Harkins was.

My hat's off to you fellows [he read]. But then, that's the trouble with me. My hat comes off too easily. There's a place ready for you beside me on the breadline. All you need to do to qualify is to show them your name on the blacklist.

He tossed the letter aside. We've still got thirty seconds of play.

The second letter he tossed aside without looking at its contents. You too can be a writer whose every word realizes a golden harvest, all you need do is to enclose a dime for further information. What tripe! He stared at the third letter. Really, this was quite a letter day.

There was no return address on the outside. It had been mailed

348

yesterday, he saw from the postmark. From town too. Who from? Well. . . . He opened the envelope.

He reached in and brought out two pieces of paper. He stared at one of these and turned it over. A twenty-dollar bill! Then he looked at the signature on the letter: Fred Onigo!

Even before he read the message, he had—by one of those fast, almost instantaneous, intuitive processes that can hardly be called thought—understood what this meant. The strikers had been abandoned. The note, brief as a telegram, read:

Use this please. Any way you like. Believe me, your friend.

He had brought an evening paper home with him, hoping that there would be further news of Lucille in it. Now, his mother temporarily thrust out of his mind, he went into the bathroom, for greater privacy, and began turning its pages. He was so sure of finding what he had known was true the moment he saw the twenty-dollar bill and Onigo's note, that he did not even hurry. All the time in the world, he told himself.

He discovered that, in the rush of the last few days, he had more or less gotten out of touch with what was going on in the world and he read headlines and sometimes lead paragraphs as they came, noting (although absent-mindedly, because of the pent-up fury in him) that Spain's cities were still falling to the enemy, the temperature reading still predicted increasing cold, the damned and double-damned football scores still occupied the sports page, etc., etc. And then, on the sixteenth page, he came across a story on Lucille.

It was a rewrite from the afternoon paper, saying the same general stuff the former had. But there was one point in addition that was not without its amusing facets.

Miss Turnbull [this point was] expressed it as her view that the sight of the picket line, with all the hatred and strife that it suggested to her, must have brought back memories of the World War, in which she served for a period of time. Miss Turnbull, who said she has

349

been suffering from a nervous malady for some time, will be confined to bed for several weeks, according to her doctor.

"The wrists, yes," he said aloud, "but this story still doesn't explain the cutting in the other place."

He continued to go through the paper but could not find what he was looking for. What the hell, he thought. He looked at the twenty-dollar bill again, then read the note. Mailed yesterday, eh? Before his meeting with us. And he didn't say a word about it to me tonight. No, it has to be in here. He's leaving town tonight for Washington, he recalled. He said so. It wouldn't be tomorrow's paper. . . . He went back to the first page, and started over again, more carefully. There it was, on the fourth page!

DISMISSAL SUSTAINED, INVESTIGATOR'S FINDINGS INDICATE

Counter-charges of inefficiency and dictatorial management made against Thornton C. Hohaley, State Supervisor of the National Authors' Project in this state, by 16 members of the Project who are on strike at present are not borne out by an investigation of all the available facts, according to Fred Onigo, of the National office.

In an interview given reporters just before he boarded a plane for Washington, D.C., Mr. Onigo stated further that it was his belief that the dismissal of Lloyd Matson, in whose behalf the strike was called, would be sustained.

He read no further. So that's it. That explained it. Again he looked at Onigo's note. *Use this please. Any way you like.* So he had been right in his estimate of the meeting this evening with Onigo. The strike had been given the full business.

"Pa," he said, shaking him.

"Huh?"

"It's ten-thirty. You're falling asleep here."

"I'm going."

He waited until his father had stumbled up and, rubbing his eyes, had gone off to the bathroom, dragging his paper after him.

"Why don't you go to sleep?" he said, in the direction of the girls' bed. Silence immediately answered him. "I mean it. I don't want to hear another damn whisper out of either of you."

His mother was still sitting at the window. He deliberately experimented with her by goading his father—who loved to sleep stretched out on the kitchen table over his paper—and ordering the girls, whose custom it was to continue to talk until all the lights were put out. As a rule, his mother considered this sort of thing a usurpation of her own privileges. She considered it that without realizing whence her anger came, and she would invariably tell him to mind his own business and watch when, how, and why—and where—*he* went to sleep. But still no answer from her.

"I ran into Doctor Grozek on the street today," he said casually, as he went over to his own bed and began to pull his shoes off. "He told me he's been meaning to get in touch with us. Don't you want to know why?"

He was improvising one of those stories that she loved to hear: How he meets the doctor. The doctor beams. He rushes forward. Can't control himself. "My God," he says. "You know, I thought your mother was a sick woman. I looked at her record from yesterday's visit she made to the clinic. Why, man alive, she's in fine health. No kidding. I was amazed at the progress she has made since the last time."

His mother had made such a visit just yesterday.

"It's pretty good news he had to tell me," he put out. "You ought to want to know what."

Once, as a boy, when he was selling papers, he had had an altercation with one of the other kids. The other boy, who had started it, had slowly backed up to the wall. He had followed, pursuing his advantage. Suddenly, as they were standing still, an instinct had led him—perhaps because of something unnatural and tense in the other's face—to look down at the boy's hands. In his left had been a knife, the blade open, pointing outward.

351

When the boy had drawn it, he could not say. He had had a peculiar shock.

Suddenly he became aware of tears streaming down his mother's face. Silent tears, while the face remained immobile, soft and eternal, like sculptured stone. He had the same feeling.

"So you are in a strike," she said, with that voice; "you have lost your job."

He had given the kids strict instructions that they were not to tell her. His father also had begged them not to. He had hoped, day after day, that the strike would be over, settled, won. Now she knew. How was not important. Neighbors maybe—his name in the papers. Today, too, he knew for certain that the strike would not be won.

"Ma," he said, "Ma—"

What could he say? The bitterness of being right, and finding that there was nothing to say!

"Don't talk to me," she said. "Who says I am your mother?"

This, really, was the first time she had ever talked to him like that. She had often cursed him, calling down on him all the manners of vile conditions—in life, in death, or in both—that the richnesses of the language had evolved through centuries when the strength and the totem of words was the Jews' sole protection. But this!

"Oh, Ma," he said, "oh, Ma!"

Oh, Mother, it's so hard to be a man. Have mercy! Be on my side! Why do you take these things so? Why did you not kill me in my cradle, keep me a child forever, if you did not want me to enter into the man's world? Why do you stand above me with the poised knife, watching to drop it if I open my eyes? Don't you know how it is outside? Do you really think that it's a simple kindly world of masters and men who are not yet masters, and that all a man need do is work hard (have you asked yourself what this work is?) until he, in his turn, becomes a master?

"Oh, Ma," he stammered, "Ma, Ma!" He dared not even

caution her that she must watch out, not get excited, protect herself against her thoughts of him, if she would not revise those thoughts themselves.

Whose fault is it that I am sick, she would ask.

"Sleep in this house, eat of our bread," she said. "But you are not my son."

He had stepped forward when she had told him that she knew. Now he went backward softly until his legs touched his bed. He sat down on it, watching her. She continued to sit where she was, looking out at the street. He lay down, without undressing, watching her silently. In the bathroom he heard Nussim gargling. The homely familiar sound, far from destroying the effect of her words on him and dissipating his fears for her now that she knew of the strike, heightened its reality. Why doesn't she curse me, he begged, in an increasing ecstasy of rooted terror. Why doesn't she scream? Why don't the neighbors get to hear about all this?

His father came out of the bathroom.

"*Nu?* Sarah? Make it night," he said innocently.

She rose and went to bed. This frightened Charlie even more. It was not right that she should react to suggestion so tamely. What was she giving up in this fashion?

He lay on his side and watched his parents' bed. In that bed, or in one like it, they had conceived him. To us is a son conceived. In what joy, in what hope! In Heaven, say the Jews, wait the souls of all those not as yet born. In joy and expectation do they wait, forever and forever until the ordained day comes and a great gong strikes, and the angels bless them and tie them in red ribbons, giving the babies-about-to-be little white cakes to nibble on, so that they may not cry or be bored in the long journey down.

And in all the beds of earth are children conceived, with what joy, in what hope! . . . What a story! What a lie! Take my life away, his soul whispered. Take my life away, or let me live. And he knew that all over earth, in every city, men (and women too) lay writhing in their beds and cursing their parents, who had given them life and opened their eyes on a hideous world, a world which they must accept because the priceless gift of life had been given them—a gift so priceless that they must spend their entire lives in paying for it. . . .

He lay there, between fear and concern, love and hate. He felt sorry for himself now, and sorry for her, sorry for everybody, and he hated himself and everybody.

Later: It seemed that Lucille and he were walking down a street. It was all very comfortable and they were talking.

"Jesus Christ, Lucille," he said, "don't you know we had trouble enough already without you blaming what you did on us? What tripe! Crap even! What plain unmitigated crap! Is there any other word for it? The union drove you out of your mind! So you slash your wrists and, as though that's not enough, you go ahead and slash your poor little unwanted unmentionable! Now really, Lucille, now—for God's sake now—*really!*"

She giggled and skipped along sideways, on one foot. "I'm a good girl, Charlie. You don't really think that I'd be giving out the real reason—and to the gentlemen of the press too—now really yourself, do you?"

He had been asleep. He was still almost asleep. His mother blundered against the side of the bed on her way to the bathroom.

"Did you hurt yourself, Ma?" he asked sleepily. He had forgotten the scene which had happened between them.

"I don't know," she said.

Her voice seemed reflective, so quiet and reflective that he concluded that she had not. He heard her go into the bathroom. Then he went back to sleep. He knew he was going back to sleep, but there seemed no reason to stop himself. Just before he really fell asleep, he thought to himself, 'So that's the reason Lucille tried the stunt.' By God, it made wonderful sense. As a writer, he got quite excited about it. Why, the poor bitch, it was her way of telling Jim Hudson something! And why at this particular time, with the strike in the news, and why blame the strikers? How simple, how simple! It was because the strike gave her the chance to blame somebody, because she was a nice girl and couldn't blame Jim Hudson, and it gave her the chance to camouflage the reason. But Hudson was who the "note" was for. And the strike let her do it without anybody being able to say that she wasn't a nice girl. For what nice girl doesn't lift her skirts and hop onto the nearest table at the first sight of a picket line? But the tampered-with unmentionable was the tip-off.

Ha, ha, ha, he thought, and hurried back to his dream, telling himself to be sure to confront Lucille with the fact that he now knew her little secret.

But he couldn't dream. Something seemed to be in the way. Everything down there in sleep was black, a black that groaned and seemed to be trying to say something. He tried to escape, to awake! He was awake. He listened. For God's sake!

He heard something. Was somebody groaning? Where? Who? It came—he discovered by slow degrees in seconds—from the bathroom. But his mother was in there! He remembered hearing her going in there. She went often at night. Her digestion was bad. She took medicines.

But *this*—what was it? Was she groaning? My God, what sort of a sound is it? He got up slowly, sat on the edge of the bed, looking toward the bathroom. It was dark in there. Naturally. She would not have put on the light. And now he could hear the sound clearer. *In,* a long shuddering prayerful in; *out,* as long, a sound, a half-gasp, a despairing regret, half-shout. Intensely agitated, he arose and went to the door. It was closed. She had closed it.

Modesty held him bound for a moment.

"Ma!"

No answer, *In, out!* The sound.

"MA!"

He flung himself at the door. It was one of those sliding doors

355

that come out from the wall. He tore madly at the handle, which was always jamming. It was jammed now. He heard his father leap up from bed, a cry of alarm from the girls.

"Ma! Ma! What's the matter, Ma?"

He flung the door open. Before he put on the light he saw her. She was lying in a half-sitting position between the bowl and the wall. She had one hand on the bowl, the other had dropped while frantically reaching for the support of the paper-rack.

His hand, in the gesture, stopped itself from reaching the light and he began to pick her up. His father was behind him. As he pulled her half to her feet, his father turned on the light. His mother's face was a foot below his.

Only her eyes were alive. They looked up at him with dreadful intensity, full of a fright and an appeal that was unbearable. The rest of her seemed dead. Her features dragged, as though they wished to follow the flood in her face, which seemed to have flown. Her arms and shoulders, her body and legs were a dead weight.

"Pa! Help me!" he shouted, still looking into her face, their eyes bound together.

Between them, they lifted her onto the bed. The girls stood in the doorway, shivering with cold, and looking on with scared quivering faces.

"Call an ambulance," he flung at Nussim.

He bent over his mother and began rubbing her hands. Not even the fingers twitched.

"Ma, can you hear me? Close your eyes if you can!"

Her eyes closed and immediately opened. She had not taken her eyes from his a moment.

"Ma, close your eyes again if you're in pain!"

Her eyes remained open.

"Did you feel it coming on or did you fall first?"

Her eyes bored at him. Frantically he rubbed her hands. Now

he understood how eyes can speak, and he knew what she was asking him, praying him to say.

"Ma," he answered her, his voice breaking, "the thing is, don't be afraid! Don't be afraid! There's nothing wrong with you!"

He heard his father open the front door and rush out. With his ears he followed him down the back steps, up the neighbors'. He heard him pound on their door.

"You'll be all right," he babbled. "I give you my word for it! It's just the *shock*. You fell down, and you're just *shocked*. When a fighter gets knocked out, it's the same way. They're all right, but they can't move for a while. It's the *shock*. Just don't be afraid!"

He heard the neighbors' door open. He heard windows in the yard going up.

He could not bear looking at her eyes.

"Please, Ma," he begged, "believe me! You'll be all right!"

Of a sudden both girls began wailing. "She's dying," Clara sobbed. "Our mama's dying."

He turned on them and drove them out of the room, menacing them with his fists. "Get out of here, you bitches!" Grabbing Clara by the shoulders, he shook her till her teeth chattered. "You little bitches, you shut up!" Back he went to the bedside. He realized with horror that her eyes had followed him, and she had seen him chase the girls and shake Clara. "I didn't hurt them, Ma. I just told them to behave themselves. They're not used to being up at this time of night. They're going back to bed now." Inwardly in a frenzy, he forced himself to appear calm. "We're going to take you to the hospital where you can rest up for a week or two and you'll get a good chance to get on your feet again." He dared not ask her if it were all right with her. He forced himself to smile at her eyes.

At last his father returned. "They're coming," he whispered.

"Ma's all right," Charlie told him cheerfully. "She's just dazed. She fell down. It's the *shock*. I felt her heart and it's beating fine.

357

You better get something to cover her with, Pa, while we're traveling. It's kind of cold outside. You'd better get a couple of blankets."

After this he took to rubbing her hands. "You rub her legs, Pa. Rub 'em toward her body. We may as well do something until the doctor gets to her. There's nothing wrong with her. It's just the *shock*!"

The girls let in the ambulance men. They lifted her. Charlie walked alongside her, holding her hand. They worked this way down the stairs slowly, sidewise. Charlie scraped through, the banisters creaking against his back. All the neighbors' windows were up. Women stood at them, motionless, neither leaning out nor standing concealed, with shawls thrown over their heads. Into the car. Careful, careful. This is my mother you are carrying.

"You'd better stay home with the kids," Charlie whispered. "They're scared."

"I'll go with you. . . . Please, Mister, one minute." Nussim ran back up the stairs. Mrs. Cohen stood on her side of the porch. "Mrs. Cohen, stay with the children." He ran back, a little gray man in pants and sweater and his shoelaces untied.

They rode to the hospital in silence. Charlie kept on stroking the hand close to him. If only she would give a little pressure in turn. Then it occurred to him that just because it was dark in the car and she wasn't moving, he must not think that she was asleep. She's awake, *thinking*. . . . She was trying to lift herself and she couldn't, he thought. She was trying to call out and she couldn't get us to hear. His body jerked convulsively, his eyes dry. He began to speak to her again.

The quiet efficiency and practiced calm of the hospital reassured him. Quickly she was lifted from the ambulance and taken into a ward. The nurse stopped them at the door.

"You men can wait there, in the waiting room," the girl said. "We'll take good care of her. We'll undress her, bathe her. The doctor will probably fix it so she can sleep."

358

"But how is she? When can we know?"

"They'll be looking at her in a minute."

They went into the waiting room.

"One of us ought to go home, Pa," Charlie said unsteadily. "The kids are going to worry. We ought to think of them. A-and you have to be at work in the morning. You ought to g-get some sleep."

He wanted to be by himself. He could not bear being looked at.

"I'll stay here," Nussim said briefly.

The nurse came back.

"Well?"

"She's in a bad way. A cerebral hemorrhage. The bleeding has stopped, but you can't tell when there'll be another one. We had very little to do with stopping the hemorrhage. Mostly, it just stopped. We can't tell when there'll be a second one."

"But isn't there something you can do?"

"We can put cold compresses on her head. That's what we're doing."

"She's in a bad way. Is that it?"

She hesitated.

"Yes. I'm afraid that's how it is."

They were left alone again. Charlie looked at his father. It seemed to him that Nussim was avoiding his eyes.

"I killed her, didn't I, Pa?" he said wildly, his voice poised on a thin high key.

"No, Charlie. You didn't kill her. Nobody killed her. She fell. It could happen any time. Besides, she lives yet."

"But if she dies, then you'll think I killed her."

"No, Charlie. What kind of talk is that?"

"But I did kill her. Didn't I? *She* thinks that."

"Who can tell what a person thinks when they're—like that? But you are wrong."

"She always hated me. She thought I did things to spite her.

She could never understand why God had given *me* to her for a son."

"That's because she never knew what to do with you. Not to understand is not always to hate, Charlie."

"Pa, she always thought that I could have saved us all if I had only wanted to. When I was a little boy, she used to go around telling everybody that I would be a great doctor. Or a great businessman."

"We live according to what we know, Charlie. Your mother cannot read. How could she understand what you wanted to do. She understands only our sorrow, our fate as poor people and as Jews. These are two curses which we carry. A great doctor heals. Jews, above all other people, can understand that. A businessman doesn't starve. Poor people know what that means. And your mother wanted the world's goods for you."

"But I understood all that. I told her it was no good. It was a difference of opinion, wasn't it? I told her I had to find my own way. I saw a world that she couldn't and wouldn't see. I wanted her to be happy too. But—b-but—"

He remembered where he was, and under what circumstances.

"Charlie. Look at me. Hide not your head, my son. I will tell you something you don't know. You will know it later, in your heart, when *you* have children. When you went away from home that time, your mother wept. . . . Yes, I know. First she wept for herself. That is true. But, afterward, and she *still* could not understand what you wanted, she wept for you. Bitter tears. I saw them. She knew then that she had not driven you away, as she thought when she wept for herself. And she knew that you had not fled from her. And, you see, you knew it too. So where was the thing between you that was not understood? She knew that what had driven her drove you too. It drives all men who must live as we do. From hand to mouth. With not an extra blanket for a child except the one on your own back. And how many extra blankets does a poor man carry on his back? And she

360

grieved for you, Charlie. For *you,* Charlie. Not for herself. She cursed herself and our first ancestors."

"But why—then—when I c-came back, she—"

"Because even though you are her son, she is still a woman who lives in a house, four walls, and knows not what you know."

"Tonight—when she told me that she knew I was on strike, she said—she said—"

Nussim sighed. "She has other children, Charlie. She has two. Little girls. Poverty drives us. Poverty is a madness. It is the world's great sickness. She was saving the money you brought in. She was beginning to dream again."

MORNING DAWNED. THE SUN STREAMED IN THROUGH THE bright curtains and they awoke to a white glare of color on the white walls. They looked at each other, remembered where they were, and immediately got up. Outside the room a fat middle-aged maid was passing toward a ward with food on a huge rolling tray.

Charlie stopped a nurse outside.

"Where can I find Mrs.—Gest?"

"Ask at the desk, please."

The girl there told him that Mrs. Gest was being kept in a private room. She gave him the number. Five rooms down the hall. From where he stood he could see into the ward—women still allowed to be together. From it came the sound of them eating. Half the door was open and he saw a group of doctors standing around a screened bed in the middle of the room. On either side of this bed women sat up in bed like children and ate their food.

"Can you tell me how she is? I mean—can we see her now?"

"She's doing as well as can be expected. Her doctor is Dr. Glanzberg. He's in the ward just now, on inspections. If you'll wait a minute, he'll be out and you can ask him."

In a minute Dr. Glanzberg came out. Meanwhile Charlie had

looked up at the corridor clock and seen that it was a quarter to seven. So she had been in this place for five hours! That's time. He took heart.

"Doctor, I am Charles Gest. This is my father. Can you tell me how my mother is?"

The doctor was a fat elderly man, very Jewish-looking, very kindly and jovial. "So. Father and son. Ha, ha. That's a title by Turgenieff. Do you know Turgenieff, young man? Or does he only know the sports page?" he threw jovially at Nussim. "We-e-ell" (why do doctors always say we-e-ell in just that way, Charlie thought with irritation; they say it that way on the afternoon radio programs too), "she's not worse. She's not better. What can I tell you? Do you believe in God? If you do, then believe it is more in His hands than it is in mine. Why should I fool you? If you don't believe in God, then you have known for a long time (your father has known it for a longer time) that we come from dust and in dust we end. And make the best of it."

"I don't ask you for philosophy, Doctor," Charlie said. . . . "I-I'm sorry." He smiled, a twist of the mouth. "We just got up. A bedside manner is pretty hard to take before breakfast."

"It's all right, my boy. A bedside manner we can very well do without after breakfast as well. But it helps, you know, to have one. A lot of people are helped by it. You'd be surprised. People you couldn't fool a penny on a business deal, and smarter people than that too—I knew a man once who had his daughter in here —this man could speak fourteen languages. A refugee, just came over from Germany. They ask you a question, and they don't listen to the answer. They don't want an answer. They watch your face. They listen to what is in your voice. That's what helps. And not only the relatives ask you the questions. The patients, too. Most of all, the patients. Here's a woman. Can you fool her an ounce on a pound of potatoes? Can you tell her what goes in a noodle soup? She would bite your head off. Yes. Believe me. 'Doctor,' says a woman sixty-five years old, 'since I have been ill my behind has broken out in pimples. Does it look to you, Doctor, like I have got pimples on my behind? Or do I think it is just because I have been in bed so long and my behind—excuse me'—they always say *excuse me*—'itches me' So? So what do I say? I smile, I make a joke, I pat her—on the shoulder; after a while, the second week, on the behind. 'Goodness me, no, those are not pimples on the behind. Those are just *scratches*. You should not scratch. When it itches, you should tell the nurse. Let her scratch it for you. She will scratch it nice, keep it smooth. . . . My dear,' I tell her, 'you've got wonderful smooth skin down there. At your age, too.' And naturally, they love it. Yes, a bedside manner is not to be despised." He looked humorously at them, one to the other. They were both laughing. "I would not advise you to see her just yet. She's—how shall I say it?—perhaps upset. If she sees you, she will want you to stay. And that's bad for her. You understand?"

"But she hasn't seen us since we brought her in. Won't she think something wrong?"

"She doesn't know much about the passage of time. She's under an anesthetic. Everything is gray to her."

He nodded briskly and walked off. "Later perhaps," he flung back.

"Well?" Charlie said. He was a bit abashed now because of his outburst of last night. Things somehow did seem better this morning. Perhaps the bedside manner. The doctor of course had worked it on them too. "Why don't you go home? I'll call up your boss, in case there was any work for you. I'll tell him you can't come down today. The kids probably stayed home from school today. They're probably worried."

"All right."

He walked down to the corner with his father and saw him off on the streetcar. Deep snow on the ground. The sun hurt their eyes. Everything was quiet out here. The hospital lay on the edge of a park, and No-Noise signs were on every corner. When

Nussim had left, Charlie went into a restaurant and called up his father's boss. Then he called up strike headquarters. Matson answered the phone. He found himself telling Matson what had happened. It was almost as though, in explaining to Matson, he too was listening. Responding to a sudden stab of anxiety in the telling, as though he were hearing the news now for the first time, he abruptly terminated the conversation and returned to the hospital.

He stood outside the room in the corridor and listened. He heard her breathing. *In, out.* She had started that again. Not as loud as when he had first heard it (last night?) but almost. What was she thinking of? How impossible that there should be nothing he could do! And in all that hospital, nobody! And this would go on, and in there she would be all by herself. With nobody to help!

A nurse came out of the room. They had been changing her linen.

"We'll call you," she said. "Why not go in there, where it is more comfortable?"

He understood that he was considered in the way here, and went into the waiting room without a word. But he could not stay there. The fact that the waiting room now contained several men and women, all of whom were passing the time in talking to each other or in staring at the opposite walls and yawning, only emphasized that there was nothing he could do. Out into the corridor again. An interne passed. On an impulse, he spoke.

"Where can I find Ferstein?"

"Oh, Doctor Ferstein?" Emphasis on the *doctor*. Respect, my tousle-headed friend. Pause. "Are you a friend of his?"

"Yes."

"Well, I guess he's still in his quarters. I just came down. He was up there when I left. Suppose you take this elevator up to the fifth floor, then . . . "

He was standing on the fifth floor, peering uncertainly at all the doors of the internes' quarters when one opened and Ferstein came out. He was a short, stocky figure with a large fore-head. Short, curly, doglike hair that ringleted his temples gave a somewhat precious cast to his features. These were otherwise large, regular, and firm.

"Well, well, Charlie! The *writer!*" he said, patting himself on his cheeks, which were freshly shaved and powdered. "What brings you here to our little love-nest?"

He gave Charlie a humorous, somewhat sardonic smile. This reminded Charlie that Ferstein had an opinion of him. He refused to accept the bait.

"They've got my mother in a room downstairs. I brought her in last night. Glanzberg's waiting on her. I wish you'd take a look at her chart and tell me—"

As Ferstein's step had not slackened, he had fallen in along-side him. The doctor pressed the button for the self-starting elevator. He was only a couple of years older than Charlie. A muffled shudder deep down in the building. The elevator could be heard coming up.

"Glanzberg's a good man. A *very* good man. I don't know that I can—"

"Oh, hell, Ben. I'm not asking the question who is better, who is good. I assume that he's good. But I just want to know how she *is*. Glanzberg won't tell me. He gives me jokes about Tur-genieff. Jesus Christ, if I want to hear jokes, I'll tell them to myself."

"All right. I've got to inspect my ward first. You wait for me at— No. Perhaps you want to come along?"

"I guess so."

"Here. You carry my stethoscope. You're a guest of mine. A visiting *doctor.* See?"

He stopped at a desk on the third floor and had a word with the nurse, who gave him a number of charts of the rooms he was to visit. Charlie watched him as he exchanged words—terse words: questions and answers pertaining to the work—with the nurse. Then as he studied the charts, the concentrated frown on his face. This, Charlie thought, is not the same Ferstein whom I knew from the Marxist Literary Forums and the Study Center. There he was an excitable impassioned fellow, contemptuous—he remembered the last meeting—of all composers but Beethoven, whose music he knew no better than he did the music of the others, but who had refused to kneel (or was it to step aside?)—so went the story—when the King of Prussia had passed. He was a precise person here. A man always looks best when seen at something he can do.

They entered into the corridor of the wing Ferstein was to inspect.

"Old people here, mostly," Ferstein said. "Complications."

He looked sidewise at Charlie. "This one in here is pretty gruesome. You can come in if you want to."

It was an invitation, but Charlie stayed outside and gave him the stethoscope. "I'll wait for you."

"As you say!"

"The bastard," Charlie thought. "This proves something conclusive to him about me. It confirms a political thought."

From up and down the corridor he could hear groans. He stood in the corridor and waited until Ferstein had come out. He felt unutterably depressed. He followed the doctor as he went from one room to another. Finally it was the last room.

Ferstein glanced at him.

"I'll come in here with you," Charlie said.

He was immediately sorry, but a form of fascination forced him to look at the man who lay in the bed. About sixty-five to seventy he was. And breathing hard—*in, out*—as he'd heard his mother. The old man was lying on his back. His eyes were open, but you saw that they weren't looking at anything.

"Gruesome, eh?" Ferstein said, following the direction of Charlie's gaze. . . . "No, he can't see a thing, don't let his open

366

eyes fool you. He doesn't even know that he's fighting for his life. But he is. He's fighting with everything in him."

"Will he—?"

"He'll be dead in an hour."

"Is there *nothing* can be done for him?"

"Well, suppose he revived. It would only be from himself, not from the illness. Another six months, say, of life! Life? What good would it do him?"

"People learn to think of their lives in other terms than the *good* it does them."

Ferstein was busying himself with tapping the old man's chest. In answer, he shrugged. He held the old man's pulse a moment. Then he laid the wrist down. The fact that Charlie could see the bare chest made this even more horrible, not the sight of the futile, wasted wrist. Only the face improves with age, and can be shown naked with dignity.

"Doesn't it affect you to hold the pulse of a man who'll be dead in an hour?"

"What a queer literary notion! Of course not. That's the way we learn. The truthful is not always beautiful. If you follow it far enough, it can become gruesome. Do you know that this old boy has a family? See what I mean? Forty years ago he *might* have been beautiful."

The repetition of the word *gruesome* was beginning to exert a peculiar effect on Charlie. At the literary forums already mentioned, he had often clashed with Ferstein—usually on matters of esthetics (on political matters he had always considered that they saw eye to eye; nevertheless, he'd avoided politics). Ferstein maintained that James Joyce was an inferior artist to the crudest worker-correspondent to the labor press because Joyce used words to disguise, whereas the worker used them to reveal. He constantly spoke of *meaning* as though it were absolute. Here is meaning. Here are men.

A ghastly smile came to Charlie's lips: "You derive satisfaction, don't you, from the fact that death is gruesome?"

"Well, satisfaction is hardly the word. Not all death is gruesome. This one *is* because the life was wasted. The old boy was a saloonkeeper. Well, here he is. See? What about Rockefeller? Don't you think his death was pretty gruesome? Where were all his millions then?"

"That's pretty literary, too, isn't it? Philosophical, even. You're passing judgment."

"Not at all. In a hospital you learn to think of *life,* not of the individual people who—let's see!—rent some of it for a while. You learn so much here of life—you'd call it death. This old boy was quite the little wiggler-waggler in his day. Probably thought he was immortal. But now, here he is. He's used up his little span of life, don't you see? Look at him—he's unconscious, finished. But look how the life is already packing itself up, waiting to get away. You see, it's the man that's dying—not life. So the point is, how does he leave *life?* Huh?"

"I asked a Christian once if all the people who lived before Christ were unsaved. He said he thought they were. I asked a southern Baptist once if colored kids would be allowed to eat at the same table with Jesus. Blake's poem gave me the idea, in case you want to know. He said, 'Christ, no.' Mohammedans don't think that women get to heaven. . . ."

"Oh, come now. You're certainly getting metaphysical. I thought we were talking sense a moment ago. This thing, as you ought to know, is altogether different. We're scientists, not mystics. Our Heaven will be here on earth. There'll come a time when all men (and women and black babies too) will be part of this kingdom. Only they'll all be kings. And they'll call each other Comrade. To show that they're all a different kind of a king. Only —before that time comes, people will have to quit leaving their portions of life stranded—they've got to quit releasing their little bits of life at the wrong destinations—"

"Destinations!"

"What?"

"Nothing. What you said, Destination—that's all. The place to which we're drawn—"

Ferstein thought that his friend was giving in. His pale face beamed. He passed a long delicate hand through his incongruous curls. "We're all through now. What do you say to a cup of coffee?"

"That old man will have—vacated his *lease* . . . by the time we've had our coffee."

"That's probably right." Ferstein laughed. "But the perception of the inevitable is the prerequisite of a clear acceptance. Once we have understood and accepted truth as it is, we can begin to change it. Thus we change the gruesome—imperceptibly —for the beautiful. The *truly* beautiful. Not that which *seems* beautiful. As for instance, a pretty woman. In other words, any twenty-five-year-old female in the dark."

In high good humor now, he began to lead the way down the corridor, looking slyly around at Charlie all the time. Charlie, who knew now why he had always hated the man, let himself be led. Ferstein took his arm. If he noticed the involuntary shudder of aversion that passed through Charlie's body at the touch, he paid it no attention. Or gave it another interpretation than the truth. He was a great believer in conversion. As to the shudder, any student of the nervous system knows that there are men so delicately constituted that the merest touch on the skin raises welts. On the other hand, there are men who can put their hands to flame and not be burned. These things can be explained.

He led the way through a low archway into a restaurant in the Nurses' Building. It was a self-service place. Student nurses waited behind the counters, spotless and white as the walls behind them. Nurses sat at their breakfasts at the tables, here and there with them a doctor or an orderly. Charlie was conscious of sparkling pretty faces, white teeth, white walls.

"How are you doing with your strike?" Ferstein asked. Carefully, he ordered ham. Eggs. Coffee. Pie. Charlie, sitting over his coffee, watched him plunge his fork, lift the food, hold it before his mouth, poised for a split second; then, with a quick pop, in it went. The doctor ate with great gusto.

"Tell me," Charlie said. "Have you heard from any of the boys in Spain?"

"Fisher's in a hospital at Barcelona. His eyes are gone. I read it in the *New Masses*. What do you think, Spain is a country spa? They don't write letters as often as that."

"You worked Fisher into going over there. Sol was a medical student too, wasn't he?"

"What do you mean, I *worked* him? Sol *wanted* to go. He knew what the struggle was about." Ferstein put his napkin down. "Are you going reactionary or something?"

"Look, Ben. Let's not call names. Not yet. . . . Tell me—"

"Why I'm not in Spain myself?"

"No. Not that yet. But look—suppose a car hits you right after we go out of here? You bump off. A little earlier than that old man upstairs. What about it? Have you used life right? I'm going by what you yourself were saying. Could you say that you'd left it off at the right destination?"

"I don't see the point of all this."

"I do. . . . You helped *persuade* Sol Fisher to go to Spain, I'll put it at that. Certainly the Spaniards are fighting for their lives. In a great cause. Self-defense is always the greatest cause. But meanwhile, here *you* are. Some day you'll be a full-fledged graduate doctor, if that car doesn't hit you as we leave here. We've talked about these things before, you know. How about that liberal old doctor at whose house you spend so many evenings? You certainly must know that he's the head of this hospital."

"I talk Communism to him, as I did to Sol."

"But it's different, isn't it? I knew Sol. We went to school together. I know the Señor Very Powerful Herr Doktor. His wife's

370

a writer, you know very well. That's how I know them. And you know that this doctor and his wife are interested in a number of things, but only from a personal point of view that you must despise. You know, as sure as you know your own name, that there's no question of this doctor going to Spain. And yet you continue to go out there. You despise me, as you would have Sol if he hadn't gone off to Spain, and you would have been pleased to pass an obituary on us if you'd found us in one of your beds one morning. But you continue to go out to see the Herr Doktor. Why?"

Ferstein's face was pale as chalk. "I suppose you think it's because I want an appointment from him."

"Yes."

"There's nothing more to say then." He got up and began to walk out.

Charlie followed him and caught up with him at the archway. "What's the use of going on your dignity?" he said, through gritted teeth. "Won't there be time enough for that when you're a great doctor yourself with a great practice and in a mood to amuse yourself with clever and mad young men who want to get somewhere in the world and know how to amuse you?"

Ferstein looked around in alarm.

"For God's sake, Gest. What's the matter with you? Don't you know we're going to be noticed?"

"You had your say back there where that old man was having his last hour of life. And now I'm trying to ask you a few simple questions—that's all that's the matter with me."

"All right. I'll tell you. I *am* trying to get an appointment. I do *not* intend going to Spain. Now or ever. I can't. I'm afraid to. I—*personally*—can't control fear. I'm still right though. I am my own proof that I'm right. The man is not important. He's despicable. It's *life* that's important. I'm not important, no matter what I do to life. You're not important."

"And your gruesome little excursion that you took me on was

371

intentional, wasn't it? It was your gruesome little way of *consoling* me, of using my mother's death (which you undoubtedly have forecast to the minute) as propaganda. It was a way of bucking me up, wasn't it? Killing all the birds at once! A way of changing reality, wasn't it?"

"Charlie! Our mothers all have to go. Sooner or later. We too will have to go some time. *I've already seen the report on her!* I was the doctor who looked at her last night when you brought her in. It's better for her that way. She's *suffering!*"

"Better! Better!" The words hammered at his brain. "You son of a bitch. What's her suffering to *you!*"

Quite beside himself he turned and ran toward the building. His mother's room was full of the sound of her breathing—*yet.* He leaned against the wall and closed his eyes.

MATSON HAD PUT THE PHONE BACK ON ITS HOOK AND TURNED to where Folinger, who had been addressing the assembled union, was waiting for him to return to the meeting.

"Go ahead!"

"Who was that? Charlie Gest?"

"Yes. His old lady's sick. He's got her in the hospital. He won't be down today."

"Well . . ." Folinger returned to the subject under discussion. "It's pretty plain by this morning's report in the paper that Onigo has doublecrossed us. For the benefit of those of you who have not seen the morning paper, I will read this item."

He read the statement that Onigo had given the press just before he boarded his plane.

"What do you think of that?"

Silence.

"It's a honey, isn't it? Washington finds that Hohaley is a pure brave maligned gentleman; that there are no charges against him outside of inexplicable delusions and intrinsic poisons in our own minds; that Matson definitely is an ungrateful swine

372

who has repaid the angels by chalking obscene slogans on their backs." He smiled bitterly and continued:

An offer of settlement has been made to the strikers, Mr. Onigo revealed, in accordance with which it is expected that [etc., etc.]

Because of the cuts in quotas of non-relief which are to be put in effect soon because of over-lapping departments, it is not expected that all of the strikers will be reinstated, Mr. Onigo stated.

These cuts, however, he emphasized, do not proceed from the fact that these people have elected to strike rather than to work. The cuts were in order anyway. Because the strikers are no longer employed with the Project, having been automatically dismissed according to W.P.A. rules and regulations that proscribe that three days absence without cause from the Project shall constitute cause for dismissal, it is not a question of rehiring them, but of hiring them in the first place. Mr. Hohaley, reached at his home at an earlier hour, had expressed his confidence of the outcome of the investigation and said that he would accept without question whatever verdict was rendered.

He was willing, he said, in the event of a general settlement, to drop all personal charges against the ringleader, Matson, in whose behalf he alleged that the strike had been called.

"I don't want to hide anything from you," he continued. "Things aren't looking up for us elsewhere. I am referring to the report of the meeting of our committee with the Social Justice Commission. If Mrs. Van Fern will give it now. . . ."

The strikers listened in silence to this report.

"We urged them to an action on our behalf. . . . A public statement of the rightness of our cause, a declaration of sympathy for the principle involved in our strike. . . . They refuse to consider the case in terms of principle. They point out the *practical* differences in a strike that involves hundreds of thousands of men—such as the Auto Workers unions—and this one, involving sixteen people. Moreover Bishop Marshall says he is leaving town tomorrow, and will be gone three weeks. *Must* be gone. And Rabbi Goldstein is ill, and can not be expected to rise from a sick bed. And Monsignor Jones is at present deeply involved in the Laughton case. Besides, the union must understand that the Commission is not a partisan body, but impartial, blind even, *passive,* you might almost say, standing with a blindfold across its eyes and a pair of empty scales in its hands. 'It will take time to test the weights dropped onto those scales.' They said finally that in any event our committee, before we could call on them again, must confer—without *pride*—with Jim Hudson on the terms of settlement. . . .''

Hennessey had a look of disgust on his face.

"I would like to hear a financial report," he said. "Frankly anything else—just now—would bore me."

Georgette's clipped tones, just a touch of the red-hot Southland in the way she met her *r*'s: "Five dollars from the Steelworkers' Organizing Committee. . . . Two dollars from Mrs. Stephenson, in advance of whatever the Garment Workers may vote at their next meeting. . . . Ten dollars from the Newspaper Guild. . . .''

That part of the report was not very long.

"However, we have promises that amount to some sixty dollars. As to affairs, the cocktail and dance thing netted us thirty-one dollars. The reception at Clarey's, however, was a flop. We lost four dollars. But then . . .''

She summed up.

"Matson's dismissal precipitated matters. We started with a 'battle-chest' of one dime, as it were. . . . Have collected one hundred forty odd dollars. Disbursements for leaflets, et cetera, were . . . The telephone bill, because of the long-distance calls, will be very high. It must be paid immediately. We can't expect the Musicians' Union, which has been so kind in the matter of rent, to . . . Five dollars this week to Matson, five dollars to George Folinger, five to Hennessey, five to . . .''

Exemptions. Don't need the money. Gest. Georgette Wilson. Olivia Van Fern . . .

"They're giving us the run-around down at the relief," Alice Tennebaum reported. "It'll be weeks before anything will be done for us, the way it looks. Johnson got mad, pounded the table and called them names. . . ."

The financial report rubbed in what they had all been thinking. Each, as he listened, seemed to be withdrawn too, listening to something inside himself. Perspectives, proportions, were asserting themselves. A far-away, yet intent, look on each face. The morning-after feeling. The Social Justice Commission. Colon. Hohaley. The relief agency. All these had been the important factors all along, the *day-time* factors, of the real world of between sun-up and sun-down. And only themselves had been unreal, cut off and intense, passionate, in the *midnight* where dreams are, ideals, impossibilities that won't admit compromise, don't understand it, don't *see* it down there. . . .

Not that each was sorry for what he had done. Not *sorry*. To be sorry did not apply. The passion does not yield; it believes in itself still. But the mind comes in, the tricky mind. Names names. Valedictory to passion. The cause burning bright in the man's private midnight, thrusting him forward through space against all known things, becomes, in the inhuman and greater brightness of the sun, of the day-time and *reasonable* world, a mere adventure. It *can* become, that is. The midnight challenges day, pits and hurls itself. . . .

Not so much sorrow then. Shame? Certainly. To be exposed is shameful. And grief enters in, the opposite of remorse. Who do not as yet fully understand their defeat turn about, blame themselves, their leaders, themselves again, alternating all these feelings with resurgent splurges of new hope, new enthusiasm, new thoughts of a victory which it seems they must have had in their grasp at some time and therefore can, will, and must reclaim. And there may also be a sense of relief. The mind is not so free as the passions. Part of the mind has always been on the other side, or has—at least—*understood* the other side. And this

375

is the time when it comes out to arbitrate and infer that nothing had ever been. . . . The greatest insult.

"Nobody has bothered to get in touch with us in regard to the results of this so-called investigation," Folinger said, in a choked voice. "The first we hear of this is through the newspapers. They give Hohaley his say. Onigo. But not even a reporter calling here to see how we react to our own murder."

"The voice of the people is too clamorous. There are too many crusades already the newspapers are fighting. I hear that the city is being disgraced by her saloons. The papers are going to fix it so you can't buy a drink after twelve o'clock. And don't forget, they've just got through driving the auto-bus boys off of the streets."

"I think we've lost the strike," Folinger said, speaking slowly. "But I'm still just as mad as the day we started—madder! I personally would vote for an attempt at a sit-in. We can't lose anything any more."

"How do you propose to stage the sit-in? Are we to go in and drive out the people now in possession?"

Folinger reddened. "We can all of us walk in. And *stay in*. The scabs will leave at five o'clock."

"And return in the morning. Will we be sitting in their seats?"

"Why not?"

"There are only sixteen of us. We can't sit in all the seats."

"We could all be sitting in the middle of the floor. All together. Just sitting. Let the scabs keep their seats."

Heads shook slowly. Too many objections.

"This action, to be successful, like any other action, must be dramatic. Hundreds of workers, holding an auto plant completely, with thousands of supporters outside, supplied for siege, with all facilities in their hands, and only the job of keeping the doors barred to invasion—these are dramatic. They win by power. We'd be ridiculous. People typing all around us. We'd look like loafers mostly. The scabs would be eating their sandwiches on the job and asking us if we'd like some lunch."

"We've got one real trump to play," Georgette said at last. "Why should we hesitate to use it? I say to release the photostats to the papers now. Or do we still expect Washington to change heart?"

"Yes. Release them."

"Matson, how about you and Georgette being a committee of two to handle that?"

"I'm willing."

"Okay."

"Now," Folinger said, "I give the following not as a suggestion but as my most earnest advice, hardly subject to a discussion. I propose that we form a mass picket line again this morning, as we did the first morning of the strike."

"Amen to that."

"Let them arrest us."

"There'll be no scabs in jail."

"By God, we'll still show 'em."

It was a sudden resurgence of feeling. All together they left the building, carrying their slogans and placards. They walked down the street. It was a quarter to nine and thousands of clerks and workers were coming off streetcars and buses and hurrying to work. They received many glances and remarks, and not a few catcalls. They doggedly took up a position in front of the Project and began walking up and down the line. Project workers were beginning to arrive. Pete Cavagni, his face rounded out now, his eyes ripe as new olives. Others. These, as a rule, averted their glances in passing the picket line, but now they came forward with expressions of joy.

"Didja see the morning paper? I hear you're coming back to work."

"Keep your line," Folinger ordered. "Keep your line. The strike isn't over yet."

377

"We've just begun to strike," somebody shouted.

They kept this up, marching and shouting slogans, until ten o'clock, when the wagon arrived and they were all arrested.

BY THE NEXT DAY, HOWEVER, THEY HAD NOT AS YET BEEN officially notified of a proposed settlement of the strike and neither had they been officially notified of the results of the investigation. In addition to this, the newspapers had refused to handle the matter of the photostats. The union, one editor said, had waited too long before using this evidence. The investigation has been made, you've been on strike three weeks now, it's old news, nobody's interested any more. If it comes into *court,* of course—that's another matter. The other newspapers gave no explanation. Their reporters had taken down the story, as the union gave it out, and then the union waited in vain for the story to appear. Indifference? Fear of libel? Whatever it was . . . Nevertheless, a sense of relief among the unionists as individuals. They just had not liked the *idea.* Shall we print it in booklets ourselves? No! Wait, wait. . . . Thus three days went by.

In this time Charlie had paid little attention to what was going on. Most of the time he had spent at the hospital. For these three days his mother had hovered between life and death, neither suffering the second hemorrhage feared for her nor regaining complete consciousness from the first stroke.

On the fourth day, when they had still not heard from either Washington or Marathon, and thus were—officially—still without either a verdict or an offer, another meeting was held. Again Folinger, at the impasse, urged that the sit-in be adopted.

"The sit-in is the only weapon left to us," he shouted. "Jesus Christ! You won't print the truth about Hohaley for fear of hurting Washington and the Project, and you refuse to understand that Washington has now become part of Hohaley. Or that Colon has. Then what's left to do? What else beside the sit-in! Aren't we ridiculous enough already?"

"There are only sixteen of us! And three of us at least must stay outside to conduct our business and maintain some sort of a picket! We'll be dragged out of there!"

"Even if they let us stay in, how do we get food? They won't let food be passed in."

"We go on a hunger strike, if they don't let food in," Folinger shouted. "Again I repeat: What do you think this is—a tea-party? We're on *strike!* In Spain they're giving their *lives!*"

His eyes lighted on Matson. Matson was another man since the strike had started. He did all that was required of him, had addressed various sympathetic groups and fellow-unions on the strike, was in all the picket lines and decisions, but seemed to be brooding, the spark and the devil out of him. Impossible to say just what he felt. Was he sulking because the initiatives had all passed out of his impetuous hands? Or was he grieving because of the disaster he had brought on all of them? Both, no doubt.

"What do *you* say, Matson?" Folinger shouted. "Do *you* think we should stick to the middle way?"

Matson looked up, flushing deeply. There was something akin to hatred in the looks the two men exchanged.

"I spoke against the strike," Matson said thickly. "I was the only one who had the courage—" His face was wrinkling and lining. He seemed painfully torn and confused. "I publicly had the courage to reverse all my stands. . . ."

"Do you think it courageous to sail your ship up to the enemy's lines and then scuttle her?" Folinger shouted. "Do you think that's more courageous than ramming her and going down with your goddam ship?"

Georgette got up. Her face was angry. Several of the strikers, swayed by Folinger's passionate utterance, were hesitating. Matson, unconsciously, had stood up, almost at attention, and was facing Folinger without speaking, almost as though he were facing a firing squad and had steeled himself not to utter a sound. At this time the strikers might have voted a sit-in strike, a strike

379

that went against the instincts—under the circumstances—of all of them.

"I'll read you a phrase from a letter received by me from National Headquarters of our union. And I *didn't* jimmy a desk to get hold of it." Matson winced. "I'm sorry, Lloyd. I shouldn't have said that. But I want to show that I'm not on your side in what I'm going to say. I think this is very apropos." She read:

Dear Sister Wilson: We have followed your strike with the greatest interest and sympathy. It certainly seems that the condition in Monroe and the state as a whole is disgraceful. But we are wondering whether it would not be the wisest thing for you now to accept whatever conditions can be obtained and to return to work. If you had succeeded, then this would have been another story. But, surely, you must see that our union (nay, the labor movement as a whole) can not proceed or rely on such essentially adventuristic undertakings. After all, our national policy is to arbitrate, not to strike. And you're bound to find yourself increasingly out of the swim. . . .

"Now listen to this! Folinger, apparently, has been arguing his point with them too:"

Monroe is not Spain, nor is an Authors' Project the same as the Chevrolet factory. . .

"I'll read no further. It's almost like mental telepathy. Twenty-five dollars is enclosed."

Folinger had listened in sullen silence. Now he got up again.

"What about our committee of 'experts' from the local unions that we consulted?" he asked. "Why did they decide it was right for us to go on strike? Why did they say we had no other way— that it was really out of our hands?"

"Why did *we* think the same way?" Georgette parried. "Why did we know deep in our hearts that we would lose, and yet never spoke out openly of our fears or what commonsense told us— except for Matson here, whose words then were even more courageous than he thinks? Well, I don't know. I think the main thing was, we had to strike a *blow*. We had to do *that,* and we shouldn't kid ourselves that we were really concerned with victory. The 'experts' weren't psychologists. Why should they be? I suppose they took our chances at our own words, and simply trimmed their sails to our own wind. I guess they sincerely thought that we could win."

"You may be right about having had to strike a blow," Folinger said bitterly. "But I'm not satisfied with the extent of the blow we've struck. I want to get Hohaley and I want to get him good. I want to get Colon even worse."

"Our original purpose was to get Matson back to work," Georgette said. "That was our first purpose. If we had had more experience, we could have struck our blow and still—"

"What's the use of these afterthoughts?" Folinger demanded. "What *is* this!"

"It came to me one day, while I was on the picket line," Georgette persisted, "that what we should have done when Matson was fired was to have continued at work, but used our lunchhour to picket the Project with demands for his reinstatement—"

"Holy God!" Hennessey shouted suddenly.

He sat straight up and stared at her, his eyes intense. Matson too sat up. Even Folinger. The dark woman had everybody's fascinated attention now.

"—In this way we would have struck our blow, kept ourselves functioning and drawing pay and doing our work, and still remained a vital part of the workers in general and the national policy of our own union. We would certainly have provoked tremendous interest in the audacity and rightness of our move. We would not have cut our local off from growth. And we might have won."

They were under a spell, waiting for what she would say next. But she was finished. What more was there to say? Here they were! Then:

"Afterthoughts," Folinger said. "Still afterthoughts!" His

pride was deeply thwarted. "I resign," he said bitterly. "Whether you're right or wrong, it's plain that as president of the union I'd make a good barker."

Georgette absently fingered the communication from the National Headquarters. Then she put it down on the table before her, type facing down.

"I suppose there's nothing for me to suggest but that we call on Jim Hudson for an official offer."

The others had all been silent up till now. At her words the discussion started up again. Everybody was now eager to send this committee along. But they were all, of a sudden, feeling kindly toward each other. It was almost as though, in coming to a decision, no matter how unsatisfactory, they had again discovered each other as human beings and friends. And they were kindest of all to Folinger, as to the most passionate and the most hurt of them all. In their kindness to him, they forgot how mortally hit they were. They tempted him, tried to draw him into the discussion. He was silent. Once or twice, as though he still could not believe the verdict, he shook his head from side to side. Violently. As if his spine jerked. . . .

"THE WAY I SEE IT," HUDSON SAID, "YOU PEOPLE SHOULDA FELT you were goddam lucky to have a Project at all, let alone—when we go and make a spot for you—you go and call a strike."

Charlie, who had seen Hudson before, but only from a distance, had been watching and listening to him with extraordinary interest. He was trying to see in him the "fine, wonderful" man that Lucille Turnbull said had proposed to her in that romantic setting in the lagoon so many years ago before she had gone off to seek a career, giving up love.

What he saw was a middle-aged wheelhorse who impressed him as an ass essentially—a politician whose reward for twenty years of faithful service it was to have been given this most inappropriate of all possible jobs, the state Czardom of the Arts

Projects. He was of medium height, thin, with a beer-paunch; blondish with thinning hair; a ruddy face that you know is well-fed but somehow never fills out, giving out a sort of sweat instead of fat; pale merry-marble blue eyes and thin meager lips that did not seem ample enough to cover his mouth, for his teeth were always visible, whether he talked or was silent. This last gave him a peculiar expression most of the time, particularly since he was constantly smiling as he talked. His puckered inadequate lips gave an effect of alum and there were his pale merry-marble eyes, and all of him somehow naughty. Not a dynamic fellow, not even a brutal fellow, just a guy who knew how to get by after he left law school, knew what the score was, and is always sufficiently in the know and the swim.

And this was the lad for loss of whom Lucille had, after twenty years of feeling jilted, slashed herself!

"Now you take when we put dough into a road project," Hudson expounded easily, well pleased with his eloquence. "You know what a friend of mine wrote me las' week? He come through here from Michigan on a bit of business, so he stops in to see me on his way to Marathon. He asks me about the roads. So I tol' him, Boy, they're fine. You go right out along State Highway 12. So when he gets to Marathon, he drops me a card. 'Jim,' he says, 'I have been on many a road, but I have never been on roads such as this one over which I have just come. It is a credit to your state, and you may quote me on this if you want to use it.'

"See what I mean?"

Hiss. He sucked in his lips.

"We put down a road—let's say we spend a hun'er' thousan' on it. When it's down, it's *down*. You can *feel* it. You can *ride* over it. It's there. The public knows what the money has gone for—"

And building roads can go on forever and there's nice profits in them for Tremaine's contractors, Charlie thought.

"See what I mean?" Hiss. The lips sucked in. They were be-

383

ginning to wait for the sound. "But what've *you* fellas got to show when you're through?"

"That's not the question," Hennessey said. Hudson being an Irishman, Hennessey had done most of the talking for the committee, on the theory that words from an Irishman would be more acceptable to the Co-ordinator. "Look at it this way, if you want to take roads as an example. Suppose, instead of concrete, sand is being put down. Suppose, instead of a road inspection, a vaudeville actor rides by on a mule and sings a song as an okay. Suppose—"

"Now wait a minute, Hennessey. That don't happen on *our* roads. Let me tell you—"

"I'm telling you about the *book* we were trying to write. I'm only *using* roads. I'll give you an example. There's a certain part of this state which is very poor farming country. The earth is practically all made up of rock. Everybody knows it. It's admitted. They teach it in school books at the agricultural schools. So, in the essay on agriculture, we mention that this county is rocky. See? Just rocky. What happened? We were told to cut that out because the Chamber of Commerce in that county did not approve it. The essay was edited by the real-estate men. . . . And that's only one example. I could give you hundreds."

"All right," Hudson broke in. He was smiling, sucking at his mouth as though it were an orange. "Look at it thisa way. I go to a tailor. See? I tell him I want a suit of clothes. See? I tell him what kind of clothes I want, and I tell him what kind of style and cut. It's up to him to make me the kind of suit that I want. If I don't like the suit he makes me, I don't have to buy it. And I can get me another tailor."

Hennessey, as the others in the committee began to fidget, tried once more. "Look, Mr. Hudson. There's a man named Rockings who maintains a private art gallery down at the State Capitol. At Marathon. It's considered one of the finest of its kind in the country, and a quarter gets you in. Okay. You know yourself that not all the paintings in that gallery have been found acceptable by everybody. And yet, the *gallery* itself—"

Hudson's merry-marble eyes twinkled. "You know what *I* think of that gallery, Hennessey?"

Hennessey, astounded at the interjection and the leering quality of it, stopped. "What?"

Hudson shook his finger at him chidingly. "You can't kid me, Hennessey. I think the same thing of the paintings in that gallery that you do. Between you and me—pardon me, ladies—I wouldn't hang them things in my bathroom."

The committee, after an incredulous moment, joined in the Co-ordinator's laughter. Hennessey laughed too. They all laughed together. It seemed as though they were all laughing at the same thing. Hudson thought so. One of his favorite sayings was to the effect that he had not been born "yesterday."

"Well," Hennessey said, "I see that we've been wasting our time on those points. I can see now that you weren't chosen Co-ordinator of the Arts Projects for nothing."

"I know what I like," Hudson said. He gave a benign smile all around. "Now that we got this far, what can I do for you? I got just a few minutes now."

When it came to the bargaining, Hennessey felt somewhat at a loss. He looked at the others. Georgette spoke up.

"We want you to reinstate all of us at our old positions. Inasmuch as Mr. Hohaley still remains state director, we insist that Lloyd Matson be reinstated as well. If Mr. Hohaley is made to resign in favor of a more experienced and conscientious director, we are prepared not to insist on the return of Lloyd Matson."

Hudson had been listening to her with slowly hardening eyes.

"You're Georgette Wilson, aint you?"

"*Miss* Georgette Wilson, Ph.D. You may call me *Doctor* Wilson, if you like."

Hudson's cheeks grew mottled. But he restrained himself. "Well, *Miss* Wilson, I'm afraid we can't do that. Some of you people don't have none too clean hands from where we see it. Now you take—"

"If you're giving us excerpts from the findings of the investigation, we would prefer to have you let us read the report," Georgette said boldly.

Charlie looked at her in admiration. The girl was a fighter, as well as a gentleman and a scholar.

"Now you take this fella Matson," Hudson continued deliberately. "He's a known Red. We have checked up on him. We have got him on record."

"Look," Charlie said. "Does Matson's politics have anything to do with it? You're a Democrat. Other people are Republicans. What's that got to do with it?"

"And some people are Jews," Hudson said. "And some people are *Nigras. I can get just as tolerant as you can, any time you want to start that game.* . . .And that aint got nothing to do with nothing neither. I was just saying that this Matson is a Red. And if you will allow me to continue, you and *Miss* Georgette Wilson, I will tell you *what* we have got on *Mister* Matson."

Hennessey belched.

"Excuse me," he said. "My stomach."

"We have got a signed affidavit here," Hudson continued. "It is the affidavit of a woman by the name of Lucille Turnbull. She is an employee of the Authors' Project who did not go out on strike when you saw fit to do so. And she has hurt herself, as you are well aware." He smiled around at everybody. "Did you know that Matson hounded her into it? Yes. He did. We have here a sworn statement from Miss Turnbull to the effect that when she repulsed Matson's overtures to either come out of the Project on strike or suffer the consequences, she was driven into a state of despair that caused her to slash herself with a razor."

386

Hudson sucked at his lips with relish, enjoying the contemptuous battery of stares of which he was the center.

"Now," he said, "I understand that you have a number of so-called letters in your possession which, according to my information, Mr. Onigo of Washington has been instrumental in keeping you from using so far. I also happen to know that the newspapers have refused to consider their publication. But I aint no fool, friends. Don't think I am. So I will now make you an offer, on condition that you turn these—photostatic copies too—over to me and promise not to use them in pamphlets put out by yourself. We will ask Mr. Hohaley to resign from his office, effective immediately, if you release these papers to us. Just in case you hold out on some of those photostats anyway. That ought to satisfy you. Matson, anyway—we have plenty on him too: postcards that are not fit to look at, money he owes to everybody in the state—is out. Furthermore we are prepared to let eight of your sixteen people return to their jobs. But there won't be no such thing in the future as supervisors or editors, except as Washington agrees to them in conjunction with this office. However, the *pay* of all former supervisors will not be cut—"

"For how long will they not be cut?"

Hudson laughed. "You tell me."

In each other's eyes, as they silently consulted, they read that they would take this offer back to the union and that the union would accept it.

"Those strikers who are not taken back will be given a chance to qualify through the regular channels for other forms of employment, if they are eligible for relief. The non-reliefers we don't take back will not be taken back anywhere at all. That's our final offer. If you decide to turn it down, I want you to know, right here and now, that not one of you will ever be returned to work anywhere in this state on WPA. We will cancel the Authors' Project before we allow Reds to dictate to us."

387

"Who are the people to be taken back," Hennessey asked, "if we accept?"

Hudson began to read from a strip of paper.

"Hennessey. Gest. *Miss* Georgette Wilson. Alice Menenbaum. Herbert Johnson. Walter Smith . . ."

"SO IT'S ALL OVER," MRS. VAN FERN SAID. SHE STOOD AT THE window of strike headquarters and looked out at the roofs of the city. There was a curious thrust of her neck, a sort of eagerness in the stance of her head. Her back was to Charlie, who was seated at the table staring bitterly at the wall. "Do you know what I shall do now?" She spoke as much to herself as to Charlie. "I shall go home now and get the house cleaned up. I've hardly looked at it for a week. Then I shall take the children out into the park and we shall go for a long walk and talk about the animals in the zoo. And I shall spend my evenings reading my books. I've got hundreds of them. I'm crazy to dip my head again into some poetry. And I shall call up my sister-in-law—she's a Countess, you know—and we shall have tea (and whisky too if she wants it)—and she can tell me all about Austria, how it looks this year. And my cousin will begin coming over again (he's a bachelor) and he'll taunt me about the strike—'the lurid episode in Olivia's life,' he'll call it from now on—and I'll tell him that he doesn't understand anything except stocks and bonds and loans and things like that, and in a short time we'll be bored of the subject, and by next year—" She broke off abruptly. "By the way, Charlie, what *was* it all about?"

She came over to the other side of the table, compelling him to lift his gaze. *"Really,* Charlie, what was it all about?"

He knew that she was talking more to herself than to him, so he did not answer. Besides, he wasn't interested. And he found that her elegiac manner, which he thought more than a bit affected at this moment, irritated him. She acted as though she were already home (and had been—for ages).

388

"Call it a dream," he said rudely.

He saw that she was hurt.

"I'm sorry," he said. "I guess I was being more interested in myself just now than I was in you."

"You mean that I have something to go back to, don't you?"

"Everybody has something," he snapped.

"*That's* it then." She was silent a moment. "Do you know, Charlie, I think this strike has been more of an experience for me than it has for any of you."

"We all think that, I suppose," he answered indifferently. He was hoping that Matson would get back so he could leave. He wanted to get out to the hospital. Mrs. Van Fern was not supposed to be here at all, but he was supposed to take care of the telephone until Matson got back. After a strike is over, there are still tag-ends to pick up.

"No. Listen to me. I mean that's why I've felt that you all hate me of late."

He looked at her now. "Who hates you?"

"You all do, don't you? I'm not sore. I've felt it for some time. I never felt it on the Project, except that some of the field workers, I thought, laughed behind my back at what I suppose they consider my queer accent. But when we went on strike I began to see it. I think it's what Folinger would call 'class-hatred.' I suppose you'd call it that too. So would Hennessey. I've felt it in all of you—"

"You've been imagining things, Olivia," he said shortly.

"Have I? Isn't it natural to hate somebody who has more money than you have—particularly when that person need not fear the blacklist as I know you all have since you saw that the strike was being lost? Not that you have an alternative," she added quickly.

"I don't know whether it's natural to hate somebody—as you put it—who has more money than you have. The presence of a sufficiency in another calls attention, I suppose, to the fact that there is more freedom of action for another."

"But it's true! I've seen this hatred crop up in many strange ways. It made me rather self-conscious, you know. At times I hated back. In a way I'm glad it's all over now. I can relax. I can be myself without feeling as though I'm on the defensive all the time. Can you understand that?"

"Certainly I can. Many's the time I've wished I was back in the days before I came to work on the Project—when everything was nice and private with me, all dreams—treacle and morning glory, as I used to put it to myself—and I didn't have a penny in my pockets and nothing but a pot to dream on. I understand just how you feel."

"You *do* have a nice way of expressing yourself! Do you talk like that at home?" she joked. ". . . Oh, I'm sorry. I forgot about your mother being ill. It must be terrible for you."

"It's quite an experience."

"All right, be haughty and sardonic. . . . About that class-hatred. I'll tell you the thing that makes it awful. You know, I don't mind being hated myself. But I got to thinking of my children. It scared me, I don't mind admitting that. If I was hated, then my children were hated. That's when I began hating back. When I saw that my children were being hated."

He thought of Janice and Clara. He thought of all the nice things he had bought for them—of all the things he had intended to buy. Not tokens of his feelings only, but things they needed.

"Look, Olivia. I can't speak for the others—only for myself. I don't hate you. I don't hate your children. I *know* your children. I like them very much. But—" He joined her where she stood at the window. "There lies Monroe. All around us. Stretches out for miles from where we can see it, in every direction." He pointed. "You live out there. I live over there. That's a fact. In itself it doesn't mean a thing.

390

"When I pass by the gates of people who live where you do and see their children on the lawns, I don't hate them. I like to see children looking pretty and well-fed and happy. . . . Jesus, Olivia! You know me. I'm a *person*. You know I'm telling the truth. . . . But at the same time that I see these children, I also see mine. Not mine, of course. I'm a man of conscience; you tell me how I could afford them. So, let's say I see my little sisters. I guess you understand what I mean—"

He looked out at the city, so apparently quiet and at peace under its roofs. "Children, I think, should be given an even break to start with. As it is, they're dependent on the parents who bring them into the world. A child has no better chance than his parents' cunning or inheritance entitles him to. What does a child do whose parents were not sufficiently cunning? Or sufficiently anything? For that matter why should a parent have to spend his entire life—his one and only life—pursuing an impossible, perhaps abhorrent course of action and thought calculated to make things, as they say, easier for his child? My father says that poverty is the world's great illness. That's true. And hatred and greed is its proper legacy, that it passes on to posterity."

Olivia, who had admired Gest and Hennessey and all the others and had liked Onigo, and had gone out on strike with them in the same spirit in which she had come here to work in the first place, not out of compulsion, but because of the thought to do these things, could understand what he was saying. She even felt that she agreed with him. But she knew in herself why things would have to remain as they are, until or unless revolution or anarchy or race madness changed the set-up or substituted something worse in its place. For in her heart, and she was ashamed of this feeling too, she knew that her agreement with his words was cheap. That she was glad that with her and her children, his problem—and his little sisters' problem—did not exist. She knew that, if pressed to the wall, she would stop agreeing with him. She would call every argument she had read, and arguments of the emotions and self-interest, to her aid, and would flaunt words like *breeding* and *eugenics,* to maintain the foundation on which her life, but not his, was secure. . . . And (she shuddered) she would even fight him. . . .

"I despised Matson, when I first knew him," she said, in a low voice. "I thought him an awful pup. A climber of the worst kind. I never could understand why people like you and Hennessey and Folinger continued to like him, even to have what seemed to me a sneaking sort of admiration for him, the foulest actor since Cyrano de Bergerac. But I've changed my opinion of him. I just now changed my opinion. I think that in Matson—people like him—you unconsciously perhaps see the peculiar gangster-messiahs of the modern world. You count on him to take things for you in the end by the sword, as your last argument. So now I will despise him—I can't help that—but I respect him too. I guess I have just begun to be af-fraid of him. . . ."

Silence. He could not help feeling irritated at the way she expressed herself, but he knew he would never hear more honest words from her than these. "If only there were a fourth dimension to the plot," he said, half-jeering. "That's the theme song. Huh? There's the rub. 'The divine right of children'—there's the lost chord."

DEEP, DEEP SHE LAY BENEATH VASTNESS ON VASTNESS THAT pressed on her, and tried to reason against the meaning of that sizzling she heard in her head. It was as though she were a ship, at the bottom of the ocean, and the water was bearing down. And at the same time that she was a ship, she was also a soul within that ship; and the soul ran from room to room and wrung its hands. The ship shook. The ocean pressed.

"The First of the Month is at hand," roars Kleinschmidtt, in the terrible yet beautiful voice of the Rabbi of Odessa, whom she hears for the last time as a child. As she sails.

Gone. Again runs the soul, from room to room.

Who sweeps the sea aside, as though it is a table-cloth? She opens her eyes. Woe is me, what faces? Closer, closer they come. Voices too.

"Stay out of her range."

"You must not excite her now. She's got her eyes open now."

In the hospital. Now she remembers. If only the pain in her head would go away. Doctors. Nurses. She fell. Suddenly she remembers everything. She was at home. She was going to the toilet. She fell down, how it hurt. Hit on the shin-bone, the little shin-bone, curdling the marrow. And then they carried her. *Carried.* . . .

"I *die!*" she shrieked. But no sound burst from her lips. And she could not lift her hands, nor turn her body. . . . If only she could turn her head a little. A little.

A doctor leaned over her.

"You're feeling better now, aren't you, Mrs. Gest?"

False, false he was. She had heard the words as her eyes had opened. Charlie stood there. Nussim. Janice and Clara. She knew it. And they were not allowed to come forward. They were told to keep out of her sight. She tried to raise herself. Oh-h-h. *Charlie,* she tried to say.

"She's trying to look around at me. She knows I'm *here!*"

"All right. But just for a second."

"Hello, Ma."

He was looking down at her. Charlie. Smiling. *Charlie, you don't understand.* My son, smile not. Run, get help!

"They tell me you're doing fine, Ma. You'll be out of here in no time."

She lay absolutely motionless. No change in expression. It seemed to him that she was even calm. But then it was as though her eyes were gathering eloquence. In her eyes, as she gathered

393

all her agony and appeal to him, he saw a dreadful anguish. Ten days! Had there been no let-up for her? And all alone—shut in!

"You're doing fine, Ma," he said. "You'll be up in no time."

Don't look at me like that, Mother. Please don't look at me like that. He trembled in every limb.

"You'll have to go now," Glanzberg whispered behind his back. "She's getting excited. She's trying to *struggle.*"

He stepped back. Two steps to the left.

"You'd better go," Glanzberg said, "she—"

"Whisper! Whisper! She can hear us." *Whisper, you bastard.*

But—again—she was hearing nothing.

She struggled, she tried to remember something. What was all this about? She tried to lift the unliftable. Lift earth! Press back the sky! Where's Charlie? *Charlie!* He was here just now! And now the ship settles, settles. The sizzling in the head. And the soul runs about. Run, little soul. *Run!* Look about. Look. Seek. Hide yourself. . . .

But as the roar grew, she remembered Nussim. Her children. She stopped. Nevermore. The end. Death, the twin, born with the other, *herself,* lying quiet in the cradle as the baby weeps and beats his fists, praying Mamma, Mamma.

"Oh, no, God," she begged, "I can't. . . . Not yet. . . ."

She knew that the sea would conquer soon. Already she felt the cold. There was no time.

Now. NOW.

"God," she said, "take care of them. *For my sake.* I beg You. Charlie. He is so wild. And me not there to watch over him. And Nussim. Poor Nussim. God, you know how hard he has worked. And he still has to work. He will have to work all his life. And for what? And not a rest, not a day in which he can smile and say 'I have nothing to worry about.' And the little ones, Clara and Janice. Did they hurt anyone, God? Say Yourself, God, did they hurt anyone?"

394

She knew that she had an unanswerable point there, and—cunningly—she repeated it.

"You know Yourself that they never hurt anybody. They will be without a mother, God, think Yourself now. Woe is us all, will this not be hard for them to bear, if You do not cherish them?

"At least until they are married, God. At least until they have good husbands, God, take care of them."

So earnestly did she pray, so much did she mean what she said, that it seemed to her that she had prevailed, that God surely would do as she asked.

She had never, in all her life, thought what God would look like. But now she had a desire to see Him. While she still had time. Before the twin began to leap, and *she* lay quiet. She wanted to see to Whom she was leaving her dear ones. And she called on Him to appear before her. But she had never seen Him before and He still did not come. God—what was He thinking!—should know that loved ones cannot be left to strangers—even to such a one as He. And all over again, to make sure that He heard her, she prayed.

That roar! That roar! As the ship burst in and the waters rushed in, waters of all the colors, she thought: He is a *man,* He will not know how to take of them.

"God," she began to scream, "take care. They will try to fool You. You can't go out to play poker. They are cunning. You will have to be there all the time. . . ."

An iron instrument had seized on the biggest tooth in her head. "Oh-h-h," she shrieked, lifting herself to ease the sudden, the *heart-smashing* pain.

But it lifted her, continued to lift, to pull, her tooth held but began to give way with a pain that had the *sound* of one high note.

"Oh-oh-oh-oh-oh-oh-oh-oh-oh-oh-oh-oh-oh-oh—"

And up, and up, and up—the intolerable pain, and the tooth

395

lifting, lifting, still held by the body, that lifted after it to ease the pain, until—*out*. And the blood rushed after it.

And she was free.

"WELL, WE WON A VICTORY," HENNESSEY SAID AWKWARDLY. "I guess you can call it a victory. The papers allowed us to get in that interpretation. There'll be another director."

The big Irishman, whose novels spoke of changing the world, professed to see some hope in this. He did not sound very convincing though.

"Her name is Dennis-Littleton. With a hyphen. A *she*. From the north part of the state. They breed nothing but syphilitics and club-ladies up there. Did you ever hear of her?"

"No," Charlie said, "I haven't."

"Probably a bitch. Anyway, it'll be a change. We won't have to look at Hohaley's fat puss any more. . . ."

They approached the Project.

"By the way," Hennessey said, "did you know that our hero has already left town? Matson's gone." He laughed. "The son of a bitch stole my hat. The last I saw of him he was huddling in this guy's jalopy. Off to he doesn't know where himself. Not a dime in his pockets, except a four-bit piece he borrowed from me. To saw wood for his keep, if need be. Or work in the coal-mines. To toil under the azure roof of farms, it may be, or on the decks of ships and in company of other questing spirits to learn the Meaning of It All. Off in an open rumble-seat, through sleet and snow, not a penny in his pockets, except my four-bits, to eat on. Not to speak of a two-dollar fountain-pen that he thinks he can get a quarter for. The son of a bitch even tried to steal my overcoat. Good-by, he says. Off like that."

"That's Matson."

"Who do you think I meant. Colon?"

Charlie shrugged. Conversation. "What about Folinger?"

"He's got himself a job in a Greek restaurant. From writing

396

Tours through Our Beautiful State to washing beautiful dishes."

"Yeah." That's where he too should be. Anywhere.

"Well," Hennessey said, "here we are."

"Jesus," Charlie said, "I hate to go back in there."

"We'd still be looking for a job elsewhere," Hennessey said. "There aren't many you and I can get that pay this well."

Charlie laughed bitterly. "I guess I don't need any persuading. You know, Hennessey, I had two hundred and ten dollars saved up in the nine months we've been here. I didn't even know I had it. My mother was saving it. I'd been persuading her to move out of where we live. She wouldn't hear of it. I got her a servant once; it still makes me laugh. She kept socking it away. She had plans of her own in mind. And the whole damn thing went for the funeral. She didn't include *that* in her plans."

THERE THE STORY SHOULD END. ACTUALLY, STORIES NEVER end. They go on for a long time after author and publisher shake hands and agree to it, and the audience says Amen and moves on to its next pastime. No matter what, the story goes on. Around it goes, and where it stops, nobody knows. . . .

Two sequels:

It was spring. Mrs. Dennis-Littleton suddenly burst through the Project door and rushed to the nearest window. One hand was clutched to her cheek, the other was closed as a fist around the arm of the man who was the bringer of the little pink slips, Jim Hudson. Perforce, he was being dragged with her.

All other motion, at this dramatic entrance, ceased. Eyes and mouths opened up like oyster shells. Mr. Black looked up from his maps and blueprints, Miss O'Hara looked up from her typewriter, her little finger freezing on the motion to punch *A*. Everybody looked up.

"Oh, look," said Mrs. Dennis-Littleton, "the *spring!* Isn't it *beauti*ful?"

Look, look! Oh, look! At the words of sweet entreaty, of command nevertheless, the workers sprang to their feet, almost as one person. Some then rushed to her side, striving to be the first ones there. Others, undecided, stood where they were. And continued to stand, in attitudes of dreadful indecision. Still others sat down again. None of them, of course, were thinking of Mrs. Dennis-Littleton. And the spring concerned them not at all just now, except as the long-heralded time that would bring this man with the little pink slips. And here he was.

"Sure *is* beautiful weather," Mr. Black said, cooing a prayerful agreement with her.

Regan, who entertained no doubts as to how *he* would stand after the names had been read, said nothing. He stood, confidently, with folded arms, in front of the bulletin-board, on which he had just pasted another "chocolate soldier"—this was what the rules and regulations were called by the workers.

"It certainly is," said the lawyer Petrie, peering uncertainly out at the dainty blushing air, wondering where his voice and assurance were, now that he needed them so desperately.

Hudson, for a while, allowed the island that he—and, by courtesy, Mrs. Dennis-Littleton—formed to be surrounded by all this anxiety, entreaty, and verbal whistling in the dark. Or, rather, spring. But soon he began to clear his throat. At that, understanding his ways, the little chocolate soldiers stuck to the bulletin-board—the little chocolate soldiers known singly as Don't-Smoke, Don't-Loiter, Don't-Speak-Above-a-Whisper, Don't-Use-the-Telephone, Don't-Slam-Your-Project, and so forth—came instantly to attention, anticipating additions to their own ranks as the human ranks fell. The people, too, at this clearing of the throat, stiffened in their watching.

"Mrs. Dennis-Littleton—" he began, in his rules-and-regulations voice.

Too late. "If there's one thing I simply adore," said Mrs. Dennis-Littleton, her voice piercing yet poignant (or poignant yet piercing), "it's spring! All the dear little buds! The bird-songs at dawn! The pigeons—so happy! so content! going coo, coo! S.J."—she whirled to tell them all—"that's my nephew. He's seventeen years old and he's on the college baseball team up home; he wrote me just the other day and he said, 'Auntie, it's leafing up here fit to beat the band. Won't you just love the spring?' and he wanted to know if the leaves were in bloom down here. Just the other day."

Mr. Black immediately spoke up. It wasn't for him to say, he said. He was the architect only, not a mind-reader, but he knew exactly how Mrs. Dennis-Littleton felt about such matters.

This reminded her of the flowers Mr. Black had got her last week on her birthday, a dozen American Beauty roses.

"Would you believe it," she told Hudson, "this bad man made me cry for the second time in a day!"

"It was nothing," Mr. Black murmured.

Everybody laughed knowingly, trying to appear as though it was nothing for them either.

"It sure is beautiful weather outside at that," Miss Kelsey giggled, in the pause that followed Hudson's clearing his throat again.

"I hate to interrupt this little party," he said now, smiling in his manner. "You people being artists and writers with—uh"— he paused slightly, in order to collect words suitable to the occasion—"artistic temperament, I guess you kin look at the leaves any time you feel like it. But me, I'm just plain old-fashioned mister rules-and-regulations, business before pleasure, and I gotta make two other Projects yet this morning."

Mrs. Dennis-Littleton got in behind him as he started for the inner office.

"Excuse me, Mr. Hudson," said Pete Cavagni at this point, "may I ask you a question?"

The chocolate soldiers swung by their skinny black necks. The warm little patches of air romping in slyly through the windows

399

seemed to rush out again. Mrs. Dennis-Littleton stepped aside, her nostrils pulling in like oars.

Hudson looked at Pete for a while.

"That's what I'm here for, to answer questions if they're within the rules and regulations," he said at last. "What is it, fella?"

"Mr. Hudson," Pete said, "I been meaning to ask you this for a long time. How long does it take for the pay-sheets to get to Marathon?"

"They put them on a train," said Hudson, very deliberately, "and it takes the train two hours and fifty-three minutes to get there."

"Well," said Pete, "how long does it take for them to come back?"

Hudson sucked at his lip. "It takes the train the same time coming as it does going."

"That aint what I mean!"

"That's what you asked!"

"You know what I mean!"

Hudson leaned forward. "Listen, fella," he said, "I don't get sore, see? Remember that. I don't get sore." He looked about him. "If anybody has got a complaint, I will be happy to be in receipt of the same from you in a letter. That way, we will all be happy."

"A letter!" Pete broke out. "That's a hot one! You're here all the time, aint you? We can't get rid of you! You're in and out of here fifty times a day! Jesus, you know what's going on!"

Suck. "I told you I don't get sore," Hudson said imperturbably, "but any time you feel you don't like your work here, I'll be more than happy to accept your resignation."

"Resignation!" Pete shouted, almost frantic. "That's another hot one! Jesus, you talk like a YMCA secretary, uh sumpin! You aint never been on relief, that's why yuh talk like that."

Hudson pulled out a notebook from a pocket. A pencil. He

wrote something down. "You won't mind if I take a few notes?"

"Take alla notes you want. I aint afraid uh you. Send you a letter! Jesus, if that aint a hot one all right! Hell, you even know how many times I went to the toilet T'ursday, the fifteenth uh las' mont'! I don't know myself, but all *you* gotta do is look at th' time-out-for-th'-toilet list fuh dat day. An' you want me t' send *you* a letter!"

Pollin, the fat old ex-banker, came forward.

"I think, Mr. Hudson, that what Mr. Cavagni is trying to say is——"

"I kin make a good guess at what he's tryin' to say. Do you have something on *your* mind, Mr. Pollin?"

The whitehaired man wrung his hands like a woman. "It isn't the rules-and-regulations, Mr. Hudson. At one time, sir, I might say, I enjoyed a not inconsiderable position in a bank and know how necessary it is to have order in a place. . . . It's not so much the rules-and-regu*la*tions. But when we're kept waiting so long for our checks—sometimes they're a week late . . . sometimes *two* weeks, why, why——"

"Anybody else?"

Nobody spoke. Hudson turned to go.

"I guess you figure I talk too much," Pete shouted. "I'm too tough, uh sumpin. Maybe I'm th' first one to get one uh dem little pink slips. Huh?"

All of a sudden, Margaret Renny walked straight up to Hudson and tried to say something, but she had grown very pale and all she could do was move her lips.

"IF I WAS A YOUNG MAN, A NICE YOUNG AMERICAN YOUNG man——"

This was supposed to be directed at Charlie. . . .

"I would buy a suit," Harry Goselkin continued, "a fancy double-breasted suit with a nice tie and a nice collar. And I

401

would buy a dime paper and a new pencil to make in it some figures—"

What the Widow thought, she did not say. The Widow no longer. She sat stony, quiet. She flicked her eyes over the kitchen clock. It rang.

"And I would go sit in the Montana—"

"What's the matter with the Washington?"

Goselkin would not be diverted. "And I would go sit in the Montana, in the restaurant—how do you say it—the *gri-i-ill*. The waiter comes along. What does he see—a tailor? A Harry Goselkin? A dragger of his own bottom? He sees a man, a gentleman, with a double-breasted suit! He gives himself a shake like a dog; bows, in other words. Hands me a menu. 'What'll it be, Sir?' He stands there. 'Gimme a cup of coffee and your special Montana sandwich—with Italian imported olives.' —'Very good, Sir! Will there be anything else, Sir?' —I say, 'Here'; push him into the hands a fifty-cent piece; he doesn't know what to do—shall he bow to the ground or kiss my feet! He stands; without words like a dummy. 'I am a big businessman,' I tell him. 'Who is registered here? Be so good as to point them out.'"

He flicked his cold cigar into Nussim's empty coffee-cup. "The waiter looks around. I take out my dime paper." Suiting action to the words, he pulled some papers from his pocket and spread them on the table before him. "See? I write!" He began to write. As he wrote, he spoke: " 'One million dollars! Two million dollars! Three million dollars! Four million dollars!' " Sitting erect suddenly; looking about him wildly: "What's this? What's this? A lady comes in! An heiress! A beauty! A *blonder*, with a pair of shoulders! A bosom with breasts! A nose that turns up at the moon! Such a one as to make a gentleman lick his piggish fingers! . . .

"I look for him. Here. There. The waiter stands at my elbow. 'Give her a table by me,' I tell him. 'I am a big businessman!'

And I begin to write. *One* million dollars. *Two* million dollars. *Three* million dollars.

"She begins to come closer. She sees a man sitting there; doesn't know who he is. One already can imagine what she thinks: Who is this man, she gives herself a question. Too bashful to stop the waiter to find out. Her mother raised her like milk; a child sweet like honey. She sits down one chair from me. Tries to order a sandwich.

" 'Ibble kibble shnibble stibble one million dollars,' I say. 'Ibble bibble hibble ribble two million dollars.' So how long does a person find it in her strength to be bashful? She cannot make her order. 'Who is this man?' she asks the waiter. Not angry, it is understood."

Harry stood up. He bent down a bit, looked back up over his own shoulder in imitation of a beautiful *blonder* becoming almost prostrate with admiration.

" 'I beg your pardon,' " he said, using Nussim as his model. He spoke in his best English, the haughty eyes blinking down out of the sly, foolish face. " 'Pardon me that I should talk like this. But I am a big shot, a businessman. I am making a little figuring what I should do with my money. It is a question of investments!' "

"Well," Charlie said, "I wasn't laughing at you. It could happen. I believe you."

"No, no. Don't laugh. A boy like you! Such a fine education! And a face, a figure! I'm kidding you like I would kid myself."

Charlie laughed. A stab of pain. How *she* would have enjoyed this, how passionately she would have entered into all this—this fairy-tale! "I'm not laughing at you, Harry. A friend of mine just did the same thing. The way it happened is a little bit different than the way you tell it, but it happened. . . . *You* remember Matson, don't you, Pa? . . . Well, he is sitting in this cafeteria in Los Angeles warming his rear and in walks this millionaire's Communist daughter—"

403

"Communist!" Goselkin exclaimed.

"Sure. Why not. She's a Communist. They—"

"Uhuh! And is she perhaps a little bit hump-backed, this flaming bargain?"

"That's funny," Charlie said. "She's not. She's very lovely. And it's a pipedream how much they're nuts about each other. . . ."

But Harry had had enough.

"Nussim! What makes him talk so foolish! . . . What does he see to laugh at! Is it not true—every day—in the papers—a lady—her chauffeur. . . . A boy! A girl!"

"May you already go blind with your boy and girl," said the Widow suddenly. Pardon us, dear reader. The ex-Widow.

Involuntarily Charlie looked over his shoulder into the next room. Every now and then he got that feeling that she'd be sitting in the chair there, looking out of the window. Of course not. What was the matter with him! Already the pain had begun to get less intolerable. It was already beginning to work down from the outside, going deep, deep into him, getting itself stacked, put away, buried in its true grave. . . . Well, times change. He'd even begun looking in the Married Columns lately, to see what Elizabeth might be doing.

Across the street a record ran down. He waited. Another one was put on. Tony keeping himself company while he got his place in readiness. Tony the barbecue man, our midnight host. A black orchestra was swinging the Blue Danube Waltz. Better put cellophane around that historic river. It's burning its pants.

University of Illinois Press
1325 South Oak Street
Champaign, IL 61820-6903
www.press.uillinois.edu